COMING SOON BY THE SAME AUTHOR

The Crying Boy
The Butcher's Daughter
Looking for Lucy

THE
LONG
WEEKEND

JANE E. JAMES

Matador
9 Priory Business Park
Kibworth Beauchamp
Leicestershire LE8 0RX, UK
Tel: (+44) 116 279 2299
Fax: (+44) 116 279 2277
Email: books@troubador.co.uk
Web: www.troubador.co.uk/matador

ISBN 978 1784621 445

British Library Cataloguing in Publication Data.
A catalogue record for this book is available from the British Library.

Typeset in Adobe Garamond Pro by Troubador Publishing Ltd
Printed and bound in the UK by TJ International, Padstow, Cornwall

Matador is an imprint of Troubador Publishing Ltd

For my girls

An invitation from the author to her two
estranged daughters:

'*If a lifetime of wrongs really can be forgiven in one long*
weekend, then meet me there'.

The Old Lighthouse
1st December 3.00PM

'*Soon, I will see them again*'

The Beach Hut at Old Hunstanton
© Mike Sherman

FRIDAY

Hundreds of years battling wind, rain and sea meant that Old Hunstanton's chalky cliff edge had all but eroded away, until all that was left was a crumbling ledge shaped like the cheekily rolled-out tongue of a whale poking fun at the North Sea.

Balancing precariously on this outcrop was an old lighthouse, as grey and uninviting as a dead seal washed up on shore. Today, a depressing shoal of cloud and mist hung over the lighthouse's hunched shoulders and, beneath it, a long way down – on the grassy sand dunes below – beach huts the colour of faded seaside rock stood wearily in line, like dusty foot soldiers.

And then there was the sea. Cold, blustery and hostile, doing for the most part a grand job of keeping away straggling visitors to the shore.

Even so, alone on the shingle a woman strolled, not exactly happy in her own company but accustomed to it. With the sound of crashing waves filling her ears, Hazel Ladd turned her face into the direction of the wind, wanting to feel the full blast on her skin.

Savouring the mouthful of salty sea air that ice-skated across her tongue, she eventually let it slip away with a sigh. Hazel was so full of sighs; each one seemed to make her stand taller, straighter and fiercer. Then she stopped staring moodily at the sea and crossed the beach to where a sperm whale had been washed up on shore.

Looking down on the giant mammal, with its intelligent peephole eyes and harmless baleen teeth, Hazel felt she shared an affinity with the sorrowful creature. Never more so when she saw the broken fin that curved protectively at its side, as if it had once kept a calf close by. Appalled to see huge chunks of the mother whale's corpse missing – no doubt hacked off by souvenir hungry voyeurs – Hazel felt an intense anger stir inside her that wasn't supposed to be there.

Wanting to forget about the whale, she began walking toward the beach huts and this time the hint of a pleasant memory played out in front of her eyes.

Coming to an abrupt stop in the sand, she stared at the peeling red, white and blue beach hut that stood on rickety stilts. It had a roof of furry moss that reminded her of the worst of tongues. Only Hazel knew the reason why this beach hut, out of all the others, was so special and why it now held her attention.

Suddenly, the beach hut door banged open and shut in the wind and a squeal of children's laughter leapt out of nowhere. At the same time, a make-believe summer's day exploded onto the scene, casting a sunny orange glow on the sand. Hazel watched as the two fictional children she was so fond of conjuring up ran down to the sea, laughing. Always laughing as they chased the sun's rays toward the clear blue water.

They could so easily trip and fall. 'Be careful,' she wanted to shout. But just as she was about to warn them of the dangers, everything went quiet again and the children disappeared into the water. There was no more laughter; just an eerie silence as the sun dimmed and the sand went back to being grey and downcast. Her vision always had the same ending.

It no longer hurt Hazel to see them go. Not as much as it should. Looking down at her boots, she wondered *why* it didn't hurt more. Surely the guilt alone should have her crawling, with bloody knees, on the gritty sand?

In reality, it had been fifteen years since she last saw them. They were the reason she was here now, for three whole days, on Old Hunstanton beach – a place she'd vowed never to return to after all that happened there. *Could a lifetime of wrongs really be resolved in one long weekend?* she wondered doubtfully.

TIRED OF BEING told she'd be gorgeous if only she lost some weight, Yvonne Ladd struggled to climb the steep hill along the cliff parade. Being gorgeous was what got her into this mess in the first place, she realised. Having been the only girl in her year at school to get pregnant at fifteen, she was still a single mum, with no job, money, prospects or any sign of a suitable husband on the horizon six years later. The extra two-and-a-half stone she'd gained since giving birth not only hindered her progress in all of those respects but also caused her to break into an unattractive sweat.

She might be a rounder, plumper version of her former self, but Yvonne still took trouble with her appearance, particularly the glossy chestnut hair that hung down her back and ended in a curl that kicked out happily at the ends. Although deeply embarrassed by her weight gain, she did not feel the same way about the cause of it – her six-year-old daughter, Una.

Looking at her now and taking in her black scarecrow hair and skinny limbs, Yvonne experienced the same shock she did every time she looked at the child. Nobody would ever mistake them for mother and daughter. That difference was never more obvious than today, when Una was desperate to reach the top of the hill and the lighthouse and Yvonne was not.

Pausing for breath, Yvonne couldn't quite decide how she felt about revisiting the lighthouse again after so long. There it was now, waiting at the top of the incline, as it had for a hundred and fifty years or more, with its conical tower that clung for dear life to the crumbling white cliffs.

She now wished they'd waited for the next bus to come along instead of starting out on this long trudge. They'd only missed the earlier one by a few seconds and tried frantically waving the driver down. But he'd gone sailing past as if she didn't exist, which was surprising seeing she was built like a Volvo – sturdy and compact and meant to last.

Just then, a battered old Suzuki Vitara soft top drove past. It might not be the sleekest vehicle in town, but Yvonne looked wistfully after it all the same, glad to find it was not a Volvo. She may never have hitched a lift in her life, but today she wished she had the courage for it. Seeming to read her mind, the Suzuki had a change of heart and came back for them, its dodgy exhaust tapping an ominous tone on the highway as it did so.

Resting a heavily tattooed arm on the driver's open window, the female behind the wheel had a tidemark of clumsy orange makeup and sported a barber shop number 2 haircut. Her overindulgence in facial piercings meant you couldn't avoid staring at her face for too long. Yet underneath the face cutlery, Yvonne immediately recognised her and the shutters came down, like a guillotine, on her own face.

'Want a ride?' The driver's voice came out as little more than a hamster-like squeak. Instead of making eye contact with

Yvonne, she winked boyishly at Una and threw her a nervous 'help me out' grin.

Suddenly noticing Yvonne's red sweaty face, she nudged open the passenger door with her Doc Marten boot.

'Get in. Looks like you could do with a lift.'

'We're fine as we are,' Yvonne snapped, hoping her racing heartbeat did not give her away. After all, this was not somebody she normally stood up to.

'There's no helping some people.' The driver slammed the passenger door shut and revved the clapped-out old Suzuki for effect.

'You should have thought about that before,' Yvonne screeched, causing the driver's left eye to bounce up and down like an unpredictable lift shaft before settling erratically in one grey corner. It was a reaction Yvonne knew only too well, one that happened only when the driver was trying to hide something.

But before Yvonne could yell anything else at her, the driver took off in such a hurry that the Suzuki's wobbly exhaust finally surrendered itself to the tarmac.

Mother and daughter stared after the vehicle. No way was the driver going to lose face by coming back for the exhaust that now bounced down the hill. Luckily, there was no oncoming traffic in its path as it gathered speed and finally disappeared from view.

'Was that really who I think it was, Mummy?' asked Una, wrapping herself around her mother's generous legs.

'I'm afraid so.' Yvonne sighed, the weight of the world on her shoulders.

SITTING IN FRONT of an ornate dressing table mirror, Hazel brushed her well-schooled hair into place while a mist of expensive perfume created a cloud of sophistication around her.

Behind her, a suitcase lay open on the four-poster bed,

5

exposing scraps of lace underwear and expensive jewellery scattered amongst flimsy tissue paper. The bed was adorned with chiffon panels and chintz cushions, creating a glamorous, movie-star feel to the room. Always every inch the leading lady, Hazel felt entirely at home in the sophisticated surroundings.

Laying down the silver-plated paddle brush, which was part of an expensive vanity set, she impatiently tapped the Patek Phillippe watch that had been an anniversary present from her dearly-loved second husband. She was convinced the watch had stopped working again and would have given anything to have Phillip here now so she could playfully remind him of all the trouble it had caused. But it wasn't the watch. It was the waiting that was proving unendurable.

'Any minute now I will see them,' Hazel reflected, her face taking on a dreamy, expectant hue. But then she had another more depressing thought. 'Any minute now the pretence will start all over again,' she reminded herself, with a frown that considerably lessened her beauty.

Not liking what she saw in the mirror, she sniffed disapprovingly before blotting her lipstick with a tissue. Annoyed further by the impression her blood orange lips made on it, she discarded it in a wisteria-patterned bin. Getting up from a velvet stool with turned-out legs, she crossed the room to the window that looked down on the sea.

From the master bedroom of Old Hunstanton's redundant lighthouse (now a luxury holiday home that had belonged to the Ladd family for the last 18 years), Hazel looked down on the matchstick-sized people below. It occurred to her that of the small dots that made up the holidaymakers, dog walkers and day-tripping folk, *one* if not *two* of them could be related to her.

'How is it possible for a mother to love one daughter and not the other?' she pondered.

* * *

TWENTY YEARS AGO, Hazel's home had smelt of sponge cake, talcum powder, nappies in soak and Charlie perfume and the light fittings above her head had quivered with the sound of children happily running around upstairs.

That was when she'd enjoyed a much simpler life as a stay-at-home mum, living in an ordinary terraced house with a wilderness for a garden that backed onto a railway line.

Those were the days she allowed *The Sun* into her home without being snobbish about it. When the family sat down to a meal every Sunday of a Bernard Matthews turkey joint, followed by an arctic roll they would all clap and applaud as if it was the nicest thing to ever happen to them. A time when she thought drinking Blue Nun and having a microwave was the height of sophistication.

As if it were yesterday, Hazel could easily recall some of the first precious moments spent in that house with her children: baking fairy cakes, reading bedtime stories, playing at dressing up and games of hide and seek. Nor did she have any trouble remembering when those moments had first been spoilt or when the terror had begun. For a second or two, she was someplace else. A place in her past she didn't want to revisit.

The nursery had smelt of cotton wool, Johnson's baby lotion and breast milk, Hazel remembered reluctantly. She'd been rocking her newborn to sleep when she first noticed the sulky-looking toddler in the doorway, clutching a toy that had seen better days.

In fact, that wasn't the only thing jaded about the child; even her clothes looked neglected. The knitted cardigan she wore had snags in it and her pale little face was sticky from spaghetti hoops.

Underneath the dirt and sorrowful expression, the three-year-old looked as if she very much wanted to be part of the happy family scene in front of her. But instead of allowing her to do just that, Hazel had sprung to her feet and cruelly slammed the door in her face before going back to cuddling her newborn.

* * *

TOUCHING THE COOL glass of the windowpane that separated her from her children – who may or may not be out there right now – and avoiding the reflection of the scowling woman looking back at her, Hazel had difficulty acknowledging her own cruel behaviour. Instead, she made a promise to herself.

'I will make it up to you. I swear. All I need is one weekend to make everything right again.' This was said with teeth so gritted that her jaw barely moved. As she relaxed it, a more carefree expression settled on her face.

'I wonder which one will arrive first?' she asked innocently of the sea, having quickly grown indifferent to her own heartlessness.

HOLDING FINGERS – NOT hands, mind, but fingers, because that was their 'thing' – Yvonne and Una stood at the archway of a ruined chapel, through which they could see the defunct lighthouse.

The archway was all that remained of St Edmund's Chapel, which had been built to commemorate the saint who first landed on the spot in 950AD. Nowadays, though, it was little more than a point of interest, signalling visitors' arrival at the lighthouse that gazed formidably down on the sea – the magical holiday home where Yvonne had spent all her summers.

It was a place that conjured up memories of spiders in corners, fish and chips eaten on a rug on the floor, "Wiley the Sea Monster" carrying day trippers out to the wash and rooms at the very top of the lighthouse that she was too frightened to enter because of the sheer drop to the sea below.

Despite being brought up by the seaside, Yvonne had always been afraid of the ocean. To her, it was a terrifying place of dirty grey water that her sister said contained human waste and that, if it got into your mouth, you had to make yourself sick, fast. Or die.

Yes, indeed, this was where all her childhood memories had been formed. And yet there was no way of telling from her expression whether she was pleased to be reminded of them or not.

A LARGE GLACIAL chandelier swung dangerously high above Yvonne and Una's heads in the lighthouse's entrance hall, as they shuffled like delicate chess pieces, across the checkerboard tiled floor, imagining they could hear the ceramic splinter under their feet.

The old fireplace, which was big enough to swallow children whole, hadn't been lit in years and was as unwelcoming as the rest of the room, which was bare as old bones. The emptiness added to the eerie echo in which Yvonne imagined she could hear the sounds of her childhood.

'Stop it Vee, stop it. Or I'll tell Mum!' a younger Yvonne cried. Then came the laughter – spiteful, teasing know-it-all laughter from another child.

Meanwhile, the grown-up Yvonne chewed off a hangnail on her thumb and waited anxiously, feeling like a wide-eyed mouse that had the predatory shadow of a bird-of-prey hovering above it.

But she didn't have to wait long. Because there she was now – her mother, gliding ghostlike down the spiral staircase and stepping off the last rung so gracefully she could have stepped into Vivien Leigh's shoes at a moment's notice. Her mother, who was so beautiful, and so impossible to outshine.

'Where's Venetia?' Hazel asked, looking around with arms outstretched as if she expected both her daughters to immediately fall into them, like nothing bad had ever happened. 'Didn't she arrive with you?'

A scowl set up home on Yvonne's face. Not only was her mother's preference for her sister hard to swallow, it was doubly hard to witness the disappointment on her face when she knew she was the cause of it. As usual.

'It's nice to see you too, Mum,' she replied bitterly, pushing past Hazel. In her haste to get away, Yvonne took the stairs two at a time, hating the way the flimsy metal steps trembled and groaned under her weight.

NOTHING MUCH HAD altered in this room in the last fifteen years, Yvonne noticed. Except perhaps for the widening waistline of a damp patch she'd once claimed resembled Princess Diana's face. Otherwise, there were the same matching velvet headboards belonging to the twin beds and the frilled B&B-style bedspreads that had been religiously turned down every evening and folded neatly back again every morning.

Not daring to invade her prickly daughter's space, Hazel watched from the open doorway of the guest bedroom as Yvonne unpacked her holdall, tossing items asunder as if they were death row inmates not worth worrying about.

'Fifteen years and all you can do is ask about Venetia.' Yvonne knew how whiney she sounded, but she couldn't stop herself. She wanted to throw everything at her mother there and then but knew she would never dare.

'What about your own granddaughter?' she demanded, pointing at Una, who was bouncing up and down on one of the beds and making a mess of the bedspread, not knowing that in this house, this was not allowed.

IGNORING YVONNE, HAZEL came in proper, somewhat startled to see the little girl using the bed as a trampoline, her faux fur coat flapping like an alarmed animal about to take flight.

Hazel hadn't noticed her properly before and was now intent on remedying that. Holding out her hand, she tried out a timid smile on the odd-looking little waif that was her granddaughter.

'Una, I'm so happy to meet you at last.' Too polite. Much too formal. Hazel hadn't intended her words to be quite so grown-up.

Awkwardly, Una shook hands with her grandmother and, as soon as it was polite to do so, pulled her hand away. Until Hazel made friends with her mother – proper friends, that is – she wasn't going to be won over.

Hazel bent down to Una's level. Her voice took on a breathy, movie-star quality.

'I never thought I'd be lucky enough to have a granddaughter, let alone get to meet her. We are going to have a lovely time here. You wait and see.'

Peeking slyly at her grandmother, Una flashed Hazel a suspicious look. 'Will we get to play on the beach?'

'Every day.' Hazel's girlish laughter tinkled like cut glass in a celebratory toast.

'And make sandcastles?' Una wasn't convinced just yet.

'Every day, if you want to.'

11

'And eat ice cream?'

'Just like your mother.' Hazel's merry eyes sought out Yvonne's, hoping to enjoy a shared moment. Too late she realised her blunder as her ever-sensitive daughter stormed into the en-suite bathroom.

'Mummy's not fat!' Una was on the warpath again, frowning at Hazel.

Resting her hand on Una's wild buckaroo hair, Hazel fought back the urge to take a brush to it.

'Of course she isn't. She's beautiful. Just like you.'

Una beamed, ready to forgive her grandmother anything and everything, not knowing that, one day, she would have to do exactly that.

'Will we do all the things you and Mummy used to do on your holidays here?' she wanted to know.

Hazel was troubled by the question. A withdrawn, mysterious look settled on her imperial features.

'Most of them, my darling. Most of them.' So distant was she in this moment, Hazel could hardly be described as being in the same room.

THE MAHOGANY TABLE was set for a formal dinner but the crystal glasses and Royal Albert fine bone china plates remained untouched. Unusually, nobody had yet helped themselves to the steaming dishes of iron-rich greens, baby carrots or sweet corn drizzled in butter. The creamy potato dauphinoise and chicken breasts wrapped in Parma ham, in their matching serving dishes, were also ignored.

Behind the glass panels of a Victorian dresser, more of the same dinner service was displayed, along with an assortment of silver ornaments that included inscribed family heirlooms and trophies that would emphatically deny any association with the Ladd family.

Elsewhere, candles had been lit in glass hurricane lamps that flickered gloomy, otherworldly shadows over the walls, creating uninvited guests for dinner. Ones Yvonne and her sister had once made up names for, such as the handsome Mr Darkly and the sexy Miss Silhouette, who used to torment the former with her sensual dance moves. Mr Naughty had been another made-up character, but his name wasn't to be mentioned out loud. Especially not three times over whilst staring into a mirror.

For some reason, the heavy drapes at the dining room window had been drawn, deliberately obscuring the spectacular view of the North Beach, which meant the room was like the atmosphere – dark and oppressive, as if the sun didn't exist outside its formal confines. An awkward silence prevailed as Hazel, Yvonne and Una sat staring at the empty place setting in front of them.

Nobody could have guessed how much Hazel wrung her hands underneath the table due to how still and straight she sat in her chair. Even Una, unused to such decorous surroundings, dared not make a sound and took extra care not to scuff her shoes against her chair.

The only one refusing to be still or silent was Yvonne. Her raised eyebrows told a story of their own as she huffed and puffed out her frustration and drummed her nails on the polished table. Hazel was pretending not to recognise her impatient, childhood tapped-out rendition of "Why Are We Waiting?" but Yvonne knew her mother's nerves were on edge just as much as hers. Finally, she threw Hazel a frosty look, purposefully unfolded her linen napkin and nodded for Una to make a start on her dinner.

'We ought to wait,' Hazel reminded her.

'She's an hour late already and we're both starving,' Yvonne snapped. She still hadn't forgiven her mother for earlier.

Again, Yvonne gave Una the go-ahead to eat, but under her grandmother's disapproving gaze, she was incapable of lifting the heavier-than-normal silver-plated cutlery.

'What will she think if we start without her? This is meant to be a family dinner.' More than a hint of annoyance had crept into Hazel's voice, but Yvonne tucked in all the same, spilling carrot and sweet corn as she went, beyond caring what her mother thought.

'We're family too, Mum. Or had you forgotten?'

At that moment, the door was thrown open and in staggered the person causing all the fuss – the driver of the Suzuki Yvonne had bumped into earlier.

Completely slaughtered after downing a dozen vodka and cokes at The Ancient Mariner Inn (where she'd run out of Mayfair cigarettes, been turned down by a bi-curious girl in tight animal print leggings *and* fallen out with the usually affable barman), Venetia Cox immediately reared up when she spotted that her sister had already started eating.

'Well, don't mind me,' she slurred. 'You just go and pig out for both of us, why don't you?'

And with that, Venetia stumbled over to a large silver urn on the display cabinet, which was engraved with none other than the coat of arms of Hunstanton's founding family, Le Strange, and promptly threw up into it.

SHE HAD STAYED away as long as possible, deliberately outstaying her welcome at the inn, where the goateed barman had made her laugh out loud with his, "What do Essex girls use for protection during sex?" slogan T-shirt. The answer, "Bus shelters", was printed on the back.

Shame about Carly, though – the 19-year-old spray tanner who, after two-and-a-half hours of flirty exchanges across the pool table, disappeared into the bogs with the same fucking barman who'd kept rudely refusing to serve her. Why the girl had suddenly gone all huffy and heterosexual on her, she had no idea. People! Honestly. No matter how hard she tried, Venetia (known as Vee for short) never understood them.

It was the same with her sister and mother, neither of whom she had ever got along with – even though she knew her mother better than anyone else, including the two dead husbands she'd already got through and her faithful little lapdog daughter, Yvonne.

But how did I end up being so different to them? she wondered. *And how come I have so much hate in my heart for my own flesh and blood?*

It was true that Vee had only to look in the mirror to acknowledge she had done a brilliant job of obliterating any resemblance to either of them. Surprisingly, she herself had once been rather pretty and could hold her own against Yvonne, but that was now a very long time ago. Since then she'd dyed her hair jet black, got her tongue, nose and eyebrow pierced and filled up most of the white space on her skin with Gothic tattoos she didn't understand the meaning of.

Having rejected the feminine ways of her sister and mother, who were, as far as she was concerned, both manipulative and deceitful, she had decided to become a lesbian. A cold, practical decision based, at first, on nothing more than a strong desire to insult her mother and shock her Barbie-doll sister. But since she no longer harboured any doubts about her sexual preferences – she doted on young uncomplicated girls in the same way she

15

would a wrinkle-faced puppy – everything seemed to have turned out for the best.

The painful absence of any such partner in Vee's life only went to prove what a lonely, troubled woman she was. For this, too, she blamed her mother.

As for her *own* blame, her punishment for turning up late *and* drunk was to wash up while the others went off to their rooms to freshen up or gorge on chocolate – depending on who you happened to be.

She still couldn't get over how much little Vonnie had ballooned since she last saw her. Alright, maybe she shouldn't have called her a pig, or as good as, but it wasn't as if she didn't deserve it. *No more than I deserve such a banging headache*, she thought wryly, as she squeamishly carried the plates of uneaten food into the kitchen. It was an undertaking that made her gag, like a worm-riddled cat, every time her mean glance fell on a slice of grey potato or piece of soggy chicken skin.

Feeling more at home in this room than any other, Vee was reassured by the warm-hearted iron range and the nautical knick-knacks on the walls that they had, as a family, collected over the years from quirky seaside gift shops. She also remembered many wet days spent over at the table by the window playing cards. Or, "I Spy With My Little Eye" – a game that routinely involved a lot of words beginning with the letter S – for sea, seagull, seal, sandcastle, shell, sun, and so on.

Back then, Vonnie had been such a generous loser; it would never have entered her head to accuse anyone of cheating at their favourite game of Snap. Although of course Vee had, for she could never bear to lose at anything. Especially not to her sister.

Loving the knotted feel of the wooden floorboards under her

bare feet, Vee shook off the sad memories that threatened to melt her heart and tried to focus instead on the chore of scraping congealed carrots into the bin, but she kept missing.

Too late, she realised, she had been barmy to come. She should have slept off her drunkenness in one of the Le Strange Arms self-catering chalets or at the very least kept on driving after the confrontation with Yvonne on the hill. What a little wildcat her sister had become. *That* certainly hadn't been expected.

Nobody need remind her how much she'd hurt her sister, but was she never to be forgiven? And what about what Vonnie had done to her? Didn't that count?

But the child. Could that scrawny fur-ball with the gobstopper eyes really be her niece? A full-of-beans gnome who was as much a part of her as Yvonne had once been, back in the day when they had been friends. Maybe one day she would get to stroke the tangled scarecrow hair and even grow fond of her (in her own laidback way).

But the only way she would now get that chance was to ignore the ominous warning signs that crawled like the living dead over her skin screaming, 'Get the hell out of here while you still can.'

NORMALLY, HAZEL HATED being exposed to the bright lights and loud music of the amusement arcade, where holidaymakers with burnt skin, varicose veins and bulging pockets full of change crowded in around her, but tonight she barely noticed them at all.

Instead, she watched Una take snapshots of elderly, blue-rinse ladies whose big bottoms spilled out of their cheap plastic seats. Every so often, she would point the camera lens in Hazel's direction, dazzling her with its powerful flash so that her eyes filled with too many suns. The Canon T80 had been in the Ladd family for as long as Hazel could remember, but she had decided to gift it to her granddaughter as a peace offering and so that Una could create a perfect family album of their weekend together.

Hazel couldn't remember a time when she had been so happy. She was delighted to have her family back together again; all she really wanted to do was a celebratory cartwheel – a gymnastic feat she hadn't attempted since she was 13. Once again, she had to remind herself to show even more reserve than usual, because it was early days yet and Venetia and Yvonne, who hadn't exactly got off to the best of starts, weren't ready to share her enthusiasm.

Aware of other people glancing pointedly at her or sizing her up in an unpleasant way, Hazel put their curiosity down to the fact that they knew who she was. There could be no other reason for their blunt fascination – none that was in the least tolerable to her, at any rate.

'See, I told you it was her.' Hazel overheard a woman in easy-iron polyester slacks whisper to her friend, a woman resembling a crossbred dog with long, straggly hair that kept getting caught up in her large hoop earrings.

'I don't know how she's got the nerve,' the Heinz 57 whined, before no doubt going off to sniff out a decomposing bone.

By now, Hazel was used to people staring, although that hadn't always been the case. Having kept a low profile in the seaside community, she had, out of shyness, turned down numerous offers to join the many clubs and associations Hunstanton boasted. But by failing to attend any of their charity fund-raising events, she had unintentionally insulted the locals, causing an irreconcilable rift she wasn't in any hurry to heal.

Consequently, she was instantly recognisable as the wealthy widowed owner of the lighthouse, who not only owned a top-of the-range Range Rover Sport but also had a whole wardrobe of fancy clothes and expensive jewellery to go with it. She was also extraordinarily attractive for her age, looking much younger than her forty-five years. Most probably they were just jealous – and who could blame them?

Even the chubby bingo caller, who wore a jazzy bow tie and tuxedo and went by the name of 'Fat Kev' (like it or not), froze to the spot when he saw her. Forgetting he had the microphone in his hand, he accidentally spluttered the word 'shit' out loud to his audience. Then, getting a laugh he hadn't bargained on, he went back to his amateur dramatics.

'Two little ducks. Twenty-two,' he chirruped, and was immediately rewarded with quacking noises from the players.

'Number eleven. It's those legs eleven.'

This time, the players wolf-whistled in as lewd a manner as was possible for the mostly celibate over sixty-fives.

Ignoring the hostile crowd, Hazel concentrated on helping Una understand the rules of bingo and together they chipped in with the usual responses, just as if they too were regular bingo players.

Voice loaded with doom and gloom, Fat Kev played out his favourite chant of the evening, 'Unlucky for some. Thirteen.' But his piggy little eyes flitted side to side nervously, like an overweight Action Man's, when Hazel's glance happened upon him, leaving him with the distinct impression that it had definitely been unlucky for him.

The truth was, Hazel was not remotely interested in the former Butlins' Redcoat, and had been looking out for someone else entirely when their eyes happened to clash.

But Fat Kev and the crowd's unfriendly reception were both immediately forgotten when at last Hazel spotted them. Perhaps

19

she could relax a little, now she could see that they weren't tearing each other's hair out.

COMPLETELY UNAWARE OF her mother's observation, or of the commotion she was causing in the amusement arcade, Venetia competitively eyed up Yvonne's scorecard, knowing that no matter who won this game of bingo, there could only be one winner when it came to their mother's affections.

Still suffering with a hangover the size of the North Sea, she felt like a scrawny rat that had gone five rounds with a pack of terriers but who'd lived to tell the tale. Most likely because of it, her mood hadn't improved any.

'Two fat ladies. Eighty-eight,' Fat Kev called out, causing Vee to dart a suggestive smirk Yvonne's way. She may as well have called her sister a "fatty", but Yvonne was giving her the cold shoulder and refusing to bite. Just one number was all Vee needed for a full house. That would show her.

'Top of the house. Ninety. Nine-oh.'

'Bingo,' Vee whooped, jumping out of her chair. Next thing she knew, she was waving her scorecard deliberately in her sister's face, so close it nearly caused a paper cut.

'You snooze you lose, Vonnie,' she hissed in her sister's perfectly formed ear. For a moment, she dwelled on how unfair it was that a girl like Yvonne, who already had everything, should also end up with quite possibly the prettiest ears she'd ever seen. But it didn't stop her sister sulkily ripping her card in two as Vee received her prize – a large, stuffed cuddly lion.

LIGHTS FROM THE funfair lit up the otherwise dark and deserted north promenade as they made their way back to the lighthouse. The tide was in and the sea was calm beside them, lapping gently at the sea wall; taller distorted versions of themselves followed behind in the form of shadows caught in the flickering light, like a family of ghosts going for a pleasant evening stroll.

Lost in her own thoughts, but keeping one wary eye on the shadows, Hazel was caught off-guard by a familiar figure selling hotdogs from a burger van.

Small and thin, with a hooked nose, he appeared to notice her at exactly the same moment she did him. For the briefest of moments, they shared a relationship that is only possible between two sets of inquisitive eyes; one in which all kinds of questions and answers are bounced silently back and forth.

Five minutes later she saw him again, this time blowing up an inflatable dolphin for a child outside one of the many souvenir and gift shops Hunstanton was famous for. There was no doubting it was him. He had the same narrow eyes, and a single golden tooth glistened from his dark mouth, as if it were a piece of burning orange coal.

This time, Hazel did not raise her eyes to his. Refusing to acknowledge his ghostly presence, she kept her gaze down instead, watching how one leg moved in front of the other; transfixed by her Charlotte Olympia jewelled pumps. She did not even bother to glance over at the man bringing in the sign from a café up the road because she already knew who he was and understood that he wanted to surprise her by being the same man all over again.

That he unsettled her was obvious. But she kept on walking all the same, not allowing a smile, tear, frown or crease to appear on her face. If she pretended hard enough that he didn't exist, she knew she could make him disappear. It only required a little deep concentration. Just a few seconds more and she would be far enough away...

'What are you looking at, Granny?' Una's voice seemed to come from a great distance, as if it had been carried along on a rain cloud.

'Nothing. Nobody.' Hazel stuttered, glancing quickly around to make sure that he really had gone.

DELIBERATELY IGNORING EACH other, Venetia and Yvonne walked in silence, avoiding being too close to the other. A good eighteen inches apart felt comfortable. Any closer than that and they would have been in danger of lashing out at each other.

Trailing some distance behind were Hazel and Una, whose voracious tongue kept diving into the candyfloss she was holding.

Every so often, Vee noticed Yvonne steal a sly look behind them, as if checking that Una was still there. What she thought was going to happen to her, in 'Sunny Hunny' of all places, she had no idea. But when her sister's ever-protective eye wasn't focused on her daughter, she was glad to see it was enviously eying up her own prized win – the cuddly lion.

Having always been highly competitive, even as a child, Vee still couldn't help gloating over any achievement, no matter how small. Knowing that the sight of her holding the cuddly lion only worsened her sister's mood made her do it all the more. The desire to tease and antagonise Yvonne was by now too deep-rooted for her to be able to stop.

Although she was tired of fighting, she still couldn't help reacting to the surly side glances her sister kept throwing her. Vee had always been this way. As soon as she found herself alone with Yvonne, with no one's attention to fight over, she was ready to forgive and forget and keen to be friends again. But not so Vonnie. Vee could never bring herself to understand why she didn't feel the same.

'Get over it, will you?' Deciding to take her on, albeit playfully, Vee nudged her sister into a pathetic little stumble, but all she got for it was a raised half-moon eyebrow and an overly dramatic sigh.

Vee sulked and fumed for just a few seconds more before thrusting the cuddly lion at her sister.

'You can have it if it makes you feel any better.'

It didn't. Instead of accepting the lion as a peace offering, it bounced tragically to the ground, landing on its whiskery snarling face. Yvonne stormed off ahead, as if it had attempted to bite off both her hands.

Quickly, Vee caught up with her and got right in her sister's face. In moments like this she was truly frightening.

'You're so spoilt. You never have been able to stand not getting your own way.' Her words caused Yvonne's jaw to drop in ridicule.

'Spoilt? You were always the favourite.'

'You've got to be kidding.'

Pointing accusingly in Hazel's direction, Yvonne screamed in her sister's face, 'She let you get away with murder and you know it.'

COMING TO A halt at these incriminating words, Hazel stared hard at Venetia and Yvonne, who were by now so caught up in their own argumentative world that they'd forgotten they were part of a foursome, a family outing.

That's when Hazel felt Una press her shaky little palm into her own Dior-fragranced hand, and shook off the ominous feeling that one day Una would remember this same perfume, a poignant reminder of her grandmother, and be reminded of suffering.

'Did Mummy and Aunt Vee always argue, even when they were little girls?' Una was desperate to know.

The question hung in the air as Hazel paused to think about that.

* * *

BY NOW, HAZEL knew where all the doors in the vast corridors led and what hospital department she would need for which particular emergency. She also knew what vending machines were reliable and which ones swallowed your money without so much as a scrap of remorse.

But on this particular visit, salt and vinegar crisps and a king-size Mars bar were the last things on her mind as she watched anxiously, fighting off a queasy feeling in her stomach, as her little girl writhed in pain while a doctor applied drops to her eyes.

'It might sting for a while but luckily no permanent damage has been done,' he advised coolly, handing the tearful toddler back to Hazel.

The bearded man with enormous hands was unlike most others Hazel came across in that he was unimpressed by her face and figure. It was not a situation she was entirely comfortable with, for she could see there would be no "winning over" of this taciturn Captain Birds Eye remnant. Hazel could not have guessed in a month of Sundays that his sexual preferences ran to excessively hairy women he met through personal columns of seedy magazines.

'A pencil in the eye?' the doctor commented doubtfully, scrutinising her daughter's medical notes and scribbling illegible warning notes in the margin – medical jargon Hazel didn't understand. All the same, she could have sworn she'd seen him jot down the words 'social services' and had to force herself not to snatch the piece of paper away so that she could shred it into tiny pieces until it no longer existed. She wished it was gone, along with the humiliating recollection.

'How did this happen, Mrs Cox?' he'd demanded. As if she was a criminal. As if he didn't believe her.

Hazel's eyes had darted fearfully to her eldest daughter, then just five years old, who stood by watching defiantly, unmoved by her mother's accusing stare. Unable to meet those unsettling eyes head on, Hazel concentrated instead on the lie she was about to tell.

* * *

FEELING SOMEONE TUGGING at her sleeve, Hazel was surprised to find Una's hand still resting in hers. She'd completely forgotten about the child, but then memories had a habit of doing that to her. Sometimes she could lose a whole hour or even a day to the past.

Now, what was it the child had wanted to know? Ah, yes. That was it.

'All sisters argue, Una,' Hazel told her.

'But they love each other really?' Una persisted, as if her world depended on the answer.

Unsurely, Hazel gazed worriedly at her still squabbling daughters, hoping against hope that everything would turn out right in the end.

NOTHING HAD GONE to plan so far. In fact, Venetia could safely say that things were turning out far worse than anticipated. For instance, why on earth did she keep picking on Yvonne, making even more of an enemy out of her when she'd come here to make amends? Why was it proving so difficult?

'Venetia, darling. You really must try to make friends with Yvonne if this weekend is going to be a success,' her mother had warned. But why must she always make the first move when Vonnie could be so stubborn?

'As always, I'm relying on you, Venetia, dear,' her mother had cajoled, not without menace.

Venetia had always hated her Christian name, thinking it overly pretentious and at complete variance with her own 'without airs' personality. In fact, everyone including Yvonne called her Vee, never Venetia – everyone except her mother, that is.

Vee didn't know if she did it on purpose, but Hazel would always articulate the word 'Venetia' in a cringing Marilyn Monroe whisper. As if by doing so she imagined the soft dreamy sound of her daughter's name on her lips would radiate some misplaced femininity in Vee's steel-toe-capped-boot direction.

Whilst her mother might still harbour the possibility of Vee turning her back on lesbianism, or somehow miraculously learning how to make daisy chains in green meadows whilst wearing a floating chiffon dress, there was in truth nothing dreamy, floral or appealing about the face looking back at her in the glass. In fact, Vee's reflection couldn't be described as anything other than ugly and devoid of charm.

She had climbed to the top of the lighthouse tower to be alone. To think. Just as she'd done all those years ago when she wanted to be by herself, knowing Yvonne would never dare follow her up here.

Vee wasn't sure that the others even knew this breathing space existed, because even HE didn't stalk her up here. It was the one place she could escape to without hearing the constant whispering of her name coming from every dark corner of the lighthouse or feeling his rank, putrid breath on her skin. This, then, was her sanctuary. A place where, during the day, the shrieking of the seagulls proved overwhelming, but at night you were gently babysat by the wind hissing through cracks in the brickwork. And, in place of a doting mother, the clunk of metal banging against metal provided a soothing lullaby.

It was dark and cold in the tower, where the rain (or mist, she had never been sure which) drizzled in slow motion down the soulless glass windows. In the past, she'd never been able to resist drawing faces on the glass, conjuring up a perfect make-believe family to whom she belonged. She'd even given them names and personalities – Clayton was the strong fresh-faced father who always had a spare knee for Vee to perch on, and wholesome Jenny was an insignificant plain-Jane of a mother who didn't attract attention wherever she went, and whose only purpose in life was to make her husband and child happy. Significantly, there had been no other siblings in Vee's fantasy family.

Not once during all her night time forays into the tower had anybody ever come looking for her; she didn't expect tonight would be any different. She had never been missed in the same way Vonnie was; whenever her sister left a room, all heads would start to glance around, agitated without knowing why, until her cheeky grin was back amongst them again.

It wasn't Vonnie's fault that nobody could help looking at her, no matter what mundane task she might be doing – whether that be a 1,000-piece shrimping-on-the-beach jigsaw puzzle, colouring in drawings in a book (careful not to stray outside the lines) or making a friendship bracelet out of glass beads. One particular summer, Vonnie had made them all a bracelet, spending hours on each one and getting the colours just right; they were meant to signify the receiver's personality.

For Hazel's bracelet, she had chosen cool blues and greens, like the mysterious ocean; for Phillip, navy for the smart blazers he wore and red stripes for his deferential old school tie. As for Vee, it had to be blacks and purples, because these "suited her moods best", Vonnie had maintained without any intention of causing offence. Even Mrs Dunoon, the "twice a week is more than enough at my age, with all those stairs" cleaner her mother employed, had not been left out, for Vonnie didn't have it in her to be unkind.

'Pink for your chubby little cheeks,' she'd told the usually indifferent, cud-chewing goat of a woman whose hideous varicose veins had been the subject of much lamented discussion in their household.

Never a day went by after that when Mrs Dunoon didn't jangle the same bracelet on her fleshy wrist, just to keep "Miss Yvonne" happy. It was true that in thinking the best of everybody, Vonnie was loved back in abundance, and there hadn't been a day in Vee's childhood when she didn't wish she could be more like her sister. More worryingly, a day hadn't gone by either when she also hadn't wished her dead.

Of course, even Vonnie hadn't been perfect. Mess with any of her meticulously cared-for possessions and she'd claw at you and draw blood if she could. But she'd always beg forgiveness afterwards with anguished, heart-wrenching sobs; 'How could I have done that to you? I am so sorry. Please say you will forgive me or I will die.'

So whilst it was fair to say Vonnie certainly did have a temper when roused, it was also true that nobody could stay angry with her for long. But then, as her mother had informed Vee time and time again, Vonnie wasn't *allowed* to get upset or angry. Something to do with the fainting fits she'd been diagnosed with as a toddler (which she was now famed for), because even an angry word or raised voice could result in Vonnie holding her breath long enough to make her pass out.

It wasn't that she did it on purpose, the doctors had told her mother, more a case of severe emotional breakdown whenever the child got upset. Therefore, "do not upset Yvonne under any circumstances" became a familiar mantra throughout Vee's childhood. This illness, diagnosed as vasovagal syncope, had become an everyday part of their lives. One that no doubt caused her mother many sleepless nights, but which turned out to be bloody unfair on a sibling who sometimes felt her sister deserved a good belt across the lugs.

Now that she came to think of it, Vee realised that instead of coming up here to be by herself, so that she could decide on what course of action might be best for her, she had done nothing but think about Vonnie.

It was the same for everyone, though. Anyone Vonnie ever came into contact with couldn't help but love her – friends, aunts and uncles, old people, hard-boiled travelling fair people, boys… especially boys, and especially as she got older. No indeed. Nobody could be blamed for falling head over heels in love with Vonnie.

Love. She'd had the word tattooed along her right forearm. Funnily enough, it had been one of her earliest tattoos and perversely one of the most painful. There it was, right next to the heart with the word DAD tattooed in its centre, in scream-out-loud capitals.

Taking a Swiss army knife out of the back pocket of her

camouflage trousers, Vee flicked out a two-inch blade and, without hesitation, dug it into the outline of the D, immediately drawing a fine line of blood that trickled down her arm into the L belonging to Love.

After spending all this time up here in the tower, she had, without realising, grown accustomed once again to the ammonia-fuelled smell of the bat droppings that formed a crunchy black blanket on the concrete floor where her boots, of their own accord, drew impressions of alien life forms.

Along with her favourite pink and white nougat from Rocky Thompson's sweet stall, the smell of beer and cigarette smoke at the Kit Kat club before it burned down or cockles soaked in vinegar in a paper cup, it was one of the most comforting smells of her childhood.

THE HIDEOUS AVOCADO circular bathtub had always reminded Yvonne of a giant green bug that would swallow you whole should you ever be fully submerged in it. She watched it fill with water now, still a little dubious about getting in, even after all these years.

Wiping steam from the mirrored bathroom cabinet with the palm of her podgy hand, Yvonne slid a clip into her long hair so it wouldn't get wet. Next, she rubbed a generous amount of Pears cream onto her round face until it shone like leftover beef dripping in a roasting tin.

Apart from a few scars here and there – one above her right eye, conveniently hidden under her eyebrow, and another, shaped like an elephant's tusk on her nose, visible only now she had removed her makeup – her skin was in fabulous condition.

She might have inherited her perfect complexion from her mother, but not her mother's astonishing capacity to modify the truth. Did Hazel seriously think she couldn't remember how she'd earned each and every one of these scars? Well, one of these days Yvonne was going to let her have the truth, like it or not. Only she secretly hoped it wouldn't be today.

Pulling an unattractive face, Yvonne poked out her tongue at her reflection. So she had great skin. So what? It was the rest of her that was the porky pig problem.

Annoyingly, the peach guest towel didn't quite fit around her ample cleavage, so she let it drop to the floor and quickly stepped into the foam-filled water before she could change her mind. She was immediately enveloped in the calming scent of lavender, but it did little to boost her mood. For as long as she could remember, her mother had insisted on having lavender bath salts in this bathroom, convinced of the uplifting effect it had on the children's moods.

Disguised by steam, the ugly plumbing and the crackle glaze tiles remained invisible, thank goodness. Not so the memories of sharing baths with her sister in this very room. There had been much splashing and laughter, Yvonne seemed to recall, and the pointing out of rude body bits when their mother wasn't looking.

It hadn't all been like an episode of *Little House On The Prairie*, though; Yvonne could still remember when somebody had tried to drown her in this bath.

She couldn't remember how old she'd been at the time, but what she did recall in vivid detail was the terrifying sensation of being held down in the water as it churned like a witch's cauldron of poisonous broth, spilling everywhere. She could remember the rising panic of not being allowed back up as if it were yesterday; the feeling of being desperate for air, frantic to know whose hands held her down.

Afterwards, when calm had been restored with the return of

her stepfather, Phillip, and she was sitting up in bed with a cup of hot chocolate, her hair still dripping wet, there had been much heated discussion and many accusations.

Yvonne was being overdramatic and must stop this exaggerating, she could hear her mother claiming. It had been a "fainting fit", nothing more.

'There is no need to call a doctor, Phillip, as no harm has been done,' her mother had insisted. *No harm done!*

The suspicion that Hazel had left them unsupervised in the bath while she went off to do her hair (in anticipation of Phillip coming home early) had been glossed over. She was not responsible. Hadn't she saved her daughter's life by scooping her out of the water and giving her a good shake to clear her lungs?

Vee's testimony that Yvonne had got her finger stuck in the tap, panicked and fainted was also dismissed as nonsense. As was her claim that she had been the one to save her sister by pulling out the bath plug, dragging her to the surface by her hair and screaming for help.

Either way, Yvonne knew that somebody was to blame for what happened to her that night and, one way or another, she was determined to find out who.

Surprisingly, Phillip never got to the bottom of what happened either, but Yvonne could remember him expressing his suspicions to her later that same night. It had been a sad moment, because it was the first time she understood they were a pair, like the birds in the hedgerow that coupled up and chased all the others away. She had grown even more panicky, thinking that perhaps it was the other way around, that she and Phillip were the outsiders – the ones being chased away.

'As much as I love your mother, Yvonne, I couldn't help

noticing how flustered she was, and that's just not like her,' Phillip had confided from the bottom of her bed.

'Not only was her hair all over the place, but her makeup was smudged, as if she'd been crying.' He'd paused at this point as if to test Yvonne's loyalty, but she'd remained silent and spoke only with giant watery eyes.

'Afterwards, when I tried to talk to her about it, she kept flinching, almost as if she were fending off blows from somebody about to attack her.'

Yvonne hadn't known what to say. She wasn't used to adults asking her for advice. So, rather than risk saying the wrong thing, she'd tucked a bit of his hair back around his ear in exactly the same way her mother did to her. That usually helped when she was upset.

'But, to the best of my knowledge, I've never known her cry, and she certainly isn't capable of getting into a fight with anyone. Not your mother,' He'd gone on to say.

Yvonne might only have been five or six years old at the time, but even she could sense the doubt creeping into his voice and wished she had a gobstopper to give him. With that, he'd shaken his head bemusedly, in the same way he did when he struggled over *The Times* crossword. As he got up from the bed, an empty whisky tumbler dropped out of his hand and rolled like a straw bale over the bumpy carpet until it came to rest against her Sindy dolls house (the one with the rooftop balcony).

She wondered if he would notice and pick it up, but he never did. Days later, she buried the glass under one of the beach huts without knowing why, except that it felt as if it had died of a broken heart the second it left his lips. But not before she ran her finger around the crystallised rim and tasted the residue of a golden liquid that made her want to retch, the same way she'd seen mullet-haired boys do outside the Wash And Tope pub.

As for Vee, Phillip had concluded she was but a child and unfortunately not one who could be relied on to tell the truth – unlike Yvonne, who, they all agreed, never lied.

'Speak the truth and shame the devil – that's Yvonne for you,' Phillip had been fond of saying.

In the absence of any real explanation, they'd all decided how lucky they were that Yvonne was fine, if a little frightened. That night, Phillip sat up with her and read her a special bedtime story – just the two of them. Yvonne seemed to remember just how much that annoyed Vee at the time, but as she wasn't the one who had nearly drowned, she had shown little sympathy towards her.

Remembering her stepfather after all this time could still make Yvonne's lip tremble, especially when she felt that the rest of the family were singling her out and ganging up on her. Gentle, kind Phillip had always been her champion: the only one to defend her from the rest.

Reminding herself that she was no longer in need of a protector – after all, she was now a mature woman with her own child to look after – Yvonne slid further into the bubbles and was about to have harsh words with herself over "toughening up a bit" (especially where her sister was concerned) when she felt something wet and warm trickle from her scalp onto her forehead.

Feeling sure it was nothing more than suds from the lavender bath salts, she quickly wiped it away before it could dribble into her eyes and make them sting. That's when she saw the BLOOD on her hand.

THE OTHERS BARELY glanced up as Hazel glided into the guest bedroom wearing a floor-length satin nightgown and high-heeled fluffy slippers that were a direct throwback to the 1980s.

Hazel liked to appear glamorous, even in her nightwear, and enjoyed the feel of the silky-smooth material against her skin.

In the distance, she could hear the eerie tapping and wailing of the oil-fired central-heating system firing up. Even so, the room was icy cold. It came to her that the sound of the failing boiler (begging to be put out of its misery) had once frightened her daughters into believing that there were prisoners trapped in the tower above them, desperate to escape. But all along, they had been the ones imprisoned – only they hadn't known it at the time.

Taking in the equally icy silence, Hazel noticed that Yvonne's, Venetia's and even Una's eyes were all over the place, anywhere but resting on each other. The silence she could cope with; the incriminations were a different thing altogether.

'This is a homely little scene,' she said, in the voice of someone about to break into the most beautiful of arias, as she moved across the room, trailing the satin hem behind her as if she were a bride on her wedding day.

Yvonne sat with her feet up in the rocking chair by the window, which had always been the most uncomfortable of seats. She had a bathrobe tucked around her and her plump little feet rested across one arm of the chair, bouncing nervously as if suffering from a trapped nerve. Her face was smeared with Ponds night cream and her nails had been chewed down to nothing since arriving here, Hazel noticed.

Kissing the side of Yvonne's cheek, Hazel felt the harsh prickle of the tired bathrobe rub against her face. Laying a hand on her daughter's hair, she allowed her jewelled fingers to pat it before moving on. Next came Venetia, who was laid flat out on one of the beds, her steel-toe-capped boots hanging off the edge, moved no doubt off the bedspread only when Hazel came into the room. In her hands she held a bulky bedtime storybook that was wider than her own measly waist. Hazel did not linger quite so long here (frightened that Venetia would inch away if she did), but she stayed long enough to kiss the top of her black head, which was scattered with grey.

At least Una greeted her with a smile. That was something. Still reeling from the shock of having a granddaughter, it was all Hazel could do to stop herself grabbing her up in both arms and shouting, 'Thank you. Thank you. Thank you,' to the highest of cliffs. Because Una was going to love her in a way her own daughters never had. She'd never been more sure of anything.

She watched her granddaughter now, wriggling around under the blanket of the other divan bed, hugging the bingo win lion and swamping it in sticky kisses. Hazel guessed that she had probably already named the cuddly toy, but wouldn't let on to anyone else – not even to her, even though she was desperately trying to be her favourite right now.

'It's so lovely having you all back together again,' Hazel remarked, even as she thought, *How cold they all are! And Yvonne the coldest of all, like a frozen bird that hasn't yet thawed.*

'And what's that you're reading, Venetia?'

Swallowing guiltily, Venetia threw a conspiratorial glance Una's way, hoping for a little silence on the subject. But, not having been brought up in the two-faced lighthouse, Una did not how to play such games.

'I was reading her the story of the race between the hare and the tortoise,' Venetia got in quickly.

'The tortoise won because the hare was a no-good homophobic gay basher,' Una spilled the beans immediately, causing Yvonne to stifle a giggle and shift about in her wooden seat, because by now her legs had gone all crampy.

Knowing better than to say anything that might hint at a reprimand, Hazel nevertheless glanced disapprovingly at Venetia; under her cool gaze, she watched her slam the book shut and start weaving the frilled edge of the counterpane in and out of her fingers, like one would a ball of wool.

Pointedly removing the book from Venetia's hand, Hazel spotted at once a telltale trail of dried blood on her wrist and their eyes met for a quarter of a second before darting away. Again, Hazel said nothing. She didn't have to; Venetia was already guiltily tugging at her sleeve in an attempt to cover up, her pallid face going beetroot in the process.

Hazel then placed the book in a cabinet housing other children's classics: a whole series by Enid Blyton, *The Secret Garden* by Frances Hodgsen Burnett, *Robinson Crusoe, Gulliver's Travels and The Chronicles of Narnia* by C S Lewis. As far as Hazel was concerned, these were proper children's stories. None of that inferior "Potter" wizardry would do for her family.

'I had planned on reading to her.' Polite as ever, there was however a warning in Hazel's tone, one that Venetia would be a fool to ignore. Especially now she had been caught red-handed, as it were, self-harming again.

'I'm sure she won't mind another story.' In the circumstances, Venetia tried to be generous.

'Tell me one about my granddad, Granny.' Una interrupted enthusiastically, leaning forward in the bed.

Hazel and her daughters exchanged wary looks. *Where had that come from? How could the child know anything?*

'Who?' Hazel could not disguise how taken aback she really was.

'My granddad. I want to know what he was like.' Una was completely immune to the adults' shifty glances.

'Yes, why don't you, Granny?' Deciding to brave her mother's discomfort, Venetia dared at last stretch her Doc Martens out on the bed.

'This should be interesting.' Pulling the belt of her bathrobe (which maddeningly did not quite meet in the middle) tight, Yvonne shuffled across the room and pushed Venetia's boot-clad feet off the bed before plopping down next to her. United for once in badgering their mother meant they even shared a lukewarm smile.

Sitting side by side, the sisters looked about the same age. There was no way of telling who was the eldest, although one was without doubt far prettier than the other. And didn't Yvonne know it?

Feeling slightly thrown by their unexpected display of camaraderie, Hazel nervously wrung her hands.

'Well, he was a wonderful husband, Una. A good father,' more confidently now, 'and he would have made a fantastic grandfather too. Wouldn't he, Yvonne?'

Venetia sprang forward, ready to do battle. 'Not that idiot. She wants to know about her *proper* granddad.'

'Proper? If you can call him that.' There was no way on earth Yvonne could prevent the unladylike sneer appearing on her face at any mention of *him*.

'That's my father you're talking about,' Venetia warned.

'Then don't call my dad an idiot,' Yvonne chipped in, looking as if she'd like to poke her sister in the eye.

'Your dad is the same as mine, you idiot. He was your real father, not –'

'Just because you didn't like him.'

'He never had much time for me. That much was obvious,' Venetia scoffed.

'That's because you never let him.' All misty-eyed, Yvonne had never been so sure of anything. 'He always tried to be a proper dad to both of us –'

'He wasn't my proper dad. Or yours.' Venetia had heard enough. 'Nothing can change that.'

'Girls! Please,' Hazel intervened, gesturing to a tearful-looking Una, who wished she'd never asked the question.

'We'll come to Phillip later, if that's alright with you, Yvonne? Let's start with Roger first. After all, Una should get to hear about both her granddads – and in the right order.'

Feeling drained, Hazel sat down next to Una and was instantly gratified to feel her shuffle up against her, attaching herself to the hook of her arm like a koala bear would a eucalyptus tree. Only when they looked exactly right together did Hazel appeal to Yvonne with the softest of marshmallow eyes.

'Okay.' Yvonne grudgingly nodded her consent. But Hazel could tell the word stuck in her throat like a handful of giant salted peanuts.

'We didn't have long together, Roger, your real grandfather.' Again she glanced at Yvonne to see if it was alright to continue, 'And I. Just six years all told. But they were some of the happiest days of my life.'

Seeing the look of disbelief on Yvonne's face, Hazel was quick to reassure her. 'Not that I didn't have such happy memories with Phillip, darling.' She sighed at the complexity of it all. 'I consider myself extremely lucky to have been loved and adored by two such wonderful men, but I don't mind admitting I really don't know what I did to deserve it.'

* * *

39

NOT ONLY HAD the church roof at St Wendreda's been repaired just one week before the wedding (after months of delay), but the rain had stopped at last, and the sun had come out. Even yesterday's trodden-down confetti had been brushed away and an upside-down smiling rainbow (the like of which nobody had seen before) had appeared in the sky. So, if anyone considered themselves luckier than most on their wedding day, it was Hazel and Roger.

They were a gloriously handsome couple. Everybody said so. Roger was good-looking in a way that somehow reminded older women of their first boyfriend, with his slim, athletic physique and shy mannerisms. Respectful to his elders, he always opened doors for women and was hardly ever heard to swear; he was a regular knight-in-shining-armour. He might not have worn a heavy chainmail suit to his own wedding, but he hadn't looked all that comfortable in the tight-fitting suit his mother had picked out for him in Burtons either. But Hazel hadn't minded. In fact, her own dress had been a surprisingly plain affair, with a scratchy lace neckline that brought her out in a rash. Then there were the miniscule pearl buttons she'd had to get Roger to do up, because her hands shook so much, and a full skirt that quivered with electricity and hissed like an angry cat whenever she moved.

She could remember the moment he'd first placed the ring on her finger and the tremendous relief she'd experienced. She wasn't sure if the feeling was due to the service finally being over, or more to do with the fact that she could at last get on with the job of being married. Either way, she couldn't pretend to be anything other than delighted at being a respectable married woman; having people address her as Mrs Cox made her as happy as a kitten with a ball of string, even if she did still giggle childishly whenever she heard it spoken.

She'd already spent hours practicing her new signature and writing out her new address, using a bold black pen for emphasis. The home she and Roger owned – or would own in twenty-five years, when the mortgage was paid off – would be her whole world from now on. As soon as she got her hands on her first week's housekeeping allowance, she intended to buy a flowery cotton apron and a pair of Marigold gloves. To top it all off, Roger's mum had agreed to teach her how to make cottage pie, Yorkshire puddings and dumplings on Tuesday afternoons.

* * *

'DIDN'T MY GRANDAD want little boys, Granny?' Una probed, in between sly sucks on the thumb she'd been told she must not be friends with any more, now that she was six.

'Oh no, Una.' Although Hazel's arm was now so numb she could no longer feel it, she would never think of disturbing her sleepy granddaughter.

'As soon as he found out I was pregnant, he brought me something pink every day, in the hope of having a girl. Some days it would be a bunch of flowers, others a pink balloon, or even a bottle of pink perfume.'

Leaving her words dangle in the air, as if they had been left there by somebody else, Hazel couldn't help think how nice this would have been had it been true. Wanting to be sure her lie had gone undetected, she glanced at Yvonne, who kept her eyes averted and was impossible to read. Not so Venetia, who hugged her own skinny waist and devoured every single word. Hazel was well aware that she could listen to stories about her father all day. Even made-up ones.

'He wasn't disappointed when we came along, then?' The

over-casual way Venetia asked the question told Hazel how important the answer really was to her daughter. Still, she flinched and hesitated before replying. Only she knew why.

'He was always saying he couldn't wait to meet you both, and as every day of the pregnancy passed, he would cross it off the calendar.'

'And he was there at the birth?' Venetia smiled encouragingly at Yvonne, wanting her to partake in the Roger Cox appreciation society.

'For both of us, wasn't he?'

'Pissed out of his head at the pub, more like.' Yvonne raised dark challenging eyes to the ceiling. Clearly, she was not buying it.

Venetia seethed, casting moody eyes around the room.

'No, Yvonne.' Hazel conceded fairly. 'He was there for both births.'

* * *

HOOKED UP TO a drip and other tangled-up medical devices, Hazel was in a bad way after undergoing surgery. Fortunately, a general anaesthetic meant she'd been dead to the world when they ripped her open and plucked out a wriggling mass of X and Y chromosomes (hers and Roger's long-awaited DNA) before stitching her back up again.

Afterwards, she'd woken up to a sterile room that resembled a jail cell, dazedly wondering what had gone wrong, because there was no baby in the cot next to her bed. When a nurse in a uniform (considerably shorter than standard NHS issue) came in, she latched on to her arm and wasn't about to let go in a hurry.

'My baby?' Hazel was so exhausted it took every ounce of her diminished strength to beg the question.

'Being given its first bottle by its father.' The pretty young thing with the impossibly perky bosom sounded awed, as if under someone's spell. Hazel didn't need three guesses to correctly identify who could have got her into such a flutter. Him... Roger.

As the nurse's words sank in, she bowed her head and allowed the self-pitying tears to come.

'You're very lucky to have such a hands-on husband. I wish more were like him.' The nurse was matter of fact.

'But I was supposed to be breast feeding and I haven't even seen my baby yet,' Hazel wailed, not wanting to be thought selfish or unreasonable; something she was increasingly being accused of these days.

Hurrying around the bed, the nurse, who had plans to meet up with an intern doctor later that evening, but wouldn't mind swapping him instead for her patient's charming husband, popped a thermometer into Hazel's sulky mouth.

'Too lazy to come out of the anaesthetic, that was your problem,' she clicked her tongue disapprovingly. 'Anyway, she's adorable. Half the ward is in love with her already.'

'It's a girl then?' Hazel's face lit up as she imagined what her baby looked like. What it smelt like. What it would feel like to hold her in her arms.

And then Roger came in, looking quite the doting husband and contented father, doing just that... holding HER newborn baby in his arms.

* * *

UNA WAS BY now fast asleep, her mouth opening and closing like an inquisitive little fish coming up to the surface for air. Tucked protectively under her arm was the cuddly lion that had

43

caused so much trouble just a few hours ago. Good luck to anyone trying to take it away from her.

Like a satisfied cat with a belly full of stolen milk, Venetia had also curled into a sleepy ball on the bed. Yawning crudely without placing a hand over her mouth and displaying tonsils, teeth and all, she was in danger of exhausting her well-mannered sister's tolerance levels.

'I remember having Una,' Yvonne suddenly volunteered, with a maternal glance at her sleeping daughter. 'It was the best thing I ever did,' she reminisced. 'Everyone was so nice to me.'

'As usual.' Although she had her eyes closed, Venetia was still ready to fight her corner if need be.

'You're just jealous.'

'Of *you*?' Not possible, in Venetia's book.

'Just because you're a sad old lesbo who will never know what it's like to have kids.'

Yvonne regretted the venomous words as soon as they came out of her mouth. Surprisingly, Venetia was not in the least bit offended by this attack on her sexuality and did not retaliate. Instead, she turned her back on Yvonne and yawned a couple more times, making it clear she was now very bored and intended to sleep.

Ashamed of herself and wanting to change the subject, Yvonne switched her attention to Hazel.

'Was it the same for you? Did you love the whole experience of giving birth?'

Not having a hope in hell of being able to worm her way out of this one, Hazel squirmed.

* * *

44

FOR HAZEL, GIVING birth to her first child meant experiencing the absolute worst of times. In fact, she couldn't have suffered more if she'd miscarried or lost the baby through her own fault. But the baby had survived and had gone on surviving – and would have done so with or without Hazel, who was from the very start made quite obviously surplus to requirements.

Like many first-time mothers, Hazel faced the task of changing, feeding and bathing a baby with a natural amount of trepidation. But to know her newborn cried instantly the second she picked it up hardened her for what lay ahead.

Of course, Hazel had been far too young to become a mother – having been almost emotionally retarded back then, she now thought. Terrified of authority and unable to assert herself in any way, she was not the slightest bit prepared for an adult world.

Brought up by a distant father who could be cruel and strict, but not altogether unkind, and a mother with bipolar disorder, who suffered from violent mood swings, she'd never experienced a normal family life. To begin with, Hazel had thought her mother's diagnosis meant the crazed lunatic who bore a passing resemblance to her was actually one day going to turn into a real polar bear. But when you took into account her mother's likeness to a dangerous man-eating predator who was also cold as ice, this all seemed to make sense. So, although she hadn't had to fight off other siblings for her father's limited affection, Hazel learned quickly that her main rival in life was her mother.

With mother and daughter choosing to ignore each other for the most part, but also competing for the attention of the same man, Hazel learned the hard way how to fight for the crusts of parental attention her father chose to throw her way, and as a result constantly craved his approval.

Unfortunately, she'd taken that unhealthy habit for a ride

into adulthood, where the men in her life made it their business to exploit her weakness.

She had lost her virginity at the age of fourteen and had never once considered that she might actually have been raped by the much older labourer, who was as beefy as a bull. She could remember him clumsily penetrating her on a playground slide, which had been wet and soggy at the bottom. Afterwards, he had even acted kindly, buying her a bottle of dandelion and burdock and allowing her to wear his silver curb chain necklace – but only for a week, mind, and only as long as she didn't tell anybody.

She didn't. Nor did she let on to anyone else that she now knew where tampons went, a humiliating detail that had previously eluded her.

Another boy her own age (who, according to her father, came from the wrong side of town) had sneaked her up to his sock-smelling council house bedroom when his mum wasn't looking. His clumsy inexperience left very little impression on Hazel, even though he'd treated her nicely, saying complimentary things about her hair and telling her how pretty she was, like a Nolan sister.

Then came the tall boy in the leather jacket with the turned-up collar and ripped jeans, who had more swagger than John Travolta and who, according to him, could have his pick of any girl at the youth club. Never doubting what he said was true, Hazel had been so dumbstruck to have been sought out by him that she had put up with him fucking her without any attempt at kissing her. Afterwards, she found out that he'd told all of his friends that she smelt like a rotten fish and wore her own mother's dirty pants.

Till the day Hazel left school – which she did without any qualifications to speak of, except for one paltry CSE in art (payment for letting her art teacher stick his tongue down her throat) – she'd never lived down the shame.

So, when she'd first met Roger, she'd been quietly optimistic. He had been quiet and unassuming, and he didn't say much, but he didn't ridicule her either – at least not in the beginning.

She'd been working in a small boutique in town as an apprentice on a youth training scheme when they first met. It was while she was dressing the mannequins in the window that she'd first noticed the boy in the sheepskin coat that was four sizes too big for him. At first, she'd mistakenly thought he'd been eying up the doll's lifelike boobies, as other weirdoes did. But she'd been wrong. Even so, it took him three weeks to pluck up the courage to speak to her and another two of walking her home before he finally worked up the courage to ask her out.

Three months later they did it quickly, so as to get it out of the way, in the upstairs room of a house party they'd been invited to. He'd been a virgin and had only ever kissed one other girl (who'd laughed when his nose clumsily squashed against hers). They married just a few months later, when Hazel was already pregnant. Although the baby was unplanned, they were both delighted. Though of course, Roger being Roger, he didn't say much at all.

And that's how Hazel, at barely twenty years of age, arrived at being a wife and mother without any real clue as to how to be either. But she *was* intelligent enough to soon realise that those early days in the maternity ward had already had a disastrous effect on her relationship with the baby.

From the day her newborn rejected her in favour of the most subordinate of nurses, there was no way back for Hazel. To be rejected all her life by those around her was one thing – to have her own flesh and blood turn their nose up at her was too horrible to contemplate.

47

Nobody had put it in writing, but already it was confirmed to Hazel she must be, *had* to be, disgusting. There was no other explanation for it. The nurses in the maternity ward did nothing to overturn that conviction.

WOBBLY ON HER feet and still attached to a drip, Hazel swayed helplessly, fighting off a stab of nausea as something wet and clumsy escaped from her pants, landing with a plop on the floor. There, for anyone to see, dirty and discarded, was her soiled sanitary towel.

As if this wasn't humiliating enough, Hazel was unable to do anything about it because the bulging stitches in her stomach meant she dared not bend down to pick it up. Instead, she sought out the hardened, wrinkled eyes of an auxiliary nurse who happened lazily by, looking for all the world as if she spent all day figuring out how to avoid doing any real work.

'Don't look at me. I ain't nobody's slave. You can pick up your own muck.' Auxiliary Nurse Kolonda Dixon tippy-toed around the offending sanitary towel and started lazily unwinding sheets from the bed. Being in a room of her own, Hazel had no one else to turn to, but she felt sure that the other mums in the main ward would, in any case, have been too scared to help her.

Red with shame, Hazel felt the stitches start to unwind like a slack yarn of wool as she slowly lowered herself into a squatting position. Hanging onto the IV bag and pole so that they didn't clatter to the floor, she grabbed the bloodied pad and stuffed it into her dressing gown pocket before somehow managing to painfully straighten up.

Nurse Dixon wasn't the only nurse on the ward intent on making her stay in hospital a miserable one. At a time when she should have been at her happiest, nursing her newborn and getting plenty of rest, there were others in that nursing circle who seemed to enjoy making her life hell. Of this spiteful group of women, Nurse Dixon was by no means the worst. That epitaph went to Senior Auxiliary Nurse, Priscilla Savage, a large woman with a dairy cow's neck and man-sized fists, who for some unknown reason was allowed to wear pink slippers on duty.

How those so-called angels ended up being such unfeeling bitches, Hazel was at a loss to know. Perhaps it was the checked uniforms they were forced to wear; perhaps they despised them so much for identifying them as the unskilled workers they were? Or was it the fact that most of them were underpaid immigrants skivvying after a bunch of comparatively well-off British women?

All she knew was that she had done everything possible to get them to be nice to her. Like the new girl in class, she had tried softening them up with chocolates left by well-meaning visitors, which they took without so much as a thank-you. But even that didn't dent their hardened hearts. She'd tried singing their praises in front of other staff, in a bid to get them on her side, but all that did was make them despise her even more for being the coward she was. Reporting them to the ward sister was unthinkable. Hazel was convinced that she'd never make it out alive if she did.

But the tears that had built up over a number of days could no longer be denied and, having reached breaking point, Hazel couldn't stop blubbing. Regrettably, the noise reached into every crook and cranny of the hospital, disturbing others. That's when Nurse Savage and Nurse Dixon burst into her room. Hazel had never had to face both devils at the same time before. Even so, nothing was going to stop her hysterical crying.

Looking down on Hazel as if she were nothing but dirty old bandages that needed incinerating, Nurse Savage tugged the curtains around Hazel's bed, creating a dark isolated little empire, while Nurse Dixon wheeled the baby's cot out of the room.

'Where are you taking my baby?' In between sobs, Hazel just about made herself understood.

'All this over nothing! You want to stop being such a cry-baby and calm down before that nice husband of yours arrives,' Nurse Savage warned. And with that, both women breezed out of the room with the baby in tow, switching off the lights and shutting and locking the door behind them.

Although she wanted to bash down the door, spit in the faces of those two witches and take back her baby, Hazel was too terrified to do anything other than cry herself to sleep in the dark.

She had to endure one more wretched encounter with Nurse Savage before finally being discharged from the maternity unit, and that just happened to be in the shower. Hazel didn't like being naked in front of other people – not one little bit, not even in front of her own husband (especially not him) – so she absolutely hated having to shower in front of the nurses. She felt so strongly about it that she'd even dared protest, however feebly, but she was told that they couldn't risk her slipping and falling over unsupervised.

So far, for her daily shower, most of the nurses had considerately kept their eyes averted. Not so Nurse Savage, who greedily scanned and absorbed every tiny fault and imperfection on Hazel's body as fast as she could put a dislocated joint back in place.

Without doubt, Hazel had put on an awful lot of weight during her pregnancy, topping the scales at a massive four-and-a-half stone heavier than normal. With the extra folds of flesh came the unsightly stretch marks she'd been reassured would fade in time. Even so, she had been totally unprepared for Nurse Savage's attack.

'A right fatty, aren't you?' she said, pointing at Hazel's offending wobbly bits. 'I've never seen so many stretch marks.'

Folding her arms together, Nurse Savage appraised Hazel as if she were a fattened piglet about to be turned into crispy pork crackling.

Every word uttered by her was as good as gospel to somebody with as little confidence as Hazel. Rather than answer back, Hazel kept her head down and concentrated instead on the woman's pink slippers. Rather stupidly, she wanted to warn her nemesis that her favourite footwear was getting wet, but Nurse Savage was by no means finished yet.

'No self-respecting woman would have let herself go like that,' was her harsh summary.

And no self-respecting woman would have allowed Nurse Savage to talk to her the way she had. But what little self-esteem Hazel had ever had now disappeared for good, like a missing child who never made it home. Closing her eyes as she stood there, naked and exposed, with water dripping down her back, Hazel knew she would remember those words for the rest of her life. From that moment onward, no man would ever be able to convince her that she was anything but filth that should be rinsed away in a shower cubicle.

Mercifully, ten days after giving birth, Hazel was finally discharged from hospital. But throughout the long walk along the vast, disinfected corridors to the lobby on the ground floor – even now still forbidden to carry her own baby, until she reached the exit – she was convinced she would be prevented from leaving.

So when the staff nurse finally handed Hazel her baby and there was no one left to interfere, she wondered why she felt nothing. Wondered why she was already looking around for someone to hand the baby back to. Wanting it out of her arms. Wanting it gone.

She must be an unnatural, terrible mother. Otherwise, why would the wriggling creature in her arms, by now so detached and alien to Hazel, only remind her of the terrible ordeal she'd suffered?

Full of self-reproach for having such ambivalent feelings toward her own child, Hazel might as well have been looking into the face of Nurse Savage all wrapped up in the baby-soft blanket. If Roger hadn't turned up in a taxi at that very moment to save the day, she may well have left the bundle by the exit and kept on walking, without once looking back.

* * *

VENETIA DOZED RESTLESSLY, her stubby eyelashes fluttering like mad as she fought off her childhood arch-enemy, "Mr Naughty", who would rear his menacing head whenever he got the chance. Hazel watched her daughter's eyelids flicker under their translucent lids and detected a snail-like trail of saliva that trickled out of her mouth and onto the pillow, staining it yellow.

But when she stole a look at Yvonne to see if she too had fallen asleep, she was surprised to find her sitting bolt upright, with a stiff and unyielding look on her face that almost took her breath away. In some ways, it was easier to take in the undeniably awkward ugliness of one daughter rather than the beguilingly soft, beautiful qualities of the other.

'What's wrong, Yvonne?' Hazel gasped, sensing at once that something was amiss.

'Why are you doing this?' Yvonne demanded. And then,

getting unsteadily to her feet, she lumbered, like an extra in a low-budget horror movie, across the room towards Hazel.

'Doing what?' Hazel shrank back in fear. She found it almost impossible to meet her daughter's eyes, which were bloodshot and sickly, like a messily shaken cocktail.

'Lying to us. You hated him!'

'Who? What are you talking about?' Hazel gabbled, struggling to make sense of what was happening. Was this real, or was she someplace else again?

'Him. Roger. You couldn't stand him.'

'That's not true. What a terrible thing to say.' Desperate to silence her daughter before she woke either of the other two, Hazel raised a warning finger to her lips and gave her a look that should have brought Yvonne to her knees. That's when she felt her daughter grab her wrist and snap it backwards, putting Hazel in a painful vice she could not escape.

'You were glad when he died,' Yvonne hissed spitefully. Her teeth ground so angrily against each other that Hazel could hear them crunch.

* * *

SHE MIGHT HATE him more today than she had yesterday, but what Hazel was going through had absolutely nothing to do with the "baby blues", as her midwife had dared suggest. A lot of women suffered from the same condition, she had reliably informed her.

'But this is no condition!' Hazel had wanted to scream, but hadn't dared to, in case her stitches came loose again, like they had last week, when they had begun oozing a fishy-smelling pus.

It had been two weeks since she'd given birth and even now

she couldn't sit, walk or stand for more than a few minutes without feeling pain and discomfort, much to the surprise of the midwife, who seemed disappointed to find that she wasn't doing as well as the other mums on her patch. There was a reason for that, but it wasn't anything Hazel could share with the woman, no matter how much she might take her slow recovery personally.

'You must make an effort to get better,' the midwife had advised her. 'Especially now you've got a little one to look after.' The woman had meant kindly, but it was all Hazel could do not to throw a bloody sanitary towel at her. Already she was sick to death of everyone pointing out how lucky she was to have such a hard-working considerate husband, who not only did a full day's work but also helped with the baby when he got home.

Once upon a time, she might have agreed with them, but nowadays it was as much as she could do not to laugh in their deluded faces. Knowing better than to do this and risk further alienation, Hazel grew more resentful and sullen instead, earning herself the unfair reputation of being thought spoilt and ungrateful. In fact, she regularly came under fire from such snide comments as, 'Young ones these days don't know they're born,' or 'A young girl like you with a husband and a healthy baby should count her blessings.'

But how was she supposed to do that when everything down there felt so raw still, as if somebody had taken a sharp metal grater to her skin, and when night after night Roger took her savagely from behind without any thought for her predicament?

'I'm bleeding, Roger. Please stop. It hurts so much. Something's not right,' she'd beg – but not too loudly, just in case the sound carried next door. Roger wouldn't have liked that one little bit.

Once, when she *did* cry out, his roughened hand had

clamped down forcefully on her mouth and nose, cutting off her airways and making her mind whirl with panic. All the while, the baby in the cot next to the bed cried as if it too couldn't catch its breath.

When she thought it couldn't get any worse, he'd hitch her bottom further in the air and plunge deeper into her, causing her such excruciating pain that it felt like she was undergoing a vaginal episiotomy. All the while he went at her, like a germ-free-obsessed housewife would a shit-stained toilet, humiliating ship-horn sounds escaped from her body.

Sex was all about colour, Hazel decided: reds, pinks and purples. A woman's exposed pink inner lips, the angry purple end of a man's penis and the flashes of raw flesh and muscle you glimpsed every now and again that the naked eye wasn't meant to see. Sex was an exclamation mark. A word that should only be written in **THE BOLDEST OF *ITALLICS*.** Sex was about babies and blood. So much blood. Such thoughts were meant to block out what was happening to her, but they did not. She may as well have been meditating about a recipe for vanilla panna cotta for all the good it did her.

The only thing she was grateful to Roger for was how reliably quick he was. He was always done within a few minutes and already pulling out, his single gold tooth sparkling under the ceiling spotlight, making his hateful mouth the centre of attention as always. Casually wiping himself on Hazel's nightdress and ignoring the puddle of blood being absorbed into the mattress, he never once glanced in her direction.

Feeling utterly wretched, Hazel gingerly untangled herself from the agonising position she found herself in and tried as best she could to mop up the congealed blood staining the backs of her thighs. By now, the baby had cried itself into a fitful, miserable sleep, so all that was left for her to do was stare defiantly at Roger's crooked nose and wish him deader than she had yesterday.

* * *

HAZEL MUST HAVE dozed off for a moment or two, because when she opened her eyes again, Yvonne was back on the bed next to Venetia, as if she'd never been away from it. They were both looking at her expectantly, as if waiting for her to finish her story.

Taking a sip of water, Hazel felt the glass tremble in her hand, but that was nothing compared to the violent hammering going on in her heart. Had she dreamt the whole episode with Yvonne, or had it been real? If so, what exactly had she been accusing her of? What misguided notion was the girl living under? Or were both her daughters in on this and sitting there together now, secretly mocking her? They couldn't know anything, of that she was sure. Otherwise they wouldn't be trying to upset her like this, not when all she wanted to do was make things right again. Hadn't she suffered enough already?

By now, she was beginning to find herself on edge all the time, in case she said the wrong thing. No matter how hard she tried to keep the peace between them, her girls could be so difficult and demanding. It wasn't really fair of them to put her through that, was it?

'Dad used to take us everywhere with him, didn't he? Even when we were babies?' Venetia wanted to know, showing an unexpected display of vulnerability that couldn't possibly be false, making Hazel doubt herself all over again.

'Oh, yes.' Still reeling from her very lifelike hallucination,

Hazel was slow to reply. 'He loved nothing more than taking you out on his own, showing you off to the world.'

* * *

IN THE SLEEPY Cambridgeshire market town – population 9,000 – where Hazel and Roger lived, everybody appeared to know everybody else. Especially if, like Roger, you had been brought up in the town and came from a large family; that meant there were plenty of brothers, sisters-in-law, aunts, uncles and extended family members to visit if you wanted to. And Roger did. Anything was better than being stuck indoors, staring at Hazel's sour face.

Since she'd had the baby, he'd hardly been able to get a civil word out of her. All she did was stuff herself with crisps, fish-finger sandwiches and burp up gasses from the fizzy, full-fat coke she knocked back all day. And to think, in those first early days, he'd been under the impression he was getting somebody with a bit of class who also came complete with a fancy bit of packaging! He'd no idea she would let herself go so soon. "Baby blues", his eye. If she thought she was going to make a fool out of him, she had another thing coming. Just how long was she going to keep this "the doctor says no sex for another six weeks" lark up? Well, he had shown her he wasn't having any of that crap, hadn't he? But the lazy bloater still needed teaching a lesson. And, knowing what strings to pull where his wife was concerned, he intended to do exactly that.

Today was as good as any other to show her. Because today, hailstones big enough to take out somebody's eye were pinging off the rooftops, and as Hazel hated storms so much, Roger was hoping for some thunder and lightning to go along with it.

Already the deserted streets were flooded and people with any sense were shut away in the comfort of their homes.

Not so Roger, who cycled determinedly along the submerged road, causing a glut of water to spray off each wheel in a pretty arch, the large sheepskin jacket he was wearing taking the brunt of the downpour.

Inside his coat, snuggled close to the sparse wiry hairs on his chest, his two-week-old daughter screamed till she was blue in the face. Literally. It was not a pretty sight. She reminded him too much of the baby's mother.

The thought made Roger grin from ear to ear. Mission accomplished. If this didn't get the bitch to sit up and take notice, nothing would.

HAZEL PATROLLED THE darkened living room – up, down, up, down – not knowing what else to do. If the rain didn't stop soon, she thought she would go crazy. Likewise, if the milk from her breasts didn't stop pumping out onto her blouse, she thought she would scream.

Anxiety.

Terror.

Frustration.

She didn't know what emotion to feel next. All of them were familiar reactions, perhaps – except for the one of feeling completely out of control. But all of them were natural enough emotions that a new mother separated from her baby would go through.

As for the threat of the storm, that was way down on her list of frightening things that could happen. She barely gave it a second thought.

Hearing the front door open and close, she was immediately

on someone's case. His case – Roger's – as he sauntered casually into the room with the screaming baby tucked inside his coat.

'Where have you been? You've been gone hours!' Calm. She must stay *calm*. But at the same time, she knew it was impossible and he knew it too.

'What of it?'

Even on a good day, Hazel hated the sound of his voice, but today there was an added menace to his words.

Deciding it safer to ignore him, Hazel undid the buttons on her blouse and exposed her painfully swollen breast. It squirted breast milk uncontrollably, like a fireman's hose.

'The baby! She's missed her last two feeds.' She mustn't beg. Mustn't let him see her weakness. Hazel held out her hands expectantly, trying to appear more confident than she actually was. But already he had rumbled her. Knowing she had nothing to lose, she was suddenly fierce.

'Just give me my baby.'

Laughing, Roger dangled the baby provocatively in her face and then quickly snatched it away again.

'I think not.' He poked an accusing finger right in the centre of her milky chest. 'You're not fit to look after a dog, never mind anything else,' he spat.

Knowing just how much that must hurt, Roger disappeared into the kitchen, still clutching the screaming baby. Soon afterwards, the muffled soundtrack to *Neighbours* trickled through a crack in the door. As if nothing untoward had happened, Roger was now watching his favourite soap on the kitchen portable, turning up the volume to drown out the sound of the sobbing baby.

Hazel was left wringing her hands and trying to second-guess his next move, so that she might yet get her hands on her starving baby. The saddest thing to happen to her today was not the storm, the fight with Roger nor the prolonged separation from her baby. It was the fact that she all too easily believed everything he'd said. Maybe she couldn't be trusted with a dog, let alone her own child?

SHE'D WAITED TILL he'd gone to the snooker hall, knowing he wouldn't return till the early hours, and that even then he might come back with stragglers who liked to gamble away their dole money on a late night game of cards.

That's why she'd picked tonight to do what had to be done. She had five hours to get there, do *it* and get back home. It would be as if she'd never left the house.

It was called Butch and Hazel was terrified of him. Perfectly aware of how intimidating the wolf-like dog was to others – its paws being the same size as shovels – Roger took pride in its colossal size. But then, Hazel often found small men had to have something to make them feel bigger and stronger than they actually were. At five feet four inches tall and weighing in at only nine stone, Roger was small in every way.

On more than one occasion, she'd caught the dog pawing at the baby lying on the changing mat on the floor or salivating over its dirty nappies. When she'd flapped her hand at it to get away, his top lip had drawn back in a snarl and Hazel had backed away, knowing that if it came to it, she wouldn't have the courage to rescue her own baby from its jaws. From that moment on, the dog knew he had her in his power and growled whenever she went to get the baby out of its pram. So, in effect, Butch became another obstacle that came between her baby and her, and this wasn't to be endured.

When she'd mentioned her fears to Roger, he'd told her she must be imagining it.

'The dog is there to protect the baby. He's family.'

Just not your family, he might as well have added. Although Hazel understood Roger genuinely believed that the dog was no threat to the baby, she wasn't prepared to take that risk. Besides, what was it he'd said? 'You're not fit to look after a dog…'

Having coerced Butch into the back of her Austen Allegro with a pork pie, she watched him slobber a jellied tongue over the baby, who was strapped into the baby carrier next to him. Knowing this would be the last time it ever got the opportunity to give her daughter a saliva bath, Hazel almost felt sorry for him.

But then their eyes met in the rear-view mirror and Butch growled menacingly, wiping away any last ounce of sympathy she might have had for him.

'Not long now,' she growled right back.

He'd barked an unfriendly response, his wild bronco eyes fixed warily on the back of her head as she drove into unknown regions – out of surly, tedious Cambridgeshire and into Norfolk, with its pretty stone walls and cottage gardens, where she came to a silent, ill-omened stop a couple of hours later.

Switching off the car headlights as she pulled into the deserted lay-by, Hazel's first task was to remove Butch's collar. To do this, she had to distract him with a whole tin of hotdog sausages. Once the bulky leather strap slid off his grizzly bear-sized neck, she pulled off the metal disc that contained their home address and slipped it into her pocket, to dispose of later. The collar she flung out of the window. Now it would be impossible for anyone to trace the dog back to them… or her.

'Walkies, Butch,' she called in a deceitfully friendly tone, and was rather surprised when he jumped obediently from the backseat of the car to join her on the tarmac. Then, on seeing his favourite ball being thrown into the adjacent field, Butch bounded trustingly after it.

Before he had any idea what was happening, Hazel legged it back to the car, threw herself into the driver's seat and slammed the door shut, making sure that all four doors were locked, even though she knew that Butch wasn't capable of turning car door handles.

Catching a glimpse of him in her wing mirror, bringing back the ball, she floored the accelerator pedal. Her safest of family cars did the first wheel spin of its life as she sped out of the lay-by, causing the baby in the back to start bawling with fright.

Hazel's own face was streaked with tears as she watched Butch give chase, a look of true panic on his face.

'Goodbye, Butch. I'm sorry.'

Watching him tire and eventually slow to a halt, it occurred to Hazel that he would have a whole array of new sounds and smells to get used to from now on: different people and dialects, trees he'd never urinated up against before, other dogs' arses he hadn't sniffed, postmen he'd never chased. In that moment, she felt more for the dog than her own husband. Even that wasn't saying much, considering that she was abandoning it in the middle of the night, friendless and alone.

But it was the memory of those menacing teeth that ultimately stopped her going back for him. When she was no longer able to see him in the rear-view mirror, it grew easier – out of sight, out of mind and all that. Nor did she need lecturing. She knew what she had done was a cold, calculating and almost inhuman thing. But she also knew that she would get over it sooner than most.

Just like the baby in the back seat would have to stop its bawling, because the sooner she learned that crying for attention until you were blue in the face didn't work, the better. Until then, Hazel had to blot out the unbearable sound somehow and resist the temptation to scream right back at it. 'Shut up. Why can't you just shut up and stop crying for once?'

* * *

GROWING TIRED FROM what must be the longest bedtime story ever, Hazel yawned pointedly. Nobody needed a good night's sleep more than she did. But, oblivious to her fatigue, Yvonne was intent on questioning her some more.

'They say the first birth is always the hardest. Was it easier the second time around?'

Although she couldn't be a hundred percent sure, Hazel felt there was more than a hint of contempt to Yvonne's tone and hated the sense of distrust that was growing between them. All she'd ever tried to do was protect her daughters from the truth, but as always they thought they knew best. Truthfully, she was starting to feel more than a little irked by it.

'A little better, yes,' Hazel ventured warily, no longer sure how much to give away.

* * *

ALTHOUGH IT HAD only been three years since she'd last given birth, Hazel was not only older, but considerably wiser. As a direct consequence, she was finding her second time in the maternity unit a completely different experience.

Feeling numb from the epidural in her spine and having been ripped open once again, but not yet able to feel the soreness, Hazel was sitting up in bed with a sense of wonder, breastfeeding her newborn. Happy and relaxed, she was everything a contented mother should be. She had every reason to hope that was how things would remain, but right now, outside her door, somewhere in the corridor, there was an argument going on.

Without being told, she knew who it was of course. Him… Roger.

'What do you mean I can't see my wife?' he demanded, sounding quite drunk. This public exhibition of shouting and carrying on was so unlike him; Hazel had to smile at how hot and bothered he sounded.

'It's what she specifically requested. I'm sure when you get her home she'll come to her senses.' Hazel could hear the wonderfully kind and sympathetic Nurse Samuels' normally rational tone being stretched to the limit.

'Damned right she will.'

Roger's threat carried right into Hazel's room, the way he intended it to – he wanted his words to box her around the ears, if he could not himself – but she could sense he was on the verge of giving up. Muttering under his breath, she heard his footsteps beat a grudging retreat.

'It's not uncommon for new mothers to behave irrationally.' Trying to be reassuring, Nurse Samuels decided to take pity on the man. She then wished she hadn't, when he stopped and banged on the walls with clenched fists, which was a good indication of how genuinely frustrated he was, and stomped off in a fury; his dirty working men's boots left a trail of mud behind.

In the peaceful silence that ensued, Hazel's grin grew wider as she looked down on the most perfect living thing in her lap and felt a stab of something powerful move inside her. She could only liken the sensation to that of a giant invasion that disconnected every organ from her body, except for her heart.

Here, at last, was somebody Hazel could and would die for. Here was somebody that would be hers and hers alone, created from all the goodness inside her and none of the bad. Hazel understood that in giving so much of herself to this new child, there would be nothing left for anyone else (unfortunate, but unavoidable). What's more, her life was about to change in every other way. She could feel it.

Once out of hospital, she would never be the same person again. As if to prove this, Hazel pushed the alarm by the side of her bed and waited for the auxiliary nurse, who was assigned to look after her, to come in.

'My baby has been sick in her cot and needs her sheets changed,' Hazel informed her haughtily, catching a trickle of milk spiralling downwards from her daughter's rosebud mouth with her finger.

Inspecting the sheet and finding nothing of any significance, the harassed-looking nurse was clearly not of the same opinion.

'It's only a tiny little spot, a bit of dribble really, not even proper sick. I'll just wipe it off and it'll be good as new.'

There and then, Hazel decided nothing would ever be good enough for her daughter and she would make sure that everyone realised that. There would be no seconds, no hand-me-downs and, perhaps more importantly, nobody would ever raise their voice to this child of hers while she was still living.

'I don't want *good as* new. I want new. If you don't change the sheet as I asked, I'll make Sister aware you're cutting corners when it comes to hygiene.'

Hazel was polite but assertive, confident of being obeyed. It was an attitude she would adopt from this day forward: one that would get her what she wanted, when she wanted it – judging by the submissive actions of the nurse, who stripped the sheets from the cot, keeping any hostile remarks to herself.

BUT WHEN VISITING time came round again, Hazel soon found that she wasn't yet in a position to have everything her own way. The only reason Roger was here now was because of her mother-in-law's relentless pleading. Hazel suspected that Roger had badgered his mother into pressuring her, because she would, after all "do anything for her boys"… except give up booze, gambling or men.

Although her mother-in-law was a self-obsessed, man-eating alcoholic – completely blind to any of her children's faults, particularly Roger's – who, despite suffering from agoraphobia, had conquered her fear long enough to visit her new grandchild in hospital, she was completely harmless. Most people would never guess that the sixty-year-old never wore any knickers and had a fancy for see-through plastic raincoats and men who came to read the electricity meter. Sometimes they even left her a little windfall of coins behind as thanks.

In spite of all that, it was easy for anybody to see that Gillian and Roger were related. It was the concord nose that did it, but somehow it looked far better on Gillian than her son. Nor was she troubled by it the way Roger was. Odd when she was the woman and he, the man.

Just then, somebody else with the same distinctive nose came in.

Her.

Strange how Hazel had never noticed before how the child was starting to look more and more like him. She supposed she noticed it more acutely now because of the separation brought about by her spell in hospital. It had been ten whole days and nobody had once considered taking the brooding, uncommunicative child to see its mother – and Hazel had been so caught up with her new baby, it hadn't occurred to her to even ask after her.

Searching for something of herself in this sullen child proved fruitless. Even someone with a degree in cognitive studies would have a hard time finding any similarities or family resemblance between her and her eldest daughter. She might as well not have bothered investing her genes in the almost alien three-year-old that had Roger's eyes, nose, jaw and forehead, not to mention all his infuriating mannerisms.

As she stared hard at the child, a familiar wave of revulsion made Hazel's stomach turn over, as if she'd just that minute knowingly consumed a pan of poisoned eggs and was already paying the consequences.

Realising that she would no longer be able to hide her real feelings where this child was concerned, Hazel gave in at last. She surrendered to the haunting images that flashed in front of her face each time she looked into those cold little eyes: the time she'd messed herself on the bed when the nurse was fitting a catheter; lying exposed with her legs wide open while a group of student doctors inspected her soiled sanity towel; being shaved roughly by a nurse old enough to be her granny and burning with shame as the woman parted her labia, all the while keeping up a dull conversation about cod in parsley sauce.

No matter how hard Hazel tried – and she *had* tried – she couldn't fight off the feelings of self-loathing and shame she'd experienced before, during, and soon after she'd given birth to the child in front of her. Nor could she stop herself from altogether absolving the child of any blame, no matter how illogical that might sound.

There she was now, as if butter wouldn't melt, dressed in a

black dress of all things. As if she was in mourning. Hazel came to the conclusion that the child must have chosen the colour on purpose, judging by the way she was glaring at her newborn sister, who, it would seem, just wasn't dead enough for her.

Since their separation, the child appeared to have grown hideously large, with a deformed-looking head that wobbled precariously on slight shoulders, like a heavy bowling ball about to go astray in a bowling lane.

Just as Hazel had earlier asked herself how she could possibly be related to this gargoyle of a creature, now, in comparison, she questioned how on earth she could be related to the angelic newborn she held in her arms.

And why were Roger and Gillian going on about how pretty the older child looked, ignoring her precious new baby in the process? Were they blind? Even the nurses were delighted with the truculent little thing, calling her "darling" and "cutie", stroking the ribbons in her hair and even daring to suggest that Hazel should enter her in the junior Miss Palmolive competition. More fool them for falling for the flirtatious upturned eyes and gappy grin she chose to craftily bestow on them.

All Hazel got – all she'd ever got – was a sullen scowl from black crow-like eyes that stated plainly, *Don't bother pretending for my sake. You hate me and I hate you right back. So let's leave it at that.*

But then, Hazel would remind herself sternly, this little girl was only three years old and could hardly string a sentence together, let alone concoct anything as vindictive or grammatically correct as that. That was another thing Hazel had been negligent about; the child was undoubtedly backward.

Sometimes it was easier for Hazel to forget her own failings as a mother and blame the child instead, going so far as thinking the word "evil" out loud in her head and reproaching herself for having bred such a monster. Of course, in her more rational moments, Hazel did question what might be wrong with her, to have such outrageous fantasies about her firstborn. Surely the child was just spoilt, completely ruined by Roger, and that was all there was to it? And yet the girl was always so keen to let Hazel know just how little she was thought of.

So far, Hazel had been lucky. Neither Roger nor Gillian had thought to plonk the child on her lap for a touching mother-and-daughter reunion. Feeling as she did, Hazel didn't think she would have been able to bear that without deliberately dropping her on the hard floor, bloodied and broken for all to see.

Instead, Roger lifted the precious bundle out of her arms and placed it in the child's lap, making a great show of how adorable they looked together and how they would *both* be his *best, favourite* girls from now on. And then, because he was too busy slyly watching Hazel, baiting her for a reaction he would never get, he entirely missed the effect his words had on the peeved three year old.

'Say hello to your little sister,' Roger went on, prompting the child until she felt obliged to hand the baby back, treating him to a whiter-than-white smile and sparkly eyes the colour of dark denim, all the while disguising her hatred of the new person in his life.

Suddenly, Hazel felt more fragile than ever, as all the old fears came back and she began to doubt herself once more. Would she really have any more say in this new baby's upbringing than she'd had with the last? Or had Roger found such a formidable accomplice in the shape of his eldest daughter that the two of them would isolate her from her new baby for good?

* * *

HAZEL FELT A familiar jolt of exclusion as she gazed down at her grown-up daughters, who were sleepily curled up together in foetal positions on the bed, as if nothing and no one would be able to pry them apart.

This had long been a familiar sight throughout most of their childhood. A whole day might have been spent arguing over some minor, or even major, misdemeanour on one or both their parts, but come bedtime, they rarely ended up in separate beds. How long they had been asleep, Hazel had no idea. But she was grateful for the respite, as they were all incredibly tired. Tomorrow, she was sure, would turn out to be a much better day. Especially after a good night's sleep.

Dropping a blanket over their conjoined bodies, Hazel realised dismally that this was going to be the longest of weekends, one that would no doubt age her considerably. Already she felt as if she had aged fifteen years.

'Time for bed,' she decided wearily, getting to her feet and walking toward the door. 'Don't let the bedbugs bite,' she called out involuntarily, for this was how she'd customarily taken her leave of the girls at bedtime. In fact, there'd been a time when they would never have let her leave the room without hearing her say it. The memory not only tugged at Hazel's heartstrings but at her downturned mouth, causing it to stretch into a sentimental smile. And then, saying 'Sweet dreams, my children,' she blew them each a kiss, just as any loving mother might.

But Hazel proved once again that she was no ordinary mother when she froze on the spot, another searching question on her lips.

70

'How could I have gladly died for one and yet have resented giving my own breast milk to the other?' she puzzled.

It was true. Hazel must face up to the fact that she'd hated seeing her eldest daughter's unpleasant little mouth fastened to her puffed-out nipple and had to turn away from the needy, knowing eyes each time she'd been forced to nurse her.

Holding the doorknob in her hand, Hazel turned off the light, glad of the cloak of darkness that settled on her shoulders in much the same way an expensive fur coat might. But just as she closed the door on her family and was about to walk away, she heard a noise.

Laughter cut short. She was sure of it. As if someone on the other side of the door had jammed a fist into a mouth to stifle an onset of the giggles. That would be just like Venetia and Yvonne, to play a trick on her, pretending to be asleep when all the time they'd been wide awake.

Annoyed, Hazel immediately threw open the door, hoping to catch them unawares, still in the middle of their little game, so she could tell them exactly what she thought of them. Seconds later, she wished she had simply walked away, pretended not to have heard. She would give anything not to have opened that door.

* * *

HAZEL INSTANTLY RECOGNIZED the washable pink rosebud wallpaper she had painstakingly hung herself, and didn't need to trip up on the fake sheepskin rug to know she had gone back in time and was now hovering in the doorway of one of the children's bedrooms in the Cox household.

Everything was at once familiar. The dappled grey rocking

horse with the genuine leather reins and saddle that Roger had bought second-hand from a car boot sale. The cherryade stains on the carpet were exactly where she remembered them. Over there, on a chest of drawers, was a pink ballerina jewellery box; its lid was open and the ballet dancer was doing a pirouette to the music of "The Dance Of The Sugar Plum Fairy". There was something eerily disturbing about the ballet dancer with the torn tutu and sad face, whose heart just wasn't in dancing.

But what really got her attention, in a heartbreaking way, was the bed with its pink butterfly quilt that matched the curtains at the window. Tucked up inside was her five-year-old daughter, whose fringe had been cut into an uneven zigzag shape (she had refused point-blank to sit still for the hairdresser), and she had crusty porridge remains stuck at each end of her grinning mouth. What was more disturbing was the sight of Roger lying alongside her, his suntanned arm curled around her ridden-up nightdress.

Sensing her presence at the door, both Roger and her daughter looked up unhurriedly. Though clearly irritated by the intrusion, Roger was not put out to find his wife gawping repulsively at him. In retaliation, he even pulled the child closer, making her giggle, making her appear to enjoy her mother's obvious horror.

At last Hazel found her voice, but it was one she hardly recognised as her own – all guttural and anguished, obviously unwilling to belong to someone as easily hoodwinked as her.

'What are you doing in there?' At last she was doing her duty, the same as any other doting mother, Hazel felt, ignorant of just how little credit she actually deserved.

For a moment, she thought he wasn't going to answer, and even hoped that would be the case. After all, how easy would it be to convince herself that she was the one in the wrong, that she had been mistaken? But of course, words once spoken could not be undone. First came the flash of a fourteen-carat nougat tooth as he yawned and stretched lazily, like a tiger at rest, then the incriminating words.

'Seeking the warmth I can't get from my own wife,' he told her cuttingly.

Funny that all she could think of afterwards – a long time after she had quietly closed the door on them and gone about the house, busying herself with trifling household chores – was what an odd verb it had been for Roger to choose. Not once in their married life had she heard him utter anything that even remotely resembled the word "seek". No. It was not part of his limited vocabulary; he would have naturally plucked a more familiar word out of the air, such as "get", to describe this act. As in, "getting the warmth I can't get from my own wife". Even then, "warmth" was horribly wide of the mark too. "Getting *it*", "getting *some*" or "getting *a bit*". Any one of these descriptions would have been more characteristic for Roger to use. Therefore, on reflection, Hazel could only assume his eloquent use of speech had in fact been rehearsed. That could only mean he had, all along, planned on getting found out.

* * *

UNDISTURBED BY THE kind of memories that would haunt others, this painful truth nevertheless jolted Hazel back into the present, where she found herself high up on the lighthouse tower. Leaning over the flimsy railings, she could see what a sheer and terrifying drop it was to the ground below, where the cliff edge and the fierce rolling waves of the sea waited expectantly.

Best then to grip the metal safety barrier as tight as possible so you didn't accidentally fall. Up here, the wind was strong enough to flatten you, like summer wheat in a breezy field, and in the pitch-black dark you could easily lose your footing. What's more, the wind speed alone could steal the breath out of your body and turn you inside out like week-old road kill.

Feeling at home on top of the tower, braving the elements, Hazel did not hold onto the railings. Nor did she flinch as the wind and sea spray toyed with the idea of knocking her down. Instead, she stared defiantly at the black sea and listened to the waves crashing against the cliffs. Sometimes, if she listened hard enough, she could almost imagine that the sea was calling out her name, urging her to throw herself into the depths of the freezing cold water, promising her an easy end to it all – easier than she deserved, at any rate.

'Not tonight,' she shushed, and immediately felt the sea back off; it knew when it was beat. Tonight wasn't for dying. Tonight was for remembering.

* * *

USUALLY SO PREDICTABLE in the way he chose to humiliate and torture Hazel, Roger's MO now seemed to have changed for good. Ever since she'd discovered him sharing her daughter's bed, he'd thrown caution to the wind and his dangerous new habits worried her more than she could say.

He'd even run the risk of being overheard by the next-door neighbours after viciously kicking in the bathroom door just to prove a point. Of course, it had all been Hazel's fault. Didn't she know she wasn't supposed to lock any of the doors? She wasn't allowed to lock herself in – away from him. Even when taking a bath.

As punishment, he'd sat on the toilet, jeans around his ankles, emptying his bowels in front of her, making her listen to every grunt and fart while she sat shivering in a rapidly cooling bath. After that, he'd slipped into the bathwater behind her, making her want to vomit. The naked scrotum rubbing against her back actually caused her to swallow a mouthful of bile.

How she hated him. Hated the way he sang through his nose; hated how he accused her of picking her arse in bed if she so much as scratched a bum cheek; hated when he deliberately urinated on her as punishment for failing to wear the clothes he picked out for her; hated the way he ate, with his knife and fork the wrong way around; hated the fact he wanted her by his side night and day, never wanting to be alone; hated the fact he was a pathetic, disgusting, cowardly little man who had even less courage than she did.

Hated, hated, hated him. And this list of reasons was by no means exhaustive.

Still, she wasn't letting him have everything all his own way. That had been proven the day he'd pushed her too far, and for once, knowing she meant business, he had actually sat up and taken notice.

On this day, the navy Silver Cross pram (much admired by family and friends) was in its usual pride of place in Hazel's living room. Here she kept her sleepy newborn wrapped in a pink blanket. Should she wake, the baby could stare, boggle-eyed, at the woolly sheep mobile that dangled enticingly above her head.

But on the day in question, when Hazel lost it with her husband, the baby had woken up extremely hungry and begun wailing almost immediately, while she was still in the kitchen frantically trying to cool the milk. Other things were happening at the same time; potatoes were boiling on the hob, the microwave was pinging and she was stirring up instant gravy with a fork because Roger would be furious if his Sunday roast was late. The eldest child, three at the time, kept getting under her feet.

Added to all of this, she could also hear Roger complaining in the living room where he was watching a particularly gory horror film. 'Hurry up and feed that baby, will you? It'll soon be dinner time.'

But the baby would not stop bawling. Then, an empty beer can was heard hitting the wall. Both Hazel's and her eldest daughter's bottom lips dropped.

'For fuck's sake. All I want is to watch my movie in peace. That's not too much to ask, is it?' he shouted.

As Hazel rushed into the room, tepid milk bottle in hand, she caught Roger about to pick the crying baby up, his eyes still glued on the telly where a family of deranged cannibals, led by somebody called Papa Jupiter, was murdering a group of American travellers.

No way was she going to allow Roger to handle her baby. He was far too angry and far too drunk. Anything could happen. Without thinking, she lashed out with the first thing that came to hand – the fork she'd used to stir the gravy.

Hardly daring to believe what she'd done, Hazel gawped stupidly at the fork embedded in Roger's hand, the tapered tines slotted in between the bone and tissue either side of his knuckle. She couldn't help thinking that this scene of blood mingling with gravy was far more horrific than anything else Roger might watch on video today.

'You crazy bitch!' He must have been too stupefied to react properly, or he would surely have knocked her out there and then.

Wishing she had a powerful chainsaw to hand rather than a useless old fork, and not knowing what else to do, Hazel quickly prised the fork out of Roger's hand, causing him to scream and leap about in agony.

Then, their eldest daughter, obviously not wanting to be ignored any longer, tumbled deliberately from her tricycle onto the floor. So now not only had the baby gone red in the face from crying but the older child was also screaming at the top of her lungs, as if she too were being stabbed. Then there was Roger, hopping around the room like a rabbit that had been shot in the arse, holding out his throbbing hand as if it might drop off, and trying unsuccessfully to stop the bleeding. The last time Hazel heard such a racket, he'd had his jeans around his ankles on the toilet. Quite honestly, she wanted to tell him what a fuss he was making over nothing. She'd had to put up with far worse.

But then he took a menacing step in the baby's direction. 'It's my kid and if I want to pick her up I'll bloody well do it,' he warned.

Mesmerized, Hazel looked at the fork in her hand for what seemed a long time – when it could only have been a matter of seconds – before stabbing him with it again.

Second time around her aim proved just as good, because it got him in exactly the same place as before, and, comically, Roger's reaction also remained the same. First there was the swearing. Then, came the dancing around the room and the inevitable grunting. Only this time, he did not take a menacing step in her direction. This time, he took a cowardly step back, glaring at Hazel as if she were the devil itself. Perhaps in that moment, she was. The next thing she knew, she was pointing accusingly at her eldest child, who was still sobbing on the floor, and letting him have it.

'You've stolen one child from me. I won't let you do it again!'

And for the third and perhaps fourth time that day – not that she was counting – she stabbed Roger with a piece of cutlery from a set bought for them as a wedding gift. Perhaps from now on he wouldn't have so much trouble mixing up his knife hand from his fork hand when sitting down to a meal. This social *faux pas* had always secretly annoyed her.

OF COURSE, IN the end she hadn't got away with it. Roger made sure of that. On the day of his revenge, Hazel had been trying to get some vegetables into her eldest daughter, who was used to surviving on an unhealthy diet of white chocolate and cheesy Wotsits. But the stubborn little preschooler wasn't having any of it, not at Hazel's bidding, and spat out the spoonfuls of carrot and peas as soon as they were forced through her clenched teeth. A stalemate had been reached at the dining table.

'Just try. It won't kill you.' Getting more and more irritated, Hazel pinched the child's nose until she had no choice but to open her mouth and swallow.

But her success was short lived and resulted in far more than she'd bargained for; a whole mouthful of undigested mush spat deliberately in her face.

'You little sod,' Hazel lashed out angrily, catching the child on the side of the head, making it bounce sickeningly like a drunken jack-in-the-box.

Horrified at what she'd done, Hazel didn't need telling she'd gone too far. My God, she could have knocked her out, stone cold dead. As it was, there were for once very real tears spurting out of the child's eyes and a shocked holding of breath that clearly wasn't part of an act. The traumatized look on her face as she held her boxed ears, like Van Gogh's *Scream*, told its own story.

But before she even got a chance to try and quiet her down or convince her that "Mummy didn't mean it", Hazel was thrown against the wall.

'Raise your hand to her again and I'll kill you.' Saliva from Roger's snarling mouth sprayed her face. She couldn't help noticing that it tasted like venom.

Having pinned her to the wall with one hand around her throat, he used the other to wipe the regurgitated food over her face. It got into her eyes, blinding her, and up her nose, suffocating her.

Hazel's terrified eyes pleaded with Roger to stop; he really was killing her. Both hands were around her neck now – squeezing, pushing – the thumbs digging in her thyroid cartilage. Already, she could sense parts of her dying – her brain, her consciousness, her desire to live. But, like a bull terrier taught to lock onto its prey, it took Roger at least another full minute before he let go: the urge to destroy had been so strong.

Gasping for breath and clawing at her throat, Hazel dropped to the floor, where she waited for the throbbing blackness of her mind to fade. She knew she had come close to dying. Already she could feel a ridge of swollen flesh around her neck where his hands had been, and knew it would take months before the mark healed. Ironically, this would be the only necklace Roger ever gave her.

But their poisoned marriage did not end there. Hazel hadn't the courage or financial independence to leave Roger. What's more, she was terrified that he would not allow her to take the children with her if she did. And then, by chance, she stumbled upon an amazing discovery that meant she wouldn't have to.

The child had a cold, a bad cold – one that kept even the likes of Roger away from her bedroom door. And that could only mean one thing – another trip to the doctor's.

THERE WAS AN oppressive masculine air to the oak and leather room that even the overpowering whiff of Mr Sheen polish and medicated tissues in a box, positioned right under Hazel's nose, couldn't compete with.

Outside, she could hear a tree squeaking loudly in the wind. She might not be able to see it from here, as her back was against the window, but she could picture it in her mind; a black ash flapping its branches gracefully, like the wings of a black swan perhaps? Anything she dreamt up was better than having to look at the bespectacled little man with horny crusts on his face, who kept jangling his stethoscope at her as if to imply she wasn't paying enough attention.

As if it wasn't enough having to be in the same room with a hideously unattractive person, Hazel acknowledged that Dr Bonner might be a well-respected family GP, but he was not the sort of man she would ordinarily allow her children anyway near, let alone perch on his suspect lap.

All the same, there she was now, giggling and squirming indecently on his knee and eyeing up a jar of lollies that already had her greedy little name on. But not even the doctor's child-friendly banter could stop her coughing or wheezing in between sniggers – harsh, hacking, distressing sounds that would grate on the most patient of nerves, especially Hazel's, as well as irritate the child's inflamed airways.

The doctor was grave and reproachful when it came to addressing Hazel. Already she could tell he had taken an instant dislike to her; had spotted the telltale look of disgust on his face when she skilfully crossed her elegant long legs in front of him. Hazel supposed he was one of those awkward types who thought beautiful people always underestimated ugly people and believed they could get away with anything – which they mostly did, in her opinion.

'The bluish tinge to her face has faded somewhat and that at least is a good sign,' he said.

Not sure it really mattered what colour her child's face was, Hazel wished he would just get on with writing out a prescription, as she was itching to escape. She hated the way this man all too obviously looked down on her. He didn't know her. Them. Or what their situation was. Must she always take the blame for everything?

'Her airways are still partially blocked, though, and she will need a course of steroids as well as the injection I've just given her. And inhalers, both the preventative and relieving kind, before she's anywhere near better.'

He presented her daughter with the biggest, shiniest lolly in the jar, but the only thing he treated Hazel to was another insinuating look.

'Lucky for you, we caught it in time.'

'I'm sorry, Doctor. I thought it was a bad cold. I didn't realise –'

'His cold. Daddy gave me *his* cold. No one else can have it, he said. Only me.' Her daughter rounded on her, pulling the life-saving nebuliser mask off her pinched little face and pinging her skin painfully in the process.

'Tell me, does anyone else in the family have asthma, chronic or otherwise?' the doctor interrupted, quite taken aback by the child's vitriolic outburst.

Hazel became aware of her own hesitation in replying long before the doctor did.

'Her father.'

'Being aware of his condition, you should perhaps have

known better. There's no telling what might have happened to this child.'

There it was again: the judgmental, sneering sigh that fully warranted a slit throat in Hazel's opinion. Momentarily pushing such delicious thoughts aside, she reflected on the doctor's alarming prognosis before looking him unflinchingly in the eye. 'Are you saying that without proper medication she could have died?'

'I think you already know the answer to that,' he warned in his most authoritative manner, not liking the way she had, for the first time during the consultation, shown any interest in the child's symptoms.

Afterwards, Doctor Bonner admitted being disturbed by both the woman's and the child's behaviours. But what really baffled him most was that instead of being understandably upset – as one would expect from a distraught mother on hearing the news her child could have died – Mrs Cox had in fact looked vaguely satisfied by the outcome; almost hopeful, in fact.

SATURDAY

S quatting on the offending avocado-coloured toilet in the en-suite bathroom, Yvonne tried her utmost to pee prettily in a refined way, the way her mother had once instructed her. 'A tiny tinkle,' Hazel would call it, if pressed to give this necessary bodily function a name at all. Because, let's face it, she could be a bit sniffy about such things. But, try as she might, Yvonne had never been able to do anything but gush ferociously like an elephant; always on edge, in case Venetia started banging on the door demanding to know if she was in the middle of a "poo" or "wee".

Supposing she was like her mother in that respect, Yvonne had inevitably grown up prudish about her private toilet habits and would refuse to respond to her sister's vulgar interrogations. Usually, Vee insisted on knowing exactly how long Yvonne was going to take because she was either in a hurry to use the toilet herself or because she wanted her sister to come and play. Now.

When Yvonne had complained to their mother about Vee's behaviour, Hazel had refused to get involved in their degrading rows, saying, 'There are enough bathrooms in this house without having to form a queue.'

Funny how, back then, it never occurred to Yvonne her sister simply hated being on her own; was in fact scared to death of being alone.

Truth was, her sister had always been "mad as a box of frogs", but for years, nobody had taken the trouble to realise it. The telltale signs had always been there, of course. Look at how she'd carried that cracked bit of mirror around with her for years, constantly getting it out and staring into it, convincing herself she was dying and that nobody cared.

'My reflection is changing. My face is dying. There, see. Why aren't you doing anything to help me?' she would howl, and then claw savagely at her face, all the while working herself into one of the terrible frenzies they all dreaded, when there was no longer any point trying to reason with her. That was when her overwhelmed mother would insist, 'An hour or two of solitude in her room is the only cure.' How many doors, elegant vases and pieces of furniture had the angry little whirlwind devastated as a result of this well-intended but misguided belief?

'I'm being abused. Poisoned. Murdered,' Vee would holler out of the window, for the whole of Lighthouse Close to hear. Yvonne remembered such incidents clearly.

'Call ChildLine before they kill me. Somebody help me, please,' she would implore of astonished passers-by until eventually her mother would, out of fear of the authorities, relent and unlock the door.

The one and only time this strategy hadn't worked was when Phillip insisted on going up to the room to remonstrate at her. Having been firmly instructed to remain downstairs, Yvonne and her mother had sat on the sofa, nervously wringing their hands and waiting for it all to kick off as they heard the door above their heads open and close quietly. But instead of launching ornament after ornament at Phillip's placid head, or rowdily attempting to throw herself out of the tower, all that bounced off the walls on that occasion was his familiar firm-but-fair tone of voice. Then came a long, drawn-out silence, as if some small person was taking time out to "think about what they had done", followed by the tread of his brown weekend brogues coming back down the stairs. Casually settling himself into his favourite armchair with a copy of *The Sunday Times*, Phillip never once spoke about what happened upstairs.

As if that wasn't enough, there was also Mr Naughty. Yvonne had lost count of the times she'd been awoken by Vee wildly flinging herself from one end of the room that they shared to the other, protesting that Mr Naughty was after her. Convinced the shadowy ghoul with skeletal grasping fingers was going to drag her through the walls of the tower to the special hiding place where he imprisoned bad children, Vee would leap on Yvonne's bed, shaking her awake and begging for help.

'Don't let him take me, Vonnie. Help me, please.'

More often than not, Yvonne would take pity on her and let her slide under the covers next to her, wrapping her arms around her trembling body and stroking her sticky little forehead, or shushing her reassuringly as if she was somebody's granny and not just a child herself.

'It's okay. He's gone now.' Yvonne had learned the hard way how important it was for Vee to be believed, so she always went along with her sister's night terrors.

'He won't come back for me?' she would beg.

'Oh, no. Not when he's got other little kids to torture.' Yvonne could remember how matter-of-fact she'd been about it all. Usually her words helped, because sooner or later Vee would drop off to sleep, her panicky hot breath so close it warmed her own cheek.

Other times, God help her, Yvonne had been too tired and grouchy to be any help. Instead, she would angrily throw a pillow at her deranged sister's head and scream, 'I wish he'd hurry up and get it over with so I can go back to sleep.' To really scare her sister, she'd even dared challenge the bogeyman man himself. 'Mr Naughty, I give you permission to kill my sister.' At such times, she thought Vee would drop dead on the spot through fear alone.

So, whilst waking up this morning to find Vee's foul fag breath on her face hadn't exactly come as a huge surprise, Yvonne was not altogether pleased to discover they had spent the night cuddled up on the same bed that had seen them through such troubled times. No doubt her sister would now wrongly assume they were all friends again, but it wasn't as simple as that. Somebody had once tried to drown her in this very room and it sure as hell wasn't Mr Naughty.

SUCKING HUNGRILY ON a crooked cigarette and flicking ash into a crunched-up beer can, Venetia sat on a low wall that bordered a fancy flowerbed and agitatedly scratched the scars on her arms.

There weren't yet many people about and those who had braved the chilly start to the day gave her a wide birth, no doubt assuming she was some homeless drunk or pickpocket. Or worse, perhaps one of the occasional jumpers who braved the barbed wire fence in order to throw themselves over the cliff edge, not the least bit comforted or put off by the Samaritan signs nailed to each post.

Vee found it amusing to people watch, inventing lifestyles for each stranger she came across, wondering at the same time what improbable tales they assumed about her – if they noticed her at all. She also had a very bad habit of likening a person to certain parts of the human anatomy; this was an instant and completely uncontrollable reaction.

For instance, the old boy over there, walking like an old soldier with a broadsheet tucked uniformly under his arm, reminded her of somebody who had just let one drop and was smirking internally about it. And the girl with the hard-as-nails face, wearing UGG boots and pushing a screaming infant in a buggy, had meaty vagina written all over her. Vee never could fathom why some people were farts; others were fannies and others still cocks, ball-bags and bum holes. Bum hole was a particularly favourite noun, reserved especially for her late stepfather, Phillip, who in Vee's opinion had a lot to answer for when it came to the division in their family.

Plucking off a purple flower head from the plentiful array of bedding plants, Vee inhaled its fresh, promising scent and felt inexplicably sad. Having no idea what the flower was called, she nonetheless felt like a wilted dandelion in comparison to its dazzling purity and vivaciousness; a bit like how she felt standing next to her sister and mother.

Vee was sure her mother would know what the flower was called, even in textbook Latin; she would also no doubt be horrified to find her daughter drinking so early in the morning, particularly in public, and especially because she was knocking back something as vulgar as working men's lager. From a can, no less.

But if it was a choice between her mother's disapproval and Wuffa's, she would definitely choose the former. Ever since she'd been a little kid, she'd been terrified by the stories of a giant wolf who was immortalised in a four-foot oak statue, its head thrown back in a baying position, that was situated in the flower bed overlooking the sea.

Legend had it the wolf had guarded the body of King Edmund after he had been killed by the Danes for refusing to renounce his Christian beliefs. Known as the "boy king", Edmund had been tortured by the Vikings and shot so many times with arrows that he resembled a hedgehog, before finally being beheaded. The dismembered head was later found in the forest before the paws of the great wolf, and as a result Wuffa's statue had been erected next to the ruins of the chapel, built to mark the spot where Edmund first landed over 1,000 years ago.

Vee could not remember exactly how many times she'd had terrifying nightmares about the giant wolf or the headless boy, but just sitting here, beside the heavily maned animal, was enough to give her the willies. You'd have thought she'd have got used to him by now, but no matter how many times she sat in the same spot, she still expected the wolf to come alive, intent on savaging her. In fact, she'd dreamt repeatedly of being carried off in his slobbering jaws as he leapt from the cliff edge and waded out to sea, where she would drown like a rag doll in the grip of his rotten canines.

Appreciating what a ridiculous and unlikely fantasy this actually was, Vee couldn't resist a childish giggle and, in retaliation, flicked a trickle of ash onto one of the wolf's mammoth paws. She even toyed with the idea of poking out her nicotine-stained tongue at him, but decided that would be going one step too far. Still, it felt good to laugh. In fact, since last night she'd been in a much better mood. Hearing her mother reveal all those wonderful things about her father had been a revelation and she couldn't help wish it had been done sooner, years ago, when there was still a chance they could all be friends. But at least now Vonnie would have to stop muddying their dad's good name and give him the credit he was due. Surely now they would all be able to move on: put the past behind them and start over.

'WHAT ON EARTH did you feed Vee all that rubbish about Roger for?' Yvonne demanded, helping herself to a large custard doughnut from the American-style fridge-freezer.

'It's difficult keeping everyone happy, Yvonne. You should know that.' Wearing a mumsy apron, Hazel stood at the kitchen sink, washing up that morning's used china teacup and saucer; her moisturised hands were encased in a pair of vibrant Marigolds.

'She'll want a statue of him erected in the flower bed next to Wuffa after this,' Yvonne grimaced, slyly licking away the telltale sign of sugar from her lips before shutting the fridge door.

Distracted by something going on outside the window, Hazel wasn't really paying attention to her daughter's concerns or her out-of-control binging. Had her mind been in the right place, she would definitely have pointed out that breakfast was only half an hour away and eating between meals was not ladylike. As it was, all she could do was crane her neck, intent on peering out of the window.

There it was now, sneaking its way around the curves in the road like a very long snake – the funeral procession led by a black hearse with a coffin inside, swamped by a "Dad" wreath in brash colours that Hazel considered tasteless.

She had no idea who could be inside the coffin or what their connection to the holiday resort might be, but judging by the number of dark cars following the hearse, the "dad" in question must have been popular. Inside one of those tinted-glass limousines was the man's family. His wife and children, all dressed in black, hands folded on laps, starched handkerchiefs at the ready as they prepared themselves for the gruelling day ahead, all the while knowing that today was just the start of their grieving process.

Peering closer in the hope that she might be able to identify members of the grieving family, Hazel's heart suddenly started banging against her chest. Inside that car was somebody she hadn't expected to see. There she was now, her legs elegantly crossed on the back seat, taking out a flashing gold compact mirror and applying a well-known shade of lipstick to her mouth. Then came the vain tossing of curls, a gesture she recognised at once. From underneath the veiled hat, Hazel caught sight of the familiar pea-green eyes that looked as if they wanted to own everything in front of them. Shockingly, it was Hazel's own image she was seeing; a younger version of herself, whose self-assurance surprised her. Next to her sat two little girls, hard to tell apart, dressed in matching black dresses with white lace collars: her own daughters. On sight of them, Hazel tore her eyes away, the horror and pain too much for any mother to witness.

Luckily the vision soon blurred, to be replaced once again with somebody wholly unconnected to her sitting in the back seat of the limousine. Supposing it only natural for her to be so easily spooked, considering she had already buried two husbands and survived two such days as this, Hazel could easily identify with how the newly-widowed woman must feel.

Almost.

Because, if Hazel was brutally honest, she had taken to young widowhood like a homeless ghost would a vacant spooky castle, and therefore her situation could hardly be described as the same or even remotely similar. Her recollection of her precious Phillip's funeral was somewhat patchy and contradictory, yet she remembered Roger's, which had taken place eighteen years ago, as if it were yesterday.

* * *

HAZEL OBSERVED THE other mourners through the haze of black net that escaped from her pillbox hat and preferred the quirky new accessory that was perched elegantly on one side of her head to anything approaching sorrow. In fact, she hoped its sprinkling of feathers would be much admired. Better that than having to witness a grief-stricken Gillian gawping morbidly into the silk-lined coffin containing her son.

Wearing stripper heels and a low-cut top that exposed her sun-damaged, crinkly skin, the older woman was being held upright by relatives who all lugged around the same cumbersome nose as she did.

'My son. My son,' she sobbed in anguish, her knees finally buckling under her as she kissed Roger's refrigerated forehead in a conspicuously inappropriate way that did not go unnoticed by certain members of her family. Then, on the edge of fainting, she was finally hauled away into a supportive huddle of family and friends where it didn't matter that, for once in her life, she wore no mascara or eyeliner.

Wondering if she'd bothered to throw on a pair of knickers for the visit to the funeral parlour, Hazel couldn't help thinking how different her mother-in-law looked without the heavy eye makeup; rather like a woman who'd lost her eyes at a game of cards.

She felt pity for her. Of course she did. Roger was her son, after all, and Gillian had never done Hazel any real harm. Even so, once today was over, Hazel had already decided that she would distance herself from her and the rest of the Cox family. It would be hard for Gillian to lose touch with her two grandchildren, but it had to be done if Hazel was to start a new life. Besides, she had plenty more grandchildren to maul.

Able to finally take her place by the open coffin now that

Gillian's drawn-out turn was over, Hazel found herself looking dispassionately at her dead husband's face. This was only the second time she'd seen a dead person – her father being the only other cadaver she'd viewed – and found the experience satisfying rather than frightening.

In death, Roger's concord nose appeared smaller, less bloated and broken-veined, which seemed to fit his face better. He looked so much nicer with the thin lips firmly stitched shut (they looked sewn up, to Hazel's inexperienced eye), which at any rate hid the golden false tooth that she had long despised for being low-class. The oversized coffin drowned him in exactly the same way his old sheepskin coat once had, she thought indifferently. She couldn't help noticing how extremely self-conscious he looked in the shirt and tie (done up too tight, judging by the folds of bluish skin bunched around his neck), which made it look as if he'd been strangled. But everybody knew he'd died from natural causes, Hazel reminded herself, and fought back the desire to do a hop, skip and a jump on the spot.

Careful. She had to be careful. People were already looking at her and commenting on her odd behaviour, her not having shed a single tear since Roger's death. But if she was in any danger of crying at all, it was through sheer relief at discovering just how careless Roger had been with his own health. She still couldn't quite believe her luck. What did she care what others thought, when even the irascible Doctor Bonner had agreed she was suffering from shock. Still, conscious of being watched and knowing it was expected of her, she bent over the coffin to say her last goodbyes.

'Don't let the bedbugs bite,' she whispered in his ear, fighting back the mouth-watering urge to spit on his downturned face. It would be such a relief when they finally nailed the lid shut on him. Perhaps then her seven-year-long ordeal would finally be over. Then, noticing that somebody had placed a photograph of her two young daughters in the coffin, she was at once furious. How dare they? What right had anyone?

Flapping out her unused handkerchief, she let her hand stray long enough inside the coffin (next to him, almost touching), to slyly tuck the photograph inside the hankie, afterwards pretending to dab her eye with it, giving her all the time she needed to slide the photograph in her bag.

Roger wouldn't need any mementoes of their life together where he was going, she decided. Nor did he deserve any keepsakes. Hazel might have lost the battle to have his body cremated and her wish to forego any religious ceremony had also been ignored, but she still felt the church service would be a complete waste of time. In her opinion, he was going straight to Hell.

THE CHURCH COULD never be full enough to satisfy the likes of Gillian, Hazel observed, even if that meant people were squeezed in like sardines while others queued out the door. After all, this was her precious son they were burying; she couldn't stop herself telling anyone who would listen, 'You couldn't find a more decent, hard-working boy with a beautiful young family to boot.'

On and on she'd whined to Hazel about how he deserved a good turn-out, with a bloody good knees-up in the pub afterwards, knowing that Hazel had all along been against the idea, preferring instead some hushed finger buffet do in the restrained local conservative club, which wasn't the Cox family's cup of tea at all.

In a way, Hazel was pleased for Gillian, who seemed delighted to have so many people turn up at the church. Perhaps now her mother-in-law could relax, knowing that the local townspeople hadn't let her or her boy down. And, as you couldn't see the wood grain of the coffin for all the wreaths and flowers covering it, nothing else needed saying. Didn't this alone prove how much her boy had been well-liked and loved by all? A fact that surely made it easier for Gillian to finally relinquish any niggling doubts she might have had about her son's mental state.

'I always felt responsible for the way Roger turned out, though Lord knows I've been as bad a mother to him as any of the others,' she'd confided dryly to Hazel.

It was the only attempt at an apology she would ever receive, Hazel realised. Even so, Gillian could never be entirely blameless, because mothers never were, were they? But she couldn't begrudge what little comfort it brought Gillian, knowing that any leftover doubts she'd had about her son could now be buried alongside him.

'It's a shame though that the vicar never actually met Roger,' Gillian pronounced loudly on the way into church, when everybody else was respectfully silent. Comically, Gillian had then gone on to suppose, 'As none of us go to church that often, not at all if the truth be told, it really can't be helped. I only hope he gives a fitting enough eulogy, as Roger deserves nothing less,' she'd hissed through badly fitting false teeth that clacked loosely in her jaw.

'But what is the vicar saying? I can hardly hear him. I wish he would speak up, be a bit more animated. Somebody ought to prompt him not to be so grave,' she complained as they settled in their seats.

'A BELOVED SON, husband and father, tragically cut down in his prime'. Reverend Pickles, with the basin-bowl haircut and propensity to spit saliva during sermons, hardly knew where to begin, having heard various different accounts of the dead man's character. Some had hinted at a drink problem, others of drug abuse. He'd even heard rumours that he'd been a wife beater.

But just looking at the attractive, demure young woman in the front pew, he couldn't imagine how anyone could – and the two adorable little ones were so pristinely turned out, in matching black velvet dresses with white lace collars. Not only would he say a prayer for them now, he would keep them in his thoughts afterwards, unaware that he would one day come face to face with Hazel again in the most unexpected and horrific of circumstances.

CLASPING HER HANDS together in what appeared to be fervent prayer, Hazel kept her eyes firmly shut, hoping to find herself anywhere but inside the gloomy confines of the church when she opened them again.

She didn't know how much more of the vicar's pitying glances or sorrowful references to herself she could take before screaming, 'Don't pity me, because I'm not a bit sorry,' out loud to a stunned, horrified congregation of mourners. But she must keep it together, if not for her own sake then for the children's, for as long as this interminable service lasted.

But what was *she* doing now, leaning forward in her seat and glaring at Hazel as if she were the devil, as if she was the one who had personally crucified Jesus on the cross, as depicted by the stone statue on the wall? Throughout the service, her eldest daughter had constantly brought attention on herself, squirming and shuffling restlessly about, whispering loudly to her sister or making faces at her older cousins two or three pews back. It wasn't as if Hazel hadn't instructed them how to behave. Look at the little one sitting there, sucking contentedly on her thumb, her huge eyes taking everything in, occasionally squeezing Hazel's hand as if it was her job to comfort her mother, not the other way around. *Why couldn't her eldest be more like her?*, she wondered dismally.

'I know what you did,' the bad-tempered child hissed accusingly at Hazel, her cheeks burning angrily.

Her timing couldn't have been more premeditated, Hazel felt, having deliberately waited until she was settled in church in full view of all these people before throwing down the gauntlet. God forgive her for sometimes thinking it served her right when… or that she had almost deserved… but no. Hazel must never, ever think such thoughts aloud, not where her late husband and daughter were concerned. Else what sort of mother did that make her?

'You don't know anything,' Hazel spoke fiercely, relieved to see a look of surprised doubt flicker across the child's sickly grey face.

And she didn't. For what could she know?

* * *

'YOU DON'T KNOW anything,' Hazel accused, spinning around to repeat the same words to a grown-up Yvonne, who guiltily dropped her eyes in shame, not knowing that a giveaway trail of sugar still sparkled on her chin.

'Venetia still feels it so badly, his passing. It was such a terrible accident and he was so young.'

'He was my father too, at least my biological father, but I don't see any need to turn him into a saint.'

'Perhaps not, but it's wrong to speak ill of the dead, Yvonne. You of all people should know that.'

'That doesn't stop her when it comes to Phillip,' Yvonne spoke quietly.

Hazel leaned back against the sink and sighed, hating to see the frown on her beautiful daughter's face.

'There was never any doubt of my loving Phillip more. You know that, don't you?'

Yvonne lifted her head, eyes glistening like a wet morning. 'But you still think of him at times? Roger?'

Sensing her daughter softening, Hazel resisted the almost overwhelming urge to reach out and push a loose tendril of her hair back behind her ear.

'Do you really need to ask?'

* * *

HE HADN'T GONE to work: a rarity for such a hard-working, exemplary employee as Roger, who prided himself on never having taken a day off sick in the last ten years. Instead, he'd stayed in bed, wheezing and whistling like a toy train, whilst his sunken eyes hung bloodshot and lazy, like a bloodhound's. Lined up on a bedside table next to him was a military line of inhalers that may as well have been lines of cocaine for all the good they were doing him.

'I feel terrible.' Like a little boy, he'd reached for Hazel's hand, wanting sympathy. Despite all their differences, Hazel allowed him to hold it.

'I think I need a steroid injection. My breathing's not getting any easier and I must be in a bad way if my inhalers aren't helping.' Agitatedly, Roger knocked down the row of inhalers; Hazel did her best not to notice.

'Would you like me to take you to hospital?' she sighed patiently.

'They'll only want to keep me in.' He shook his head vehemently, as she knew he would, given that he hated being among strangers.

'Give the doctor a ring. If you tell him how bad my asthma is, he'll come out.'

Nodding, Hazel took leave of her husband. She did not linger, as one might have expected her to. Nor did she turn back for one last look as she reached the door. She simply walked out quietly and sedately, leaving Roger with the surest of impressions that she'd be back in a few minutes with a cup of tea and news of the doctor's imminent visit.

HE MUST HAVE been dozing in and out of consciousness for hours, all the while expecting to find her there next to him whenever he woke up. But there'd been no sign of her since she'd gone downstairs to make the phone call. What the hell was she doing down there all this time? What could possibly be keeping her? He'd tried thumping on the floor, but was too weak to make any significant impact – or raise hell, as he'd have liked.

'Hazel? Hazel, can you hear me?'

Nothing. Absolutely nothing. She must be on the phone chatting to his mother or hanging out the washing, unable to hear. But, come to think of it, he hadn't heard a peep out of the children either.

'Yvonne? Venetia?'

Nothing. It was so still and deathly quiet in this house, you'd think somebody had died.

Realising at last that something was up, Roger was left with no choice but to clamber feebly out of bed and see what his treacherous family were up to. Finding it increasingly difficult to take in air and wheezing with each intake of breath, as if a giant wrestler had him in a chokeslam, he moved at a snail's pace out of the room, dragging his useless legs behind him.

Downstairs there were yellow post-it sticky notes everywhere, stuck on everything. What the fuck? Had she gone mad? Only a few days ago he'd heard Hazel marvelling at what a wonderful invention they were, but was she really that forgetful that she had to leave notes for herself?

But it turned out the sticky notes weren't reminders for Hazel at all. They were for him. And not the common old, "your dinner is in the oven" variety, either.

In the cutlery drawer, stuck to the fork Hazel had once stabbed him with, was one of the blasted notes with Hazel's neatly joined up schoolgirl's handwriting on it. "Remember this?"

Another was stuck to the laundry basket next to a cotton pair of Hazel's pants. "Proof that my dirty knickers do not stick to the wall," she'd jotted down. All right, maybe he shouldn't have said that. He'd known how much it upset her at the time, but sometimes she was so up herself that she needed bringing down a peg or two. Although Roger didn't test them this time by chucking them at the wall, he was unable to resist smelling the gusset.

Stuck to the toilet seat was another. "Nor do I pick my arse in bed but I did pick a complete arse to marry." note. If Roger hadn't felt so under the weather, he would have burst out laughing. Thought she was being clever, did she? Until now, he'd no idea Hazel even possessed a sense of humour, but even he had to concede that he might just be able to drum up a bit of admiration – respect, even – for this newly comical, spunkier version of his wife.

Until, that was, he came across one that really got his goat, stuck to where the telephone should have been. "Doctor suggests you seek the warmth you can't get from your own wife in HELL, where there is plenty of heat to go around."

Instead of cutting the telephone cord and leaving behind any incriminating evidence, she had, wherever she had gone, actually taken the clunky BT rotary dial phone with her. She had in the end turned out to be a rather clever girl; he had to give her that, although he wasn't sure how or when this had come about. But he'd fucking kill her anyway. Mark his words, he would. And he'd mark her too. Maybe he'd mark all three of them while he was at it. Show them once and for all who was boss in this house.

'Bitches. All of them fucking sly, backstabbing bitches,' he managed to roar, before being overcome by the inevitable coughing and gasping that racked his body and threatened to close off his airways. Already his breathing was very rapid and the chest pain was becoming unbearable, like a herd of wild horses stampeding across his chest.

Aware that if he didn't find help soon he could be in danger of going into the "silent chest" stage of asthma, which was a particularly dangerous sign, he began crawling laboriously on his bare knees. He eventually made it to the front door, only to find it locked and the key missing. The door having no modern, Yale-style lock but an old-fashioned one that could only be opened with a mortise key meant there was no way out.

Once again, Hazel had dared defy him; she knew she wasn't meant to lock any of the doors, at least not without his permission. Unable to bear being locked in, particularly in small, claustrophobic areas such as this windowless hallway, Roger had always seen to the locking of doors and was most particular about it. He'd even been known to go off on one if Hazel accidentally locked the bathroom door to pee.

Having inherited shades of his mother's tendencies toward

mental illness, Roger had never confided to anyone – not even his own wife, and certainly not his man-eating mother – how one of her many male visitors had once shut him in the damp outside toilet of their 1940's council house and taken his childhood from him over the porcelain privy.

Knowing that it was the worst possible way to go – shut in a cold, dark space no bigger than Butch's decrepit old dog kennel – Roger nevertheless didn't have the strength to do anything about it. Slumped against the wall, his one regret was failing to keep his promise to leave an everlasting mark on his wife, not knowing he already had.

His fingertips had already turned blue to match his lips and his lungs had tightened so much there was not even enough air movement to produce the wheezing anymore. He had arrived at the critical "silent chest" stage; he didn't need telling what that meant.

The only thing to keep him company in his last minutes was the ticking of the plastic cuckoo clock Hazel had hated the instant she unwrapped it on their wedding day. Perhaps it was because of that he'd insisted on giving it pride of place on the wall, even though he'd later discovered it originated from China and not Switzerland. He didn't know why he'd been unable to resist antagonising his wife so much, only that it was in his nature to do so. And look at how she'd repaid him! By clearing off out for the day rather than staying home and taking care of him.

And so he waited, hoping to catch a glimpse of her hand appearing magically through the keyhole as she turned the key in the door, using the same finger he'd once put a slither of cheap gold on, belatedly realising he couldn't remember the last time he'd seen her wear it.

And so he listened, hoping to hear the sound of her high-heeled shoes tripping over the gravel as she returned home, wishing he'd given her the money to have them re-heeled when she'd asked.

But all he saw was the dead-looking eyes of the cheap plastic cuckoo that hung lifelessly on a metal spring, and all he thought he heard was the creak of the eighth step on the stairs, as if someone or something was creeping down them to hurry him along into the next life.

As Hazel had suggested in her note, he already knew where he was going. There would be no surprises.

DOWN IT WENT jauntily, like a lifeboat being lowered from a big liner into the sea below. Everyone stared at the coffin as if they hadn't seen it before, although it had been on display both at the church and in the hearse that led the procession of mourners to this very churchyard.

It was very different, though, watching it actually being put to rest in the hole in the ground; for those family members hovering around the edge of the grave, it meant never seeing Roger again.

Though she didn't know it yet, Hazel would be reminded of this moment many years later, at a time in her life when she'd grown bored of social networking and decided to temporarily deactivate her Facebook account, only to be confronted with a warning that instantly made her think of her late husband being lowered into the grave, with the caption "Roger will miss you" underneath.

Another thing Hazel would not miss in the slightest was the depressing mourning colours everyone wore. Black coats, dark grey suits and black armbands for those who hadn't the funds to rush out and buy anything black. She for one definitely planned on never wearing anything but the brightest of colours after today.

Just another hour or so and it will all be over, she told herself as she watched Gillian making a spectacle of herself for the hundredth time that day; flirting madly one minute, leaning on the arm of this or that man, and sobbing hysterically the next. There she was now, honing in on Hazel, her arms outstretched, wanting to share her grief with 'The one other person who loved him as much as she did.'

Attempting to bear-hug some life into her daughter-in-law, Gillian couldn't help noticing that something was different about Hazel, although she couldn't quite put her finger on what it was exactly.

'You've done something to your hair, dear?'

'A few highlights,' Hazel nodded.

'Very cheerful, I'm sure.' Gillian was not sure she approved. 'And the suit is new, isn't it?'

'Only the very best for Roger.' Hazel wished with all her heart that she had a large glass of wine in her hand. In fact, her hand felt quite empty without one, even though as a rule she didn't like alcohol that much.

'I'll be glad when it's over, myself,' Gillian whispered sympathetically, noticing that Hazel looked as keen to get away as she did. 'I'm starting to have palpitations at the thought of staying any longer,' she confided even further. After all, if she couldn't trust her dead son's widow with this information, who could she trust?

'I think the vicar is ready for us.' One of Roger's many brothers – Hazel couldn't be sure which one – came and took hold of Gillian's sinewy elbow, diplomatically guiding her toward the open grave. Meanwhile, Hazel looked around for her daughters, who were being entertained by Great Uncle Basil, an old favourite of theirs who no doubt had a comforting bag of Werther's Originals somewhere in his pocket, judging by the see-sawing action going on in the girls' mouths.

'Venetia. Yvonne. Come over here please, there's good girls,' Hazel called.

The little one ran over straight away, pleased to be reunited with her mother, but the eldest hung back, her eyes on fire, looking as if she'd like to disobey but not having quite enough courage to do so.

Handing them each a long-stemmed red rose, Hazel and her daughters joined the rest of Roger's family at the graveside. Although she would have preferred to skulk in the background like some very distant third or fourth cousin, she found herself unexpectedly propelled to the front of the queue, expected to be the first to throw soil on top of the coffin.

Holding onto her youngest child's hand, Hazel watched, mesmerised, as the clods of earth bounced off the wooden coffin below. Then came the turn of the red roses as they floated downwards, their pungent scent almost overpowering as their fragile petals scattered into potpourri when they collided into the coffin.

But no matter how hard anyone tried, it proved impossible to coerce Hazel's eldest child into giving up her red rose, and long after they'd conceded defeat she continued to hang on to it as if her life depended on it, her little thumbs dotted with thorny pinpricks as a result. Rather than hold onto Hazel's hand like her little sister, she stood alone and kept a wary distance, refusing to smile even for Great Uncle Basil.

But when Gillian decided to reclaim the show once again by sobbing loudly and sucking on a brown paper bag in order to help her breathe through her palpitations, attention was at last diverted away from her difficult child. For once, Hazel was able to forgive Gillian for her histrionic outbursts.

'He wouldn't have liked it one little bit. Not being covered in dirt like that. He was just like me in that respect. Claustrophobic, wasn't he, Hazel?'

Later, after the inevitable fight between two Cox brothers that had to be taken outside the pub; a domestic over someone's husband looking down another woman's cleavage; and many cups of tea, several cases of beer and half a dozen bottles of sherry later, Hazel was finally able to say her goodbyes to a tearful Gillian.

'Do you think it wise, Hazel, to take them on holiday so soon, when their father's only just died?'

Hazel glanced at her two daughters, who were by now as tired and grumpy as each other, the littlest one barely able to keep her eyes open.

'I'll take them away the same time every year, so they never forget.'

Happy with this homage to her son, Gillian decided that she had enough on her own plate to worry about. Hazel knew best how to take care of her own children.

'God bless you, dear; that would have been so important to Roger. Them not forgetting the day he died, but remembering it.'

Fondly kissing her mother-in-law's cheek and leaving the last impression her nude lipstick would ever make on the older woman's doughy skin, Hazel could only think how much more important it was to remember that it had also been the day they first discovered that Hunstanton's defunct old lighthouse was up for sale.

JUST A FEW days later, they arrived in what could only be described as "glorious Technicolor" at the old lighthouse, overlooking the North Beach, that now boasted a wind-warped "Sold" sign outside.

Sporting a sophisticated new look, with a whole head of platinum hair and a bright cerise mackintosh to go with a new, livelier shade of lipstick, Hazel couldn't have looked younger or more radiant if she'd tried.

Overdosing meanwhile on pigtails scraped tightly into multi-coloured hair bands and wearing matching clothes as they always did, her two daughters were dressed in bright yellow plastic raincoats and Neapolitan ice-cream-coloured ra-ra skirts.

Playing piggy in the middle, Hazel held on to each of her daughter's hands as they crossed the road from the bus stop into Lighthouse Close. Then, once they got to the white picket gate that opened into the front garden of the lighthouse, she stopped to gaze up at their new holiday home and felt a familiar buzz. Although the sale of the lighthouse had not yet been completed, the owners, in this case Hunstanton Town Council, had in the meantime agreed to let it to her on the proviso that she paid cash when her husband's numerous life insurances paid out, no doubt taking into account how the young widow's considerable fortune would be an asset to the town.

'What do you think, girls? Isn't it fantastic that it's ours?'

The little one was all sunny smiles and eager to go anywhere, so long as she could take her yellow and green Care Bear toy with her. Not so the eldest, who had predictably never needed a comforter in her life – no bear or rag doll had ever stood a fighting chance of being cosied up to her. Proving that was still the case, she snapped her hand away from her mother's and crawled under the nearest parked car, refusing to come out.

WAFTS OF COOKING smells crept invasively into every corner of every room and on every level of the lighthouse, as fresh coffee gurgled away in a percolator and lemon and cinnamon pancakes sizzled in a frying pan on the six-ring hob. Arranged like a still life oil painting, an assortment of fresh fruit and healthy mueslis was laid out on a blue and white checked tablecloth on a table over by the window.

Like an overanxious wife, with freshly applied lipstick and a powdered nose, Hazel came to the door of the kitchen and called out in a voice brimming with forced homeliness, 'Breakfast is ready!'

As if they'd been summoned by the most efficient of school matrons, all three of them came into the kitchen at the same time, dragging their feet like unenthusiastic boarders who didn't know how to be anything other than belligerent.

Hazel cast a quick eye over Venetia's grey, rodent-like face and was not altogether surprised to catch a grateful nod of recognition from her. Although she couldn't stop wishing her other daughter was as easy to please, it didn't stop her sending a warm, appreciative smile back. Talking about Roger had obviously gone some way to restoring a semblance of friendship between them at least.

But Hazel wasn't the only one to detect Venetia's mellowing. Yvonne had also seen the look that passed between them and, judging by the hostile look on her face, instantly felt ostracised by it. It would always be one foot forward, two steps back when it came to her girls, Hazel couldn't help observing.

Oblivious to her sister's scrutiny, Venetia rolled her eyes hungrily when she saw all the yummy food and quickly grabbed a chair, staking her "head girl" place at the table. Una, meanwhile, rubbed crusty sleepies out of her eyes and settled the soft lion toy into a chair of his own, all the while whispering to him in a secret language made up especially to exclude the adults.

Only Yvonne lagged behind, pulling a sour face, obviously not the least bit impressed with the continental offering.

'This hamster food is all very well, but you can't beat a proper fry-up.'

Seeing her mother's crestfallen face – after all, she had gone to so much trouble – Venetia surprised herself by coming to her mother's rescue, turning on Yvonne in the process. 'And you can't beat some people. Talk about ungrateful.'

'It's alright, Venetia.' Hazel glanced appreciatively at her daughter, wishing she could mime a silent "thank you", knowing if she did that Yvonne would surely spot it and have something else to brood about.

'Really, it is.' She was quick to assure Yvonne at the same time, so she wouldn't take offence. But really it wasn't and everyone felt it.

Grabbing a copper-based frying pan from a hanging rack above her head, she commented, 'I should have guessed someone would prefer something more traditional. It's not too late though. I can soon rustle up some bacon and eggs.'

Then, turning her back on her family, Hazel proceeded to slide thin slithers of streaky bacon out of a greasy packet and crack eggs into the pan.

WATCHING HER MOTHER retreat into her "wounded victim" role, as she was prone to do whenever anyone injured her feelings, Yvonne caught Venetia mouthing the word "idiot" at her through a stuffed cheek-full of muesli and realised she was not only an idiot but a fool – and a jealous one at that.

It was one thing to dismiss her sister's bad opinion of her, but Yvonne could not feel the same way about her own daughter, who was also clearly shocked by her outburst. Yvonne fought back apologetic tears and felt deeply ashamed. How could she have been so deliberately rude when she always insisted on the best of manners where Una was concerned?

For something to do other than die of excruciating embarrassment, Yvonne piled pancakes soaked in maple syrup on hers and Una's plates, all the while knowing she no longer had the stomach for any food, all the while wondering why on earth she'd acted in such a spoilt, thoroughly nasty way.

After all, who was to say she had any real reason to feel such antipathy towards her mother and sister? For all she knew, she may have got the whole drowning-in-the-bath incident wrong all those years ago. Perhaps it had been just as everyone always claimed – nothing more than an accident. It wasn't even as if she could be one hundred percent sure of anything that happened that night. When was she going to grow up and stop blaming everyone else for something that probably never even happened? Or at least, not in the way she thought it had.

Realising she was similar in ways to her mother and sister in that she too was capable of holding a grudge, Yvonne wished she could stop whining about who her mother's favourite daughter was and just accept whatever relationship Hazel *was* prepared to offer, because deep down she was desperate for Una to get to know her grandmother – and that was never going to happen with the way they were all carrying on. She was hardly setting a good example to her child, she realised. They might be a family who didn't know how to forgive, but they were also a family who didn't know how to sit down to a simple meal together. Perhaps it was time for her to take the first step in making amends where her family was concerned. Otherwise, she was in danger of ending up being bitter and resentful and the very sort of person she least wanted to be.

HER MOTHER LOOKED more carefree and relaxed than she had since the start of this long weekend, Yvonne decided, as she watched her roll up her white pedal pushers and paddle barefoot in the shallows – a thing she never usually did.

Wearing a silk headscarf that revealed a teasing glimpse of platinum curls beneath, Hazel looked every inch a blonde Hollywood bombshell putting on a wide, practiced smile for a smitten camera crew. Unsure if her mother was entirely ignorant of how she appeared, Yvonne watched her dangle a pair of nautical stripe deck shoes in one hand and swing a plastic beach bucket in the other, laughing girlishly as she watched Una chase after seagulls on the sand.

Lagging just a few steps behind and feeling like a baby elephant in comparison to her trim mother, Yvonne had also taken off her shoes but chose to remain on the sand strewn with squashed mermaid purses. Dodging the razor-sharp clam shells that could slice through skin, she never once strayed into the water, but would every so often hop about on one foot and swear under her breath; she was finding the pebbled beach painful terrain on the soles of her feet.

Una, on the other hand, seemed to love the wet mushy sand that stuck like cement to her naked toes and said she never wanted to have to wear shoes again. The only thing she loved more was washing off the sand in a tide pool and starting all over again, watching her toes fill up with the magical quicksand as she ran from one cove to the next. Una also went to great lengths to explain she hadn't as yet seen or felt any evidence of the crabs

Yvonne had warned her would nip spitefully at her toes, nor had any of the seagulls attempted to land in her hair and start making a nest. Rather than frighten Una, the cautionary tales Yvonne had told her about the seashore only succeeded in enthralling her daughter all the more. In fact, Una was finding the beach everything Yvonne did not. Wonderful. Exciting. Adventurous.

But Una also wanted everybody to be friends. So, having sidled over to Yvonne, she'd whispered something wet and salty in her ear and then thrown herself down on the ground, knees sinking in the gritty sand as she made a start on the sandcastle her grandmother had promised to help make. In order for that to happen, Yvonne would now need to keep her earlier promise too. Watching her daughter fill her beach bucket with wet heavy sand, Yvonne decided it was now or never.

'Mum,' she called tentatively, shyly.

Coming to a standstill, Hazel turned around with a bemused expression on her face, not sure she had heard right. And who could blame her? After all, when was the last time either one of her ungrateful children had addressed her with anything like affection? Yvonne could argue that she couldn't remember a time when her mother had last deserved it either, but thinking like that would get them nowhere. Instead, she hobbled towards Hazel on her bruised foot, actually smiling.

'Wait up a bit, Mum, will you?' Yvonne felt her mother had every right to look distrustful after the way she had behaved that morning.

'I thought it would be nice if we could stop for a rest and a chat.' Yvonne pointed to a section of barnacled hull, the last remaining bit of wreckage belonging to the *Sheraton* trawler ship that drifted ashore in 1947 – the same deserted shipwreck where Yvonne and Vee had played at pillaging pirates many years ago, and which now provided a convenient seat for fatigued beachcombers.

SITTING SIDE BY side on the rotting wood, Yvonne and Hazel had linked arms and were now looking out to sea. The wreckage itself reminded Yvonne of old dinosaur bones, while the blood-orange sand was littered with heavy stones she would not have been able to pick up by herself. The clouds, in comparison, had all the appearance of a badly put together jigsaw puzzle – the likes of which her sister might have hurriedly attempted, she thought fondly.

Turning her attention to her mother, Yvonne noticed that Hazel had thrown a cardigan over her shoulders and slipped on a large pair of tortoiseshell sunglasses, and would have been delighted to know she could easily have been mistaken for someone famous. In sharp contrast, having youth *and* beauty on her side meant Yvonne needed no such fancy accessories, did she but know it. The slight breeze tossing her chestnut curls starboard-bound was flattering enough.

A few yards away, her brow furrowed in concentration, Una was digging out a moat around her turreted sandcastle. Every so often her pink little tongue would pop out of the corner of her mouth and stay there, a sure sign she was engrossed in the task at hand. Soon she would ask for her grandmother's help to finish it, but not yet… not yet…

Smiling down on Una's soggy, sand-knotted hair and seeing how happy she was with her gangly limbs exposed in her pink Disney Princess swimming costume, Yvonne experienced a warm sensation radiate through her. The same kind of feeling you got lying on a rug in front of a log fire or tucking into homemade toad-in-the-hole.

'This is nice, isn't it?' She was sure her mother felt the same, but needed to ask. After all, she had to start somewhere.

Agreeably, Hazel patted her daughter's hand and sighed contentedly. 'Yes, darling, it is.'

'Lovely, peaceful, family time,' Hazel added. Then, smiling softly, she did what she had been longing to do ever since arriving in Hunstanton – reached over to tuck a wayward strand of her beautiful daughter's hair back behind her ear where it belonged.

'I'm glad we came this weekend.' Yvonne confided, leaning against her mother, comforted by the familiar Dior perfume that lingered on her clothes. 'And I want you to know how sorry – oh my God, it can't be.' Yvonne's attempt at an apology was cut off as surely as Hunstanton's own boy king's head had once been. The lovely, peaceful, family time Hazel had been relishing was brought to an abrupt, unwelcome end.

Because hurtling across the sand towards them was Venetia's clapped-out Suzuki, discharging explosive shotgun sounds from where its exhaust should have been and spraying waves of sand in its wake. Finally, it span to a dangerous halt just a few feet away, causing Hazel and Yvonne to jump off the ship's hull in alarm.

'Are you out of your mind?' Yvonne shouted, pulling Una to her feet and quickly inspecting her skinny torso in case she'd been hurt.

Throwing open the passenger door, Venetia leaned across the ripped seat that oozed foam stuffing and grinned expectantly, as if this kind of sensational arrival deserved nothing less than a round of applause.

'Vehicles aren't allowed on the beach, Venetia. You know that.' Hazel was always more tense when both her warring daughters were together at once.

'Oops.' Laughing, Venetia gesticulated for Yvonne to climb aboard. But instead of her sister's face looking back at her, all she got was a dark cloud threatening to spoil her fun.

'Oh, come on. You know you want to,' she wheedled.

'Can we, Mummy, please?' Yvonne had no idea where Una's adventurous side came from. She certainly hadn't inherited it from her. Still, seeing how thrilled she was at the prospect of going for a drive on the beach, and in a Suzuki 4X4 of all things, Yvonne was sorely tempted.

'Una would love it.' Venetia was quick to take advantage of her sister's weakness.

Seeing how things were likely to go, Hazel put in her two pennyworths. 'Don't do it, Yvonne. It's not safe. It could roll over or something.'

Then, realising Yvonne had made up her mind and was already tugging Una towards the vehicle, Hazel stomped her foot as if she were an angry sheep in a field.

'We'll be fine, Mum. Vee will be careful, won't you?'

Venetia wasn't so sure about that, but nevertheless nodded her assent. Anything, if it meant they could finally be on their way.

After helping Una into the Suzuki, Yvonne climbed ungainly aboard herself; the three of them were crammed in front seats originally intended for two, with not a single seatbelt between them. Bunched scruffily together, they looked like a family of itinerants on the prowl for scrap metal.

'Well don't blame me if your sister ends up killing you all!' Hazel shouted as the Suzuki plunged forward, its wheels spinning on the sand, before it raced off toward the shoreline, leaving Hazel alone on the beach.

HAZEL ANGRILY PACED up and down, stirring up ripples of wet sand beneath her feet. She couldn't get over it. Not when things had been going so well between them. No wonder the sun had gone in and the weather had turned grey and cold to match her mood. In fact, it almost felt as if a large black hand had appeared in the sky and was now making her dance like an angry puppet, forcing her to churlishly kick out at the sand.

Never having been able to stand it when her daughters shut her out of their lives with their secret gestures and childish whispering and giggling, Hazel sometimes felt the one thing getting in the way of her relationship with her children was her children.

As far as she was concerned, her rage at being left alone on the beach had been justified. It felt just the same as when her mother and father – always whispering together – had conspired against her.

Indeed, she had felt the same kind of betrayal watching them redecorate the Christmas tree in their lounge after her father had told her "how wonderfully Hazel had decorated it and wouldn't change a single thing on it". But later, when she was supposed to be tucked up in bed asleep, she'd watched them through a gap in the door as they re-hung every bauble.

Years later, she had attempted to involve her own children in decorating the tree, hoping to make it a family ritual they would repeat every year. Hazel would put on a Christmas album that invariably included Cliff Richard's track "Mistletoe and Wine" to get them in the mood, pour some mulled wine for herself and open a packet of sticky dates for the children. But all efforts to prepare for this festive family tradition ended in disaster with everyone, including herself, in tears. There would always be squabbling over the best baubles and someone – usually the eldest child – would end up poking out the eyes of the angel tree topper if she didn't get her own way. And when the eldest's attempts at strangling her sister with the silver tinsel failed, she would even stamp on the fairy lights, leaving behind a trail of dead bulbs.

Realising that no malice had been intended, Hazel didn't blame Yvonne for abandoning her alone on the beach, but she couldn't deny being hurt all the same. Then again, Yvonne had always been an unknown quantity, capable of surprising them all at times. At least where Venetia was concerned, you could rely on her being surly and uncommunicative most of the time.

Having now had a few minutes to calm down, Hazel was able to see things through more rationally, but she couldn't deny having been furious with the pair of them at first. Why, even her poor darling grandchild hadn't escaped her unprovoked wrath, for Hazel had called her some terrible names out loud in her head! But again, on reflection, she could see that Una hadn't played any part in the treachery; she could hardly have refused to go along with her mother and aunt, not even when it was plain for them to see that she wanted to stay with her grandmother.

Yes, Hazel had wanted to lash out – retaliate, even. But she couldn't really have trampled Una's sandcastle and moat, could she? Had she, out of spite, really stomped all over her grandchild's lovingly made fortress – flattening it into nothing? And if so, why couldn't Hazel remember? If so, had anyone seen her?

Lifting her bare head, her hair all wild and loose now she had lost her scarf in the tide pool, she did a crafty 360-degree scan for observers. Luckily for her, the only other mammal on the beach was a mange-ridden stray dog. Hazel and the flea-bitten canine sized each other up, the same thing on both their minds – were they in any danger from the other?

'Get away from here!' Hazel's unnerving scream came out of nowhere, surprising and scaring the dog into a bark. It curled its lip and raised its hackles in alarm, making it appear twice its size and far more aggressive.

'Go on, I said!' Hazel's only other experience with dogs had left her terrified of coming into contact with their sharp teeth and slobbering jaws. So, with considerable force, she threw a large pebble at the dog, catching it mid-thigh. Yelping, the emaciated animal bolted off in the opposite direction, giving Hazel a wide berth – anything to avoid slightly barmy holidaymakers.

'Dirty, disease-ridden thing.'

Knowing her granddaughter would be horrified to learn her grandmother was capable of hurting another living thing, Hazel was nevertheless relieved to see the dog flee with its cowardly tail curled firmly between its legs. But then, feeling sorry for it, she guiltily wondered when it had last eaten. Even Hazel wouldn't see an animal starve to death if she could help it. Forgetting for the moment that she had in fact abandoned Butch to a similar fate, she remained convinced that her granddaughter would not believe her guilty of any unnecessary cruelty to an animal. And that's when the idea came to her – how she could get her granddaughter back on side, so she would never be tempted to leave Hazel on her own again.

Of course, she'd have to tell Una about the dog wrecking the sandcastle, but she doubted the soft-as-a-boiled-egg child would mind that much. Most probably she'd want to adopt the poor thing and find it a warm bed in the kitchen next to the range.

They could have such fun together, taking it for walks and picking out a name; it had been years since the Ladd family owned a dog. *Lucky, Sandy or even Laddy sounded like good contenders*, Hazel thought, getting thoroughly carried away by the idea. Now that the sun had come back out again, she must find Una at once so that she could tell her all about it.

ABOUT A FOOT deep in water, the Suzuki had come to a standstill in the middle of the surf, waves lapping at its blue and silver two-tone bumper. Its windows were steamed up with smoke and a child's smudged handprint was clearly visible on a rear pane of glass.

Inside the Suzuki, Venetia and Yvonne kicked back their heels, their feet lazily parked either side of the dashboard and steering wheel. Puffing on a cigarette, Vee made popping sounds with her mouth as she blew out circles of smoke, marking the already heavily stained ceiling. Meanwhile, Una sat cross-legged on the dirty floor in the rear of the Suzuki, coughing pointedly when the smoke spiralled her way.

At first, Yvonne had been glad of the opportunity to make friends with her sister, but she was now having doubts as to whether it had been a wise thing to do, leaving her mother alone on the beach like that. She hadn't meant to be selfish or thoughtless, but it must have come across that way. And no matter how much she told herself that the apology had been as good as spoken, she didn't know if Hazel would see it that way. It wasn't even as if coming away with Vee like that had achieved anything, because here they were, sitting in silence, with nothing to say to each other.

Irritably batting the cigarette smoke away, Yvonne couldn't help taking her bad mood out on her sister.

'Is that it, then? I thought we were in for more excitement than this. Even old people park up on the beach, usually with a flask of tea and sandwiches.'

'I did promise Mother I'd look after you,' Vee laughed

118

graciously. 'Besides, we could always stay here and wait till the tide comes in – see where it takes us.'

'Don't say such things,' Yvonne warned, shuddering at the thought.

'Would we float, Aunt Vee?' Una was at once interested and maybe even a little frightened.

'Your aunt's the floater.' Yvonne pointedly pinched her nose and wafted away an unpleasant imaginary smell, making Vee laugh. 'You smell like one anyway.' Yvonne pushed playfully at her sister.

'And you should have been flushed away a long time ago!' Vee came right back at her, never expecting to see her sister's face fall.

'I very nearly once was.'

Confused, Vee shrugged off her sister's sudden melancholy, having no idea what she was going on about.

Although Una had initially joined in with their grubby laughter, she had no idea what was supposed to be so funny, and in that respect she was in danger of being excluded from their special jokes in the same way Hazel was. But, unlike Hazel, Una could not tell her mother and aunt how very unfunny she actually found it, nor order them to bed early when they continued to annoy her with their cloak-and-dagger whispering and private gestures.

'See that girl over there, the one with the dog and the ginger boyfriend?' Vee gestured to a couple walking a wiry miniature Schnauzer. Wearing matching tracksuits, each half of the couple carried a dog poop bag in their hand and energetically followed the dog's arse around as it squatted, changed its mind and squatted once again, only to have yet another change of heart and cock its leg instead.

Just watching these shenanigans made Vee want to get out of the Suzuki and beat the dog to death. Talk about having the piss taken out of you – and by a dog of all things.

'What about her?' Yvonne wanted to know. She couldn't see anything unusual about the couple and their dog – nothing that warranted her undivided attention, anyway.

'I bet she likes the smell of her own farts,' Vee half whispered.

In the back, Una's bottom jaw dropped and she could do nothing but hold her breath in disbelief. She couldn't quite believe half the stuff her aunt came out with and felt sure her mother would now object to such crudity, but instead she seemed to be taking it in her stride.

'You think?' Yvonne mused.

'Definitely an under-the-sheet sniffer,' Vee confirmed with an authoritative nod. Then, deliberately raising her bottom off the torn seat, she faked a noisy fart and laughed, earning her a disgusted look from her sister.

'She's far too pretty and sweet for someone as foul as you.' Yvonne couldn't resist the spiteful dig.

'Are you blind?' Vee wound down her window to take a closer look.

'Flat chest. Chunky thighs. Smelly twat,' was her expert summing up.

'There's no need to be crude,' Yvonne hissed, aware that her cheeks were burning with embarrassment.

'Built-in twat nav, that's what I've got,' Vee gloated, pretending to sniff the air.

'Oh my God, I think she heard you!' Yvonne slid down in her seat, conscious of the fact that the woman was now looking in their direction.

Giggling hysterically, Vee also ducked down out of sight, but she needn't have bothered – the woman's glance seemed not to take them in. Instead, she finally captured a piece of poo hanging from her dog's arse, but had to give it a good tug before it eventually dropped into the bag.

'Poor woman,' Yvonne murmured sympathetically, but truthfully she was more worried about whether her own twat was smelly, rather than the woman's feelings.

'You're too nice. That's your problem.'

'My problem is not being too nice. It has never had anything to do with being too nice,' Yvonne replied matter-of-factly.

Frowning, because she somehow suspected Yvonne of being all subtle and deep, Vee offered her the remainder of her cigarette, along with some sisterly advice. 'You need to chill out more.'

Finally giving in to temptation, Yvonne took a tentative puff on the cigarette and immediately choked on the fumes.

'Wait till I tell Granny!' Having never seen her mother smoke before, Una didn't know whether to be shocked or impressed by her daring.

'I think it's safe to say she's already not very happy with us,' Yvonne giggled, inhaling for a second time.

'So what's new?' Vee was of the same mind.

'Do you remember that time we got lost on the beach and she got so mad I ended up being sick down myself?'

Vee nodded, remembering the incident well. 'You always did know how to avoid a good telling-off. And I got the blame, as usual.'

'THAT'S BECAUSE YOU WERE TO BLAME!'

Now the shit really had hit the fan, because whilst they had been wrapped up with the woman and her obsession with her dog's bowel movements, their mother had crept up on them and was now glaring at them through Vee's open window.

'BOTH OF YOU WERE!' Hazel added, trying to keep things fair.

One look at her mother's stony face was all it took for Yvonne to guiltily pass the cigarette back to her sister, hoping that she hadn't been spotted. No such luck!

'And you've been smoking. You know how bad it is for you.' Hazel seemed cross and concerned all in the same breath.

'Why doesn't anyone worry about *my* health?' Vee continued lazily inhaling on the cigarette.

'Because nobody has ever been able to stop you doing anything you wanted,' her mother countered.

Thinking that her mother had a fair point, Vee decided to keep her trap shut, but then she happened to spot her sister's naughty caught-in-the-act expression and began to splutter out loud. Unable to smother her own laughter, Yvonne joined in and soon they were honking like geese while their mother looked on frostily, clearly wanting to throttle them by their stringy, bird-like necks.

'Did they really get lost on the beach, Granny?' Desperate for them all to be friends again, Una interrupted before any more damage could be done.

'A long time ago, yes,' Hazel finally conceded, glowering at her still giggling, infantile daughters.

* * *

TWO CHILDREN IN matching old-fashioned swimsuits wrestled like gladiators on a deserted pebbled beach that you'd think belonged exclusively to them. Surrounding them, like an ancient Roman coliseum, was Hunstanton's famous red rock and white chalk cliffs, rich in fossils belonging to dead sea-creatures.

The gulls squabbling among the rocks seemed to jeer and cheer the children along, taking the place of the bloodthirsty Romans who would once have watched gladiators fight to their deaths.

Both girls were extraordinarily pretty and roughly the same build. There was never any doubting that they were closely related, but although they might look the same age, there were in fact three years separating them, the sisters being six and nine respectively.

You could watch them playing on the sand all day till you felt as dizzy as they did; their playful laughter was as deliciously cheerful as a three-ounce bag of liquorice allsorts. There was, however, no way of telling them apart, only so far as that one was being twirled around on the sand while the other was doing the twirling.

The one being twirled around was suddenly let go of and off she went, still laughing but spiralling dizzily like a miniature hurricane, until she careered off and landed with a heavy plop in the sand, her head striking a large protruding piece of rock as she did so.

Sprawled out on the beach that was as gravelly as any well-maintained urban driveway, with her gangly legs pointing in opposite directions, the child, obviously knocked out, did not get back up again.

THE CHILD WHO had been doing the twirling was now snuggled in an oversized blanket outside the Royal National Lifeboat Institution, where well-meaning members of the public stood helplessly by, wishing they could do something to help.

In the background, a team of competent RNLI crew wearing bright orange overalls were preparing for "a sea shout" by getting the Atlantic 75 B-class rescue boat ready. Once they'd been given all the correct information, they would set sail and start a shallow water land search for the missing child.

Meanwhile, other crewmembers attempted to comfort the remaining child as she sobbed hysterically, snot pouring pitifully out of her postbox-red nose. One of the volunteers had brought her a paper cup of steaming sugary tea. Another had wiped her nose for her, on a menu from The Boathouse Café of all things, which was adjacent to the station in Sea Lane. Only the leader, whom everyone referred to as "Coxswain", seemed insistent on questioning her. But as he reminded the child of a cartoon dog with his large ears, long face and sad, expressive eyes, she was never going to take him too seriously.

'Can you tell us where on the beach it happened? It's vitally important –'

'She's dead. I saw her. She's never coming back,' she finally blurted out, disinclined to have her moment of fame end too soon. Then, seeing the terrified look on everyone's faces, and the way they held their breath not wanting to believe, she frightened herself into being sick down herself.

THE GIRL WHO had been twirled around on the beach sat up groggily and immediately wished she hadn't, because it felt like a carousel of wooden horses was galloping around in her head. Grimacing in pain, she tenderly stroked her bruised, soggy scalp and was horrified to see her fingers come away covered in coagulated blood.

Immediately she retched, throwing up that morning's sugary breakfast cereal, amazed to discover that the crisped rice bubbles still continued to snap, crackle and pop hours after being digested.

Pulling herself somewhat unsteadily to her feet, she was

bewildered to find herself alone on the beach, with not a soul in sight – or perhaps more worryingly, not an adult in sight. Because everybody knew that a sister was no good to you when you were hurt and afraid. At times like this, you needed a grown-up's help – even she knew that.

Finding her land legs at last, she took a little stroll along the beach. Shielding her eyes from the sun, which seemed too low in the sky, as if it had fallen down a flight of steps, she scrutinized the horizon. Fearful that the sun's dwindling flames were about to go out, she was terrified of being left alone in the dark, of becoming just another stretched-out shadow on the sand, like the sinister silhouette made by the striped cliffs. Unusually, everywhere was deathly still and silent, as if all the everyday sea creatures had scampered away to hide. Not even the squawk of gulls broke the hushed calm.

With her bottom lip quivering, tears soon filled her eyes. 'I'm not meant to be on my own.'

Then, gazing down, she noticed a multitude of different-sized trampled footprints in the sand. Weirdly, these smudged imprints seemed to bounce happily along, whereas the ones she now made in their wake were down in the dumps by comparison. Wondering which tracks might have been hers and which ones were her sister's, she started to follow them, certain they would lead her back to the main beach.

NOW THAT HAZEL had arrived on the scene, having been fetched from the beach hut by a frantic passer-by, the child who had done the twirling was forgotten in the background as the RNLI volunteers rushed to fetch her a cup of something hot and sweet for her nerves.

Close to collapse, Hazel felt swamped by all the attention

and unable to catch her breath. All she wanted was somewhere quiet to crawl into, a safe haven where nobody would worry her with all this detail. She wished Phillip were here to take care of things. He would know what to do, how to behave and what to say to these officious, meddling people. Feeling overwhelmed by the situation, she found herself longing more for his presence than her missing child's. Because not only would Phillip find her, he would also make everything right again.

Then, from out of nowhere, came the unexpected but longed-for sound.

'Mummy.'

Everyone, but most especially Hazel, turned to stare at a surfer, wearing Union Jack shorts and a smug grin on his fuzzy face, as he waded cockily through the crowd toward them. Holding on to his bronzed hand as if he were her new best friend, and chewing on the piece of Wrigley's gum he had given her, was her missing child.

Catching sight of her mother, the child who had been twirled on the sand excitedly broke free from the boy's hand and, none the worse for wear – apart from a small cut on her face and a lump on her head that already felt the size of a hardboiled egg – ran into her mother's welcoming embrace.

Once everyone had all but gone and her darling child had sobbed out the whole story, Hazel's thoughts turned to her other sour-faced daughter, sitting dejectedly on the wall with a vomit-stained blanket wrapped around her.

Not looking the least bit sorry, she stared back boldly and insolently, her legs jangling merrily beneath her as if she were doing some sort of high-spirited jig in her head.

'You said she was dead. You said you had seen her and she was never coming back!' Hazel screamed accusingly, her words echoing shrilly among the rocks, scaring the gulls into abandoning their nests and causing the last of the onlookers to stop in their tracks.

* * *

THE LIGHTHOUSE GARDEN had uneven bald patches of lawn where wild rabbits grazed and could sometimes be seen re-ingesting their black viscous droppings. Occasionally, if you were quiet enough, you would see a young rabbit peer inquisitively through the long blades of grass before dashing back to one of the many burrows in and around the garden.

Surrounding the garden was a wall made of local carrstone that had been built low enough to allow onlookers to see the sea beyond. Unfortunately, this also meant that walkers exploring the cliff path could peer over the wall into the garden to stare at Hazel – something that had always incensed her, particularly on days like this, when she had her family with her. Sometimes she would glare right back at the voyeurs, satisfied only when they looked shiftily away or moved reluctantly along. But always – *always* – it seemed to Hazel, they would take one last sneaky look back over the wall before finally disappearing from view. When it came to such diehard peeping Toms as these, Hazel wanted to run at them screaming, 'Haven't you ever seen a happy family?' before pushing them over the cliff edge.

But today there were no walkers on the cliff edge as yet, so Hazel could relax and enjoy the time spent with her family, as well as bask in the rays of a surprisingly warm midday sun. Forgotten about for now was the earlier incident on the beach, when her daughters had abandoned her. In fact, all three women seemed to have put it behind them for Una's sake; she seemed particularly susceptible to their differences of opinion. No doubt later on, when the child was asleep in bed, the same old unfinished squabbles would resurface again, but for now Hazel could unwind with Leo Tolstoy's *Anna Karenina*, whose complex flawed heroin she felt a deep connection with.

Whilst lazily sat around the picnic table sipping cloudy lemonade, she was also able to keep one attentive eye on her granddaughter, who was all over the brown dog from the beach like the hundreds of tiny Lilliputians who once tied down the giant in *Gulliver's Travels*. Having decided to forgo his life of freedom, which had consisted mainly of mange, thirst, starvation and beatings, the dog had no trouble succumbing to the new life of luxury he'd been promised on first being captured by Una on the silent walk back from the beach this morning.

Meanwhile, the sound of bat meeting ball could be heard in the background as Yvonne and Venetia played a game of rounders. Bowling a mean underarm at her sister, Venetia was in her sporting, sweaty element whereas Yvonne seemed nervous of both wooden bat and hard, leather-encased ball, often putting up a hand to defend herself against the strike.

'That was a no ball,' she complained.

'It so wasn't. Stop being such a girl!' Venetia aimed another fast and furious ball.

'I am a girl!' Squealing, Yvonne dived out of the way of the approaching high-speed ball, allowing it to bounce energetically into the long grass behind her. 'I don't know why I ever let you talk me into this.' Sulkily throwing down her bat, Yvonne knew exactly why she'd let Vee talk her into it: the same way she could talk her into anything she didn't want to do. Vee could describe a petrol forecourt and make it sound like an exciting place to go visit. That's exactly how Yvonne had been wheedled into giving this savage ball game a go.

'One more go. Come on, I'll be gentle,' Venetia coerced, running to retrieve the ball.

'And then it's my turn to bowl.' Finding a middle ground, Yvonne picked up the bat once more, oblivious to the fact that her sister had got her own way yet again.

Watching the game of rounders from the other end of the garden, Hazel and Una shared an appreciative smile, equally relieved to see everyone getting along.

'Are you glad I told you about him?' Hazel nodded toward the dog, whose coat now shone like bright copper, having being bathed in Wash & Go shampoo out of Yvonne's toiletry bag and brushed to within an inch of his life by Una.

'He's the best dog in the world, Granny.'

'And have you decided on a name?'

Taking a break from brushing the dog's glossy undercarriage, Una shook her head. 'I'm not sure yet. I still like Laddy but I also quite like Lucky.'

'You should call him Butch. Now there's a blast from the past,' Venetia called out, innocently enough, but Hazel was quick to think the worst. After all, it had been many years since Roger's dog exited their lives and she'd been so sure they wouldn't even have remembered him. Was Venetia having a pop? Hazel couldn't be sure, but if she was, two could play at that game.

'It doesn't suit him at all. He's far too gentle,' she answered quite sharply and then turned her attention back to her grandchild. 'But Wuffa would be a nice name, Una. Don't you think?' Deliberately, Hazel did not glance over to see what affect her words had on her daughter.

'Or Mr Naughty,' Yvonne giggled, getting where her mother was coming from.

Put off her stride by her sister's and mother's juvenile suggestions, Venetia's aim faltered, allowing Yvonne an opportunity of actually hitting the ball at last. Ignoring her sister's little victory dance as the ball span high over her head, Venetia only had eyes for Una who kept chanting out loud the word, 'Wuffa, Wuffa, Wu –'

'Don't say it a third time. Everybody knows what happens when you do that,' Venetia squawked in alarm, completely missing out on the fact that her sister was now finishing a whole circuit and was about to tap her bat victoriously against the last post.

'She wouldn't really call it that, would she?' Venetia wanted to know.

'I think it could suit him.' Hazel was casual, not over persuasive. After all, it had to be her granddaughter's decision.

'I won by the way, not that anybody would notice,' Yvonne grumbled, trailing her bat behind her, miffed that her triumph had gone unnoticed. Not that moaning would do any good either, because as usual Vee was centre of attention, being her usual demanding self.

'I can't believe you would suggest it, knowing how I feel about that statue,' Venetia fumed, ignoring her sister.

'Really, Venetia. Everything isn't always about you, you know.' Hazel was all aloof, insincere calm.

'No. And he's MY dog.' Una was unexpectedly spiteful, her eyes glowing with sudden venom.

Surprised to find herself squaring up to this usually docile child, whom she had been in danger of getting attached to, Venetia pointed an irate finger at her rebellious niece. 'Well, if that's how you feel, little Miss Furball, you can stick your precious, flea-bitten mutt where the sun don't shine.'

Before Yvonne could jump in and warn her sister not to speak to her daughter like that, the dog lunged forward and started barking. Straining against its brand new collar, he was making it clear to everyone in his new family where his priorities lie; he would give up his life to protect Una.

Cowardly taking a few steps back, Venetia grabbed the bat from Yvonne and adopted a defensive position with it.

'Gentle, huh?' She was at first scathing and then more threatening. 'Don't you come near me, Wuffa.'

'He doesn't like Aunt Vee because he knows how bad she is,' Una sparred.

'Who told you that? Was it your mum?'

'Vee!' Yvonne was righteously indignant.

'Granny, then? I bet it was.' Seeing Una's guilt-ridden expression, Venetia was sure she was on the right track.

'It all makes sense now, the pair of you joining forces.' Then, pulling a suitably spooky face, she said with emphasis, 'She's all smoke and mirrors, your granny. Better watch out she doesn't practice any of her black magic on you.'

Seeing the frightened look on Una's face and no longer liking the direction this quarrel was going in, Hazel intervened. 'That's quite enough, everybody.' Then, worried for her grandchild's safety, she put out a restraining hand, meaning to take the dog by the collar, but she snatched it away again when it snapped nervously at her.

'Seems like he doesn't like Granny, either.' Finding the situation nothing but comical, Yvonne hooted out loud in what was, for her, a very unfeminine way.

Una scrutinised her grandmother suspiciously. 'What bad

things have you done, Granny?' She wanted to know, because it never occurred to her to doubt her dog's judgement.

Fortunately for Hazel, she was able to avoid answering such a particularly loaded question; the dog chose precisely that moment to break free from Una's hold and proceeded to chase Venetia around the garden, nipping sadistically at her heels.

Joining in the chase, Una stumbled along in third place, trailing after the dog and her aunt and falling flat on her face when she made a hasty grab for the dog.

Una wearily hauled herself back to her feet. 'Come back, Laddy. Come back,' she called, finally settling on a name for him.

'All we need now is the Benny Hill music to kick in and this scene would be just perfect.' Yvonne was in stitches, laughing so much it hurt.

Swinging the bat in one hand and hopping madly from one nibbled ankle to another, Venetia was just about able to keep far enough ahead of the dog to avoid being seriously bitten, but she wasn't sure how long she could keep up the pace.

'Get it away from me. I'm warning you. Somebody stop it, will you? This is so not funny, Yvonne. Mum, do something, please! Furball, I'm gonna rip your dog's head off when I finally get my hands on him,' Gnashing her teeth like a comic book character, Venetia had something angry to say to every one of them as she raced like a mad March hare around the garden.

'Oh, Vee. He's only playing,' came Yvonne's voice of reason. It had already dawned on her that the dog was not really about to harm her sister. 'Honestly, he wouldn't hurt a fly. He's just a baby himself.'

But Venetia would not listen.

And that's when the sickening thud of bat on bone was heard and a spray of blood spurted out of the dog's mouth, creating a crimson zigzag pattern on somebody's lambswool cardigan lying forgotten in the grass.

The instant the rounded end of the bat came into contact with Laddy's jaw, breaking off two lower premolars, one upper canine and one lower incisor teeth, he fell to the ground, writhing in pain and crying like a fox in heat, a long, drawn-out vulpine wail. The kind of sound that made your heart skip a beat.

Decidedly shaken, Venetia stood frozen to the spot, unable to do anything other than look on in bewilderment, firstly at the blood-stained bat in her hand and then back again to the scene that was unfolding around her.

Having thrown herself down by her dog's side, her knees grazed green from the churned-up grass, Una sobbed hysterically into its fur, fingers kneading his belly as if she was a suckling kitten.

'He's fine, Una. Honestly. Just a bit winded… and toothless, that's all.' Kneeling beside her daughter, Yvonne carefully examined the dog, who was already showing signs of recovery, weakly wagging its tail and bravely trying to sit up.

'Do be careful, Yvonne. He could just as easily turn on you,' Hazel warned, hiding behind Yvonne, not daring to get too close to the salivating dog.

'He was only protecting her!' Clearly niggled, Yvonne darted accusing looks at both her mother and sister.

'I wish I'd had someone like him to look out for me when I was younger,' she threw in for good measure.

'I didn't mean it. I know I said… but I wouldn't really have hurt… it was an accident.' Telling herself she must not cry, Venetia was in danger of breaking her own self-imposed rules.

'I hate you, Aunt Vee. All you do is hurt people.' Una levelled a surprisingly grown-up hateful stare in Venetia's direction. Seeing her sister's utterly dejected expression, Yvonne took pity on her.

'Una, darling.' Yvonne felt she ought to try remonstrating at her unforgiving daughter, but soon found she didn't have the heart for it. One look at Una's angry, tear-stained face as she picked up the dog's missing teeth from the ground, storing them safely in her balled-up fist ('For the dog tooth fairy, for later'), was enough to persuade her of that.

'It's true, Mummy. You said so yourself.' Una was desperate for the two of them to be of the same mind.

Torn between sister and daughter, there could only ever be one winner, one side.

Nodding in agreement with her daughter, Yvonne could not bring herself to witness her sister's wounded look of despair.

'Why don't you go and fetch us all some fish and chips, darling?' Fetching an elegant snakeskin purse out of her handbag, Hazel went to extraordinary pains to be kind. 'I'm sure we'll all feel better when we've had something to eat,' she smiled encouragingly, patting a note into Venetia's reluctant hand.

'Fine.' The word came out like a sharp scratch inflicted by a cornered cat. Then, never once looking up from her boots, Venetia stumbled like someone drunk towards the white picket gate in the wall, the note scrunched up tightly in her hand.

FLYING LOW AND keeping level with the Suzuki, giving Venetia sideways glances with its predatory eyes was, of all things, a barn owl. Though she could hardly believe it herself, Vee felt this unusual sighting had to be an omen, and not a good one, because you hardly ever saw a barn owl in the middle of the day, let alone rubbernecking you on the highway.

Already she'd had to swerve several times, narrowly avoiding a parked car and hitting the kerb, because it was freaking her out so much. There it was now, its elongated talons stretched out behind it like a jumbo jet's engines, waiting for a meal to fly by so it could impale it to death. Its heart-shaped face with its witch-like nose remained expressionless as it locked eyes with Vee, flapping its wings and soaring sporadically in its bid to keep alongside the Suzuki.

Why is it so intent on following me? she wondered. *And what does it want? Is it a warning... a premonition perhaps? Has my mother sent it?* Shuddering at the implication, she could feel the steering wheel vibrate in her trembling hands.

As a child, she'd heard lots of old wives tales about owls – mainly from their old cleaning lady, Mrs Dunoon, who had never been able to resist trying to frighten her, particularly with the one about how an owl heard hooting at night was meant to result in the death of a child – a fact that had terrified Venetia as she lay in bed, listening to the shrill twittering outside her bedroom window, wondering who out of her and Yvonne might be dead by morning.

Another fact, long associated with folklore, was that an owl was supposed to be the only creature that could live with ghosts. So, if one was found nesting in an abandoned house, it must also mean the house was haunted. As the lighthouse had for many years housed one owl nest after another, that sure as hell meant their holiday home had every chance of being haunted. Could that be why things had gone so wrong for the Cox family since buying it? she wondered.

On a more pleasant note, she was also able to recall an old nursery rhyme from her childhood, taken out of a bulky picture book that had been read to her and Yvonne on hard-to-sleep nights.

'A wise old owl sat in an oak. The more he heard, the less he spoke. The less he spoke, the more he heard. Why aren't we all like that wise old bird?'

Repeating back the singsong verse to herself somehow cheered Vee up. After all, how could she be in any danger from a nursery rhyme or old wives tale? Or a barn owl, come to that? But still the premonition that something bad was about to happen would not go away.

Could it be that something supernatural was manifest in their lives – a ghost's meddling influence, perhaps? Or was a more human influence to blame? As far as she was concerned, that Jekyll-and-Hyde devil child of Yvonne's had to be a suspect after her recent behaviour.

Determined to get to the bottom of the mystery even if it killed her, Vee put her foot down on the accelerator and overtook the owl.

'Eat rubber, big bird,' she cackled, revelling in the look of astonishment on the owl's wounded, white-as-a-ghost face as it realised that this was the end of the road. Never before had Vee seen a bird look so hacked off as she put distance between them.

'Not so wise now, are we?' she shouted.

'WE DON'T NEED Dartington Crystal for fish and chips,' Yvonne admonished, removing a pair of elegant water glasses from the table and accidentally letting them clash together, causing a pinging melody to vibrate around the room.

In the middle of placing blue willow-patterned plates on the kitchen table and sharing out cutlery, Hazel stopped what she was doing to stare at Yvonne, the corners of her lips twitching in a half smile.

'Perhaps not,' she admitted. But then, surprising her daughter, she gently took the glasses out of her hands and placed them back on the table. 'But standards are something that must be kept up.'

Feeling she had been outdone, Yvonne couldn't leave it at that. Instead, she took an ordinary, everyday glass from the drainer and slammed it clumsily next to her own place setting at the table.

'You don't have to try and be clever, Yvonne.' Hazel said, sounding tired.

Seeing that there was no malice in Hazel's expression, Yvonne hung her head. Her mother was right, of course. She had been doing exactly that.

Pulling out a pair of chairs – one for herself and one for Yvonne – Hazel sat down.

Noticing how weary her mother looked, it suddenly struck Yvonne that she had never paid much attention to the fact that Hazel was aging, the same as everyone else. One day, not far from now, Yvonne would be the more beautiful of the two. Perhaps, in twenty or thirty years' time, her mother would be totally dependent on her and Venetia. Warmed by the thought, Yvonne welcomed the prospect of looking after her mother in her twilight years – though she couldn't for one minute imagine Hazel as a weak old woman who clung to her daughters for her every comfort.

Gesturing for Yvonne to sit, Hazel inhaled the scent on a white linen napkin folded limply on the table and then expertly refolded it until it sat up and paid attention in a starched, soldierly fashion.

'I've always loved the smell of fresh linen and the cut and sparkle of the best crystal.' Tapping the glass with a French manicured nail tip, she listened animatedly to the twinkling sound. 'And there's nothing better than the gleam of freshly polished cutlery.'

Seeing Yvonne's glazed-over, bored expression, Hazel felt

pressured into offering an explanation, of justifying her love of inanimate objects.

'As you get older, you learn to appreciate these things more. Get to realise how important they are.'

'Why?' Yvonne felt obliged to say something.

'Because all these sights, sounds and smells are part of my past. As much a part as you, Venetia and Una are. One day, they will be part of your past too. That's why they matter so much.'

'More than being happy?' Yvonne was not convinced, even though she found herself looking over the linen, crystal and silver with new eyes.

Surprised by the question, as if the possibility of happiness was so far out of her reach that it had become a hopelessly unattainable dream, Hazel likened the emotion to not being able to reach out and touch the stars or planets; never witnessing one of the tsunamis you read about in the newspaper; never experiencing the tremors of a major earthquake in some far flung foreign country; never standing under a cascading waterfall and feeling its teardrops on your eyelids. No. As far as she was concerned, no matter how much you fantasised, attaining happiness was just as improbable.

'You can't have everything.' Hazel sounded sad, her tone of voice flat.

'Not when you're you.' Seeming to genuinely understand her mother, Yvonne reached across the table and took hold of her hand. For one brief moment, they shared something special.

'I don't know why you always let her bully you.' Hazel couldn't help ruin the moment, causing Yvonne to snatch her hand away again.

'You mean on the beach, I suppose?'

'That, and everything else,' Hazel nodded.

Looking out of the window, where she was able to catch a glimpse of blue sea in the distance, Yvonne thought long and hard about what her mother had inferred; it wasn't nice being reminded how weak and pliable you were. After all, if she was so easily intimidated by others, it didn't paint a very pretty picture of her as a mature woman with a daughter of her own to care for.

'You know how unstable she is.' Hazel's warning was as subtle as a finely-spun spider web, invisible to the naked eye until it tore gently across your cheek.

'No more than you or I,' Yvonne responded mysteriously.

'What's that supposed to mean?' Hazel was at once indignant, earning herself a sceptical look from her daughter.

'You know exactly what I mean.'

VENETIA SUNG ALONG to the Olly Murs "Troublemaker" track playing on the funfair's loudspeakers and strutted to the lively chart topper as if she were a young John Travolta straight out of *Saturday Night Fever*.

John Travolta without the leather jacket, she might add, because she foolishly hadn't brought along her own vintage leather jacket and now had goose pimples erupting all over her white skin. Having chosen to park on the green and take a stroll through the fair before cutting through to the Vegas Fish Bar on South Beach Road, she kept her head down and avoided eye contact with other fair-goers, aware that her strapless vest not only showed off her tattoos but also her nipples.

But she needn't have worried, because among the fair people her appearance went unnoticed; tattoos and piercings were fairly commonplace here. They probably mistook her for one of them. It was a thought that secretly pleased her. The fair-goers didn't pay her a blind bit of notice either. Besides, after all these years coming to Hunstanton, people must be used to her by now.

There on Rocky Thompson's sweet stall, dishing out all kinds of pick n mix sweets, was the old lady whose name she still did not know but who had been here for as long as Vee could remember. Although she must be in her seventies or even eighties, the silver-haired lady had by all accounts worked on the stall since she was a nipper and continued to work twelve hours a day, seven days a week, during the holiday season. Vee and Yvonne had always wanted to know the woman's name but never dared ask, fearful on the one hand of being told to mind their own business and on the other of breaking a spell of sorts. Knowing would be different to not knowing, they reasoned, so they'd remained unanimous in not wanting to risk change for the sake of it. Childhood was already fragile enough.

So different to her sister, who hated the noise and bustling crowds, especially in the summer months when the fair was at its busiest, Vee had always loved the sights and sounds of the status – her mother's word for it, not hers. In particular, she liked the way you could lose yourself in a crowd and the constant jostling that sent you colliding into one person after another, rather like being in a live game of Pinball at the amusement arcade.

Then there were the smells: the burnt tang from the candy floss machine that whipped up Disney-pink clouds of sugar before being sealed in grotesque clown face bags; the waft of fried onions that sweated under a heater all day long; and the pong of overcooked burgers that could still make Vee's mouth water even though her mother swore that they were made out of horsemeat or badgers or worse. And then there were the holidaying kids. How could she have forgotten their peculiar smell? The recollection made her laugh out loud because it made her sound like some evil, crooked-nose witch straight out of a scary movie. Although it couldn't be denied that she had inherited a bit of a beak from her father, no way did it make her resemble anyone belonging to the Land of Oz. Besides, even Vonnie hadn't escaped the cursed Cox nose.

Vee didn't have anything against the children, per se – her niece was the one exception – but the little blighters did have their own individual smell: a concoction of talcum powder, deep-fried chicken dippers, fizzy pop, ketchup and baked beans. *No wonder so many of them are fat these days*, she thought unkindly, spotting a couple of them now on the dodgems, going way too slow and being far too timid to do any actual bumping. On the whole, they were mostly unattractive fat kids belonging to even fatter parents whose arses were too big to fit in their seats.

Startled by the angry sound of a text message suddenly popping into her inbox, Vee took out her Smartphone and looked at the screen, which boasted a picture of her and her sister on the beach in matching swimsuits. It must have been taken about fifteen years ago because they looked as if they couldn't have been more than six and nine respectively. The message was from Yvonne. "Hurry up with the chips".

'Shit.' Vee put the phone back in her pocket. She'd better get a move on or, like the song said, she'd be in trouble.

HER STOMACH GROWLING angrily, Yvonne kept picking up her phone and putting it back down again as she checked constantly for new messages.

'I can't believe how long it's taking her.'

Sipping a china cup of Earl Grey tea, Hazel raised her eyebrows as if to say, *Can't you?* Then she gently put the cup back on its saucer and squeezed in a little more juice from a slice of lemon.

Her mother wasn't fooling anyone, least of all Yvonne, with this silent treatment – acting like she was too scared of saying anything in case she got her head bitten off.

'Mum, me and Vee, we're just trying to get to know each other again. We were close once.' Yvonne hoped unrealistically for her mother's understanding.

'You were never close.' With her nose in the air, Hazel got up from the table, taking her cup and saucer with her.

AS USUAL THE ducks got under her feet in the Vegas Fish Bar car park. They were popular with customers, though Venetia couldn't understand why – all they did was shit everywhere, waddle confidently over to you, and scuttle away should you call their bluff and approach *them*. Vee was often temped to remind them of that. 'Look. You approached me first,' and then, 'don't you know you weren't brought into this world to eat kebab and chips?' Watching hungry customers give up their grub to the ungrateful ducks never failed to annoy her. And she never tired of despising the ducks for wagging their tails as if they were sausage dogs with docked tails wanting to be taken for a walk.

At the entrance to the fish bar people sat at picnic tables wearing hoodies, leggings and flip-flops that exposed crusty, scaled feet and brittle toenails in desperate need of fungal treatments. Some staked their place at tables, greedily tucking into their chips, while others formed irritable queues, staring at their own blurred reflections in the glass-fronted fridge that was stocked with bottles of Tango. No doubt most of them were staying at Searles holiday camp just around the corner, and a few of them had dogs that rudely robbed them of their battered sausages left right and centre.

On the ground there were spilt chips, some of which had been trodden in, with distinct trainer marks in the potato mush. Ripped open discarded ketchup sachets leaked freaky Halloween blood on the seats and wasps hung around the overfull bins, as they did every year.

Inside the fish shop, Vee's nose overdosed on the overwhelming acidic vinegar smell. That, combined with the ugly brown doner meat, which simultaneously turned and burned at the same time made her crave for something healthy – like an apple, or a stick of celery with soft cheese hanging perilously off the end. Unlike her sister, she'd never been a big eater and had been known to survive for days alone on strawberry-flavoured Angel Delight and prawn cocktail crisps. And fags – that went without saying. Who could live a day without them?

Deciding that fish and chips were a bad idea, Vee turned around and walked empty-handed out of the shop.

LYING ON HER back on the white leather sofa, glancing at pictures in a celebrity magazine and munching her way through a green apple so glossy it looked positively photoshopped, Venetia pretended not to see her sister standing huffily in the doorway.

Arms folded crossly for effect, Yvonne glared furiously at her, impatiently waiting for her to look up.

'Selfish, that's what you are. Just because you didn't want fish and chips doesn't mean the rest of us didn't,' she fumed, then flounced like a spoilt child out of the room.

If awards could be given for flouncing, Vee felt sure her sister would take home first prize every time and needn't have to worry about any competition. But at least now her sister was gone she could finally drop the pretence of being interested in the fake orange breasts flaunted across the magazine's pages, and in doing so caught her mother's glance across the room.

Vee couldn't believe it. Was that really an amused smile on her mother's face as she relaxed in the leather armchair, leafing through her book? And did she actually have her legs tucked up under her in an uncharacteristically casual way?

Although the sitting room had a cool, minimalistic feel, it was rescued from being too cold and aloof by the gold lamps that illuminated Hazel's mature skin perfectly. No doubt that hadn't happened by accident, Vee guessed correctly, admiring the way her mother's warm, peachy skin tone thrived in such lighting.

But then, the whole setting had been designed especially to suit Hazel's complexion; from the muted dove grey walls to the pistachio rugs on the floor. Vee had to admit that her mother had done a wonderful job of creating an inviting, welcoming feel to the room. One wall was entirely taken up with books, enough to satisfy the most avid of readers, while dual aspect windows shared identical stunning coastal views. Even if you weren't much of a reader, like Vee, you couldn't help feeling tempted to grab a book off the shelf and settle down in a chair overlooking the sea for an hour or two.

Then there were the tastefully-arranged crystal-cut vases of flowers placed strategically around the room, making sure your view was always slightly obscured by white petals and green stems that in turn generated a hazy, romantic effect... *mood-enhancing*, Hazel called it. Though Vee could not name a single flower in the room, she knew they were invariably expensive and without exception had to be white, because coloured flowers in the house were considered vulgar – at least by her mother.

Surprising Vee out of her appraisal of the room and causing

Hazel to quit her comfortable position, the dog came bouncing in with no other purpose than to sniff intrusively at their crutches. Both women froze fearfully, allowing the dog to do as it wanted, neither daring to speak out. But Vee in particular was most put out to find a blood trail from the dog's slobbering mouth on her combat jeans.

'Laddy, come,' Una called from the doorway, looking like a child of the ghetto and glaring at Vee as if she alone had been responsible for sending young children to work down the coalmines. Clearly, Vee wasn't to be forgiven just yet – if at all – for hurting her precious dog. Even Laddy appeared to be holding a grudge; although he wagged his tail excitedly, he left behind a rancid trail of Pedigree Chum farts when he trotted out of the room.

Making sure her mother didn't notice, Vee poked out her fag-stained, pierced tongue at the child. No way was she letting this prissy little niece of hers have it all her own way. All she got in response though was a sneer before she flounced off in a very similar way to her mother, but Vee felt this was better than nothing. It was better than being ignored, at any rate.

'You realise of course the dog is going to have to go.' Hazel did not look up from her book.

Not sure where this conversation was going and not entirely sure she wanted to, Vee found herself suddenly transfixed by the magazine headline: "My football-playing boyfriend leaked photos of his scrotum to some slag called Kimberly".

'I know I can rely on you to see to it.' Hazel still did not look up from her book.

'What about Yvonne and Una?' Vee's eyes flitted guiltily to the door. See. She did have a conscious.

'We know what's best for them. We always have.' Maddeningly, Hazel still did not look up from her book.

CREEPING ABOUT ON tippy-toes and constantly checking over her shoulder to make sure she wasn't being watched, Venetia took the dog's lead down from a hook in the kitchen, handling it gingerly lest the chain jangle and give her away.

Her heart beating madly, as if it was being pumped by an over-enthusiastic tyre salesman, she felt she might die of fright before she got to the other end of the kitchen. Clearly not cut out to be a thief or kidnapper, she could honestly say that living life on a knife edge like a criminal wasn't for her. Yet, before today, she'd have imagined she might be rather good at it.

Pressing on regardless, she inched her way forward until a faint rumbling sound was heard. Stopping to listen more intently, she wondered, *Could it have been thunder?* There it was again, a low growl, coming not from outside at all, but being emitted from the kitchen. Perhaps her mother had left the gas on? Perhaps her mother had left the gas on, on purpose... in which case, they were all about to die from carbon monoxide poisoning.

Discovering that it was in fact the dog in its basket growling toothlessly at her approach, Vee realised it still had canines enough to do her damage.

'Want to go walkies?' Half-heartedly jangling the lead, Vee could tell by the way it eyeballed her and curled its lip that she was wasting her time. She didn't have to be an expert on animal behaviour to know that if she got any closer, it really was going to bite her.

'What are you doing, Aunt Vee?'

Jumping out of her skin, Vee didn't know whether to be angry with her niece for creeping up on her or grateful because at least now she wouldn't get bitten, not now the dog's owner was here. But where the fuck had the kid come from?

'Mind your own, Miss Marple.' Vee guiltily dropped the lead on the table, hoping that Una wouldn't notice.

'Who is Miss Marple?' Una pointedly ogled the lead, not missing a trick.

'You can't call yourself a proper detective if you don't know who she is.'

'What's a detective?'

Sighing, Vee gave up. Who the hell was she trying to kid, anyway? No way on earth would she have been able to get rid of Una's dog. Even if it had been stupid enough to go with her, she would probably have ended up just taking it for a walk around the green before bringing it back again.

Watching Una curl herself protectively around the dog, like a boa constrictor about to squeeze and swallow its prey whole, Vee was seriously beginning to think that there was something supernatural or even malevolent about the child. A child who could hide in corners and surprise you out of your wits was no ordinary child.

Reminding herself that it was her mother who had got her into this predicament and not Una's fault, it occurred to Vee that she was acting like a puppet on strings to her mother's whims. Otherwise, why would she even consider getting rid of a pet dog by means fair or foul, and risk getting caught and alienating her sister and niece forever? Anyway, why didn't her mother do her own dirty work? *It wasn't as if she wasn't capable of it…* Vee had to stop herself in her tracks from thinking such thoughts. She wasn't ready to go there just yet.

She realised that she wasn't capable of hurting the dog – or any other living thing, come to think of it, not any more – not since the last time, but again, Vee didn't want to be reminded of that either. Anyway, she couldn't even begin to comprehend what her mother had expected her to do with the dog. Tie it to a railway track, or put it in a weighted bag and throw it in the sea, perhaps? The thought made her feel physically sick.

Whatever was happening in this house between the three of them had little to do with a stray dog: of that she was certain. But there were secrets in this house and discoveries to be made. Vee had every intention of digging them up like old bones – this time at her own bidding, not her mother's. She would be her own puppeteer from now on.

HOPING THAT VENETIA was soon going to do something about that blasted dog, Hazel was keen to find the rest of the family and suggest doing something together this afternoon so as to keep the coast clear for her.

The sooner the dog was gone, the better; rather than bring her granddaughter and her closer together, as she had hoped, the savage little thing was now ironically keeping them apart. After all Hazel had been through, there was no way she was going to allow anything to get in her way now.

Of course, this would mean planning an outing somewhere Una wouldn't be able to take the dog, as well as convincing her to leave Laddy at home – which wasn't going to be easy, she realised. Persuading Yvonne to come along too whilst insisting that Venetia stayed put was just as daunting a task. Really, her children could be quite difficult just for the sake of it at times.

Having gone upstairs to her bedroom to change into a slim-fitting pair of dark jeans and a white cotton shirt with a silk scarf tucked inside the collar, Hazel was in a rush to get back downstairs when she saw IT.

'Is anyone up there?' she called into the square-shaped hole in the ceiling, not really expecting an answer because NOBODY

EVER went into the loft. In fact, she couldn't remember a time seeing the hatch open, even when Phillip was alive.

They were a house of women, after all, and whoever heard of the gentler sex being interested in what Hazel considered to be men's territory? In her opinion, women had no business poking their noses around in lofts, sheds, workshops or garages – all of them dusty, masculine places, filled with old suitcases, cobwebs and the smell of sawn wood.

So there must be another perfectly plausible reason why the loft hatch was hanging open with the ladder pulled down, like a pair of knickers, exposing secrets.

'Is anybody up there?' she called again, irritably this time. In response, a thud and a heavy sliding sound resounded immediately above her head, like a body being dragged across the floor.

Throwing herself against the wall in fright, her eyes popping in alarm as if she were a fish being skewered alive, the ominous sound awakened something terrible in Hazel's memory, immediately taking her back to a terrifying time in her past. A time and place she'd pushed to the furthest corner of her mind, the way she had as a child pushed a pin in a map to locate the furthest foreign country away from her hometown.

* * *

HAZEL WAS FEARFUL of being left alone with her mother in the half-timbered Tudor-style house where she'd been born, knowing that it was only a matter of time before something would go terribly wrong without her father there to supervise the two of them.

After all, everybody knew that her mother's bipolar condition wasn't improving; she was capable of having one of her turns if she so much as came into contact with her little girl's skin. Apparently, her mother had never forgiven Hazel for being born the wrong way around, resulting in a painful breach birth. What her mother also held against her was the fact that she'd been born a girl. Because the sexy piece, with giant breasts that swung like church bells and eyes that sometimes crackled like fireworks, could not tolerate being around members of her own sex – not even her own daughter.

Nevertheless, Hazel had been told by her father to "make sure and watch your mother" while he was away on business for a few days. His long list of instructions had included: not answering the door to strangers, remembering to water his prize cactus in the conservatory, informing the school secretary she had diarrhoea if anyone phoned to check on her absence, and to make sure that her mother never left the house. Reluctantly, she had agreed to all of his demands, providing that he write down the correct spelling for diarrhoea, just in case she was quizzed.

So, at just eight years old Hazel was expected to dutifully cook, care and clean up after her mother, who in turn never even looked at her if she could help it. When her father had warned her not to let her mother out of her sight, it also meant that she too would be a prisoner in the house, with no school or playtime for her. Not that she minded the latter; she wasn't particularly good at establishing friendships. Her awkward attempts to make friends with girls her own age usually ended in live rounds of spiteful laughter or accusations of Hazel having a plum in her mouth – whatever that meant, because she didn't even like plums. Instead, she preferred seedless grapes and Pink Lady apples peeled and cut into slices. Sometimes the cruel Kays, Tonis or Maxines of the world would even give her a little push for daring to think that they would be friends with the likes of her.

150

But, quite used to spending long periods of time on her own, she hardly noticed time go by in the large dishevelled house. In fact, she was surprised to find her father had already been gone a day when the knock on the door came. Sitting on the bottom step of the stairs chewing her thumb, Hazel prayed that the two shadows behind the glass, who kept on insistently ringing the doorbell, would go away and leave them alone.

'Who is it?' her mother hissed down the stairs, her serpent-like voice able to twist and turn around corners in a bid to interrogate Hazel. That's when the pamphlet popped through the letterbox and landed on the thick pile carpet Hazel was supposed to vacuum each day before nine o'clock. Too ashamed to admit that she still did not know how to tell the time properly, she had no idea if the hoovering was overdue or not and had nobody to ask.

Knowing that her mother would also have heard the rattle of the letterbox, she picked up *The Watchtower* and admired the photograph of a mixed-race family of different ages lording it over the front cover. The Jehovah Witnesses in the picture certainly looked far happier than her own miserable family, she thought crossly. But then again, these saintly children in their gingham dresses and lace bonnets didn't have to live alone with a polar bear, did they?

Across the page in red capital letters was the caption, "Soon, He will come to end all suffering". And, remembering how unwell her mother had looked in bed this morning with her rank, fishy breath and large paws that swotted her away when she tried to bring her a cup of tea, she supposed she ought to go upstairs and see her.

Thinking that the pamphlet might bring her mother some comfort and never knowing what a disaster this would turn out to be, Hazel placed it on the icy eiderdown on her parents' bed and then retreated to her own room, never once turning her back on her mother in case she pounced and tore out her shoulder like she'd seen the polar bear do to the poor walrus on the telly.

For lunch, not realising that it was actually 4 o'clock in the afternoon, she grilled herself two fish fingers – only two, mind, because her father frequently warned her that three was considered greedy. To go with it she heated some beans and whisked up some instant mashed potato with dangerously hot water from the kettle and then sat alone at the formal dining table with a silver fork in her hand and a stiff linen napkin across her lap. To keep her company, she lifted the needle on the gramophone player and allowed it to fall gently on the scratchy black vinyl record that came out of a sleeve with a beautiful woman on the front, who wore chandelier earrings and had a Bridget Bardot-inspired hairstyle. She could listen to Barbara Streisand singing "Someone To Watch Over Me" all day long.

Afterwards, she sat for ages in front of the misted mirror on the mahogany chiffonier, staring at her reflection in the damaged glass and wondering if she was pretty. She knew that other girls in her class at school had fathers, and sometimes even mothers, who told them they were beautiful, but they all looked the same to Hazel, with their identical ditsy print dresses, blonde curls and velvet headbands.

Hazel's own hair was brown and straight, with not a curl in sight, and her clothes were practical rather than pretty. For instance, today she had on a pair of elastic waist slacks and a matching tunic she could remember wearing to one of her father's relative's weddings. It never occurred to Hazel that her father's relatives were her own flesh and blood too, or that she had any claims to family other than her own mother and father. To have assumed that the lively cocktail-drinking lot from Surrey, who spoke with a twang like her father and made it abundantly clear that they disapproved of his lower-class wife, might have been interested in her wellbeing would have been unthinkable.

The wedding day had been made all the more special, she remembered, because her mother, sick once again, had been left at home. Perhaps because of this fact, Hazel had been allowed a few sips of sherry and could even remember being cuddled for the first time by a woman who wasn't Miss Tuppins from the corner shop.

Another first had been stealing the show itself when she took to the dance floor and boogied along to "Save All Your Kisses For Me" by Brotherhood of Man. Having spent hours practicing the dance moves after watching the group perform on *Top Of The Pops*, she'd given the performance of her life at the evening reception and had everyone up on their feet, clapping. More importantly, from across the hall she also noticed her father's usually mournful, disappointed expression light up with real pride.

She could also recall being told she looked "very nice" in her navy outfit with the white trim, but that her brown rubbery shoes did not match. Looking at the same shoes that were now two sizes too small and pinched her toes, Hazel didn't care for them either, but she cared very much that she'd only looked "very nice" and not "pretty".

She could hardly have known that just a short while later, all her vain superficial thoughts would be knocked sideways out of her; neither was she aware that she would do something unforgivably bad that would ruin everybody's lives forever. It all began innocently enough, when she crept upstairs and sat on the top step of the stairs to "watch her mother", as she had been ordered. But instead of coughing, snoring or farting – the usual sounds that drifted out of her mother's bed when she wasn't awake and screaming blue murder – she was forced to listen to a chillingly strange racket, coming not from her mother's bedroom at all, but from somewhere above her head.

From where Hazel sat, she could clearly see that the door to her parents' bedroom was wide open and there was nobody inside. She didn't know what was worse; her mother being there and having to keep an eye on her, or her mother not being there and *not* being able to keep an eye on her. How could she carry out her father's strict instructions if she couldn't see her? If her mother was, in fact, IN THE LOFT?

'Soon, He will come,' her mother squawked hysterically from the open loft hatch. This was followed by a thud and a bump, then a painfully slow, dragging noise that sounded truly terrifying to Hazel's impressionable ears. After all, she had been raised unsupervised on horrifying episodes of *Tales Of The Unexpected* and had even seen James Herbert's spine-chilling film adaptation of *The Rats*, so she already had a very good idea of the kind of thing that went on in lofts.

'I don't think you're supposed to be up there!' Hazel found her quivering voice at last.

'What would you know, little Dolly Poppet?' Her mother's barmy face swung back and forth like a deranged monkey hanging out of a tree – so much so that Hazel expected a banana to land on her head any minute.

As far as "Dolly Poppet" went, this was not the first time her mother had called her by the name. Having no idea who Dolly Poppet was, Hazel nonetheless felt that the name conjured up someone rather exciting; somebody she'd like to get to know. She felt confident that Dolly must be a brave, clever little girl, capable of outwitting adults.

Noticing *The Watchtower* poking out of the top half of her mother's almost indecently transparent nightdress, Hazel was glad to see that the picture of the smug little girls in their gingham dresses was all contorted and screwed up: just how Hazel felt.

'Soon, He will come and end all our suffering,' her mother was saying.

'Who?'

'Jesus, of course. He's coming for us all. Me. You. Your father.'

Hazel wasn't sure she liked the idea of anybody coming for her. Not when there were unfinished chores around the house – the hoovering, for instance, and the cobwebs she couldn't reach even with a feather duster. Nor had she washed up her lunch plate – but she didn't know if that was a deadly sin or not.

'Coming to rescue me after all these years. All these lies. Is it any wonder I went mad? Any wonder HE sent me mad?'

Her mother finally referring to her own madness was definitely something new, but Hazel didn't know if it was a good sign or not. Later she would make a note of it in the "things to tell father" book.

'It's all his fault, you know.'

'Whose? Jesus?'

'Stupid girl,' she cackled. 'Your father made me like this with his lies. He's a bigamist, you know. That's a sin in God's eyes.'

Hazel had no idea what a bigamist was, nor was she about to give her mother the satisfaction of asking.

'Look in his desk drawer if you don't believe me. Everything is in there.'

Now who is being stupid? Hazel thought. Not only was she banned from going anywhere near her father's study, let alone his locked desk, she had no idea where he kept the key.

'In the sock drawer.' Her devious mother seemed capable of reading her mind. To Hazel, that was far more terrifying than her insanity. But was her mother really crazy, she often wondered, or did she put it on a lot of the time? Because there were times that she acted perfectly normal, attempting to have a heart-to-heart with Hazel like any regular mother.

'Take my advice, Hazel, and get out as soon as you can. Marry the first poor bugger to come along if need be, but don't stay here, whatever you do, or you'll end up mad like me. He'll see to that.'

As this was the only piece of advice her mother had ever given her, Hazel felt obliged to carry out her instructions. So, keeping one ear on her mother's intermittent howls and squeals coming from the loft – she had by now regressed once again – she rummaged through her father's sock drawer in the bedroom until her hand brushed against a sharp silver key. Feeling a tremor of panic run through her, she held the key against her pounding heart before creeping back downstairs, holding her hands over her ears to shut out her mother's manic accusations that purposely nudged her down every step.

The curtains were kept permanently closed in her father's dark dusty study. Had they been open, the view outside would have been of a meticulously pruned hedge and a crumbling stone terrace where they'd never once had a drinks party, like other people in their quiet, middle-class street did, often on a Friday night around 6 o'clock. Hazel knew all of this because she enjoyed spying on them through gaps in the hedge, watching pretty ladies wearing rouge and lipstick and listening to the clunk of their glasses with ice in them. 'Another G&T?' somebody would encourage with a giggle. Their world not only sounded delightful to Hazel's ears, but it smelled wonderful too, of L'Air du Temps perfume by Nina Ricci.

But the world *she* knew – the one she belonged in, no matter how cruel, cold or isolated it was – irrevocably changed as soon as she opened the album in her father's secret drawer. Even as she took it out and felt the embossed cover, with the words "My Family" printed on it in her father's mean, stand-up-straight handwriting, she knew that there was no going back, but she still couldn't stop herself from opening it. The album was her destiny. She felt it in her breath, her bones, her saliva.

The awkwardly posed-for photographs looking back at her from the pages might have been of her father's dead relatives, for all she knew; particularly the sepia portrait of a tall woman with a long neck and fierce eyes who resembled a camel but whom she instantly knew to be the other woman in her father's life. Her mother had been telling the absolute truth about her father living a life of lies.

There were the three of them now, a trio of thieves and liars, all with her father's downcast eyes, pictured at various stages of their childhood. In the girl, she could even see something of herself, except this spoilt "Dolly Poppet" had blonde ringlets and clearly had no trouble with the three R's in the same way Hazel did, because there was a handwritten note on lavender-scented paper addressed "To Daddy", with a self-portrait of the girl wearing a crown and a postscript that read, "When you're next home looking for a princess, you'll know where to find me".

The hatred rose up inside Hazel like a shaken can of fizzy cola about to explode without warning over her unsuspecting, despised relatives.

How could he? How could her father have made a princess out of an ordinary living breathing girl, who was so wholly unconnected with her and her family, when she had only ever risen to being a "chucky egg" or a "little ducky" in his eyes?

There was no other girl living, more than Hazel, who wanted to make it as a princess in life. As a result of her father's ultimate betrayal, she would hate this girl and her two lookalike brothers for the rest of her life, along with the one they no doubt called mother but whom her father could thankfully never call "his wife". Now she knew the truth and extent of her father's wickedness, Hazel understood exactly what his frequent business trips were really all about. For time spent away from her and her mother was time spent with them – that family, his second, illegitimate family, begot by a bigamist just as her mother had proclaimed. She cursed him like no child should. She cursed her mother, too, for opening the can of worms that grew fat gorging on her lost innocence.

'You're a liar.' Much later, Hazel had stood directly under the loft hatch with a long pole in her hand, handling it as if it were a spear she was about to thrust into her mother's skull. There she was now, hair a silver grey from the dust in the loft, baring her teeth in a predatory way as she laughed outrageously, tickled pink by her daughter's sulky denial. 'You're not my mother. You're a polar bear, living off human flesh,' Hazel accused sullenly. 'And you can stay up there until you're sorry.'

With that, Hazel aimed the hooked pole at the loft hatch and managed to pull it shut on her mother's pug-like face, not caring if she never saw or heard from her again. As far as she was concerned, no adult was to be trusted from now on. They were all hateful liars, out for themselves, and no better than the bogeyman.

For the rest of that very long weekend spent by herself, Hazel kept busy spying on next door's guests over for a drink, brushing her hair one hundred times a night as she'd been taught, reading herself a bedtime story out loud, learning to clip her own toenails on folded-up newspaper, heating up soup and learning by default how to open a tin of pilchards without losing a finger. Her time alone was only slightly marred by the dulled, entrapped sounds of her mother's insane goings-on in the loft and the various thuds, bangs and scrapes that grew fainter as time went on.

By the end of the weekend, Hazel, having grown immune to her mother's pleas to be let out, could no longer recall exactly when she'd last heard her voice. But she was fairly sure it died out altogether some time ago, for she had now got used to the house being silent.

Along with the stillness came a welcome sense of release that meant whenever Hazel had to go spend a penny she no longer worried what her mother was doing to relieve herself; likewise, when Hazel dished up boiled egg and soldiers for supper, she forgot to consider if her mother might also be hungry; when she washed between her legs and brushed her teeth at night, it no longer occurred to her that her mother might be starting to smell or missing her favourite Palmolive soap. If "out of sight, out of mind" was good enough for her father, it was good enough for Hazel too.

In fact, during that lonesome period, she never thought of her mother again – or her father, for that matter – as she became lost in the routines of the house and its demands on her time. It wasn't until she saw the headlights of her father's Hillman Hunter pull onto the gravel drive late on Sunday evening, her thoughts turned to his tea.

More like a neglected wife than a dutiful daughter, Hazel couldn't imagine his other woman dishing up anything as jolly as the cucumber sandwiches with the crusts cut off and shop-bought scones with strawberry jam and cream she hurriedly prepared.

But her father wasn't the slightest bit hungry and even went so far as to sweep a china cup and saucer from the table onto the floor, where it smashed into three solitary pieces that he would have to glue back together again later. For now, all he wanted to do was brush off Hazel's stuttering excuses as to where exactly her mother was hiding. When she'd remained stubbornly tight-lipped, he'd gone in search of his wife himself. In fact, he'd been so uncharacteristically furious when he eventually found her in the loft, barely alive and even more doolally than usual, Hazel thought he might kill her.

'Luckily for you, she's still alive.' He'd screeched like an overfed greedy gerbil that had escaped from its cage only to find all the food was stored inside the bars of the prison it had escaped from.

Quite prepared to sacrifice herself to her father's homicidal rage, Hazel dramatically gave herself up to the idea of dying at his hands. However, since her father never did anything spontaneously, she knew she could be in for a long wait, while he made up his mind as to a suitable method for seeing the job through.

No way was he capable of strangling her and watching the life drain away from her eyes as he applied pressure to her throat. Stabbing was out of the question, due to his being adverse to the sight of blood, whilst drowning would have been his last choice, seeing as how he was afraid of water and unable to swim; she doubted very much he would go ahead with asphyxiation by exhaust fumes, as they had no garage. Being a respectable, mild-mannered man who always paid his bills on time and never so much as grumbled if he received a parking ticket in the post, it was unlikely that he had imagination enough to choose any other way of getting rid of her. Besides, knowing what she now knew, Hazel couldn't see why it should matter to him if her mother lived or died.

'What have you done?' He'd demanded on first discovering his wife in a pile of her own vomit and bodily excretions, jabbering on about Jesus.

'What have *you* done, you mean?' Hazel barked right back, no longer afraid of the weak liar of a man that was her father.

Later, coming across the ashy remains of his private photo album in the fireplace, he realised that his young daughter had finally discovered his secret and that somehow it had driven her to do this to her own mother. After that, it became relatively easy to convince himself that she was now on his side and that everything would be alright from now on. Mistakenly, he felt that between the two of them they would come to some sort of mutually beneficial arrangement for the future. The child might even prove useful to him.

Hazel blinded herself to the fact that nothing was right nor would be again, especially when her mother was afterwards institutionalised indefinitely in the sanatorium. She was all too aware that her father was all she had left in life. This somehow left Hazel feeling more afraid and insecure than if she were an orphan.

* * *

AT FIRST SHE'D been convinced that it was her mother's face looking down on her, but Hazel's alarm wilted as fast as a snowdrop caught out by an early frost when it became clear that it was Venetia's peaky white face she was seeing in the loft hatch, not her mother's.

Consequently, it had been Venetia up there all along, making that dreadful racket. Venetia, who, oddly enough, had a look of her maternal grandmother about her, now she came to think of it. So it shouldn't really have come as any surprise when she mixed the two of them up.

'What are you looking for up there?'

'Nothing.'

'I thought I heard something.' Hazel was at a loss to understand why her daughter was behaving so suspiciously. If she didn't know better, she'd swear Venetia was playing a game of cat and mouse.

'Something?'

'I'm not sure what. Just something.' Hazel felt wrong-footed.

Comically, Venetia turned her head one way and then the other, listening out for non-existent sounds.

'Take your pick,' she shrugged. 'There are bats and mice to choose from. Oh, and an owl of course.' Venetia placed special emphasis on the world "owl", though Hazel couldn't for the life of her imagine why.

'We're about to go out.' Hazel tucked her shirt into her jeans and tightened her belt, surprised to find she'd lost an inch from around her already slender waist. 'I'd really rather prefer you not to go climbing around in the loft. Anything could happen to you up there, especially when you're alone in the house.' Hazel's voice faltered as, once again, she was reminded of her mother.

'You know what to do while we're gone, don't you?' Hazel appealed, as if she were a slippery customer in a butcher's shop wanting more than her fair share of breaded ham.

'I have my orders.' Without a smile to take away the sting, Venetia saluted.

'Don't be contrary, Venetia. This is something we have to do for Una, otherwise I wouldn't dream –'

'For Una?'

'Of course. What other reason could there be? The dog is clearly a danger to her. And look how it went for you,' Hazel added as an afterthought.

'Yes. Very dangerous,' Venetia nodded in her mother's direction, but it was as if she was looking right through her and not at her at all.

'I'm glad we're agreed on that, darling.' And then, almost tearfully, her mouth twitching with emotion, 'I'm so pleased I have somebody I can rely on,' Hazel confided. 'I must just go and get my purse before we leave.' With that, Hazel headed towards her bedroom door, leaving Venetia wondering what the hell that one-woman show had been all about.

SITTING ON THE edge of the four-poster bed, a handful of chintz eiderdown clutched in her shaky grasp, Hazel's hands fluttered like fine sails on a boat as she fought back unshed tears from her childhood.

'Five more minutes. Then I'll be fine,' she promised herself, sitting stiff as a ramrod when all she wanted to do was abandon her mask of sophistication, throw herself lengthways across the vast bed and bawl like a baby.

Even now, after all these years, she couldn't think about her father without dissolving into tears. If she put her mind to it, she could hear their song playing in the background – "Save All Your Kisses For Me" – as well as see him sitting in a cloud of cigarette smoke, his eyes watery with emotion as he supped a pint of black bitter, looking dead proud of her.

Of course, the last time she'd seen him, he'd been laid out in a coffin in the chapel of rest. Remembering how it hadn't felt right, standing there with a new life growing inside her, looking upon the face of a dead man, she had noticed a flurry of gold and brown autumnal leaves collecting in the window. No doubt they'd been whipped into a frenzy by the wind – they'd seemed desperate to come inside, though Hazel couldn't for the life of her understand why; all she wanted to do was escape the cloying room and the putrid sweet-and-sour smell emanating from her father's rotting corpse. After that day, Hazel would never again touch Chinese takeaway.

Hearing the wind pick up outside her own elevated window and feeling it coil its way around the tower, it wasn't hard for Hazel to imagine those same leaves dancing in the glass of her bedroom window. Only this time, they formed a leafy shape of her father's well-remembered face – his mournful disappointed expression and all.

* * *

IT WAS THE last time she would ever see him. But she'd barely been given a full five minutes to pay her respects before that lot shuffled in, with their sniffling noses, red eyes and fake gold wedding bands they weren't entitled to wear. The mother. The slut. The whore. The stealer of husbands and lives.

You can look down on me all you want but you'll never be his proper wife, only a pretender, Hazel had thought maliciously, her hand tightening into a fist, for she was grown up by then and wanted to lash out the same as any other scorned woman.

It was true that the other woman in her father's double life had looked down on Hazel; a resentful sneer was never far from her face. But it was also true that the two older boys, adults themselves now and even more like their father, with their wintry eyes and mild-mannered sighs, looked at her more kindly, as if they were genuinely interested in getting to know her. They had grown up knowing all about their father's other family and had every sympathy for their half-sister. Had Hazel known this, it would have crushed her; ever since she'd uncovered her father's secret, she'd imagined how much the three devil's spawn must envy her, her being the only legitimate child born out of a proper marriage.

Coming face to face with the grown-up version of her father's favourite princess, who had disappointed everyone in the end by turning out rather plain and ordinary, was the next worst thing to happen. The girl looking back at her, not with enmity but with curiosity, was a good head shorter than Hazel and the blonde ringlets she'd once tossed about so playfully had turned brown and fluffy like a pet dog's ears. If you'd put the two young women side by side, there would have been no competition. Hazel would have won hands down, and not only that, she would have walked all over the weak little creature – high heels and all.

Consumed with jealousy nonetheless, Hazel's eyes raked over the freckled skin on her doll-like face and would have scooped out her eyes with a spoon given the chance. How she stopped herself from shouting out, 'You're a bastard. You should never have been born,' she would never know. Only later did it hit her, like a punch in the stomach from a southpaw, that she might as well have been talking to the child growing in her own belly.

She could no longer remember if she had stopped taking the contraceptive pill on purpose or whether it had been an accident. Besides, it hardly mattered any more, seeing as she was three months gone with her wedding day already settled. Her plan to marry into Roger's large family meant never having to be alone again – a piece of advice once given her by a crazy woman she'd taken to heart. As well as a husband, Hazel would also inherit brothers, sisters, nieces and nephews galore who in turn would be uncles, aunts, and cousins to her own baby. Not knowing how quickly she would outgrow the Cox family, it never entered her head that they in turn might never truly accept her as one of their own on account of her having ideas above her station. Luckily for her, Roger did not feel the same, because as soon as she'd broken the news to him about the pregnancy he'd suggested they move in together. But Hazel had been horrified by the idea.

'If I'm good enough to live with, Roger Cox, then I'm good enough to marry,' she'd haughtily stood her ground. No way was she going to budge.

Having looked at Hazel rather quizzically, as if he'd just received an unexpected win on the horses, Roger hadn't supposed in a million years she'd deign to marry him and that's why he'd not had the courage to ask before. He'd always felt that Hazel was out of his league, too good for the likes of him, even if she didn't realise it herself.

Back then, Roger had still been under the impression Hazel was a normal, level-headed girl – a tad spoilt, perhaps, but one who'd enjoyed a perfectly ordinary childhood. So it must have surprised the hell out of him the day she stabbed him with the fork and he realised he'd got far more than he bargained for. Hazel made sure he never found out about her mother being locked up in the sanatorium or her humdrum father's spectacular double life.

After what happened in the loft, which now seemed another very long weekend ago, her mother had been allowed home occasionally for special events such as Easter and Christmas, but her father always made sure that he was home for these visits. Ignored as usual, Hazel did not miss her mother's company in the slightest, but suffered from increasing loneliness with her father away "on business" so often.

Believing her to be a strong, practical girl, capable of more or less bringing herself up, her father had no qualms about leaving Hazel on her own. After all, as breadwinner of the family, he was responsible for providing for them; where would they be without his blue-collar job as clerk of the works for an engineering firm that had several depots and offices dotted across the east of England? Even if that did mean constant travel and uncomfortable nights spent in budget hotels next to the noisy motorway, when he'd much rather be under his own roof, tucked up asleep in his own bed. He'd say all this without once meeting Hazel's eye, because they both knew it was a charade he would play each time he packed his soft saddle-brown leather holdall that grew more creased and weary each time it was taken out. But it wasn't only the bag that suffered; her father permanently had the look of a wounded, exhausted hound that couldn't go another step. Hazel wondered if the constant lies were weighing him down; of course she knew exactly where he was going and to whom on those little trysts of his. Surely more of the same lies awaited him there, because it wasn't possible that his other illegitimate family knew Hazel, her mother or the half-timbered house even existed.

Never having pretended to be a godly or righteous man, her father was nevertheless a dutiful upright citizen who was respected within the community. But being old school, he washed his hands of household chores, considering such menial tasks as washing, darning, cooking and cleaning to be beneath him. 'Women's work,' he called it. With no other female in the house, these jobs fell to Hazel to do. In return, her father expected her to give up any silly notion of working for a living as she got older and look after him, the house and her mother instead. He certainly never expected her to marry or fly the nest.

Gazing down on his dead face, which looked odd without the usual Woodbine propped up in it, Hazel wished that she could tell him what she'd been planning all along. That he wasn't the only one capable of keeping secrets, or of having another life outside the house. Tomorrow. That's when she'd been saving it all up for. When she was going to let him have it. But now she was too late. The high blood pressure that had pursued him all his life – no doubt compounded by the excess baggage of having an illegitimate family tucked secretly away – had finally tracked him down. A lifestyle of booze and fags hadn't helped, either. Hazel could smell the fags on his breath now, as if he'd just puffed out a smoke ring in the air – the way he once had to make her laugh and clap.

Why couldn't they have left him alone? she wondered viciously. If anyone was to blame for his death, they were. Especially her. The camel. Making him cleave – a word Hazel remembered from Sunday school – to her, with her three bastards.

She wasn't entirely happy about being pregnant herself, nor having had to pretty much force Roger's hand into marriage; unlike *her*, they did have plans to marry before the baby started to show, so that no one could accuse them of having a shotgun wedding. Hazel wasn't about to ruin her special day, planned for tomorrow, just because her father decided to keel over and die from a heart attack in the middle of watering his cactus. Nobody need know, she decided. She would not even tell Roger about her father's death. Nor that he'd spent his last few minutes kneeling on the conservatory floor, clutching at his heart and clawing at Hazel's hand for all he was worth.

'You must phone them, my other... you know who I mean. We wouldn't want them to worry. It isn't fair on them.' But her father had been pleading with the wrong daughter. No doubt the other one would have run to do his bidding. Not Hazel.

Instead, she'd torn her hand away when he'd least expected it, and right in front of his eyes she'd emptied his beloved cactus onto the floor, compost and all. The last thing he would have seen before he died was Hazel jumping all over it. After that, she'd unplugged the phone. They could find out about his death in the papers for all she cared.

That's why the camel had been so cold toward her in the chapel of rest; she knew that Hazel had done her out of her God-given right to say goodbye to the man she loved. But as far as Hazel knew, a woman who lived in sin with a man – who she wasn't married to, even if she'd born him bastards – didn't have any rights, and that suited her down to the ground.

'You must be Hazel.' After looking Hazel up and down and finding her wanting, the other woman – Helen was her name – had proceeded to talk over her father's coffin as if they were about to sit down to a cream tea.

'And you must be Hell,' Hazel had fired back. At least, she hoped she had. She could hardly remember now. But even if she hadn't, she'd been practicing saying those same words and rehearsing that scenario in her head for more than half her lifetime.

* * *

HAZEL SAT UP and wiped her eyes, careful not to smudge her mascara. Outside the lighthouse, seagulls wrapped in feathery grey duffel coats with black gloved wings tucked inside their pockets, seemingly screeched, 'Five minutes are up, Hazel!' More reliable than any alarm clock – and any man!

He'd let her down badly and she still felt injured by it. Long after her father had been buried and put to rest, if such a thing could be said of a man like him, a solicitor had written to her out of the blue. A Mr Metcalf, who was one of three partners working for a firm in Norfolk specialising in wills and probate. She remembered his name only because he'd signed the letter with a very elaborate M attached to his signature. It had been shaped like a bird soaring upwards into the sky.

On discovering that her mother and father had never actually married, due to the fact that he had previously married a Miss Helen Hunt of Sandringham five years prior to meeting her mother, Mr Metcalf found himself in the unfortunate position of having to inform Hazel that her dearly departed father had in fact committed bigamy by marrying her mother in an unlawful ceremony two years before Hazel was born. Furthermore, he also had to advise her that there had been no suggestion of a divorce taking place or being sought by her father prior to his marrying her mother.

It turned out she'd been "Daddy's dirty, dark secret" all along. She likened the feeling to the way she'd instinctively kept quiet about the blood-stained knickers hidden at the bottom of her mother's laundry basket. Even though she'd only been eight years old at the time and it was far from her turn yet, Hazel had been aware of having to collude with her mother about such secrets. Things you didn't tell men about. She guessed that was how her father had felt about her. She knew without being told that there was no secret album locked away in a drawer in his other family's home with *her* picture inside.

All this time, she'd thought of her father's other family as,

They. Them. The Illegitimate Lot. The Pretenders. The Devil's Spawn. Bastards. The Slut. The Whore. But she might as well have been applying the names to herself and her mother; it turned out that she, Hazel, was the *real* bastard and her *mother* the whore. All this time, thinking they were the superior family, in spite of how much time her father spent with the other lot, only to find out they – she – was second-class, inferior, illegitimate. As such, Mr Metcalf had gone on to say, they had no claims to her father's estate, which meant the half-timbered house that had been her home would be auctioned off and any outstanding balance distributed equally between the legal wife and her children. Hazel and her mother would not see a penny.

Realising that her father never provided for them came as a real shock to Hazel. She couldn't understand it when he had clearly loved and admired her. Look at the way his eyes had gone all watery and emotional that time she'd danced for him at the wedding! Nobody could have denied the adoration in his eyes then.

But then, the more she thought about it, the more it didn't make sense. Slowly, it dawned on Hazel. The tears and the choked emotion hadn't been for her at all. All along, they'd been meant for someone else...

After all these years, Hazel could still remember the song off by heart. She sang the words out loud now, each lyric stabbing her throat like a thousand shards of broken glass. The song had been about a three year old but Hazel was six when she danced at that wedding, and now she came to think of it, the song had long been a favourite of her father's before she'd latched on to it. That could only mean one thing...

The song was for Tara. All along, it had been their song – Tara and Eric's song – and nothing at all to do with Hazel, who

171

had somehow managed to bulldoze inadvertently in on their act. Tragically, there could be no other explanation. Likewise, all her father's feelings and emotions had been invested in her younger, three-year-old half-sister. Knowing this sunk her.

But what hit her even harder than her father's disloyalty was the realisation that she had never been truly loved at all. Not by her father, her mother or indeed either of her two dead husbands.

While she'd grown into a beautiful woman, she couldn't in all honesty claim to have been loved by any man, not in the true sense of the word. Beautiful women were promised many things: wealth, fame, expensive jewellery, designer clothes, fast cars and luxury houses – but never love, not in the way an ordinary girl could expect. Not in the way her father's plain legitimate daughter could expect.

Well, at least Hazel had seen to it that neither of her children would suffer the same fate. Nobody would ever be able to call them "bastard" or disinherit them. She might be guilty of letting her children down on a grand scale, but nobody could accuse her of failing them on that count.

It went without saying that she had imagined being a wonderful mother to her brood of children and giving them a fairytale childhood they'd never want to exchange for adulthood. But, in reality, that never happened to children born into dysfunctional broken homes. Those who suffered most as children only went on to create more misery by breeding more of the same disturbed troubled children, she'd found. Look at her. Look at Roger. Look at her own children.

On the surface, Yvonne might appear to have it all; no doubt she was a devoted and loving mother, but her child, Una, born out of wedlock, had no father and no proper home to call her own. What hope was there for her when her own mother had no career, no independence, no prospects and no self-respect?

As for her own mother, Hazel had no idea if she was still institutionalised or if she were dead, but she decided many years ago that "wanting" to find out as opposed to "actually" finding out were two different things entirely.

After all, Mr Metcalf had never written to Hazel about her mother in the same way he had her father, including a copy of his death certificate for her records. Until the day the A4 size document dropped in her lap, she'd never once had anything to record before. But she'd made a habit of collecting them ever since.

Birth certificates (Yvonne and Venetia), christening certificate (Yvonne only, no Venetia, but Hazel couldn't remember why), marriage certificates (Hazel to Roger, Phillip to Hazel), death certificates (her father Eric's, Roger's and Phillip's) – all exactly in that order; that's how Hazel's world had unfolded, and nobody could criticise her for recording it like that. The only thing she could be sure of was that there would be many more certificates to record in future.

Nowadays she had her own family album and secretive locked drawer to store them in, along with photographs, newspaper clippings and an obituary or two.

HAVING NO IDEA how close she was to what she was actually looking for, Venetia was reminded of a game she'd played as a child, hers and Yvonne's very own version of find and seek.

'Hot. Hotter. Burning,' Yvonne would shriek her encouragement, unable to contain her excitement if Vee got anywhere near the carefully hidden object. Or, 'Cold. Colder. Absolutely freezing,' if she veered off course in her search for whatever her sister had hidden in the secretive crevices of the lighthouse.

But without Yvonne here to guide her, Vee didn't have a clue where to start looking and instead gazed hopelessly around her mother's bedroom, wondering if inspiration would leap out at her like a dog with a ball.

Outside, she could actually hear a dog barking. Stealthily, she crossed to the window and looked down on the garden, careful to keep away from the glass because the last thing she needed was for her mother to look up and see her in here.

What she saw outside made her grin from ear to ear as it became clear that her mother's efforts at getting Una to leave the dog behind had failed. There was Una now, with the dog circling and yelping excitedly around her as they jumped onto the back seat of the milky white Range Rover. Yvonne and her mother were already seated in the front, adjusting seats and looking at reflections in mirrors.

"Inept" would have been the word her mother would have chosen for anyone else who had fallen so short of her expectations. Vee liked the way the word made her draw back her lip in a fancy snarl.

Watching her family disappear out of the drive and down the hill until the luxury car became no grander than a milk float in the distance, Vee prowled the room, her eyes on the door, wary of being caught out even though she knew she had the lighthouse to herself. Still, the feeling of being watched persisted. Knowing she shouldn't be in here was enough to give her the willies and God help her if her mother ever found out.

Silently easing out a drawer in her mother's dressing table, Vee's greedy fingers pried guiltily amongst the expensive underwear. It came as no surprise to see that her mother favoured

French lace in feminine hues of pink; she had always opted for elegance over practicality. Personally, Vee couldn't see how the material could be anything other than scratchy and uncomfortable and preferred men's cotton boxers to anything else.

In another drawer she came across Hermès scarves, several pairs of leather gloves with impossibly thin fingers she would never be able to squeeze her own clumsy digits into and glossy champagne-coloured tights in unopened packets, still with the extortionate price tags on.

But what really piqued her interest was a red and cream suede jewellery box that took pride of place on her mother's bedside table. It had been one of her mother's many presents from Phillip, bought from Aspinal's in London during one of their regular trips to the city. It had been around so long that it somehow felt part of the family. Inside there were gold earrings, several cameo brooches and an Astley Clarke cocktail ring that had been another present from Phillip. It was worth a small fortune – enough for a deposit on a house for most people. God alone knew what her mother had done to deserve so many extravagant presents. But, then again, Vee had seen the way she sometimes looked at Phillip when she wanted something. The look reminded her of someone who was about to suck cock. She knew she shouldn't say it, but it had been downright disgusting the way her mother carried on with her wet bottom lip and drowsy eyes, luring men into the bedroom for heaven knows what. Shuddering in revulsion, Vee simply couldn't bear the thought of her mother having done "that" with her real father.

Wondering if her mother's first wedding ring – the one her father must have given her – was anywhere amongst her collection of jewellery, Vee eventually dismissed the idea. Of course her mother wouldn't have kept it, it not being of any real value. Nor would she have thought to save it for either her or Yvonne when they got older. Nevertheless, Vee's fingers weren't ready to give up the sentimental notion just yet and so they searched, of their own accord, among the jewellery. When they came across an ornate skeletal key secured right at the back of the box, hidden in the cream suede lining, she knew it hadn't got there by accident. Sliding the key out, Vee held it in the palm of her hand, wondering what it would reveal and if she was really prepared for what she might find. It wasn't too late to call off the search.

But her right eye kept flickering over to one corner of the room, drawn to a cream French armoire whose double doors were kept shut and firmly locked. Not once had Vee or Yvonne seen inside what they called the "secret wardrobe", fantasising it contained long fur coats that, if you groped your way through, revealed a doorway on the other side that promised adventures in Narnia where Aslan and Mr Tumnus lived. The locked wardrobe might have been a gateway to the lands and stories they'd read about as children, but it had always remained forbidden to them.

The key turned smoothly in the lock, as if it was used to being opened on a regular basis. This surprised Vee, as she'd imagined that whatever lurked inside was something her mother chose to forget about. And they all knew how good she was at that.

Pulling open one of the doors, Vee was childishly disappointed to see just one measly fur jacket wrapped in cellophane, hanging from a bent wire hanger. So much for all the wonderful luxurious fur coats they'd imagined locked away inside. Nor was there any sign of a door or gateway of any kind – not that she'd ever let on to Yvonne, who would be so disappointed.

On the rail next to the solitary fur was a simple black Hobbs skirt suit. Vee didn't need to touch it or hold it to her nose to know that it smelt of her mother. On the floor underneath the suit was a pair of black kitten-heeled shoes, positioned like two pawns waiting to checkmate each other. The ensemble created a garish image of an invisible woman wearing the dark suit, fur coat and shoes, all dressed up with nowhere to go and shut inside the wardrobe for years. But when Vee thought about it more seriously, she realised that this was a funeral outfit, taken out only when somebody close to her mother died. She may well have worn it to Vee's own father's funeral, but Vee was too young to remember.

Another discovery on the shelf above the rail was a hatbox with a black-netted pillbox hat peeping out of one corner. The hat indisputably went with the outfit and was no doubt something her mother would have hidden her dry eyes behind while others wept.

Unable to resist wanting to try on the hat, Vee found the Fortnum & Mason hatbox surprisingly heavy as she carried it over to the bed, spilling the contents as it landed. What came tumbling out was a large photo album, envelopes stuffed with certificates and loose newspaper clippings; some neatly folded and others screwed into a ball, looking as if they'd once been fired into a bin.

'Bingo.' This find was far better than any cheap soft lion toy from Thomas's Bingo Hall.

Sitting on the bed, her knees dissolving into the spongy memory foam mattress that did not recognise anybody's imprint but her mother's, Vee peeled back the sticky pages of the photo album, careful not to rip any of the photographs inside – particularly the older ones that had become creased over time.

Here was a life she had never been allowed to see before. There was her mother, as a child, recognisable only by the wounded eyes that were clearly out for revenge and the fact that she looked as if she might be about to throw something at someone. *God help whoever who had upset her*, was all Vee could think, with a knowing smile. In the picture, her mother wore a trouser suit and held a lucky horseshoe charm in her hand. So the photo had been taken at somebody's wedding, Vee figured correctly.

She was gobsmacked to discover that her mother's hair was naturally brown and, in this instance, long and straight – it was nothing like the legendary butter blonde waves she now sported. The heavy cumbersome shoes she'd clearly been made to wear were unsuitable for a girl her age, and Vee found herself wondering who had inconsiderately chosen them for her. In the background, a man in a dark suit stood smoking a cigarette, close enough to be somebody important in Hazel's life but not close enough to watch out for her; his eyes weren't resting on her. There was something about his hunched shoulders that made Vee think that he was depressed or, at the very least, resigned to a life of melancholy. He had the posture of a man who had been badly let down.

She was pleased to see pictures of her and Yvonne as babies, even though she couldn't tell who was who without turning the photograph over and reading what was written on the back. But there were no photographs of her father; no memories of him to take out and turn around, as she'd first hoped. Any evidence of him had been cut away, crossed out or even obliterated, though there were plenty of Phillip in his model businessman pose, dressed in one of his customary striped banker's suits, showing off an olive tan and George Clooney hair. Annoyingly, there was one of him in a pair of trunks taken on his boat, exhibiting a spectacularly toned masculine body; another of him skiing in the Alps, against the backdrop of a snow-covered mountain, which reminded Vee of an iced bun; and one of him in tennis whites, gamely swinging a racket. Each one made her want to retch. *Was there nothing the man couldn't do?*, she thought sarcastically. Having always resented her stepfather for being alive when her own father was dead, Phillip's death had not come soon enough for her.

Her mother and sister may never have got to hear what he'd said to her that day he'd come up to her room to remonstrate at her, but she remembered it word for word. Alright, she may well have been having a right temper tantrum at the time and been completely out of control, but even she hadn't deserved what he'd said to her. After all, she'd been but a child herself back then.

'I will have you taken away. Put away,' he'd threatened, and for once in her life she recognised that she had met her match and was no longer in charge. Now it was her turn to know what it was like to feel bullied, to be the victim, and she hadn't liked it. Truthfully, she'd been absolutely terrified.

'I will say you are a danger to yourself and others and you will be locked up in a home for bad children where you belong. Because I will not allow you to hurt this – *my* – family any more, is that clear?' Phillip was careful not to raise his voice even once.

She'd nodded tearfully, not daring to meet his eye, knowing that he meant every word. What's more, she knew he'd do it quickly – have her incarcerated in some loony asylum before her mother and sister ever got a chance to step in to help her, because that was the way he worked.

One other word he'd said to her to that day. One other word, made up of two syllables, which began with a vowel and ended with a consonant. A word constructed of simple enough letters, which had the power to rip out her heart. A word he'd only ever repeated to her once, a word he wouldn't forget in a hurry, not even on his deathbed, because what came around went around. That much had been proven.

Disregarding the other pictures of Phillip, Vee fast-forwarded through the album until she hit on a selection of photographs that did interest her. She found herself catching her breath, for there, on the page, were memories both pleasant and painful to see.

Her and Vonnie on the dodgems when they were young, violently trying to bump into each other and ignoring any other drivers in their deadly pursuit of each other. Looking closer, Vee could swear that Yvonne looked a bit green and sickly, as if she had been bumped *too* hard, *too* many times. Guiltily, she glanced away, at another photo. This time, they had been captured the instant they exited the ghost train ride – mouths hanging open in fear, hair standing on end, laughing hysterically out of relief.

Vee felt her throat dry up from screaming just as it had back then, imagined the fake cobwebs and dangling plastic spiders caressing her face; saw the pair of illuminated ghoulish eyes waiting for them at the end of the tunnel as the train rocked toward the exit, which couldn't come soon enough for Yvonne, who never stopped screaming the whole time she was in there. It was only when they got outside that they started laughing, and even then Yvonne remained shy of the life-sized zombies and skeletons standing guard at the entrance.

True to her word, Vee never told her mother about her sister leaving a puddle behind on the leather seat, nor how she had clung on to her for dear life throughout the whole ride, though she might have teased Yvonne about it afterwards. She couldn't really remember. But their mother must have been waiting outside; ready to take their picture the minute they came out, wanting to capture their laughter on camera. That had been such a motherly thing to do; Vee couldn't help but be impressed.

Reluctantly, she realised that she ought to give her mother more credit for trying to give them a happy childhood; the summer of the dodgems and the ghost train had probably been their best holiday ever. And their last, as it turned out, because after what happened they hadn't come back to Hunstanton again. Not until now. Instead, their holiday lighthouse had been let to other families for carefree seaside summers. That's why the album ended abruptly where it did. Why there were no more holiday photographs.

Hidden inside the hatbox was a pink jewellery box, the type that had a pop-up ballerina inside and played music whenever the lid was opened. It felt vaguely familiar, as if it had belonged to either her or Yvonne; it certainly looked well used. But rather than open it to find out what was inside, Vee's fingers avoided it. There were some things she wasn't meant to know – not yet. Instead, she unravelled one of the screwed-up newspaper cuttings, marvelling at how ink from nineteen years ago could still stain her fingers. As she rolled it out even more, a face known to her was revealed. Her father.

In the picture, Roger kneeled in front of a Christmas tree, surrounded by presents wrapped in gaudy paper with fat golden bows attached to each one. Not only did Vee wonder which present might have been hers, she thought it unlikely that he'd wrapped them himself, even though he held one of the packages in his hand, grinning as if to say, *Look what I did*. The brown velvet curtains hanging against the window confirmed what Vee already knew: that the picture had been taken at their old house in Laburnum Grove, somewhere she could just about remember if she put her mind to it. But the hint of gold twinkling from Roger's mouth was fresh in her memory, as was the monster of a nose she could tell he was conscious of just by the way he held his head, hoping to make it appear smaller for the photograph – but it clearly didn't.

Underneath the picture was the caption "Friends and family devastated by sudden death of local man, Roger Cox (thirty)". This, then, was Roger's obituary; Vee could hardly believe that her mother had kept it all these years. Unable to resist running a maudlin finger over her father's creased face, she quickly scanned the words.

There was the customary mention of relatives and who Roger was survived by. Vee couldn't help smiling when she saw her name had gone before Yvonne's and she bet her sister wouldn't like that one little bit, coming second and all. The date and time of the funeral was given in such a casual unfeeling way that Vee felt injured by it. Tuesday 14th March. The day that changed her life.

She read on. A list of interests, including fishing and pool; where he went to school; what engineering firm he worked for; his favourite pub 'The Quiet Woman', which had been but two doors away from their house. There was nothing odd about the report at all. Nothing leapt out of the pages screaming "conspiracy".

So she read it again. Slowly, and more carefully this time. Thank God she did. Because there, in column two, on line fifteen, were the words she'd always known existed. "Mr Cox collapsed and died after suffering a chronic asthma attack at home." And that was it! No more detail than that? Infuriatingly, Vee supposed that the newspaper had chosen to whitewash the ugliness of death or, in this case, something more sinister. But wait a minute, there was more…

"Mr Cox's body was discovered by his widow, Hazel (twenty-six), who said, 'He was fine the morning we left on a family outing to the seaside. We would never have left him had we suspected anything was wrong.' Contributions in memory of Mr Cox can be made to Asthma UK," the paper went on to meddle.

'We would never have left him had we suspected anything was wrong.' Vee repeated these words over and over in her head as she mulled over what this implied. She might have been just a little dot at the time, but she knew enough of her father to know that he would not have allowed them to go on a day's outing to the seaside – or anywhere else without him, for that matter, regardless of whether he was fighting fit or not.

There was definitely something not right here. Something Roger would have wanted her to know. And then she felt his presence in the room, as surely as if he was kneeling on the carpet in front of her, holding out a present, whose ribbon she would sadly never untie. Yet strangely he would not come close enough to touch her, preferring to keep his distance. How she longed for him to put his hand on her head or say a kind word in her ear, but he did neither of these things. Even the whispering she sensed around her could just as easily have been the wind playing kiss-chase around the tower – she couldn't make out any words in the uncertainty. But, in spite of the confusion, she remained convinced that her father was here with her. That he had, in fact, never left her.

So, she had been right all along about there being a ghost meddling in their lives. No doubt her father had good reason for trying to stop them becoming a proper family. Perhaps he was even trying to protect Vee from something menacing that loomed just around the corner. Either way, real or imaginary, he was here now. Roger's ghost. She wore him like a white sheet tucked around her, with cut-out holes for the eyes, mouth and nose.

And then it hit her. What he had been trying to tell her. What she had long forgotten.

THEY WERE HALFWAY around Blackbeard's adventure golf course on the seafront, which included, among its many attractions, a rope bridge and pathways made of artificial mushy pea-green lawn that your heels sunk into. Judging by the boredom on Hazel and Yvonne's faces, the eighteen-hole course was a tad over seventeen holes too long.

Armed with a club, Yvonne went glumly through the motions of being a willing participant as she teed off from the ninth hole. Every so often, she raked a hand agitatedly through her chestnut hair, a sure sign that she was feeling miserable. That it was only a question of time before she let everyone know it.

'It's not the same without Vee,' she complained, ignoring the way her ball bounced off one of the life-sized pirate statues and spiralled hopelessly into the bunker.

Knowing that it would take forever for Yvonne to hit the ball back out, Hazel sighed and gazed longingly at the nineteenth hole in the distance. She wasn't enjoying herself anymore than Yvonne, but at least she was making an effort. Her head was thumping and she could do with a cup of tea and a couple of painkillers, but after this they also planned to visit the Sea Life Sanctuary. It was the last thing she needed and on top of that, she had no idea what they were supposed to do with the dog while they were inside. Chain it to the railings, perhaps, in the hope that somebody would steal it? Hazel was slow getting over the fact that her granddaughter had been so stubborn, flatly refusing to leave the dog behind, but she supposed Una took after her mother in that respect. What could she do about it? She could hardly have changed her mind or refused to take them out on this agenda-filled day after all.

Her granddaughter was doing a "me-hearty" pirate laugh and squawking, 'Shiver me timbers,' while pretending to swing a sword, but Hazel was finding it hard to focus when every time one of them hit the ball the dog barked and lunged to the end of its lead, nearly pulling Una over each time. The child would have her arm pulled from her socket at this rate.

'She didn't want to come, Yvonne,' Hazel stressed for the third or fourth time since their arrival in town, careful not to snap, even though her patience was fast wearing out, like a cheap pair of shoes in need of new soles. What was wrong with just spending time with her, she wondered? Surely they could, between them, manage one day without Venetia?

'Well, I don't know why.' Clearly miffed, Yvonne was obviously taking her sister's refusal to accompany them personally. 'It's not like she's got anything better to do.'

The dog yapped as Yvonne took another putt, sending her ball deeper into the sand until only the tip of its grainy white surface could be seen, as if it were a bobtailed rabbit disappearing down a hole.

'Well, whatever it is, she's probably up to no good.' The words rolled spitefully off Hazel's tongue before she could stop them. The day was going from bad to worse and she didn't know how to fix it. As it was, it felt like The Sex Pistols were playing "God Save The Queen" inside her head. If only that bloody dog would stop barking.

'Why would you say that?' Yvonne scowled.

'No reason,' Hazel shrugged innocently.

'She tried to steal my dog,' Una piped up, quizzically appraising her mother and grandmother, as if they were strangers who had come to tea. People she was supposed to be nice to on the surface, then gossip about as soon as they left.

'She did not.' With one last violent whack, Yvonne smashed the ball out of the bunker. It rolled easily to the next hole, a pirate's head wearing a tri-cornered hat. The ball was meant to enter his evil, leering mouth and roll off his tongue into the hole. Yvonne figured that she'd need more than a little good luck with that.

Watching Una's face turn vinegary, as if she'd just swallowed a whole paper cupful of pickled cockles, Hazel came to her granddaughter's defence.

'She did, Yvonne.'

Glancing at her daughter, hoping for a bit of backup, Yvonne was surprised to see the narrowed eyes, creased forehead and hands tucked stubbornly in pockets – a posture she knew too well, and a mood her daughter wouldn't be talked out of easily, not even with the promise of midget gems and ice cream.

'She probably just wanted to take it for a walk.'

Hands on hips now, Una pulled even more of a sceptical face, 'Aunt Vee?'

'Why don't you just face it, Yvonne? Una's telling the truth.'

Dropping the club, Yvonne marched over to Hazel and took her to one side, out of Una's earshot.

'Have you put her up to this?' she hissed. 'Lying about the dog? About Vee?'

Hazel shook off Yvonne's insistent hand. No matter that this was her daughter; nobody was going to manhandle her. She wouldn't stand for it. Being second best was another of the things she wouldn't stand for.

'Why do you think she wanted to stay behind on her own, thinking that the dog was going to be there? You don't think Venetia was ever going to forget that it went for her, do you?'

Jealousy got the better of Hazel and made her tell the lie. *A sort of lie*, she justified, for all she was really guilty of was omitting her own part in the plotting. Unlike most people, Hazel never worried unduly about telling lies, nor did she concern herself too much with what effect they had on others; as soon as the untruth was out of her mouth, it no longer belonged to her, nor did it have any further claim on her. At least, that was her way of looking at it. Rather like a game of tag, she felt – whoever got tagged last with the lie was "it".

YVONNE'S RED ANGRY face blanched under the truth of what her mother was saying, because it just wasn't in her sister's nature to forget, nor let anything go. Still, that didn't mean she believed that Venetia was capable of hurting an animal or doing something awful to get rid of it. She just wouldn't. Not even for the sake of revenge. Although Una was on her mother's side in this, Yvonne just wasn't buying it. The child must have been mistaken.

'You want to make friends with us, but you're still trying to keep me and Vee apart, is that it?'

'You don't understand!' Hazel sounded heartbroken.

'Oh, I think I do. The whole idea of this weekend wasn't really to make amends, was it? You can't be happy unless we're at each other's throats.'

Hazel drew back shakily, so much so that even the dangly pearl earrings she wore swung against her neck with her trembling.

Yvonne could swear she did it on purpose to make passersby

think she was some frail, timid lady being shouted at by an uncouth, fat chav in leggings.

'You don't know what she was capable of… I had my job cut out just making sure you were… I don't trust her,' Hazel finally volunteered.

'You don't trust anyone!' Aware that her voice was rising, Yvonne couldn't stop herself, even though people really were stopping to stare now. Soon, somebody would come over to try to rescue her mother, as they always did. Even Una had moved away, clearly embarrassed to be seen with them, while the dog had thrown its head back like Wuffa and was now howling.

Next, Hazel's eyes filled with tears and her head wobbled on her shoulders. If she had a crucifix handy, she'd no doubt bring it poignantly to her lips and kiss it. It was all too much for Yvonne, who felt she'd done absolutely nothing wrong – as usual.

'Do you know what?' she addressed the judge-and-jury crowd, as well as her mother, for they were all involved now. 'I've had enough of this.' In the back of her mind, Yvonne hoped the crowd wouldn't misinterpret her words to mean "enough of this – adventure golf", for that would be truly embarrassing – people would think she couldn't handle a game of crazy golf without going crazy herself.

'I'm not staying a minute longer.' Doing a military about-turn, Yvonne reclaimed her unwilling daughter and dragged her by the hand towards the exit, ignoring the way the dog's lead tangled around them as if they were a pair of crabs trapped in a fishing net.

'Come on, Una. We're going back to the lighthouse.' She refused to use the word "home" in her mother's presence.

'What about the Sea Life Sanctuary? You promised. And

Granny said I could feed the sharks,' Una protested, dragging her heels and leaning back on her flip-flops.

'I think we've seen enough man-eaters for one day,' was Yvonne's last parting shot.

THE WALLS OF the lighthouse's entrance hall echoed with the same squabbling and tears it had grudgingly grown accustomed to since being owned by the Ladd family. Feeling like Hazel had earlier with her headache, the whitewashed walls winced with each scream and the tower itself would have upped and moved further along the cliff if it could, to escape the ruckus. Added to the mix this summer was the constant yapping of the dog, whose yelps chipped incessantly away at its cement, like a claw hammer intent on demolition.

'I want to stay!' Una clung on to the metal staircase and refused to budge, like a piece of washing on a line being blown about by the wind.

'The dog can come too. I've already told you that,' Yvonne told her exasperatingly. Already she had given up trying to physically pry her daughter away from the staircase and was now looking at the walls, as if they might be able to come up with a better way of convincing Una into leaving with her. Now.

'Laddy won't leave here. He told me. This is his home,' Una cried angrily, dangerously close to wanting to kick and lash out at her mother. As if to emphasise his agreement, the dog quit barking and lie down on the spot, his head resting adoringly on his paws.

Where had her gentle, sweet-natured daughter gone? was what Yvonne wanted to know. Ever since they'd arrived here, she'd seen and felt such change in her. Look at how she'd turned on Venetia, like an angry little hyena, over the dog. Up until recently, it had been unheard of for Una to be unkind to anyone. That's why they needed to get away from here, soon. She felt it in every goose pimple.

Raising her eyes to heaven, she spotted her mother hovering anxiously on the stairs. Their eyes met only for a second, but Yvonne could immediately tell that she was desperate to be forgiven. That she would say and do anything to make things right again.

'Happy now?' Not knowing what else to do and realising that her mother didn't really deserve all the blame, but unable to forgive her all the same, Yvonne burst into helpless tears and dropped her hastily packed holdall on the floor.

'Things have gone horribly wrong since coming here,' she flung accusingly at the walls, the tower, her mother and even at Una before running up the steps, passing her mother on the way and ignoring her outstretched hand. Only when she was back in the guest bedroom on her own, and only then, would she wish she could take back the words and grab hold of the proffered hand. She had never felt so in need of a hug.

AS YVONNE WENT in one door on the landing, Venetia came out of another, her face a puzzle, wondering at first what on earth was going on. But the door to the guest bedroom slamming with such fury could only mean one thing where her sister was concerned.

'What have you done now?' There was open hostility in Vee's just-woken-up hamster eyes as she challenged her mother.

Hazel sighed dramatically, 'Talk to her, Venetia. Make her see sense.'

Then, dismissing her daughter as if she were little more than a servant, Hazel stepped elegantly down the stairs, her head held high, her dainty feet finding their own way on the metal rungs as if they'd never had any help in their life before and didn't need any now, thank you very much.

VENETIA STARED AFTER her. It was unbelievable, the way her mother expected everything to be solved in her absence. Later, she would act as if nothing had happened. Pretence to her was as necessary as the most expensive face cream.

Watching her reach the bottom of the stairs, Vee saw her hold out a hand and a captivating smile to her granddaughter and Una accepted both at once, responding with a partner-in-crime smirk of her own. As if by magic, she was finally able to let go of the staircase and went with her grandmother into the kitchen. Vee couldn't help but marvel at the way their feet silently crossed the tiled floor, not making a single sound, like a pair of Siamese cats on ice.

THE SUN WAS low in the sky, creating a glimmer of light that shone like a lone candle on the water, while the hazy blue and orange skyline looked unreal, like an oil painting in a gallery. Sadly, the onset of dusk also meant that the family-friendly sand had turned into something black and lifeless, resembling a dark, inhabited desert.

Seated in a striped deckchair, Yvonne watched twilight 'happen' from the decked balcony area of a beach hut raised on stilts. Behind her, the red, white and blue painted doors of the beach hut were propped open and somewhere inside she could hear the squeal of an old-fashioned kettle getting ready to let rip. She twirled a handkerchief in her hand as if she was about to miraculously produce an intricate origami swan from its folds, but she only sniffed tearfully into it, determined to keep up the mood.

The setting sun reminded Yvonne of a perfectly fried egg, runny with oil but soft and yolky in the centre, and her stomach twisted with hunger. Given the choice, she'd have hers with thick rounds of bread and butter with dollops of brown sauce on the side. Venetia would have ketchup, of course, her eggs scrambled and her meagre slice of crust-less toast would come with just a thin scraping of margarine. Even then, she wouldn't be able to finish it all, abandoning it after just a few nibbles, like a skinny rat wary of being poisoned. That's how different they were, Yvonne realised.

She had once likened Vee to a flying saucer melting on the tongue – a fiery, fizzy sharpness that attacked your senses with angry flavours that faded all too quickly, whereas she was more like an unassuming humbug, not so intense and with a much milder taste, but one that rolled pleasantly around your mouth for longer, making sure you got your money's worth. Years ago she had tried to emulate her sister's eating habits in an attempt to be as slim and athletic as her, but found it impossible to keep up. Vee literally starved herself, preferring fags and booze to proper food, which she could easily live without. Rather predictably, Yvonne felt that she had spent her whole life trailing after her sister in one way or another, the slow chubby one who always lagged behind.

There she was now, coming out of the beach hut, looking gaunt and cancerous, like somebody who had a furball they couldn't cough up. Carrying two mugs of steaming tea and accidentally sloshing the hot liquid over her shaky hands, Vee unceremoniously thrust one into Yvonne's lap. Never in a million years would she admit to having scolded herself or resort to running her hand under a cold tap; pain was something Vee brushed off, just as she would an unsolicited canvasser in an indoor shopping centre.

'Get that down you,' she ordered unsympathetically.

After a brief power struggle with another deckchair, Vee finally managed to get it open and took a pew next to her. Then, curling her stick insect legs under her, she took an unladylike slurp of tea, lit up a fag and observed the same sunset Yvonne had been admiring, her eyes widening in what appeared to be genuine awe. Even the cigarette paused momentarily at her mouth as she contemplated the splendour directly in front of her.

'Whenever I come here, I can always smell boiled eggs,' Vee said at last.

The laughter escaped unwittingly from Yvonne's grimly set mouth and lifted the bad mood spell she'd been under. How could she have thought her sister, of all people, was about to come out with anything meaningful or poetic over a sunset?

'You have to eat boiled eggs at the seaside, everyone knows that,' Yvonne told her.

Vee pulled a rotten egg face and then, as if by mutual agreement, they both turned to stare out to sea.

'Do you ever wonder where Mum got the money to buy the lighthouse?' Vee asked after a few minutes.

'From Roger's life insurance policy, wasn't it?' Yvonne was surprised Vee didn't know even the most basic of facts when it came to their family history.

'Why do you always insist on calling him that?'

'Vee, let's not argue. I hardly knew him.'

'He was still your dad.'

In order not to rock the boat – after all, Vee had come running to find her when no one else had – Yvonne nodded an acceptance she didn't feel. Giving in to her sister came naturally, almost an obligation of sorts, in the same way she felt duty bound to eat the unappetising pith of an orange as well as its juicy segments, not wanting it to feel left out.

'And what about this place?'

'Well, Dad – I mean, Phillip – obviously.'

Yvonne wasn't sure she liked the suspicious expression on her sister's face. It made her look mean, like a thief who'd pretend to mind your bag and then disappear with it as soon as your back was turned.

'What are you getting at, Vee?'

Vee looked away. 'I can still remember the first time I saw this place. It didn't look a bit like it does now.'

Feeling suddenly cold, Yvonne sunk further down in her chair and massaged some warmth into her bare ankles, not able to understand why the sight of the sun sinking lower in the sky should make her tremble.

Keep talking. She must keep talking – then she wouldn't have to think about it.

'All those spiders,' Yvonne remembered suddenly, grateful to have something else pop into her mind. But then, mindful of how terrifying they were with their eight-legged awfulness, she visibly shuddered.

* * *

IT HAD BEEN a perfect day, the day they saw the beach hut for the first time. Hot. Sunny. Still. Too hot and too sunny for her sister, whose salmon-pink pelt frazzled easily, like crispy bacon, along with her temper. But not Yvonne, who loved feeling the warmth of the sun on her skin and watching it turn from a marshmallow yellow to the same colour as a terracotta garden pot within days of arriving at the seaside.

Her mother had appeared so much younger back then, fresh-faced and glowing with girl-next-door prettiness as she swept out dust and cobwebs from the run-down beach hut, unaware of the appreciative looks men in trunks swung her, trying to get noticed. Even more striking though was the permanent smile on her face as she threw her heart and soul into the mammoth cleaning task, for once not caring about the smears of dirt on her face or the traces of sticky cobweb in her hair. It was lovely to see her looking so casual and approachable, in a pair of jeans and an oversized shirt of Phillip's, with the sleeves rolled to the elbow, her hair in a ponytail with a life of its own that whipped her in the face whenever she moved.

'This is all ours from now on. Nobody but us girls are allowed!' she'd whispered, as if sharing a delicious secret with her dearest, best friend, afraid that someone might overhear.

'Not even Phillip?' Venetia was hot on her mother's heels, not sure if she trusted what she was hearing.

'Just us. Aren't we lucky?' Hazel confirmed with a girlish grin, refusing to acknowledge just how ugly and inhabitable the beach hut actually was.

Now Yvonne came to think of it, there was a haunted look about her mother that she hadn't noticed before – as if she herself couldn't wait to be free of Phillip, if only for an hour or two. But that couldn't be right, could it, because her mother adored her stepfather and went out of her way to please him? You only had to see the way she second-guessed his every mood to know that. If Phillip was in need of refreshment, you could bet your life she'd already be on her way with a G&T sloshing with ice; if he misplaced his newspaper, she'd find it within seconds and never minded the way the inky broadsheet stained her fingers; she'd even fetch his slippers for him if need be. And she'd be able to tell from just one quick glance at his clean-shaven face what sort of day he'd had at the bank and how best to act.

Yvonne supposed a lot of her mother's cosseting was due to the fact that Phillip had rescued them from a life of poverty and provided them with a lifestyle most people could only envy. She knew this because she'd once heard her mother tell him so, repeatedly, before going down on her knees and slipping off his shoes, leaving Yvonne to wonder why he'd never learned to untie his own laces. Later, when she'd confided the details to Venetia, her sister claimed to have seen far worse – their mother actually stooping to unzip Phillip's trousers! Yvonne had refused to believe it, of course, even going so far as to accuse her sister of lying, which did not go down well. But Vee didn't know everything. She did not know, for instance, that all the money they'd got from Roger had been spent on the lighthouse. All of it, gone. Even if she had, she'd never have been able to get her head around the fact that they were supposed to be nice to Phillip.

Whilst the lighthouse had been in excellent repair when they'd first bought it, they could hardly say the same for the decrepit beach hut nobody had been near in years, which the council had practically given away for free, according to Phillip, who'd purchased it from them.

It was going to need some money spending on it for sure. Even Yvonne could see that. The weathered doors hung off their hinges and the balcony railings were rickety and broken, while a slimy green moss covered every inch of the sunken roof. Even parts of the decking had gaping holes where somebody's feet, luckily not their own, had gone through. Underneath the beach hut was a shaded area of grey rippled sand littered with shells, discarded pop bottles, the odd sock or flip-flop and sometimes a dead rabbit with a decapitated head.

This was to become her and Vee's own private den, where they would peel their boiled eggs that always tasted of sand, hide from their mother as they sometimes did and dare each other to urinate patterns in the sand.

But on this particular day at the beach, they had been instructed to be on their best behaviour – though Yvonne couldn't see how this was possible, when they had been made to dress in matching swimsuits, as usual, which was so unfair considering that there were three years separating them. It wasn't as if they were twins, which was exactly what people would mistake them for, dressed as they were. Yvonne could remember sulking madly about this even though Vee wasn't the slightest bit put out about it. Secretly, Yvonne suspected that her sister even liked the idea of them looking alike. She had sneakily taken to waiting till Vee was dressed before changing into a different swimsuit or dress so they did not match, like the pair of antique silver candelabra displayed on the fireplace mantel. But, as usual, Vee outsmarted her, thinking it a hoot to change back into exactly the same outfit Yvonne was wearing and only make an appearance when she knew it would be too late for her to do anything about it.

One thing they did agree on, though, was what a pleasure it was, seeing how happy their mother looked. At least, Yvonne hoped her sister felt the same. Usually so formerly turned out, looking for all the world as if she was permanently on her way to a wedding, it made a pleasant change to see their mother's coral nail polish chipped and to know she smelt of bleach and cleaning fluid rather than the expensive Dior perfume she usually wore. Even her hands were dry and scaly from a morning dipped in hot soapy water, Yvonne noticed. Even so, they remained completely overwhelmed by her charm and vivaciousness – and who wouldn't be? Already, the only thing Yvonne wanted to be when she grew up was "as beautiful as her".

'I thought we could paint it blue,' Hazel had suggested cheerfully, waving a regal hand at the beach hut and smiling at both her children.

'Red!' Yvonne giggled.

'White!' Vee gave her a spiteful little push just to show who was boss.

'How about all three?' Hazel laughed, and Yvonne and Vee nodded their approval, dumbstruck all over again by the movie-star quality of their mother.

'And when we're done tidying up, I'll boil up some eggs for tea.' Thinking this a wonderful thing to do for her children, possibly the start of a family custom to be repeated religiously every summer, Hazel was oblivious to the look of disgust on Venetia's face.

But then, handing each of them a feather duster so that they could "get stuck in" – a pink one for Yvonne and housewife yellow for Venetia – she was quick to notice Yvonne shuddering as she peered inside the beach hut.

'There are spiders!' Yvonne gnashed her teeth, hanging back warily. She'd cower behind Vee if she had to; no way was she stepping foot inside. Even her sister knew never to tease her with a spider, realising that she'd get her eyes scratched out if she did.

'We'll carry them outside,' Hazel tried and failed to reassure, and then, seeing this was never going to work, continued, 'Venetia, that can be your job.'

Venetia scowled, not the slightest bit impressed, and Yvonne guessed that her sister would later MAKE HER PAY for having been given such preferential treatment.

'Can we go and play first?' From an early age, Venetia had

grown accustomed to bargaining with adults in order to get her own way. The same couldn't be said for their mother who, clearly outmanoeuvred, rested her hands on her slim hips and bit worryingly on her lip, looking doubtful.

That's when Yvonne first noticed a scab on her elbow that was partly hanging off. One of those "not quite ready to be picked" scabs, Yvonne decided; she couldn't help being a bit of an expert in everyday injuries of that kind.

But seeing the blemish on her mother's skin saddened her enormously and made her want to cry – the same way it did when she watched her take out her purse in a shop, leaving Yvonne to fret anxiously over whether she would be made to put something back if she didn't have enough money. Of course, her mother always had enough cash, and plenty of bank cards as back-up, but it didn't stop Yvonne worrying all the same; she'd once seen something similar happen to on old lady in Azam's store in town and it had broken her heart a little.

The image of the lady shopper was still very vivid in Yvonne's mind, on account of the fact that she'd smelt like a dog blanket, was about a hundred years old and had a hunched back that made her barely taller than Yvonne. Oddly enough, they'd worn the same pink tube socks, although she made a point of constantly pulling hers up while the lady did not – and that was the only irritating thing about her, Yvonne felt. She could also remember being fascinated by what she had in her basket – a pack of granny-size knickers, a high-visibility vest, a plastic spider, a mixed bag of pink shrimps and foam bananas and some fur-edged slippers.

Having slid the candy necklace she was intending to buy onto her wrist, Yvonne played with it as if it were an abacus to while away the time. Unlike her sister and mother, she didn't mind queuing. In fact, it was rather pleasant standing next to the old lady while a sullen teenage boy with a wire cage over his pointy teeth served the people in front of them. But, then again, it was highly unlikely that her mother would ever set foot in Azam's store; she deemed it common and little more than a junk shop, which it was of course, and cheap, too. Nowhere else could Yvonne buy fake dog poo to hide under her sister's pillow and pretend it came out of Wuffa's bottom, a whole bag of drumstick lollies to share around like a gracious princess when she felt so inclined, a sherbet fountain just for herself, a t-shirt with a pony's head on it and a whole pack of jazzy knickers with the days of the week printed on them and *still* have change left over from her pocket money.

But the old woman didn't have enough pocket money. That was the problem.

'Oh, dear,' she kept saying, 'oh, dear.' She counted out her change on the counter, stacking it into wobbly piles that looked as if they were about to topple over drunkenly, like the disabled driver who kept tipping out of his mobility scooter on the south parade. Suddenly, Yvonne detected a feeling of mutiny and impatience amongst the queue that hadn't been there before; it no longer felt like a nice place to be.

'Are you sure it's as much as that?' The lady who couldn't straighten up because of her hunched back was unable to make eye contact of any sort, which acted as an open invitation for the shop assistant to be rude.

'The till is never wrong,' he told her smartly, as if he were Luke Skywalker yielding a light sabre.

'I could have sworn I had enough. Three pounds and fifty-three pence, you say?' She pushed the pile of coins toward him, hoping it might be enough.

It wasn't.

'You've only got three pounds and three pence.' He spoke loudly as if she was deaf, although she was not, and then he pushed the pile back toward her and the coins finally toppled over onto the counter. By now there were raised eyes and foot tapping everywhere Yvonne looked.

'I'd better put something back then, I suppose.' The lady wasn't going to be quick about it, everyone could tell as much, and the shop assistant was already looking for his next customer, when –

Yvonne placed her fifty-pence piece on the counter in front of the lady and felt pleased that the shop assistant on closer inspection had bad acne; she couldn't think of anyone who deserved it more. When she said bad acne, she meant BAD acne; he had three blackheads the size of Walnut Whips on his chin and they were all about ready to explode their vanilla cream centre.

Glaring at Yvonne as if she were one of the slithery replica snakes they sold, the shop assistant was about to tell her to take the coin back, that this was not allowed, that it was cheating, but she beat him to it.

'You dropped it,' she told the lady, who shakily inspected the coin to make sure that it was real. Some things she could do, like feel hurt and injured by other people's treatment of her, but others she could not; like express her gratitude face to face due to the fact that she was unable to look up.

'Bless you, sweetheart. It's good to see that there's some honest folk left in the world.' She would have said more, but the shop assistant rushed everything through the till and her items were packed and thrust into her hands before she knew it.

'Your mother would be so proud,' the old lady told her,

before shuffling towards the heavy exit door that nobody held open for her.

After dutifully returning the candy necklace to the sweet section, Yvonne lingered in the store for as long as possible, because she did not want to bump into the little old lady outside. She did not want to witness her despair and humiliation, or her gratitude, which would have been even harder to bear. It was too much for someone like Yvonne, who took home the world's loneliness, sadness and dejection as if it were a stray kitten found in a sack by the roadside. Nor could she get out of her head the woman's words, 'Your mother would be so proud,' because deep down she suspected that her mother felt quite the opposite.

It wasn't that the old lady reminded her in any way of her mother, but Yvonne somehow felt that she had let them both down by not doing more. She could have shown more loyalty to her mother. She could have held open the door for the old woman. She knew this. Her mother knew this. Even the little old lady had known this. But they had honoured the little kindness she had been prepared to give and protected her from any disappointment they felt.

That's why what her mother was saying to them now actually meant something else entirely. She was sure of it.

'For just a little while, then.' Hazel was agreeing to Vee's request to go off and play. 'But you must stay together. No going off on your own,' she warned, in her serious voice, the one that caused Phillip's tongue to hang out when he thought nobody was looking. Then she'd tugged out a cobweb from her hair, turned her back on them and gone back inside the beach hut, her shoulders suddenly stiff like a mountain ledge, whereas moments ago they'd been soft and round like a heart-shaped pillow. A few seconds later, Yvonne heard the sound of a sweeping brush scraping the wooden floor. It sounded lonely to her ears, as if it missed the company of other sweeping brushes.

Intuitively guessing that her mother felt disheartened by their lack of enthusiasm for cleaning out the beach hut – Yvonne had to admit they had been less keen than the most reluctant donkey on the beach, forced into giving spoilt children like her and Vee rides on its sunken back – she wished too late that she'd had the courage to brave the spiders and Vee and stay behind. But, as always, her sister was there beside her, prompting her to do whatever it was she wanted and not caring a jot for anybody else's feelings.

'Let's race, Vonnie,' Vee squealed, grabbing hold of her hand and tugging her toward the beach.

And so they'd ran, as only the young could, tripping and laughing all the way down to the sea. But even when there was so much fun to be had, Yvonne still remembered to glance over her shoulder, hoping for one last glimpse of her mother. She wasn't disappointed; there she was, standing outside the beach hut, holding up a hand to shade her eyes from the sun so that she could see them better.

Even from this far away, Yvonne could tell that her mother looked anxious, as if she might at any second call them back from the water. Wanting to reassure her, Yvonne waved merrily. 'See – we are fine,' she wanted to shout, for all the good it would do, because there was no way her mother would hear her from all the way out here. Just before being distracted by Vee kicking water in her face, she felt sure that her mother had been about to wave back or even call out to them. Perhaps she'd wanted to warn them of potential dangers lurking in the water – wasn't that what mothers were supposed to do? But in spite of the worry lines that appeared on her mother's face, she had gone back inside without saying anything and Yvonne had gone back to wading through foamy white breakers in order to trail after her troublesome sister. When she did catch up with her, she was going to make her pay for upsetting their mother. It wasn't often Yvonne lost her temper, but when she did, somebody usually got hurt BIG TIME.

* * *

NOT WANTING TO remember any further forward than this, Yvonne noticed that the sun had by now almost hit the deck. Citronella tea candles had been lit all around her, creating a flickering orange birdcage effect.

The insect repellent did nothing, however, to put off the mob of angry mosquitoes that descended on them – their insistent buzzing was a warning as they darted from one sister's flesh to another, testing their scent and waiting for the right moment to bite. Inside the coop, the pungent aroma of burnt sage and wet grass – smells synonymous with the cannabis plant – blended with the saltiness of the sea breeze whilst tidal waves spluttered exhaustedly, having completed a nightly raid on the beach, robbing it of its pebbles.

Yvonne swatted away a mosquito that had just landed on her bare ankle. 'You were so mean to me back then,' she told her sister. It wasn't an accusation; just a fact. The fact it came out of nowhere came as no surprise to Venetia.

'Says she. Phillip's little princess,' Vee scoffed, a can of beer in one hand, a joint in the other. Unfazed by the "flying bedbugs", she was sprawled out on a wooden steamer with a blanket wrapped around her.

Splat. Yvonne crushed one of the little critters. It left a black squid ink stain on her arm. Later there would be an itchy, volcano-shaped weal in its place. They had always been more attracted to her skin than anybody else's; she suspected they left Vee alone because of the cannabis smoke.

'It's only the females that bite. Did you know that? And they won't feed on just any old human blood, you know.'

'That's why they're not bothering me, right?' Vee teased, holding out her tattooed arms as a test.

'Before you say it, it has nothing to do with whether you're fat or thin. I read all about it. They need it for their eggs. That's why the blood has to be special.'

As soon as fresh buzzing was heard, they both froze, waiting to see if the marauding mosquito would land on Vee's exposed flesh. As it hovered like a helicopter over her gothic skin, Yvonne could have sworn that its hideously long tongue popped out for a taste before snottily turning up its antenna and promptly taking off again.

'I never did get a look in when you were around.' Vee tucked her arms back under the blanket and went back to being quiet and thoughtful.

Yvonne sighed hard. She knew she had been unkind when there'd been no need and now she felt bad about it. She had no choice but to suffer. It didn't look as if Vee was going to help her out any time soon. But what was she doing, rummaging around under that blanket? Anyone would think she was trying to escape from a zipped-up tent, like in the horror film Vee had once made her sit through, where the werewolf had slashed his way inside so that it could eat the lone female camper.

But in reality Vee had been retrieving a piece of crumpled-up newspaper from her jeans pocket and was now handing it over, her eyes meeting awkwardly with Yvonne's in the process.

One look was all it took for Yvonne to pounce on it – an old newspaper cutting with Roger's picture on it.

'Where did you get this?' Yvonne couldn't pretend to be anything other than gob-smacked. In fact, she was reeling from the discovery. Roger's – her father's – obituary, after all this time. Amazing.

'Read what it says there.' Vee stabbed an accusing finger at a certain paragraph, as if that alone condemned someone to being burnt alive.

Doing as she was told, Yvonne read on but, unlike Vee, was unable to make anything big out of it.

'So?'

'She killed him, Vonnie. Mum. I know she did.'

Yvonne's mouth hung open in amazement. Where the hell had that come from? She almost wanted to laugh out loud, thinking that this was some sort of wind-up, but then, seeing the loco look in her sister's eye, she knew she must stamp on this quickly before it got out of control.

'What on earth are you talking about? It was an accident. Everybody said so.' Yvonne pushed hard at her sister and gave her a nasty pinch with whatever skin she could grab hold of. But Vee wasn't having any of it and easily swatted her off, like she was the blood-sucking insect all of a sudden.

'She intended on killing me but she ended up killing Dad instead.' As soon as the damning words were out of her mouth, Vee started coughing and choking. If she didn't know better, she'd swear that her words were already after revenge.

Working herself into a right state, Vee then started to shake violently and her breathing took a sudden turn for the worse.

Gasping for breath, she grovelled in her pocket a second time and took out an asthma inhaler, but her jittery fingers could not grasp it long enough to bring it to her mouth.

Retrieving the inhaler from Vee's hand, Yvonne pressed it in between her lips, which were now climbing the colour chart to the brightest of blues. It was not the first time she had done this for her sister. She hoped it would not be the last.

'You must try and stay calm, Vee,' she shushed, stroking her damp hair; suddenly she had a livid temperature and her skin burned all over like molten lava. Acting quickly, Yvonne held her finger down on the release button and was reassured to hear a hissing sound fill the air as the gassy compound found its way into Vee's airways.

Within seconds of receiving her life-saving medication, Vee felt well enough to push her sister off and was soon squawking like a parrot that had to have the last word.

'Killing Dad, instead of me – that was the only accidental part,' she insisted, still intent on going on with her story.

But by now, all Yvonne cared about was seeing her sister's sick-bucket face turn a nice prawn-cocktail colour again and that she no longer squeaked like a plastic toy whenever she breathed.

'How many times have you been told to give up smoking?' she admonished, thinking what a mother hen she sounded and then found herself laughing with relief. Vee couldn't help join in too, although her laughter sounded unreal because her voice hadn't yet returned to normal. As it was, she sounded as crackly as a seashell held to somebody's ear. It wasn't until Yvonne plonked herself down next to Vee and forcibly brought her skeletal body into her arms – this time, she wasn't taking no for an answer – that she realised how upside down she felt herself, no doubt a result of the panic and fear brought on by her sister's sudden asthma attack.

They stayed wrapped up in the blanket and each other for one minute. Then two. Then three. They were sisters who hated each other. Together, they were poison. But deep down, when it really counted, they knew how to look out for each other.

'Do you have any idea what it was like never being the pretty one, never being the favourite?' Vee asked wretchedly, resting her head on Yvonne's reassuringly plump bosom that rose and fell, rose and fell, as soothing as whale-song.

Yvonne shook her head. 'No.' She wished it were otherwise, for she felt sorry for Vee, but she was glad they were back on familiar ground; this sort of talk was something she'd cut her teeth on.

'Knowing your own mother didn't – doesn't – love you?' Vee went on. Yvonne felt the gulp lodge in her sister's throat as if it were her own.

'She does, Vee. I'm sure of it.' Yvonne was not lying. Usually if she wished for something hard enough, it became real in the end. She was not the spoilt one for nothing.

But Vee shook her head. No way was she going to let her sister convince her otherwise. Not unless she had something bigger and better than that.

She did. Because Vee was forgetting something…

'You're her firstborn. Special,' Yvonne reminded her. It was hardly a surprise to either of them.

FROM HER POSITION at the lighthouse window, Hazel could see an orange glow hovering like a dragonfly over one of the beach huts on the sand below. Their beach hut, of course, it had to be, with her girls inside. Always, there was so much distance between them. They might only be a few lit candles away, but it was still too far out to reach over and blow out their flames, as she'd like to do.

In fact, she sometimes felt it would be easier if they were extinguished from her life altogether. She was growing tired of constantly being undermined and having her position as head of this family challenged. Once again, they had excluded her. Once again, they had shut her out. There were no prizes for guessing who was to blame… her eldest daughter as usual.

'Venetia.'

When would it stop, she wondered, this hatred and bitterness, the spite and jealousy that reared its ugly head whenever they crossed paths? Would this rivalry go on between them until one of them was dead? She might never have been a mumsy-type of parent, although she'd always done her best, but life had treated her unfairly, she felt. Look at the way Venetia was always on her case, looking over her shoulder and hoping to exploit any weakness she found. She was the metaphorical piece of apple that got stuck in your back teeth that you couldn't dislodge, no matter how hard your tongue pushed against it. Because of her, she'd been unable to form a proper relationship with anyone else – including Yvonne.

And then, all along, Venetia had the most off-putting ability of being able to see right through Hazel, laughing out loud at her pretensions of wanting to be classy and stylish. But what was so wrong in wanting to better oneself? she wanted to know. Certainly, with her around, Hazel had never been allowed to grow as a person; Venetia acted as a permanent reminder of her past, never letting her forget for one moment where she came from.

Well, if Venetia had never outgrown the hatred she'd felt for her on first sight, then the feeling was mutual, Hazel decided. What's more, she would no longer put up with having to fight for every scrap of time she wanted to spend with Yvonne and her granddaughter. You'd have to be mad not to want to be around Yvonne; every hour with her was like playing a game of skittles, enjoying a Mr Whippy with a flake or munching on a pineapple ring in batter. Yes indeed, it was impossible not to fall head over heels in love with the girl. Hazel could remember a time when even the travelling gypsies offered her a whole lot of cash in exchange for the laughing "little angel", whose smile was like the sun and whose "beauty couldn't be eaten with a spoon", whatever that meant.

'If there are no children, there is no luck,' one of them had told her. For a long time afterwards, Hazel had kept Yvonne under lock and key – just in case.

But, while there was no denying that Yvonne was extremely soft-hearted where any animal or other living thing was concerned, and could even be moved to tears by a plastic bag with a tear in it, she barely gave her mother a passing glance. It never seized to amaze Hazel that for all her goodness she could be so cold and indifferent when it suited her. It seemed to her she had been poorly repaid for all the love, time and patience she'd invested in her youngest daughter at the expense of the eldest. You only had to look at the way Yvonne preferred her sister to anybody else, even though Venetia had bullied her mercilessly throughout most of her young life. Hazel had fought so hard to keep some distance between the two of them, trying to keep them apart as much as possible so that Yvonne wouldn't get hurt and land up in the hospital yet again. But did anyone thank her for it?

Venetia might have been born wanting to hurt people, but all she'd ever got in return for protecting Yvonne was the odd piece of kindness thrown her way while Venetia got all the adulation and loyalty. Sometimes the realisation made Hazel feel physically sick, making her want to lie down on the floor and moan like a drunken whore living in a shop window.

That reminded her of the time she had actually been called a whore and not one of her children or even her husband had come running to defend her. Truthfully, though, the name-calling hadn't upset her as much as it should; after all, she hadn't hesitated in stealing Phillip from his first wife. Nor did she feel any regret afterwards, not even when she saw for herself the devastation felt by the broken family left behind.

It was hardly her fault that his plain fat wife had been foolish enough to invest all her time, money and efforts in the house and children, letting herself go in the process. This had been a terrible mistake, considering how likely divorce was for a first wife, who usually ended up half the woman she had once been, with only half the proceeds from a house to show for her many sacrifices. As such, wasting sympathy on such women was alien to Hazel.

Besides, their need of Phillip had been greater than anybody else's. She could hardly be blamed for finding herself widowed at a very young age, with two fatherless children to raise; that's why it had been so important for Phillip to choose her over his other family. She had worked hard to see he had. That was another thing she had done for her thankless children – got them a father and a good provider to boot, even if she did have to steal him from somebody else. Disappointingly, Phillip hadn't turned out to be man enough in the end not to hold it against her, and may even have stopped loving her because of it. But never Yvonne, whom he loved more than his own biological offspring, who were in his own words, "embarrassingly overweight, molly-coddled and too much like their mother".

Hazel didn't believe other parents when they said they didn't have favourites. She was convinced they were liars; she knew more than most how impossible it was to love two children the same. She would even go as far as to say it was impossible to do anything *but* favour one particular child and despise any other for getting in the way of that love.

No doubt Venetia was doing exactly that right now – getting in the way of what Hazel wanted, plotting against her and filling Yvonne's head with untruths, hoping to turn her against her own mother.

Aware that time was running out for all of them, Hazel glanced at the clock, realising that they were not coming back any time soon. No doubt they had forgotten her the minute they escaped through the door. When had she ever been able to stop them running off to the beach together? It was unlikely that they'd be back before the early hours.

Still, she had spent such a long time *not* being their mother, a few more hours wouldn't hurt, she supposed. She couldn't even remember a time when something or someone hadn't tried coming between her and her children. At first it had been Roger, then Phillip, and now it was –

'Venetia.'

Who was she kidding? It had always been Venetia. But Hazel was determined that she would not be beaten by her. From tomorrow, she meant to take back control, even if that meant exposing Venetia's true colours to her sister. She would not allow Venetia to push her out of Yvonne and Una's lives; nor would she allow Yvonne to keep on deserting her whenever she felt like it. She was not a whim to be pushed aside like a dress that was no longer fashionable.

The way Hazel saw it, Yvonne was her last chance of being taken for the good, worthy person she craved to be, so she couldn't afford to fail. She must stay positive – upbeat, even – because she wasn't going to let anything get in the way of her becoming a good mother in the eyes of the world. If she could say she loved at least one of her children and did good by them, then that was as good as loving oneself... and almost as good as being loved back. Tomorrow marked the last day of their long weekend together and ultimately her last chance at redemption. Woe behold anyone caught trying to spoil it for her.

Meanwhile, tonight was to be a sad night. She'd already made up her mind about that, feeling as she did that she was spending too many nights alone in front of her bedroom window. Knowing that she wouldn't settle until her daughters were back in the lighthouse – home, where they belonged – she must, in the meantime, do things to make her feel less depressed and abandoned. This generally involved compulsive little rituals she found as reassuring as being driven in a smart car by a handsome man in an expensive suit – such as loosening her right pearl earring first and then the left, always in that order; or folding a neat triangle in the toilet roll whenever she went into the en-suite bathroom; or counting the number of perfume bottles on the vanity unit that were still more than half full. Seeing a near-empty bottle was never good news, because Hazel hated running out of anything and the threat of it was enough to make her over-anxious.

That's why she kept replacement items for important everyday items she could not live without, such as her favourite shade of Chanel lipstick, her Dior perfume, Floris of London's Seringa bath essence, Clinique's uplifting firming skincare products, Molton Brown shampoo and conditioning sets and Norfolk lavender bath salts, to name but a few. But the list wasn't just confined to beauty products – she also had in reserve jars of capers and Kalamata olives, Gentleman's Relish, Andalusian olive oil, Portuguese sardines and packets of English salted butter – all favourite supper items she never actually got around to snacking on. The trouble was, she sometimes got carried away by her phobia and ended up with surplus stock, which inevitably had to be thrown away. But her obsession would go on regardless, for she must have a reserve no matter what. She simply could not be left empty-handed, with nothing... the thought was too terrifying.

It was a shame one couldn't have children in reserve for nights such as these, she thought. Nicer, brighter, more considerate children who were much kinder to their parents and who wouldn't have left her alone.

Entertained by the idea, Hazel allowed herself an indulgent smile as she slipped her earrings into the palm of her hand and walked over to the red and cream suede jewellery box that had pride of place on the bedside table, even though she hated it; she had expressed how vulgar she thought it was the same day Phillip insisted on buying it for her. But what did she care if it cost him what would be the equivalent of £595 today? If she'd considered it cheap and nasty, what had that said about the way he viewed her?

She felt for the key hidden inside the cream lining, as she did every night of her life – another of her addictive little customs – for she always enjoyed the practice of putting her jewellery to bed. Like precious babies wrapped in a blanket, she would kiss each item goodnight before closing the lid. Her Astley Clark rose-gold ring always went in a certain place, as did the white-gold Tiffany heart tag bracelet, the Boodles diamond blossom pendent, the Theo Fennell humming bird earrings, the yellow gold green rainforest ring and the Swarovski pearl necklace. All things she loved to take out and handle when no one else was around; they never murmured in protest or resisted her hands the way her children did.

But the key wasn't in its usual place. It was still inside the lining, that much was true, but it had been put back much further, where it would have rubbed against the clasp belonging to the pearl necklace. Nobody but Hazel could have detected the slight variance and yet there was no question of her being mistaken. Earlier today, somebody had been in her room. They had dared handle her key, the key that until now had only ever known her own soft touch.

For a fleeting second, she knew what it was like to feel true fear. The last time she had been this scared was when she ended up on the wrong side of town on a rundown council estate, where grubby children played outside and already looked like hardened criminals capable of assault, theft or – dare she say it – even rape.

Then, her eyes narrowing, she looked from the key in her hand to the cream armoire in the corner of the room and wasted no further time worrying whether that same person had discovered what the key was for, because it was obvious that they knew everything by now. Or thought they did.

During those long years on her own, when her daughters were still refusing to have anything to do with her because of what she had done, she'd occupied her mind by reading everything she could get her hands on, providing that it was considered appropriate reading material for her age and sex. On a daily basis she had devoured books on gardening and growing vegetables, yoga, Greek mythology, gourmet cooking, and, it went without saying, *all* the English classics, particularly anything by the Brontë sisters or Jane Austen. In fact, during her academic stage she'd even gone on to gain a 1:1 in English Literature from the Open University and mastered Microsoft Office as well as the internet. But once she realised she wasn't as stupid or ignorant as the men in her life had led her to believe, and was in fact as clever as the next person, the thirst for education somehow lost its appeal. But one quote she did remember from this time – which was entirely appropriate to the situation she now found herself in – was by George Bernard Shaw, who'd once said, 'If you cannot get rid of the skeleton in the closet, you'd best teach it to dance.'

Because of course it was obvious to her who had invaded her space, and whilst she couldn't help grudgingly admire their audacity, she knew she would take great delight in seeing them "dance".

But then, thinking of the ballerina jewellery box and the secrets waiting to pop out as soon as the lid opened, she wondered if the interfering little minx had been brave enough to poke her nose into the darkest corners of their family history, or if she had saved the box for later, like she would an unexpected birthday present, not wanting to spoil the surprise.

Knowing her eldest daughter as she did, Hazel suspected that the latter was probably true in her case, and that meant her secret was still safe – *their* secret, she corrected herself – for now. This meant she would be able to sleep easy in her bed tonight, but she doubted if the same could be said of her troubled offspring.

VENETIA HAD NEVER been able to pass her mother's bedroom door without wanting to know what was going on behind it, and tonight was no exception. No matter that it must be three or four o'clock in the morning and that she was as drunk and as high as she'd ever been.

In fact, the short walk from one end of the landing to the other seemed to be taking forever, as if she was deliberately moving in slow motion, trying to prolong the agony of never knowing anything about the woman who was supposed to be her mother. Beer sloshed and spilled from the glass bottle she was carrying onto the floor; she'd long since given up trying to guide it to her thirsty cracked lips, if indeed they still belonged on her face. She might have lost them coming up the stairs for all she knew; she didn't feel real right now and she wasn't at all convinced that she could lay the entire blame for that on booze and weed.

Using the wall for support, she edged closer to the ornate oak door with the glass door knob that captured your reflection whether you wanted it to or not, and couldn't ignore how cold and moist the plaster was against her shaky fingers. The building had no heartbeat, no warmth – and never had, she feared. Her mother's bedroom happened to be on the coldest of all the floors.

Each time Vee stopped to rest, with her spiky back flat against the wall, she closed her eyes wearily and fought off the desire to sleep standing up. Then, forcing herself to reach out a hand that pulsed with ugly blue veins, as if a map of the London underground was going on under her skin, she was about to grope for the doorknob when she heard a sound come from within.

Holding her breath for far longer than was good for her, she listened again. There it was. She knew she'd been right the first time. It was the muffled sound of her mother weeping.

Convinced that her blood was moving so slowly around her body because it was terrified of reaching her own heart, Vee was incapable of doing anything other than listen.

'What have I done? God forgive me. What have I done?' her mother whimpered pitifully, in between long, drawn-out sobs that would have melted the hardest of hangmen's hearts.

Knowing she would not be able to move away from the door without looking through the keyhole, Vee felt that she must witness her mother's misery for herself, to know it was real.

Hearing it was a very poor second. In spite of her drunkenness, she was very much aware that nothing good ever came of doing what she was about to do. She'd watched enough scary movies to know that.

Crouching down till she resembled a small child struggling to tie its own laces, Vee lost herself to a wave of drunkenness that saw her sway dangerously from side to side. Forgetting where she was for a moment, she had to fight hard to regain her full senses. This was not the time to fantasise about Carly the spray tanner, wearing a cut-a-way swimsuit on Hunstanton beach, she reasoned.

It was perhaps due to her drunkenness that she also found the distorted image of her reflection in the glass doorknob completely hysterical. It reminded her of one of those fun-house mirror shows, where everybody – including the beautiful – was made to look ugly and deformed. Peering more closely at her upside-down reflection, she could only identify as belonging to herself one inflamed nostril and part of a translucent eyelid that appeared as paper thin as a butterfly's wing.

She was about to put her eye to the chilly grey metal of the keyhole to peer inside when she felt a tremendous thud vibrate through the door, which startled her so much that she ended up falling backwards in a heap against the opposite wall. Picking herself up quickly, as if her life depended on it, Vee became aware of two things at once. One; her mother had stopped crying. Two; it was her body that had fallen against the other side of the door. There was no other explanation. Unless…

But Vee stopped herself right there. She'd already been accused once tonight by her sister of being absurd and having far-fetched and fanciful ideas and she wasn't going to let that happen again. So, deciding it didn't matter what her mother might be guilty of, there was no fucking way she was going to leave her injured or even, God forbid, seriously hurt on the other side of that door.

Striding purposefully toward it, she gave the doorknob a good rattle in her hand, but of course it would not turn. Next, she rapped on the door – softly at first, and then more insistently.

'Mum? Are you alright? It's me, Venetia. I thought I heard something.' She listened for a response but all that reached her spinning ears was an eerie, floating silence that seemed reconciled to how haunting and menacing it actually was, as it seeped through the brickwork, like a strange fog made up of bad people's breath.

Trying not to be afraid, Vee bent down to peer once more through the keyhole, but this time she didn't get anywhere close to seeing her despised reflection in the glass – it was already filled with a blackness that loomed behind her, a shadow that was as instantly recognisable as it was terrifying.

One minute it was there and then it was gone. 'Venetia…' Its voice sashayed like an eel up the darkened concrete stairwell to the tower above. 'Venetia,' it implored again, pausing on the stairs like a creature stuck in a bog as it waited for her to catch up. Knowing she had no choice but to follow, Vee traipsed spellbound after it.

HAZEL'S EYES GREW wider as she peered through the misty glass of her bedroom window at the black, dream-stealing waves that crashed against the shore below, where they constantly invaded the sandy coves and inlets, who, like her, were never left in peace.

She had brushed her blonde hair one hundred times with the silver paddle brush until it gleamed like light oak, brushed her teeth for a full three minutes before rinsing and dabbed a spot of Dior perfume on both wrists before slipping on a soft, grey, satin negligee that clung to her curves in exactly the same way quality beer would a pint glass. Now she was watching a distressed boat out at sea.

She was pretty sure that there was just one man on board. Wearing a reflective lifejacket and a waterproof wind-breaker that clung to his body in an almost indecent way, he clung onto the side of the boat as it bounced up and down in the waves. Unshaven, haggard and soaked to the skin, he was clearly exhausted. Hazel guessed he must already have spent hours alone at sea. If a rescue boat didn't arrive soon, he would lose all hope and give up the will to live, she deduced expertly.

Hazel wished there was something she could do to help the solitary sailor, but she had only just finished applying a pearl polish to her fingernails and didn't want to smudge them by picking up the phone. Besides, she was used to this particular man, whose gold tooth glistened on the ocean like a searchlight, turning up in the most unwanted of ways to disturb her.

'Hazel. Hazel,' he kept calling, through a torrent of sea spray, his mouth opening and closing like a sinkhole in the distance. Hazel couldn't help thinking how small he looked out there, like the smallest island on a world map, and the thought made her smile.

Pressing a flexed, rigid finger on the glass, and reflecting on how it looked as sharp and sleek as a pencil, she drew a circle in the fogged-up glass and as it went around, so did the boat. As she twirled her finger into a faster loop, the boat got caught up in the turmoil she'd created and started spinning faster.

'Help me, Hazel. Help me.' His calls grew fainter and fainter as finally the boat got swallowed up by the heartless ocean and he disappeared beneath the water, along with his twelve-foot vessel.

AT THE TOP of the tower, there were shadows everywhere. The smoky silhouettes even bounced their own shadows back onto the white walls so that Venetia hardly knew how to identify the one that really mattered. But all the same, she felt its presence all around her. She knew its smell, the texture of its hair and could guess exactly where the top of its head and soles of its feet would be if she reached out and groped for it in the blackness.

'Is it really you?' She found her voice at last and hardly recognized its high-pitched, frightened tone.

Like a sedate priest shuffling along a corridor, one of the shadows flitted across the room in front of her, causing her to move suddenly and drop the beer bottle she'd forgotten was still in her hand. Miraculously, it did not break. Instead, it started twirling around on the concrete floor. Her name whistled through the open glass spout as it picked up speed and started spinning faster and faster, faster and faster.

Then, all at once, the shadows vanished from the walls and Vee automatically sensed that IT too had been cast out of the tower along with them. At the same time, the beer bottle came to an abrupt stop on the floor in front of her.

She found she wanted to move but couldn't. Wanted to scream but couldn't. The only other thing she became aware of, besides the fear that had crept into her bones, was the three pairs of eyes glaring ominously at her from a nest under a concrete pillar. Having never seen a family of barn owls before, Vee was appalled to see a fourth owl sprawled out dead at the furthest end of the nest, well away from the others, its ghostlike face turned toward her, its eyes gouged out and consumed, with a broken wing pointing accusingly in her direction.

Then, each of the owls shook out its feathers and began hooting at her in a wild disarranged way. And all Vee could think was, *An owl heard hooting at night always results in the death of a child*. She fled from the tower, stumbling down its concrete steps as fast as her flimsy legs would take her.

LATER THAT NIGHT, trapped somewhere between sleep and consciousness, Venetia tossed and turned like an out-of-control concrete mixer, wrapping the sheets so tightly around her that she resembled a mummified corpse.

In her nightmare world she was a little girl again, back in the bathroom of the Cox family home, reliving a time and place she'd mislaid rather than simply forgotten, like a lost sock found in the rubber trim on the washing machine door.

During her night terrors, she was somehow able to recollect the smallest and most inconsequential memories from her childhood. In this case, she vividly remembered that the normally pristine bathroom sink had been full of bottles of medicine and packets of tablets. Her mother had her back to her, ripping open foil pill packets with her teeth and manically flushing the contents down the toilet. Lined up on the windowsill was a row of asthma inhalers, identical to the ones Venetia used herself, and her mother was emptying them one by one, holding her finger down on the release button until the gassy compound was extinguished, creating a halo of mist through which Vee could clearly see her smiling.

'Where is Daddy?' Since she'd first learnt to talk, there had only been one question on her mind; it must have driven her mother mad. But, judging by the wild, unhinged expression in

222

her mother's eyes and the suggestion of laughter that threatened to tumble out any second, perhaps she already was.

Ever since she'd been born, Vee had been made aware that her mother didn't have any time for her. Didn't like her. Never had. The feeling was mutual.

Much of this was due to her being an August baby, she felt; or at least that's what her teachers used as an excuse for her doing badly at school. Not only did they blame her backwardness on being one of the youngest pupils in her class, but considered her terribly stunted, almost retarded for her age – a detail her mother had never forgiven her for. As if determined to rub her mother up the wrong way, she had remained on the small side right up until adulthood, never outgrowing her sister as she was supposed to, being the eldest. All of this had come about because she'd been born prematurely, had very nearly died when her mother could not be bothered to push down anymore and only survived when the doctors performed an emergency caesarean. Her mother had been trying to asphyxiate her long before she was born and the asthma she'd suffered from all her life was due to her having arrived a sickly, puny little thing with weak lungs.

As a result, Vee felt that her mother had never been able to look at her properly, at least not without glancing quickly away again. There was always too much injured disappointment in her eyes and Vee, as always, was the cause of it.

As she was in the dream. 'Go back to bed,' her mother warned, turning her back on her as if she didn't matter, rejecting her all over again, while she carried on releasing the last of the life-saving powder.

'You shouldn't be doing that.' Too clever for her own good, despite what the teachers said, Vee realised that whatever her mother was doing could also mean trouble for her. She didn't like the idea of that one little bit.

But then, not knowing how to stop her mother from doing what she was doing or understanding quite why it was so important that she MUST stop, her eyes filled with desperate tears and her heart with a dread that she was still too young to comprehend, but she knew it centred on her father's anger and disapproval and ultimately his withdrawal of affection. It was the danger of this – and more – happening that resulted in her wetting herself, right there on the spot.

The shame of bedwetting was already deeply embedded in Vee's mind, due to having witnessed her mother crossly throwing back the bedclothes and pulling horror-stricken faces as each new damp spot on the mattress was revealed, but this was far worse. This was an experience she couldn't leave behind in childhood, like other embarrassing clangers, such as when she'd choked on beetroot and had to be held upside down while someone whacked her on the back, or the time she fell into a patch of stinging nettles and had to be smothered in calamine lotion for a whole week, which made her resemble a hairless baby rat.

It was almost a relief when her mother sniffed through her nose the way she did whenever something disgusted her and waved a finger at her, ordering her to go back to bed. Vee didn't need telling again, that was for sure, and the burning shame lent a turbo boost of cartoonish speed to her graceless little legs as she sped upstairs to hide. From who, she couldn't quite remember.

It was at this point that her dream decided to take her in another direction entirely, with both Mr Naughty and Wuffa metamorphosing into real-life monsters, alternatively grabbing and sucking her into the walls of the lighthouse or carrying her off in a set of giant slobbering jaws down the cliff edge into the sea beyond. Next, regular as clockwork, came the headless "boy king", who had been shot so many times with arrows he looked like a game of Ker-Plunk and who kept plucking out the blood-tipped arrows from his body while crying for his lost head.

Such was the bizarre nature of her dream that she was then transported into a shitty owl's nest, talon-deep in regurgitated mice bones, where she was the biggest of a pair of owlets intent on pushing aside and pecking to death her smaller weaker sibling. She might have been a cute cloud of white fluff but she was deadly too, justifying her brutality as a way of ensuring her own survival and punishing her good-for-nothing parents for failing to supply the nest with enough food.

Just as she was about to take another chunk out of her cowering sibling or perhaps even push her out of the nest for good, the dream ended and Vee woke up, her wide predatory eyes blinking ten to the dozen, just like an owl who'd been disturbed out of its slumber.

SUNDAY

Slowly taking in the fact that sunlight was leaking through the curtains like ribbons of runny egg you wanted to dip a soldier of soft bread into, Venetia realised two things at once – one, it was morning and two, the curtain fabric was unfamiliar. Where the hell was she?

Amazed to discover that she was in the duck-egg, toile-de-jouy bedroom – her mother's pride and joy and, as such, a place she had never been allowed to sleep before – she did not have time to admire the soft fabrics and decorative cupids that adorned the walls. She was immediately on her feet, throwing back the satin bedcover and inspecting the sheets. Venetia was relieved to find that there was not a damp patch in sight – she couldn't imagine what her mother might have said, had she made the mistake of wetting the bed at her age – and in this bed, of all places. No doubt she'd want to kill her.

At first a little groggy and unable to make head or tail of most of her nightmare, the one thing Vee *was* sure of was the chilling fact that her mother had, that day, planned on killing her but ended up accidentally killing her father instead. It was doubly hard to take, knowing that her mother hated her enough to do away with her, leaving her to suffer an unimaginably slow death, *and* that she was inadvertently responsible for her father's death when things had gone wrong – which they clearly had. It was just as she'd told Yvonne. 'She intended killing me by taking away my medication but ended up killing Dad instead.' Didn't all the evidence point to that poisonous conclusion?

Irritably throwing herself face-down on the tangled bed, Vee stared at a crack on the ceiling that was probably as old as she was and only just stopped herself from debating whether "ceiling" was a feminine or masculine noun in French before realising that she had gone to bed fully clothed.

In hindsight, she had probably exposed too much of herself last night anyway. Being reminded of how easily Yvonne was able to get her to open up like a can of pilchards that couldn't wait to be unravelled hurt like hell.

Although it had felt right at the time, she now hated the idea of having been vulnerable and undressed, so to speak, in front of her sister, revealing her layers of angst and wearing her animosity as if it were her bra and pants, for all to see. She had always been far more comfortable in her own surly, resentful skin, attacking other people before they could attack her, like a grumpy dog that hadn't been taken for a walk in a while. Vee didn't make excuses for herself. That's just how she was made. Besides, if she wasn't gobbing off at the world, who the fuck was she?

And, more importantly, why the fuck wasn't anyone listening to a word she said, no matter how loud she shouted? Usually she could get Yvonne to do anything she wanted, but her two-faced sister was standing her ground for once and refusing to hear a word said against their mother. She wondered if she would see things differently if she let her in on a few home truths – secrets that didn't show her mother in a very good light. But, and it was a big but, if she did that – if she told Yvonne EVERYTHING – she wouldn't come out of it very favourably either.

Either way, despite Yvonne's lack of support, Vee remembered in detail that day in the bathroom and what her mother had done. There was nothing anybody could do about it, no way of unpicking her memory like a badly-knitted scarf, even if she wanted to. Was it only yesterday she'd felt her father close to her, whispering secrets in her ear as if she were a little girl again? Even without his help, she would have been clever enough to work this out for herself. Her mother may have made the mistake of underestimating her, but at what cost, Vee wondered, and did that mean she had finally got the upper hand over her? The thought of witnessing her mother's downfall after all these years caused an amused tugging at the corners of her mouth and a twinkle of merriment in her eyes that had nothing to do with last night's giggle weed and more to do with the way she wanted to cackle out loud, like a hen straining to lay a double-yolk egg.

If her overindulgence in the wacky backy had contributed to her being needy and soft with her sister on the beach last night, she was going to make sure it never happened again. After all, she was the eldest: the toughest, the firstborn – for what it was worth – and as such it was up to her to lead, to set the right example.

As the eldest, she'd like to go into the corridor right now and box her younger sister's ears for all the fuss she was making. By the sound of it, Yvonne was crashing into walls as if she had just stumbled out of a horror movie and was being chased by demons. On that thought, Vee couldn't get the image of her sister in a plunging white nightgown bearing two bloody bite marks on her neck and being hunted down by Count Dracula out of her head.

'Where are you? Can you answer me?' Yvonne called out

spookily. 'Are you in there?' She jangled the doorknob to the room which, disturbingly, Vee couldn't even remember locking.

'What the hell is going on out there?' Vee demanded, finally swinging her emaciated legs off the bed.

'It's Una. She's gone. Disappeared. I can't find her anywhere,' Yvonne bawled back, her voice echoing, as if it came from inside the walls of the tower – a thought that made Vee shudder involuntarily.

So many spiteful thoughts entered Vee's head before she even made it to the door, she couldn't keep up with the pace of her own hateful mind. First off, she reminded herself that this was no sweet little Miss Pears they were talking about; her niece was more like Linda Blair from *The Exorcist*, with her rolling eyeballs and snarling grin. All right, so far she hadn't seen her do a 380-degree turn of the head, but there was still time… And, secondly, if the Furball really was missing, which she very much doubted, Vee felt that it wouldn't necessarily be such a bad thing.

SO MUCH HAD happened since waking up to find Una missing, Yvonne could now barely remember what her own disturbing dream had been about, but she sensed it had something to do with playing on the beach with her sister; of them twirling each other around on the sand until one of them grew dizzy and spun out of control.

They had laughed a lot, she recalled, but the day had ended badly, with them getting lost, separated from each other. Remembering how frightened she'd been at finding herself alone, she had been even more terrified to see the sun setting on the sand, knowing it would soon be dark and that she wasn't meant to be on her own.

Like Una wasn't meant to be on her own.

Yvonne had woken up from one nightmare and plunged headfirst into another; this was actually happening. Her daughter was missing. What on earth could have happened to her? Where was she? For all she knew, somebody could have sneaked in during the night and kidnapped her. Surely she hadn't just wandered off on her own – a more innocent option – like she once had? She could be on the beach right now, lost and terrified, crying for her mother. The thought was unbearable.

She must calm down. She must think. Ever since springing out of bed this morning, woken by a premonition that something was wrong, she had been behaving like a whirlwind. All she could think was, *My daughter's bed is empty. My daughter's bed is empty.* The eiderdown on the bed that matched her own was neatly folded in place, as if Una had never laid her head there.

But in the early hours of this morning, when the sisters had crept in on tippy-toes so as not to disturb their mother, she had checked on her then and she'd been absolutely fine. In fact, Yvonne had gazed in awe at the beautiful child she had created, thanking her lucky stars over and over again for the gift of her. Never did a day go by when she wasn't grateful for every second spent with the sleepy-headed little angel who slept on her back, no matter how many times Yvonne put her on her side. Sometimes Yvonne would sit by the bed, not wanting to scare her should she wake, but drink her in all the same, stealing her breath from her like a cat would a baby in a pram. It felt so good being part of her daughter's world. Her own reasons for motherhood were best not expressed out loud, for they weren't complimentary, either to herself or her mother. She hadn't been a perfect daughter anymore than – Yvonne stopped herself before it hurt to remember.

But until coming here, to the lighthouse, she had never known

Una do anything like this. She had never even wandered off in the shopping centre like other kiddies did, to stick a sly finger in the pick n mix or linger alongside a Thomas the Tank engine ride that had countless children crawling over it. Nor had she once thrown a strop when she didn't get her own way – like the time she'd wanted to give her Barbie bicycle to the gypsy children whose caravan was parked on a scrap of wasteland near their home. Even when Yvonne reminded Una how many months it had taken her to save for that bike, which was supposed to be a very special Christmas present, she'd still wanted them to have it. When Yvonne had refused to budge, it had been left to rust in a shed out back, acting as an expensive reminder that her daughter's generosity outweighed her own. But when money was tight and you were a single parent relying on state benefits and looked down on as scum by the rest of the working majority because of it, it was no wonder that her hard-heartedness had got the better of her.

Until coming here, Una had never been anything other than a good girl, obedient, kind and gentle… all the things she most cherished about her. She had to find her. *Had* to. Then they would leave here and never come back – and she would polish that bloody bike until it shone like new, and together they would march it down to the gypsy children with the wide eyes, grubby clothing and starved smiles.

After searching under beds and in wardrobes and checking in the airing cupboard on the landing where the gurgling water tank lived – the one her and Vee used to think came to life at night, like the tin man from *The Wizard Of Oz*, to guard the hallways and landings – she decided to enlist Vee's help. Funny that she should think of Vee first, before her own mother, when she needed help, but her mother slept heavily. 'Like a vampiress,' Vee used to giggle whenever they peeked into her room to spy on her. Once they'd even tried holding a mirror over her mother's face to check for a reflection, but they had bottled it when she grumbled aloud in her sleep – something about a "skeleton", she seemed to recollect.

But that didn't matter now. All that mattered was finding her daughter and getting the hell out of here. Maybe, just maybe, she'd take her long-suffering sister with her. *If* she helped find Una, that is.

Having always felt guilty where her sister was concerned, Yvonne had gone out of her way to make it up to her over the years, allowing herself to be bullied in the process and accepting the bites, scratches and bruises inflicted on her out of jealousy for being "everybody's favourite". Only she knew the truth; that of the two of them, she was in fact the strongest, and truly independent of their mother, whereas Vee was stuck in a sulky adolescent stage of childhood – on the one hand stamping her feet and demanding her mother's love, and on the other acting hard as nails and pushing her away, all the while pretending to hate her, when nothing could be further from the truth.

How she wished things could have been different for Vee – for all of them, in fact; her mother's obvious preference for her had always been unwelcome and she resented the way that she showered every ounce of love on her when Vee went without. If she could do one thing for her sister, she would prove to her she *was* loveable deep down and deserving of any normal mother's love. There was still a place in her heart for her mother, and sometimes pity for her overwhelmed her, but on the whole she had learnt to distance herself; she had taken a step back from her mother's clingy, claustrophobic adoration and drew closer to her sister instead. Together they had been "Team Cox", a nickname Yvonne hated, but one Vee refused to change. Regardless, they were a united front, capable of running rings around the most astute of adults and a formidable "opposition" to their mother's controlling dominance.

Back then, she might have despised her mother, and with good reason. But since having Una and discovering for herself just how difficult parenting could be, she probably judged her less harshly than before, particularly when she herself couldn't imagine loving another child anywhere near as much as Una. Nor would she want anyone else to come between them and spoil what they had. Whilst understanding her mother's motives a little better now that she was a mother herself, especially when she considered how she often pretended to favour Vee in a pathetic pretence of making them feel equal, she still couldn't be excused for what she had done to Vee – nor for blatantly trying to cause a rift between her and her sister, who grew closer anyway, just to spite her.

This might not be the time and place to make plans for her screwed-up sister, but perhaps soon the three of them could go somewhere they could breathe freely for once, without the threat of their mother peering hawk-like over their shoulders. Yes. That's what she would do: feed her sister up a bit and see that she got some sleep for a change. Yvonne was convinced that a little spoiling was all Vee needed to feel normal again and put a stop to the wild accusations of last night.

But all that would happen later. For now, she must, simply MUST, insist on Vee helping her. Without her sister, she didn't think she'd be able to do this.

HAVING BRAVED THEIR mother's displeasure (she hated being woken early) by tapping on her door and even daring to try the door handle, which was locked, Venetia and Yvonne had gone downstairs, where they found the dog.

Having already made a mess of the kitchen door in his attempts to escape, Laddy had left a pile of shredded wood and sick piled up in front of him and was proudly wagging his tale, as if he deserved a bone for his trouble. But when Yvonne tried to pull him away from the door, he started howling and was right back at it, trying to dig his way out before she could do anything about it. It went without saying that Vee did not go anywhere near the dog. Vee did not touch the dog. Vee did not even *look* at the dog. It was already distressed enough without her putting its back up.

Yvonne said what they were both thinking.

'She wouldn't have left him behind.'

WITHIN TWENTY MINUTES of leaving the lighthouse, they had covered the bus shelter, the public toilets and the Cliff Top Café and Shop, where they used to buy their Walls ice creams and lollies. In fact, they had searched everywhere a child might hide and were now speeding along the North Beach in Venetia's beat-up Suzuki.

'She's got to be at the beach hut. We should have gone there first.' Yvonne forced herself to smile, because if she wished hard enough for it to be true then it would happen.

Vee hoped so too. It wasn't as if she was having a change of heart about her niece, but seeing her sister heart-broken like this was not good, so the sooner the kid was found the better. Putting her foot down on the accelerator, Vee didn't want to think about what it would mean for all of them if it turned out that Una *wasn't* at the beach hut.

This couldn't happen again. It just couldn't.

IF THE CHILD didn't like her anymore, then she no longer

liked the child. It was as easy as that for Hazel to brush off the affection she'd previously felt for her granddaughter, on account of no longer being idolised or admired by her, the loss of which she couldn't and wouldn't recover from.

From her position in the queue by the sea dragon rollercoaster ride, everywhere Hazel looked, people were laughing and having fun – everyone except her granddaughter. Instead, Una scowled at the teenage girls with their bare brown bellies as they squeezed past her onto the roulette ride. When she wasn't pulling faces at them, she was frowning at the boisterous older boys, being bounced to high heaven on the grasshopper ride, some laughing until they looked as if they were about to throw up.

Hazel would have thought that the child would have been pleased to spend time alone with her grandmother; unlike other children here on holiday, Una didn't have a single friend to play with – except Laddy, who had, through necessity, been left at home today.

'You wouldn't want him to be frightened by all the people and the noise, would you?' Hazel had coerced kindly. But of course, the child had taken it all the wrong way.

'I don't want to leave Laddy behind,' Una had grumbled.

'In that case, I will just have to go by myself to the funfair, won't I?' Hazel had bargained unfairly. She was determined to give Una the best day out ever. 'I suppose I'll just have to get used to being lonely and not having my family around me,' she'd sniffed. 'An old lady like me who never means anyone any harm.' So overcome was she by this admission, Hazel had to fight off the threat of real tears. For once, she'd managed to get her own way, because Una had at last reluctantly agreed to accompany her.

But it wasn't Hazel's fault that the much younger man with the checked shirt and long sideburns had come to stand by her, looking as if he wanted to win her a goldfish in a bag or buy her a hotdog – or something. It wasn't her fault that she was more youthful and glamorous-looking than other people's grannies. And it certainly wasn't her fault that Una grew more and more fearful of the terrifying-looking sea dragon's head the nearer they got to it, lest it breathed fire on her.

SOMEBODY HAD BEEN to the beach hut, but it wasn't Una, and whoever it was had turned it into a crime scene. Not only had the doors been prised open, but the glass windows had been smashed, leaving pyramid-shaped piles of crystal debris everywhere. The gingham curtains had also been shredded and the crockery broken, leaving Venetia and Yvonne's scantily clad flip-flop feet to dance amongst the sharp porcelain pieces.

The sisters rolled disbelieving eyes at each other, reluctant to communicate their shared thoughts. Could this be the work of their mother? Had she allowed herself to get so overwrought when they stayed out late last night that she'd flown into a rage and wreaked havoc on the beach hut just to spite them?

'You don't think –?' Yvonne was about to say the word they both feared but Vee cut her off.

'No.' Vee shook her head vehemently.

But no amount of her sister shaking her head was going to stop Yvonne becoming suspicious or thinking the way she did now, when only last night Vee had been adamant that their mother was no more than a cold-blooded murderer. In fact, she was beginning to think that Vee was hiding something from her and was becoming increasingly irritated by it. If Yvonne found out that Vee had lied to her about something as important as this – her own daughter going missing – there was no telling what she might do to her.

AS USUAL, WHENEVER Hazel put a foot outside the protective walls of the lighthouse, people stared, all the while nudging each other and rudely pointing in her direction. She'd have to be inhuman not to notice their ugly twisted faces do comical double takes as she stood innocently enough among them. As always, she chose to ignore them. Pretending was just one of the ways Hazel was able to make it through a whole day, especially when she felt alone and vulnerable.

Like now, when she was being ignored by her ungrateful little granddaughter and attracting the likes of the man stood next to her with Elvis hair and the ugliest, fattest pair of lips she'd ever seen on somebody's face. Truthfully, he looked as if he had a big swollen vagina slapped across his face. The thought tilted Hazel in the direction of being dangerously close to laughing – but not in a good way, she feared.

He didn't know her – that much was obvious – or he wouldn't be stood chatting to her now about his passion for bird-watching as if she were a normal everyday person.

But who was the real Hazel? Even she wasn't sure any more. Was it the sweet loving granny out for the day with her granddaughter, patiently listening to some lonely soul rattling on about river warblers and woodchat shrikes (all rare Norfolk birds apparently) because he had nobody else to talk to, or was she the woman who only came out on special occasions, like a witch's costume on Halloween?

Instantly falling for the appeal of being considered a loveable, friendly granny who had time for everyone and never had a bad word to say about anybody, Hazel smiled warmly at the bird-watcher from Dersingham whose self-interested heart she was about to break.

'You'll have to excuse me. I promised my granddaughter a ride on this.' Hazel patted him on the arm as if it really hurt to say goodbye. Then, reaching over to take hold of Una's hand, she quickly ushered her granddaughter into one of the waiting carriages that made up the sea dragon's long green tail.

'I don't want to,' Una complained, dragging her heels.

'It will be fun,' Hazel said firmly, unpeeling Una's clenched fists from the safety barrier, convinced that she would love the ride once it got going.

'I don't want to!' Una stamped her foot.

'I SAID IT WILL BE FUN.' Cruelly narrowing her eyes and raising her voice, Hazel came close to actually shaking the child. Everybody in the queue fell silent and started to shuffle awkwardly, not knowing where to look. Choosing to ignore the look of confused disenchantment that flitted across her gentleman friend's face, Hazel could only suppose he was put out to discover that she was old enough to be somebody's grandmother.

OVER ONE HUNDRED motorbikes of every size, design and colour were parked on the green in the centre of town. Leather-clad bikers, looking like blue bottle flies in their oversized black shades, were stretched out on the grass, licking ice cream in an attempt to stay cool.

Meanwhile, crowds of holidaymakers with burnt patches of exposed skin congregated around the bandstand where the Hunstanton Concert Band, dressed in smart black blazers and green ties, played Bernstein's "The Magnificent Seven" and bored toddlers smeared with high-factor sun cream cut their baby teeth on multi-coloured sticks of rock.

As Yvonne and Venetia fought their way through the throng, careful not to trip over crawling babies wearing oversized nappies and food-stained bibs, they searched every young girl's face in turn, hoping each time that it would be Una, growing more and more despondent each time it turned out not to be. Only five minutes ago Vee had wanted to rest – 'Just for a few minutes' – but Yvonne was having none of it.

'She could be miles away in that time,' she had stressed, even though she too was exhausted and sweating buckets in her long black tunic and sticky leggings.

She accidentally knocked into one of the bikers who leaned proprietarily against a mean-looking black Yamaha V Star motorbike and watched in horror as the blob of ice-cream slid from his cone onto the grass, where an opportunist seagull instantly swooped on it.

'Stupid fat bitch,' he called after Yvonne, tossing away the empty cone in disgust and attracting the interest of other bikers in the process.

'Take no notice, Vonnie. He's not worth it,' Vee volunteered, aggressively giving him the "up yours" sign while Yvonne slipped red-faced through the crowd, never once glancing back over her shoulder.

She had no idea that the biker hadn't actually been talking to her at all, but to his even chubbier girlfriend that he "couldn't give a shit about", whom he liked putting down in public, and the tears came all the same. Even now, when her own daughter was missing, such words could floor her; she didn't need her sister to remind her of how stupid she was. She knew she should be used to it by now – being overweight was something you never really escaped from. How many times had she repeated the mantra to herself 'You eat to live, not the other way around,' without it making a jot of difference to her lifestyle? You could avoid eating in public all you liked but people still liked to point and stare. Yvonne couldn't even walk past a group of people her own age without worrying that they were judging the way she looked or guessing how many takeaways she put away in any one week. *Why are people so cruel?* she wondered.

CHUG. CLUNK. WHIR. The sound of the rollercoaster as it began its steep climb triggered a sickly knot in Una's stomach that would only unravel once she was back on firm ground. Not daring to fully open her eyes, all she could see in front of her were yellow warning signs telling her to keep her arms and legs inside the car. Hardly daring to move now that they were some fifty feet in the air, Una tugged at her granny's sleeve.

'I don't want to, Granny.'

'You'll be fine,' Hazel told her somewhat indifferently, glaring at the people on the ground who in turn were looking back up at the ride, eyes squeezed together in opposition to the sun, their mouths hanging open like flycatchers.

'But I'm scared.' Troubled by the way her granny was scowling, as if she too was a dragon about to breathe fire on the crowd, Una tried to take her mind off how far away the ground was and how small and ghostly the people looked down there.

Then a bright white light flashed in front of their eyes, dazzling them momentarily as the on-ride camera automatically took their picture, capturing Una's wide-awake horror just before they began the descent.

'I don't like it, Granny,' she pleaded, clinging on to her grandmother. But instead of being sympathetic or reaching out to hold Una's hand, Hazel shrugged her off and held up her arms, mimicking the other thrill seekers on the ride.

'Get ready, Una,' was her only advice.

But Una did not want to get ready. She wanted to get off,

right now, before it plummeted downwards, catapulting her out of her seat and into the crowd. As the car hovered at the very top of the incline, Una screamed as it finally spiralled downwards. As the wind whipped her hair into a frenzied attack on her face, she carried on screaming while the car corkscrewed loop after loop in the blue sky, leaving behind a trail of cloudy somersaults which would have spelt out "terror" had it been a hire plane displaying a personal message banner behind it.

The mixed messages she was getting from her granny were even more confusing; one more questioning look at her cold profile was enough to convince Una that there was something wild and distant about her, as if she were a hundred miles away, unaware of her surroundings – or her own granddaughter.

Ever since stepping onto this ride, her granny had changed, become different somehow – and then at last it came to her. This woman wasn't her granny at all, but an impostor. Her real granny would never have made her come on this terrifying ride nor frighten her half to death for the fun of it. Once more she locked eyes with the woman sitting next to her and this time she was sure she was looking into the eyes of a ghost, or a devil, even – something definitely not of this world. When Una next opened her mouth to scream, it had nothing whatsoever to do with a fear of rollercoaster rides.

YVONNE RECOGNISED THE screaming as soon as she heard it. They'd been heading in the direction of the funfair, walking along the part of the beach where children were given rides on ponies whose dejected muzzles scraped low in the sand. She'd been scanning faces as they went, hoping for a glimpse of Una's crow-like hair among the many strawberry blonde heads of the other children – with no such luck.

There it was again. A high-pitched, scared-stiff shrieking that stood out among the racket of pop music and humming generators powering the funfair rides. And not only that; it simultaneously had every dog in the vicinity howling and barking.

Looking up, Yvonne could just about make out Una's diminutive face in one of the cars belonging to the sea dragon rollercoaster ride. Not only did she look frozen with fear and white as a ghost, but her face was covered in thick, black hair, so that she resembled the infamously creepy girl from *The Ring*.

'Una!' Yvonne exclaimed, clamping a hand over her mouth in disbelief.

Not far behind, Venetia spotted Una at almost exactly the same moment and likewise clamped a hand over her mouth.

'Mother!' she exclaimed.

LOOKING AS IF she was about to spew vomit in every direction, even though she was now back on firm ground, Una snapped her hand away from her granny's possessive grasp and threw herself into Yvonne's arms, where she promptly burst into tears.

Obviously, the rollercoaster ride had been too much for her. Anyone could see that. Anyone except Hazel, that is, who squeamishly turned her head away as Una threw up a barely digested hotdog.

'What the hell do you think you were doing, bringing her here without telling me? I've been going out of my mind with worry. And I can't believe you let her go on there. What were you thinking?' Yvonne demanded, wiping her daughter's mouth with a crumpled emergency tissue recovered from the sweaty waistband of her leggings.

'I thought it would be nice to let you have a lie-in for once!

Can't a granny take her own flesh and blood out for a walk without asking permission?' Hazel seemed determined to wrong-foot Yvonne. 'Besides, it's just a fairground ride, Yvonne. Just because you had a bad experience once doesn't necessarily mean Una is going to,' she wheedled.

Although she would have denied it and kept on denying it, it was obvious to anyone with half a brain that Hazel was being defensive. That typically meant she wouldn't admit to doing anything wrong but would instead point the finger of blame elsewhere. It was a ploy Yvonne was familiar with, but there was also something else going on here that she couldn't quite grasp – couldn't quite remember. But her mother seemed to want her to – otherwise she wouldn't have brought it up.

What was it her mother had said? 'Just because you had a bad experience once.'

Feeling suddenly and inexplicably mesmerised by the rollercoaster ride as it began its descent once more – this time with a new bunch of joy riders on board, all screaming excitedly and holding their arms above their heads – something deep down inside twigged for Yvonne.

* * *

IT HAD BEEN another gloriously hot day in 'Sunny Hunny,' Yvonne remembered, and as usual she had been bullied into doing something she didn't want to do just to keep her sister happy. She had been five at the time, Venetia eight, and old enough to know better.

They had been strapped into the sea dragon rollercoaster ride by the handsome David Essex lookalike who always winked at them whenever they walked past. The one Yvonne secretly had a soft spot for… It was something to do with the cheeky grin and daring twinkle in his eye, even though Vee thought he was as gross as the hairy Sugar Puff Monster and looked ridiculous in his "kiss me quick" hat.

As the car lurched forward on the rickety track and began its long climb to the top, Yvonne could already feel that morning's toast and jam, washed down with weak sugary tea, start to make its way back up as if it were a passenger in a high-speed lift.

Perhaps if she kept her eyes shut tight, she told herself, she'd be alright, but all too soon the car reached the top of the rollercoaster ride where it wobbled precariously, causing her to snatch hold of the metal bar, fearful of falling out.

She glanced nervously at her sister. The plucky look on Vee's face hinted that she'd done this many times before, but it was a first for Yvonne and so far the experience had not been a good one. She still couldn't get over how high up they were or how small the people seemed on the ground. If she wasn't so scared of letting go of the bar, she would reach out and grab a handful of cloud as a souvenir or maybe even have a word in God's ear about her sister's bullying.

As if she was able to read her thoughts, Vee turned to smile disarmingly at her before showing her what to do.

'Hold out your arms. Like this,' she demonstrated happily, holding her arms flat out to the side, mimicking an aeroplane.

Glad to have someone show her what to do, Yvonne grinned back, full of trust and admiration as she did as she was told, holding her arms rigidly out to the side.

'Get ready to scream,' Vee advised playfully.

No more delaying then. It was time to go. In the split second before the rollercoaster ride plummeted, Yvonne saw the look on her sister's face change. It was no longer full of laughing encouragement and sweet smiles – but something else entirely. Pure evil.

At the very last second, Vee slyly changed her position, lifting her arms upwards toward the sky – out of harm's way. That's when Yvonne finally noticed that everyone else on the ride had already adopted the same position. Too late, she spotted the yellow warning signs in front of her, telling her to keep her arms and legs inside the car. Yvonne's left arm struck the metal framework of the track and flicked back at an awkward ankle – limp, bloody and broken.

Only then did she open her mouth to scream.

* * *

NOT QUITE ABLE to get her head around what had happened, Yvonne gawped at her left wrist – the one that had never healed properly after the break – as if it held all the answers. Then, no longer able to deny what had happened to her, she stared, aghast, at her sister.

'I spent a whole summer with a broken wrist because of you,' Yvonne stabbed an accusing finger in Venetia's bony chest, surprised by how easy it would be to push her over altogether. 'How could I have forgotten that?' she wondered out loud as Vee stared guiltily at the ground, shuffling her feet.

'All that crap last night… I don't know why I ever listened to you.' And then, gesturing at Hazel, 'Mum was right about you all along and so was Una when she said that all you do is hurt people.'

'People are listening, Yvonne. Do try not to be so dramatic,' Hazel hissed, aware that people were eavesdropping on their argument.

But Yvonne was having none of it. 'Everyone said I had only myself to blame. But it was you all along!' she shouted at her sister. And then, unable to stop herself, she landed Vee a hefty smack in the face with the back of her knuckled hand.

'So what? You probably asked for it,' Vee retaliated, holding a hand to her stinging face – a reminder of how dangerous her sister could be.

Completely oblivious to anyone else – Una, her mother or the fairground visitors who, by now, had stopped to stare – Yvonne was about to land her sister another blow when Hazel stepped in between them, using her height to tower over and intimidate Yvonne.

'I won't let you hurt her. No matter what she did,' she warned fiercely.

At a loss to understand why her mother should suddenly be so protective over Vee, it took a full minute more before it dawned on her.

'You knew! All this time you knew. Yet you covered up for her.' This sickening revelation was almost enough to dampen her rage, but not quite. 'And it was you who tried to drown me in the bath,' she confronted her sister again. 'You who held me under.' She made another grab for Vee, but this time her sister was too quick for her. Managing to dodge out of the way, she cowered behind Hazel.

'That's it. Hide behind Mum, like you've always done!' Yvonne bawled, not caring who heard.

'What the hell are you talking about?' Vee raged, ready to fight back now that she'd had time to recover from her sister's unexpected attack. Now she was being accused of something she HADN'T done.

'You covered that up too, didn't you?' Yvonne was in her mother's face now, close enough to notice a smudge of lipstick at the corner of her mouth and to inhale her Dior perfume. She knew that, for as long as she lived, she never wanted to smell it again.

'You're not making any sense, Yvonne. When did you nearly drown in the bath?' Hazel made light of it.

'Stop lying, the pair of you. I know what you did!' Yvonne squealed in fury and then, like a savage wildcat, flew at her sister, tugging out stubbly shorn strands of hair from her head and beating her kidneys into submission with a flurry of hard jabs.

And then Vee was somehow free and ready to fight her corner. Squaring up to each other like squabbling cab drivers arguing over a fare – it would be a claws-out, blood-drawn, hair-pulling spectacle of a scrap if it ever really got going, the kind of fighting only done by girls. It would no doubt end in a screaming rolling mass of bodies on the ground if it was allowed to escalate.

'Stop it I say. This minute,' Hazel bellowed in a way Yvonne and Venetia had never heard before. Looking down, each daughter was surprised to realise that their arms had been imprisoned by their mother's surprisingly strong hands. They were going nowhere soon. For each of them, it was a case of either give up the fight now or lash out at their mother before continuing.

The first to make up her mind, Yvonne angrily thrust off her mother's hand and stormed off, pushing onlookers aside and tugging a sobbing Una along behind her. The tears would come later. Right now she was bloody furious. Right now she felt capable of killing the pair of them, so it was just as well that she quit now.

Hazel stared after her, wondering should she stay or go, but Venetia was struggling to breathe in the aftermath of all that conflict and was in danger of suffering an asthma attack any minute.

AS MUCH AS Venetia's lungs felt like they were on fire, she would not take her mother's arm or rest against her, as she seemed to want her to. Not if her life depended on it. She might have disgraced herself in public but she still had more pride than that.

All they needed, she felt hysterically, was a copper to come along swinging his truncheon, ordering the crowd to, 'Move along, nothing to see here,' in a slapstick, seaside humour kind of way. But now there was nothing much to look at, except for a sick, anorexic-looking girl who couldn't breathe without help and a mother who had just burnt her bridges with one daughter and didn't even have the consolation of being wanted by the other. So the unimpressed mob slunk away to gossip about *that* woman who'd stood in the middle of the fairground, making an exhibition of herself.

'What was all that about Yvonne drowning in the bath?' Hazel was quite obviously still confounded by Yvonne's weird and wacky accusation.

'I have no idea,' Vee gasped, puffing exhaustedly on her inhaler. 'But…' She deliberately waited until she was able to stand tall without any threat of passing out hanging over her, for her next words were important.

'Even if it's true, what Yvonne said, about you covering up for me, I want you to know I never wanted your help. I still don't.'

REFUSING TO COME out from under the bed, where she'd sought sanctuary the minute they arrived back at the lighthouse, Una continued to sob loudly, using the edge of an eiderdown to noisily wipe the snot from her nose. Kneeling on the floor beside the bed, Yvonne had already tried all manner of persuasion to get her to come out, but nothing was working.

The only one of their party having a good time was Laddy

who, believing all the shenanigans to be part of some eccentric, human-devised game, leapt happily from one bed to another, yelping and pawing at imaginary rabbits under the duvet and tugging at the eiderdown with his teeth until it started to fray.

'Una, please come out for Mummy, there's a good girl,' Yvonne pleaded, glancing around the room in the hope of alighting on something that would coax her daughter out. A bag of fizzy cola sweets, a Double Decker chocolate bar or the bingo win lion toy would do – although now she came to think of it, her daughter hadn't played with that in a while.

What she hadn't wanted to see was her mother, but there she was all the same, standing in the doorway, wringing her hands and looking nervous. Straightaway, Yvonne noticed that she'd changed into a matronly champagne-coloured two-piece outfit and wore a single strand of pearls at her neck, as if by appearing older and frailer she was more likely to be forgiven.

'I'm so sorry, darling. I wasn't thinking straight,' Hazel admitted tearfully.

'You've scared her half to death!' The sudden surge of pity she felt for her mother must have softened her tone because Yvonne had intended on shouting the words.

A small white hand shot out from under the bed and grabbed hold of Yvonne's wrist, causing her to jump and reminding her of a similar disturbing scene involving a child actress in *The Sixth Sense*.

'She didn't want to hold my hand on the ride. Only when we got off and she saw you and Aunt Vee coming toward us.' Una's muffled snivelling was barely audible under the bed, but both Hazel and Yvonne heard every reproachful syllable.

'That's not true, Yvonne. I wanted to teach Una to be brave. Knowing how sensitive you were as a child, I didn't think it would hurt to try and toughen her up a bit.' Not once did Hazel glance over to where her granddaughter lay hidden under the bed, her red indignant nose poking out from under the eiderdown. Not once. Nor was there a scrap of truth to her words – or at least that's how it seemed to Yvonne.

'And you're beginning to scare me too. What's wrong with you, Mother?' Yvonne blinked away tears, wishing that she could just as easily erase all the bad childhood memories that had come back to haunt her over the course of this long weekend.

'Don't you think you might be overreacting?' To take the sting out of her words, Hazel experimented with a girlish laugh. But this only made Yvonne angrier.

'Why didn't you stick up for me back there? You used to say you were always looking out for me, trying to keep me out of the hospital.'

'I always tried to protect you from your sister!'

'Well, I don't see any evidence of that. Not when you let her get away with murder. You've always let her do exactly what she likes.' Yvonne was on the brink of screaming again.

'Keep your voice down, Yvonne. There's no need –'

'There is every need. You say one thing to her and another to me. It's what you've always done, played us off against one and another.'

'That's sometimes how it is with daughters.' Usually so eloquent, Hazel found herself stumbling over her words. 'Always trying to keep the peace. You don't know how hard I tried…'

For several reasons, Hazel stopped right there, mid-sentence. Firstly, because she suddenly felt extremely hot and feverish, yet her skin shivered as if an army of soldier ants had just crawled over her, tickling her with their hundreds of black eyelash legs. Secondly, because she sensed that somebody was standing immediately behind her.

VENETIA.

Glaring at them. As if they were both traitors.

If Yvonne couldn't help thinking that her own daughter was like a macabre character in a sinister movie, her sister in this moment was spine-chillingly frightening in her resemblance to the vengeful, social outcast Carrie White in Steven King's *Carrie*, who was going to see them all burn.

'Why don't you take your black eyes and black mood out of here? You're casting an unlucky shadow on all of us,' Yvonne warned darkly, narrowing her eyes until they were hateful slits.

Doing exactly that, Vee went into another door on the landing and closed it quietly behind her, surprising Yvonne, who would have expected her to blow her top as she normally did, the results of which usually involved the slamming of doors, broken windows or wreckage of some kind or other – if not a police incident number.

But even with Venetia gone, her mother remained a bundle of nerves, with fear scribbled all over her face like telltale graffiti.

'Are you scared of her? Is that it?' At last, Yvonne felt she was onto something. If only she could get her mother to confide in her, tell her the truth…

Trembling from head to toe, Hazel shook her head in denial, but Yvonne did not believe her. Thinking fast, she was almost certain that her mother must have found out about Vee's accusations and suspicions. If so, that would explain why she was acting so scared around her, frightened of what she might say or do next.

'Scared of what she knows then?' Yvonne persisted excitedly, and then corrected herself in case it worried her mother even more. 'What she *thinks* she knows?'

Right in front of Yvonne's eyes, her mother metamorphosed

251

back into the cold, distant creature she knew so well. As her mother returned to a familiar world, where lies were what got her out of bed in the morning and sent her to sleep again at night, she also regained her composure.

Yvonne's disappointment couldn't have been more crushing as she watched Hazel fasten eyes resembling a stormy North Sea on a spot just above her head, as always looking over, through, or past anyone who got in her way or who troubled her with questions and demands. As children they'd grown used to their mother abruptly informing them, 'Do not question me,' and anyone foolish enough to doggedly persevere would soon find themselves alone in a room, wondering where on earth she'd disappeared to.

'Scared of my own daughter. I hardly think so,' Hazel sneered. And, as if she were a dazed swan that had just recovered from flying into a brick wall, she shook out her feathers and gracefully exited the room.

'We'll be leaving on the midday bus, Mother,' Yvonne shouted after her, her mind quite made up.

WHY MUST I always be looking down on the world from this tower that has become like a prison to me? Hazel wondered dejectedly from her bedroom window as she watched a skier out on the water lose his footing and take a tumble into the gloomy, freezing-cold North Sea.

Shivering as if she too felt the cold grey water ripple over her skin, Hazel was envious of the boats bobbing about on the water with happy families aboard. Some were nothing more than inflatable dinghies, with parents untangling fishing nets for their children, whilst the more glamorous sun-seekers powered around on speedboats, creating streams of frothy water around their sterns. But they couldn't really hold her attention for long, not when her own daughter and granddaughter were crowded into the bus shelter across the road, herded into a corner by a multitude of other holidaymakers also making the return journey home. She hoped that they didn't have to contend with chewing gum stuck to seats or the stench of urine in corners of the shelter, as was often the case when travelling by public transport.

She could not believe they had actually gone and left her, having tiptoed quietly out of the lighthouse without making so much as a sound. For all Yvonne's talk of getting the bus home and never coming back, Hazel had not really believed that she would go ahead and do it. Naturally, she'd been upset – furious, even – but she had got over far worse before. As a result, Hazel was finding it hard to accept that this might be the last time she would see her, or that it could be another fifteen years before she was to be forgiven again. Fifteen years was far too long – another lifetime, in fact. How would she be able to bear it? Surely Yvonne would come to her senses? And if not, what was Hazel meant to do? Go down on her knees and beg?

There was the Number Ten bus now, with its distinctive green and blue livery, pulling alongside the bus shelter in Lighthouse Close. It was three minutes early, Hazel noticed, glancing at her watch. As usual she had run out of time, left things too late. Why hadn't she listened to Yvonne or taken her seriously for a change? She could only suppose it was because her youngest daughter had spent most of her life complaining about one thing or another – if it wasn't her sister bullying or hurting her, it was the way Hazel supposedly overpowered her with her claustrophobic love.

Now, with Yvonne walking out on her and Venetia refusing to talk to her, once again she had nobody to love *or* hate.

AS THE BUS drew up alongside the shelter and holidaymakers carrying suitcases, sticky-faced toddlers and collapsible buggies started climbing on board, Yvonne glanced up at the lighthouse where she knew her mother would be watching. She felt her shadow rather than saw it, but her presence was there all the same.

Wedged tightly into a corner of a hard wooden bench that smelt suspiciously of urine and had patches of old chewing gum stuck to it, Yvonne gestured for Una to remain seated.

'We'll wait till everyone else has got on,' she warned, in a panic all of a sudden as to whether she was doing the right thing.

Resigned to remaining indefinitely in the bus shelter, Una proceeded to learn Old Hunstanton's bus timetable off by heart but didn't forget to offer Laddy some of the bone-shaped dog treats she'd brought along for the journey, which he turned his nose up at anyway because he was on a hunger strike. Laddy wasn't looking forward to being an urban dog, preferring his coastal life here in Hunstanton, where there were seagulls to chase and acres of sand to run about on. From what Una had told him of his future life at Number 13 Drybread Road, he understood that dogs were to be kept on a lead at all times, were subject to yearly injections by vets, had to obey all kinds of laws in relation to the Dangerous Dogs Act 1991 or risk having their testicles cut off and, more astonishingly, were supposed to pick up their own excrement from the street. Taking all this into account, Laddy doubted that he would pass muster.

Watching Una's feet swing impatiently on the bench and Laddy's fur crawl with nervous uncertainty, Yvonne was beginning to worry that she may have been mistaken about all that had gone on, particularly the near drowning. Could it have been a figment of her imagination, brought about through a very real fear of something *like* that happening to her? It might not sound very feasible, but both her mother and Venetia had been so terribly convincing. She would have been able to spot Vee's guilt a mile off, she was almost one hundred percent sure of it.

So, although it was highly unlikely, she was now starting to wonder if she could also have been wrong about the rollercoaster ride and Vee's malicious part in it. Had she got it so terribly wrong? she wondered. Was her memory really that blurred? And if so, did that mean she was losing her mind?

Having only a minute or two left to make up her mind, Yvonne sprung to her feet, surprising a bark out of Laddy and causing Una to accidentally scatter the remainder of the dog treats on the ground. By now everybody else was on the bus, settling into seats, storing luggage or fighting over window seats. The driver, who hated his mind-numbingly boring job, looked straight through Yvonne whilst pointedly drumming his fingers on the wheel.

Realising that he would go without her if she dawdled any longer, Yvonne took hold of Una's hand who, in turn, sensing that they were finally on their way, yanked the dog forward. Together they exited the bus shelter and went to stand on the pavement. A few more steps and they'd be on the bus. Yet Yvonne still hung back, her feet unable or unwilling to budge.

Thirty seconds later, the bus pulled away from the shelter. When it got to the end of Lighthouse Close, it headed towards town to pick up more passengers en-route to King's Lynn. Once it arrived at that destination, Yvonne's planned route would involve a wait of twenty minutes before the next bus departed for Wisbech in The Fens, which would involve another short stop at that bus station before travelling on to its final destination of

Warboys in Cambridgeshire. All told, the journey home would take three and a half hours.

THE JOURNEY HOME actually took Yvonne less than three and a half minutes because it was a very short walk from the bus shelter to the lighthouse. Now she stood in the grand hallway, feeling broken and humiliated. But no matter how hard Yvonne had tried to leave, she'd found she simply could not do it.

What had been stopping her was as much a physical constraint as well as an emotional one, she suspected; when push came to shove, it felt as if her feet had been tied together, as surely as she was tied to her mother, her sister and the old lighthouse. To prove this, her ankles were red raw, as if actually having had heavy chains rub against them. Only after the bus had pulled away, leaving them behind on the pavement like travellers unable to pay their fare, did she find the pain lessen and that she no longer felt like a Geisha girl, with painfully tight bindings applied to her feet.

All the pain and uncertainty were forgotten about when her mother came gliding towards her, rustling as she always did, as if she was wearing a satin prom gown and not a simple pair of white slacks and sailor-style top. Not yet able to get over the fact that she had chosen to stay, Yvonne's eyes welled with self-pitying tears.

'I got so far… and I then found… I couldn't leave,' she admitted.

NOT ALLOWING YVONNE'S melancholy to put her off, Hazel closed the remaining distance between them and pulled her daughter into her arms. Now she had got her back, there was to be no more pretence between them. No more lies. Of that, she was determined.

'I would do anything for either one of my daughters but only one is truly special to me,' Hazel whispered in Yvonne's ear. At the same time, her glance fell on Una and Laddy, who seemed to have become increasingly shabby and neglected-looking in the short time they had been away. Furthermore, there was a suspicious smell of stale urine about the child that caused Hazel's nose to wrinkle.

Unaware of her mother's silent condemnation of Una, Yvonne relaxed into her comforting embrace and wept from sheer relief. She hadn't been abandoned after all, it would seem. In that moment, she couldn't imagine wanting to be anywhere else in the world – not Bali or Lapland and certainly not on a grubby, overcrowded bus on her way home to a two-bedroom council house that had graffiti sprayed on its walls and a patchy bit of communal grass where youths smoked weed and spat.

'You understand what I'm saying, Yvonne?' Hazel's face blazed with intensity as she searched for the understanding she needed to see mirrored in her daughter's eyes. 'Because it's incredibly important you do,' she insisted. She only gave in when, at last, Yvonne nodded to show that she understood.

'Yes, Mum.' It felt so good being close to her mother again, Yvonne would have agreed to anything. But in this instance, she realised only too well what her mother was implying – that she was the beloved, adored, daughter, the truly special one. Hadn't Yvonne always known it and fought against it? But from now on, she would fight no more. If that meant hurting her sister, so be it. It wasn't as if Venetia didn't deserve it.

Like a crazed granny at a wedding with too many children presented to her all at once, Hazel repeatedly kissed her daughter's cheek and forehead like it was going out of fashion. And then, just in case Yvonne couldn't see through her tears,

Hazel placed a protective arm around her shoulders and gently guided her up the metal rungs of the staircase.

They climbed the staircase without so much as a backward glance at Una, who had her head down and was looking dejectedly at her scuffed shoes. 'We have so much to talk about, you and I,' Hazel told Yvonne, making it clear that no one else was welcome at this longed-for mother and daughter reunion.

But as they reached the top of the stairs and were about to go into Hazel's bedroom – a place she rarely allowed anyone else to enter – Hazel couldn't resist one last look down the stairs and felt at once affronted by the way her granddaughter resembled an unwanted urchin with only a stray dog for company. Left behind and forgotten about, Una seemed no longer to belong to hers or Yvonne's world, with her dark, wary gypsy looks and frowns.

HAVING PACKED CUCUMBER sandwiches with the crusts cut off, a bottle of lemon barley squash, boiled eggs and a flask of tea into a straw picnic hamper, they had decided to mark the end of the weekend the same way they always did – with a trip out to sea.

That's why they now stood outside Hunstanton Boat House, where cream teas and jugs of ice-cold Pimms were being served from a balcony overlooking the choppy North Sea and a showy display of smart boats and yachts were moored in a high-to-low price range. Yvonne found herself giggling, just as she'd always done, at the sight of grown men in wetsuits and snorkelling gear, waddling around awkwardly as if they'd messed themselves. But as nobody else seemed to share her amusement she fell silent again and couldn't help thinking that if Venetia had been here, they would have rolled about in laughter. As it was, her mother seemed on edge again, constantly glancing up and down the beach and crinkling her eyes against the sun, whereas all Una could do was sulk at having had to leave Laddy back at the lighthouse. In fact, she'd hardly spoken a word since they'd come back from the bus shelter and had even refused to hold her granny's hand on the way here.

Stood beside a slipway with a tractor launch carrying a boat named *The Sea Princess*, they were as usual waiting for the missing member of their party before they could embark.

'She's not coming,' Yvonne sighed, although she couldn't think why she should be the slightest bit bothered, after all she'd done to her.

'She'll be here.' There was a sharpness to her mother's voice that hadn't been there an hour ago, Yvonne noticed.

'How come you're so sure?' Intrigued by her mother's certainty, Yvonne genuinely wanted to know. But Hazel didn't get a chance to respond, because there she was now, slouching dejectedly toward them, hands deep in her pockets, head nodding in rhythm to whatever music she was listening to on her earphones.

VENETIA.

With a face like a wet weekend.

Nobody spoke or acknowledged her presence. It was enough that she was there.

POSITIONED ELEGANTLY BEHIND the wheel of a 24-foot Maxum Sports Cruiser powerboat, Hazel had a silk scarf coiled expertly around her hair and oozed millionaire's confidence in her oversized Ray-Ban sunglasses.

Venetia, Yvonne and Una, on the other hand, looked as miserable as sin and sat as far apart from each other as was possible in the generous cockpit that could comfortably seat eight people.

As the tractor launch began its descent down the slipway, both Yvonne and Una nervously gripped onto the side of the boat.

'It's a bit like a rollercoaster ride, don't you think?' Vee taunted spitefully, flicking a bogie from her nose onto the deck, knowing it would annoy her sister.

Ignoring her, Yvonne concentrated on reassuring her daughter, who had drawn closer to her out of fear. No doubt she too was being reminded of her terrible experience on the rollercoaster ride.

'Everything will be okay. You wait and see,' she told Una as the boat plummeted, splashing into the water and causing the sea to ripple around them. Delighted, Hazel and Vee laughed out loud, enjoying the sea spray in their faces. Not so Yvonne and Una, who already looked a little green around the gills with seasickness.

TWENTY MINUTES LATER the boat was far out at sea with its engine switched off, idling lazily – as were its passengers, who either trailed a hand in the water or stared moodily out to sea, lost in their own thoughts.

As *The Sea Princess* undulated like a bolt of silk on the calm water, a mist swirled above them through which ethereal, magical creatures could easily be conjured up.

But *Wiley the Wash Monster*, seen in the distance, was definitely not an apparition as it stormed toward them, snarling through shark-like fangs painted on its bow. The ex-military vehicle, used as a landing craft by American forces in Vietnam, was a 60-seater craft that now transported tourists from the sandy beaches straight into the sea, travelling at 8 knots. It was a popular and unusual attraction and the noise of the engines could be heard back on the prom even from out here.

But instead of waving at *Wiley* as she normally would, Una cried out in wonder as she caught sight of a family of seals basking on an island of sand flats. They all tried to stroke the inquisitive seals' heads as they popped out of the water to say hello, like marine life jack-in-the-boxes.

Cheered up no end by the seals and their pups, Una was almost back to her usual sparkly self, taking pictures of the glistening sea mammals and their fluffy cotton-wool babies that resembled newborn lambs.

'They've got whiskers like kittens,' she exclaimed, delighted by the way their prickly hairs tickled her hand.

'Phillip used to say that seals could sleep under water. That they could even swim to the surface to breathe without waking up,' Hazel informed them proudly, still easily impressed by her late husband's knowledge.

'Phillip used to talk a lot of shit.' At the very mention of *his* name, Venetia's face grew dark.

Instead of biting back, Hazel leaned over the side of the boat to see the seals better and enticed them closer with high-pitched noises, like she would a kitten with a ball of wool.

Sensing trouble afoot, Una went to sit cross-legged on the floor of the boat, right in the middle of a puddle of water that had flooded in when they first launched.

Dipping a hand in the picnic basket, she took out a boiled egg and rolled it around on the floor of the boat, just as she'd been taught to do by her mother in order to loosen the skin. Then she carefully unwrapped the shell in one long curly piece to reveal a perfectly rounded white egg, which she balanced daintily in her hand. As she bit into it, anticipating the pleasurable moment when her mouth would fill with hard-boiled yolk, she wondered why everything in life couldn't be as sunny, smiley and yellow as the middle of an egg.

All she'd ever wanted for her mother was a life full of yellow and there was nothing wrong with that – unless you happened to be in Hunstanton, a place that tricked you at first into thinking that everything was all bright and colourful, like her painting-by-numbers set, until it got to know you better. Then, once it relaxed in your company and had you in its trap, and only then, would it reveal its true palette – all gloomy greys, blacks and darks – a shadowy world you couldn't see through for all the smoke and mirrors, just like her treacherous granny, who had once been described as such by her aunt. Glancing fearfully at the black-as-night cloud hovering over the boat like a giant vulture, Una shuddered. There was no fighting the feeling that the murky sky was about to close down on them, as surely as if it was the lid of a coffin.

'So how come you never included your precious Phillip on our boat trips or days at the beach hut?' Vee was obviously spoiling for a fight. And, whilst she might not be her sister's favourite person right now, Yvonne's curiosity was nevertheless roused.

'I always wondered the same thing.' Yvonne was far gentler on her mother, but she wanted an answer all the same.

'I thought the time spent together, just the three of us, would bring us closer,' Hazel offered, ignoring their look of shared incredulity. 'Unlike Roger, he understood how important it was for a mother and her daughters to have time alone,' Hazel deliberately provoked her eldest daughter.

'You dare to speak to me about my father?' Vee challenged.

'Yes, Venetia, I dare. The question is, what are you going to do about it?' The feral look on Hazel's face was not one you'd want to cross in a hurry. Not even Vee dared. Suddenly the atmosphere around them felt menacing, as the murky water wriggled in what looked like a black mass of evil-eyed snakes and serpents; and from even further out at sea came the sound of a nerve-jangling howling that grew closer and closer.

As the boat juddered against an unexpectedly large and blustery wave, all three women clung onto each other, joined together reluctantly in a row of ghoulish bunting, eyes wild and startled-looking as they held on.

LOOKING FROM ONE alarmed face to another – from her granny to her mother and lastly her aunt – Una was certain that they would each save themselves first if the boat sank, leaving her to drown.

But on hearing the desperate howling again, even closer this time, Una realised that she had not been abandoned by everybody. Like the others, she had been hearing the distant cries for a while and wondered what sort of demonic creature it could be coming from. But now it was so much nearer, she was sure – it was him, it had to be.

'Laddy. It's Laddy!' she squealed excitedly, jumping up from the bottom of the boat and hanging over the starboard side, hoping to catch a glimpse of him. But her female relatives, still glued to the opposite side of the boat, did not even flicker an eyelash of interest. Obviously they did not believe her. As adults, they would of course dismiss the idea of such loyalty coming from a dog. After all, it wasn't possible for a dog to swim all the way out here, nor have the intelligence to know in what direction they had sailed, let alone break out of the lighthouse to come find Una. So, instead they hung their grown-up, impassive heads and avoided eye contact, intent only on seeing out the squall and nothing more.

'Go back, Laddy,' Una called frantically, suddenly worried that in trying to save her, he would end up drowning himself. 'Go back to shore where it's safe,' Una urged. She couldn't see him through the mist but she could hear his paws going ten to the dozen in the water as he fought against the strong current. But then, all at once the sea went still again and Una was thankful when her beloved pet stopped splashing about in the water, no doubt having turned around and started doggy paddling back to shore.

NOW SHE WAS out of danger of being flung overboard or savaged by Wuffa, who was the only beast she knew who could emit the blood-curdling yowls they kept hearing in the distance, Venetia detached herself from her mother and sister and got straight back on the horse, like a determined rider would after a fall.

'I don't know how you can even bring yourself to say his name out loud,' she sulked petulantly.

'Why's that? Because Mum is supposed to have murdered him?' Yvonne spat derisively.

'Stay out of this. This has nothing to do with you,' Vee growled.

'Nothing to do with me?' Yvonne fumed. 'He was my father too, as you're always at pains of reminding me.'

'You don't even care what she did to him,' Vee whinged, sensing she was losing the battle.

Pointing at their mother, Yvonne cried, 'She didn't do anything. It's all in your mind.' Wildly, she circled a "loco" finger in the air, intimating madness.

Narrowing her eyes at her sister, who always had the power to make her tongue-tied in an argument, Vee turned on her mother instead.

'You think I won't tell her?'

'Tell me what?' Yvonne was immediately suspicious. She never could trust the pair of them together.

SITTING CASUALLY, AS if about to be served scampi and chips in a basket with a wedge of lemon, Hazel took off her headscarf and let her platinum curls fall loose. Next, she crossed her legs as if she had all the time in the world, before smiling indulgently at her children.

'Well, why don't you, Venetia?' Hazel's response wiped the smug smile off Venetia's face. For a second or two, it felt damned good to watch her eldest daughter squirm, as she'd so often been made to.

Knowing she'd been outclassed, Venetia felt her cheeks burn as she darted a sly look in Yvonne's direction before shaking her head defiantly at her mother. This conversation, like her battle-weary Suzuki, was not going in any of the directions it was meant to. Fearing that everything was about to slip away from her, she could hardly believe her mother would push her to go through with this. After all, she had so much more to lose.

'You'd love that, wouldn't you? Well, I won't do it.' She put on a brave face.

'Do *what?*' Yvonne demanded impatiently.

'If your memory is as good as you think it is, Venetia, darling, perhaps you can remember what your own father did to you?'

The long pause that followed and the fear displayed on Venetia's face, which contrasted sharply to the confusion on Yvonne's, left Hazel in no doubt that she did indeed remember.

'I know you do, Venetia. I can see it in your eyes.' There was an element of gentleness to Hazel's voice that neither of her daughters had heard before, except perhaps from the cradle.

When Venetia didn't come back with any response at all, simply shuddered and looked away, Yvonne was more than a little surprised. It wasn't like her sister not to retaliate.

'What are you on about? Will somebody please tell me what the hell is going on?' Yvonne pleaded, fixing her eyes on her mother.

Hazel raised her eyes in a noncommittal way, as if to say, *Ask your sister*, but when Yvonne looked to Venetia for an answer, Vee turned her back on her and childishly put her hands over her ears, like a child in trouble who sensed a spanking was on its way but didn't want to see or hear it coming.

* * *

BAD MEMORIES WERE kicking in and there was nothing Venetia could do to avoid them. Not even Yvonne's persistent questioning in her ear, so close she could smell her sherbet Dip Dab breath, could stop her from going back.

She and Vonnie had always been under the daunting impression that as soon as you started talking about the dead, they sat up in heaven and started paying attention. Furthermore, if you ever told lies about them, they would pay you back in your dreams tenfold and make you wish you'd told the truth.

The truth was in front of her now and she wished it were a lie. But she wouldn't be telling lies about the dead if she were to finally speak, now, about what Roger had done to her.

In her mind, she was able to conjure up a picture of her bedroom in the Cox family home, which stood in front of a noisy railway line that carried businessmen in smart suits and women in tight pencil skirts to London. She could remember running to the bottom of the garden at three minutes past every hour to wave at them, like she was one of the railway children. They seemed to live privileged lives in comparison to hers.

Her bedroom had been painted a hideous shade of pink with embroidered butterflies on the curtains and bedspread and she could also remember owning a pink ballerina jewellery box she'd once dropped on purpose in the hope of breaking. Because, let's face it, a girly pink diamante world was not somewhere she belonged. To be fair, though, her mother couldn't have known that back then, nor guessed, that her firstborn would turn out to be a lesbian who preferred Doc Marten boots to Jimmy Choo heels and combat jeans to Amanda Wakeley gowns.

But at five years old, she hadn't known any of that either – all she knew was that she was different to her mother and sister. Different to anyone else she knew, in fact. Wasn't her mother always telling her so? 'Why aren't you like other little girls? Why can't you be nice?' Or invariably, 'Leave your sister alone. How many times have I told you not to hurt her? What have you done to her now, you bad girl?'

She could remember the first time she'd laid eyes on Yvonne and that car crash had taken place in the hospital. After nine months of waiting, she could recall being terribly disappointed with the fat wriggly worm and had nearly been sick in her mouth when she'd been made to hold her. Despite everyone telling her how wonderful it would be to have a baby sister to play with, she hadn't shared their feelings. Firstly, because everybody made it clear from the outset that she wasn't *allowed* to play with her, and secondly because of the way her usually cold-hearted mother looked so tenderly at the new baby in her arms, even if she did have a round face like a pizza. She didn't need to be told that her mother had never held her that way. Not once. Not ever. And the hatred she felt for her sister because of it sprung instantly to life, like a field of poisonous weeds that hadn't been there yesterday. Venetia may as well be poison, the way her mother looked at her.

As if it were yesterday, she could remember her mother shouting, 'If you keep on pulling such ugly, cross faces, nobody will love you.' But she'd been wrong. HE had loved her anyway, no matter how ugly she was.

He had loved her so much, he liked nothing more than to crawl into bed beside her, especially when her mother was rocking little Miss Tiny Tears to sleep in the next door nursery. Often she'd try to stay awake and wait for him, pulling back the bedcovers in readiness if she so much as heard a single footstep on the stairs. She could always tell it was him and no-one else by the way he avoided the creaky eighth step – the sound grated on him, he said.

Usually, he'd strip off his clothes and fold them neatly on the cream wicker chair she hung her own dressing gown on, before getting into bed in just his pants, which had hard scratchy seams that rubbed against her soft white skin. Then, he'd snuggle up to her and blow raspberries on her exposed, round tummy and she'd laugh and laugh and laugh – a real belly laugh that only surfaced again later in adulthood whenever she was hopelessly drunk on cider. Although she hated most of the other stuff he'd done to her, she never minded the kissing or the closeness, which she didn't get any other time because her father wasn't that expressive during daylight hours. Only at night would he let her twirl a lock of his dark hair around on her finger until it left behind a spirally curl in what would otherwise have been a head of dead-straight hair.

'How about a little kiss for Daddy?' he'd say, puckering up. 'That'll keep the bedbugs away.'

Vee hadn't known what a bedbug was and didn't like the sound of them at all, but if anyone could keep them out of her bed it had to be her daddy. Privately, she'd wondered if the bug he was actually referring to was in fact her mother – it was no secret he didn't like her any more than she did – but then, if that was the case, why did she get the impression that he actually wanted Hazel to come into the room? Because he was never more pleased than if she opened the door and caught them in bed together.

'What are you doing in there?' Her mother would gasp, as if she too were having one of the many asthma attacks she and her father suffered from.

'Seeking the warmth I can't get from my own wife,' he would tell her, as if that was an end to it. And that's when she realised how much he loved her, because usually her mother could get any man to do exactly what she wanted. But not him. Never him. He belonged to her – for hadn't he told her all along she was his "special girl"?

After her mother had shut the door on them and gone away, she hadn't felt so special any more because there had been pain – indescribable pain, a sort of pain that wasn't intended for her until at least another fifteen years later. All she could do to block it out was follow her mother's movements around the house. First, she'd heard her light elegant step on the eighth step on the stairs, but only after she'd hovered on the landing for some long time. Next, she'd heard her opening kitchen cupboards, finding a favourite Earl Grey Teabag and popping it into a china cup. She could hear the kettle whistle as it boiled and afterwards the tinkling sound of the cup as she stirred her tea (no milk, no sugar, just a squeeze of lemon, thank you). Vee couldn't be sure, but she also thought she heard the sound of the biscuit tin being twisted open and the chair scraping back as her mother put up her feet for a rest. Perhaps she had fancied a custard cream to go with her cup of tea while Vee was upstairs doing *her* job – what a wife *should* be doing with her husband.

* * *

SHE WAS BACK on the boat, and safe again – for now, anyway. In the short time she had been away – metaphorically speaking – Venetia felt she had at last grown into her body, which now seemed to fit her better.

Though she'd never admit it, she was starving hungry in a way she'd never experienced before and could easily demolish a whole bag of chips with mushy peas and curry sauce if it was put in front of her, and probably manage a deep-fried fishcake while she was at it. As ridiculous as it seemed, even to herself, she also felt able to breathe properly for the first time in years and no longer felt the urge to light up, which was another first for her. The unfolding of her grubby secret to her mother, sister and niece had at last brought her some peace and went some small way to a kind of acceptance of what had happened to her. Regardless, her mouth must have moved of its own accord, a bit like a ventriloquist's dummy operated by somebody else, for she couldn't remember voluntarily recounting her story out loud. Still, the words had come spewing out all the same, like molten lava erupting out of a volcano that was in a hurry to wipe out the people living below it.

What had also happened to her was what should have happened all those years ago. Firstly, she was crying, and secondly, somebody who wanted nothing from her, and who wouldn't hurt her, had their arms wrapped protectively around her – YVONNE. Her baby sister.

As Vee and Yvonne clung together, sobbing on each other's shoulder, *Wiley the Wash Monster* sailed closer and inquisitive sightseers took pictures. Yet everyone aboard *The Sea Princess* remained oblivious to them and their intrusive Nikon cameras. Thankfully it wasn't long before the ship changed course and sailed away again, blowing its horn in an inappropriately cheerful send-off.

'YOU KNEW. YOU knew and you did nothing.' Feeling like she wanted to murder one or two people, Yvonne was immediately on her mother's case. How could she?

'You're siding with her! After all they put me through?' Hazel was infuriatingly indignant.

'Put *you* through!' Yvonne was astounded. Talk about taking the biscuit!

Deciding it was best not to tackle her mother right now, because she might just push her overboard if she did, Yvonne tried to soothe her sobbing sister instead.

'Poor, Vee. I'm so sorry. Why didn't you tell me? And why go on protecting him, making him out to be a saint when all the time…' Yvonne imagined her sister's emaciated brittle body would snap with all the heaving and weeping.

'Despite all he did to me, I always came first with him. I was his "one and only". Something I've never been since,' Venetia admitted shamefully.

'That's not true.' Patting her sister encouragingly on the back but avoiding the prominent backbone that made her fingers recoil with revulsion, Yvonne felt her sister's pain and rejection so keenly, she imagined she could easily die for her.

'IT *IS* TRUE,' Vee screeched bitterly, green snot hanging out of her nose like a lizard's innards.

271

'And I wanted it to stay that way, that's why I let him. I was as bad as he was –'

'You were just a baby, Vee,' Yvonne shushed her, feeling brand-new tears well in her eyes. It was too much, all of it, too much – and heartbreaking for all of them. But before she knew it, her sister was shrugging her off and wriggling out of her maternal grip.

'You don't get it, do you? Had he lived, he would have come for you next. And, being my little sister, I would have had to protect you and risk turning him against me. Because nobody was allowed to let anything bad happen to Vonnie, were they?' Vee spat hysterically, hatred spilling down her chin like a jar of Cow and Gate's porridge on a baby's bib.

'You need to calm down, Vee, or you'll make yourself have an asthma attack,' Yvonne warned, putting out a restraining hand as Vee got agitatedly to her feet. For now, at least, she would refuse to take what her sister said personally.

But Vee slapped her hands away in a surprisingly strong manner. Now that Yvonne came to think of it, there were none of the usual telltale signs of asthma evident on her sister's face – no blueness, no gasping or tightness of breath. Usually, when put under this much emotional stress, she'd be on the floor by now, unable to breathe and needing urgent medical attention.

'But I never got to be the hero and save my sister, did I?' Vee paced a tight circle, like a leopard in a small zoo enclosure, and rubbed at old scars on her arms that only reminded her of yet more miserable times.

'Because he died. And even if he hadn't, I would have forgiven him anything. Because he was the only one who ever loved me.' Vee glared defiantly at her mother before slouching exhaustedly on the pontoon boat seat.

'THAT'S NOT TRUE.' Hazel was all restrained but her angry denial was unleashed as she got to her feet. Having had a spell of listening and assimilating all that was going on around her, she now felt that it was her turn to have her say, and to do that she needed centre stage.

'Yes it is. You practically admitted it this afternoon. Only one truly special daughter, you said.' No way was Yvonne going to allow her mother to confuse and bamboozle her sister a minute longer. But, whatever way she might have expected her mother to react, it wouldn't have been with crazed, malevolent laughter that overwhelmed the small boat and made her think that a spotted hyena had leapt aboard. In the right circumstances, the creepy "revenge will be mine" cackle would have been funny, but it definitely wasn't now.

'You think this is funny? Jesus Christ, what kind of mother are you?' Yvonne was finding her mother's behaviour hard to stomach – it was far worse than the seasickness she always experienced out at sea.

'The sort who wanted her own daughter dead,' Vee threw a scathing glance at her mother. 'It was me you were trying to kill, wasn't it? Not Daddy?'

Wanting to shake her eldest daughter out of her pig-headed obstinacy but deciding against it, Hazel held out both arms in an imploring gesture. 'You've always been wrong about that, Venetia.'

'See. I told you. Nobody was murdered after all!' Yvonne swung around, wanting to share the good news with her sister. But her hopes were soon dashed, because her mother wasn't through talking yet.

'I always intended killing him. Never you, you foolish child.' There was no doubting the naked, unabridged honesty pouring out of Hazel's eyes as she stared intently at Venetia, wanting her to know the truth at last. But, shocked to her very core, all Vee could do was sit goggle-eyed, like an unresponsive wooden doll that hadn't been wound up in a while. Her mother's unexpected revelation would take far longer to sink in than it would for the boat to perish at sea.

'Wouldn't you have done the same, for Una?' Eager to have a collaborator on board, Hazel was impatient for Yvonne's opinion.

LIKE HER SHELL-SHOCKED sister, Yvonne was also having trouble taking it all in. At first, she'd dismissed her sister's theory that their mother had unintentionally killed their father, and that she had all along intended on killing Venetia. Yvonne had defended her mother, thinking Vee insane. But now, if her mother was telling the truth, it turned out that Vee was partially right after all, in that their mother had killed their father, and that it was no accident. That she had never wanted to kill Vee in the first place was the only good news she'd discovered today, but now she had openly admitted to killing their father. And not only that, she wasn't the slightest bit remorseful about it, even if he was a – no. She couldn't say the unthinkable word out loud. Not just yet.

Before she could even consider responding to her mother's question, she had to think about this, because right now all her childhood memories and beliefs were crashing down around her. Their father was a paedophile *(there, she'd said it)*, a child abuser of the worst kind and their mother, *her* mother, was a killer. A cold-blooded murderer. There was no other way of looking at it, even if there were exceptional circumstances that drove her to it. The one thing nobody would be able to tell Yvonne was how the hell had she been protected from all of this? And how had she lived among them without knowing? Alright, she may only have

274

been two years old when it first started, but God, she had slept in the bedroom next to Vee when their father raped her – when she was barely five years old. Just one year younger than her own daughter.

UNA. In the midst of all this unimaginable wreckage, she had forgotten about her own daughter. Wanting to put that right straight away, she glanced apprehensively over to where Una stood leaning against the opposite side of the boat and sensed that a great distance had been created between them, as wide as an un-sailable ocean. Alarmingly, she couldn't help noticing how her daughter's eyes resembled the seal pups' in that they were as cold as an unlit fire, and that the fear in them matched their terror of being clubbed to death by marauding man. It broke her heart to see most of the seal pups now snuggled up safely to their warm blubbery mothers on the sand flats whilst Una stood alone. Yvonne wished she could put her arms around her and draw her into her own podgy body for warmth and reassurance, but there was no time – no time for anything other than THIS. THE SITUATION they were in. So, instead she concentrated on her mother and sister and pushed Una to the back of her mind, promising herself that later, when this was all over, she would make it up to the child.

THE CHILD HAD given up wondering if her mother would ever glance her way again without looking through her with those cool disinterested eyes of hers, and resigned herself to spending the remainder of the boat trip in isolation. In fact, she now found the lure of the sea much more interesting, especially now that Laddy was on his way back.

At first she'd thought it was another seal wading noisily through the water, but it was definitely him. She'd recognise his streetwise coffee-coloured eyes anywhere and the ragged pink tongue lolling out of the side of his mouth. Trouble was, he looked as if he was starting to tire and he was still a good way off. If he could manage to swim as far as the boat, she'd be able to pull him aboard to safety.

'Come on, Laddy. You can make it,' Una willed him on. On hearing her voice, Laddy, on the point of giving up, yelped joyfully and swam harder. As she leaned further over the side of the boat, arms outstretched to grab hold of him, Una was amazed to discover that the lapping seawater smelt of perfume – a sweet, floral fragrance that reminded her of her granny's Dior perfume. In fact, the scent was so distinctive, Una could remember the first time she'd smelt it – that night on the north promenade after she'd won the cuddly lion at bingo, when her mother and aunt had as usual been arguing.

SHE WISHED HER daughter wouldn't lean quite so far over the boat. It was disconcerting to say the least, especially when she had never been taught to swim. But Yvonne knew better than to tell her so when she was in the distant, morose mood she was currently in.

Besides, she had more important things to worry about than a petulant child used to having things her own way. Such as, what was it her mother had wanted to know? Oh yes, 'Would she have done the same for Una?' – that had been her probing question. And, yes, without a shadow of doubt, she would KILL anyone who hurt Una. But there was no way she was going to admit that now and let her mother think that she could wriggle out of things as easily as that. Besides, their situations were irrevocably different, so it was wrong of her mother to try to use such comparisons in her argument.

'It was still murder,' Yvonne insisted, albeit half-heartedly, not really having much faith in anything any more.

'You weren't the one at risk,' Hazel retorted sharply.

'From her, I was,' Yvonne pointed accusingly at her sister.

'And who could blame her for that? All those years…' Hazel's glance softened as it fell on Venetia and her eyes grew watery, losing some of their dazzling greenness.

'Never being able to hold you – love you – it tore me apart,' Hazel went on, in the same theatrical vein.

Ordinarily, Yvonne would have been one hundred per cent certain that her mother would only ever have used such passionate words about her, but she couldn't ignore the fact that she was looking straight at her sister as she said it. Watching her go all gooey over Vee caused something inside her to snap. How could her world suddenly transform into such an unrecognisable place?

'What are you saying? That *she* is the favourite daughter all of a sudden?' Yvonne screamed.

'There is no sudden about it,' Hazel arched a perfectly manicured eyebrow, reminding Yvonne that this was a woman too lazy to pluck her own eyebrows who instead paid an Indian woman in traditional dress (because that was the current trend among rich, middle-class women) to scrape them off with something resembling cheese wire.

'You had to be looked after, pandered to…' Hazel shook her head in annoyance, as if she had just remembered all this.

'Mum, don't,' Vee piped up weakly, hoping to put a halt to Hazel's vitriolic attack on Yvonne. But there was no stopping it; it had waited too many years to surface.

'Precious. That's what you were. Nobody was allowed to say a word out of place where you were concerned,' Hazel screeched.

Vee stumbled dazedly to her feet and took a few tentative steps towards her sister.

'Don't listen to her, Vonnie,' she pleaded. But Yvonne backed away, confused. Besides, if her mother had any more to say then she wanted to hear it. No longer would she tolerate being lied to, nor did she want to be protected from the truth. If her sister could face cruel harsh facts then so could she.

'You had everything you could possibly want, while my own little girl –'

'As soon as we get back to shore I'm going to take Una and go because you're lying. Trying to send me mad!' Yvonne screamed at the top of her lungs.

IF UNA DIDN'T soon grab hold of his soft brown fur and haul Laddy out of the ocean, he would disappear under the water once more, and he probably wouldn't have the strength to fight his way back to the surface again.

'Come on, Laddy. You can do it!' Una's throat burned from calling out the dog's name. Yet none of the others paid any attention, locked as they were in their own private battle on the other side of the boat, screaming terrible things at each other no child her age should have to hear. As it was, they probably thought she was making everything up and didn't believe that there was any dog drowning in the water just a few feet away.

Risking her life for her dog – and she couldn't think of anyone else right now she would do the same for, not even her own mother – Una leaned further over the side of the boat until she was perilously close to the water's edge and at last managed to grab a handful of fur as Laddy frantically doggy paddled closer. But a wet dog, even if there was hardly anything of the skinny mutt, was a lot heavier than Una imagined and as she clung on to the wriggling heap of bones, whole tufts of his fur came away in her hands, reminding her of one of her mother's friends who'd lost her hair after battling cancer.

But, like her mother's friend who'd later lost her life to the disease, Una knew that she would also lose Laddy; she couldn't physically manage to haul him onto the boat by herself, nor could she hold on to him for much longer – and they both knew it. Sending her a silent apology with eyes that were once as bright and shiny as two-pound coins and were now starting to dim, his tail nevertheless continued to wag limply as she held him. As he cried and protested beneath her gentle hands, it seemed to Una that he was saying sorry for failing her, for no longer being able to protect her from the crazed aunt who'd knocked out his teeth with a rounders bat.

Dipping her nose into his familiar wet dog smell that still didn't camouflage the scent of perfume that lingered in the air, Una watched his tongue roll out as he attempted to lick her face one last time. But she couldn't get close enough to let him and that seemed to be his only regret as he started to let go of life.

'No, Laddy,' Una sobbed, desperately trying to hang on to the scruff of his neck as he slipped further away from her. And then she felt her own wobbly legs go from under her as she slipped overboard into the freezing cold water, where she would never be parted from her dog again.

'YOU WON'T BE taking Una anywhere,' Hazel laughed callously, continuing her quarrel with Yvonne. 'Because there *is* no Una. Look around you. Where is your precious daughter now?'

Although she didn't trust her mother as far as she could throw her, Yvonne panicked all the same, scanning every inch of the boat with alert eyes. But her mother had been telling the truth, for there was no sign of the child. In fact, the only sign that she'd ever been aboard was the camera left behind on the pontoon seat.

'UNA. UNA!' Yvonne screamed, rushing to every side of the boat, desperately searching the water. But, by now, there wasn't a single out of place ripple on the calm sea.

'No. No!' Yvonne screamed. This couldn't be happening, could it? How was it possible for her daughter to go missing twice in the same day? Only this time there was every chance she had gone into the water. This time there was every possibility she was lost forever.

'She can't swim,' Yvonne spun around to appeal first to her mother, who remained so cold and impassive that she might as well have been in a salon, having her nails done, then her sister, who wrung her hands and rambled incoherently, like a crazy person in an asylum.

'She can't swim!' Yvonne hollered, seizing hold of Venetia and shaking her, making her sister's outsized head bounce on her scrawny shoulders. 'Vee, come on, snap out of it. Help me,' she begged. But Venetia turned her head away and didn't even attempt to wipe away the tears that poured down her haggard face.

'I'm sorry, Vonnie,' Vee told her, meaning it, but she still made no effort to help.

'Help me find her, Vee. Help me find Una. She's got to be out there somewhere!' Yvonne did what Vee wouldn't do for herself – wiped away the ugly tears that hung around on her face like dirty dishwater.

Not able to stand it a second longer, Hazel jealously tore Yvonne away from Venetia and sent her sprawling into a crumpled heap on the floor of the boat.

'Don't you get it yet?' she demanded furiously, glaring at Yvonne as if she were an old panty liner stuck to the bottom of her Ted Baker handbag. 'There is NO UNA, because there is NO YOU. You died on the beach that day.'

SUDDENLY REALISING THAT her hair was sopping wet and that she was shivering with cold, as if she'd just been dunked in a swimming pool by the class bully, Yvonne was amazed to discover that she was wearing the same old-fashioned swimsuit she'd worn on the beach as a young girl. Not only that, but Venetia was also drenched to the skin and spookily wore the same swimsuit. Once again they matched, just as they had when they were children and had been made to dress like twins in the same outfits.

'No way. No. How did this happen? This can't be true!' Yvonne couldn't wait to wiggle out of the wet material that smelt of slimy seawater.

'You remember that day on the beach, don't you, Yvonne?' Hazel probed.

Yvonne shook her head. 'This is not possible. None of it. It can't be...' She backed away from her mother, until she was dangerously close to the edge of the boat.

'Vee? Tell me it isn't true,' Yvonne implored, with huge, childlike eyes that would ordinarily cause grown men and women to swoon, but not her mother and definitely not her sister.

Unable to meet Yvonne's eyes, Venetia glanced guiltily away, like a child caught crayoning on magnolia walls.

'You already know the answer to that, so please don't ask me,' Venetia shook her head sadly. Then, a teardrop the size of a grape formed at the corner of one of her eyes. Mesmerised by the enormous tear, Yvonne watched it fall onto her sister's bony knee and then drip onto her left ankle with the skull and crossbones tattoo on it, before finally trickling over a newly formed blister on her little toe. What happened to it after that? She could only suppose it evaporated, disappeared into thin air, like her make-believe daughter.

By now, there was no longer any point trying to deny the reality of her situation – Una had lived purely in her imagination and only for as long as her mother and sister would allow it. She'd been no more real than the dog, the game of rounders or the teardrop on her sister's face – because since when did Vee shed real tears? Looking from her mother's forbidding face to Venetia's guilt-ridden expression, she guessed that there was more to come…

'I died on the beach that day?' Yvonne tried out the preposterous words on her puzzled tongue and found as soon as they were spoken, no matter how hesitantly, nothing seemed quite so much of a mystery any more.

* * *

HAVING WALKED FOR what seemed like several miles in the wrong direction, Yvonne only stopped snivelling and wiping snot from her nose with the back of her podgy hand when she noticed water lapping around her ankles.

So far, she'd trudged along the beach with her head down, retracing somebody else's trampled footsteps in the sand. At first she'd thought they must belong to her sister, but now she wasn't so sure. Because, glancing up, she noticed the shoreline was a long, long way off – she could barely even make out the lighthouse from here. She knew she wasn't meant to be out here on the beach alone, but what frightened her more than anything was how low the sun was in the sky. It looked as if it was about to put its pyjamas on any minute and get ready for bed, which could only mean one thing – soon it would be dark. And she definitely wasn't supposed to be out on her own in the dark. She was sure to be in a whole lot of trouble when eventually she did make it home, because she'd already broken two of her mother's rules today. But that would be nothing compared to what Phillip would say when he saw the dried blood in her hair or the vomit on her swimming costume and found out who was responsible.

Blinking away fresh tears, Yvonne felt her bottom lip threaten to wobble. She wanted her stepfather, Phillip. She especially wanted him to come striding confidently toward her with his bleached-white-teeth smile and throw her up in the air to make her giggle, but if she couldn't have him then her mother would do just as well, even if it did mean a telling off. She would even be pleased to see Venetia right now, although it was her fault that she was out here in the first place, having run off and left her when she'd fallen and hit her head. She might have died when her head cracked against the stone, for all her sister knew, and yet she'd still left her. And the twirling-until-you-were-dizzy game had all been her idea too. If they hadn't been playing that, she would never have fallen in the first place.

Earlier in the day, she'd been angry with Vee for making her go off and play when she'd wanted to stay behind with their mother. Vee had been just as livid with her for being given preferential treatment over who should carry out the spiders from the beach hut. But after playing the twirling game on an isolated part of the North Beach, she'd thought her sister had got over that. Obviously, she had been wrong. Obviously, Vee had all along planned to punish her and enticed her to the beach just so she could carry out her plan.

But if Yvonne was in for a telling off, Vee must be due a spanking – and the seriousness of what she'd done would probably have her mother and Phillip arguing over who was going to administer the punishment. Luckily, Yvonne had never had to go through any similar ordeal because she had an unusual disorder that meant that nobody was allowed to raise their voice to her, let alone their hand. Something to do with the fainting episodes that could occur any time, any place, anywhere, if anybody so much as upset her – "vasovagal syncope", the doctors called it, only for Vee to laughingly rename it "vagina sin cock" – but not in their mother's hearing, and certainly not in Phillip's, for he had always said how lucky they were that Vonnie hadn't made the most of such a condition when plenty of other children would (this had been said with a significant look in Vee's direction). But then, Phillip would say that, because as far as he was concerned Yvonne was the reason God made little girls in the first place, and had once gone so far as to suggest that He must have been in one foul mood the day he created her sister.

As Yvonne felt the water rush in between her bare toes, she noticed the wrinkles in the sand where the sea, which usually trickled into pools, had all but disappeared. The sea had gained pace and she was pretty sure that the tide was coming in because the water was now up to her knees.

All at once, she was scared and bewildered. Being six and therefore quite grown-up (as far as she was concerned), she might be old enough to understand what the tide coming in meant but, because she was *only* six years old, couldn't quite grasp why it would choose to do so now when she wasn't home yet. Too late, it twigged. All this time she must have been walking out to sea rather than back to shore and soon the water would be up to her chest. Soon, all the disgusting wiggly, wormy sea creatures she detested so much would be swimming in and out of her fingers and eating plankton out of her ears. She felt a surge of panic at the thought of them and the biting crabs that might latch on to her long hair with vice-like pincers that would drag her under until her mouth was full of revolting salt water.

But even more terrifying than knowing that her sister hated her enough to want her dead was the knowledge that she could not swim. Vee had always been the brave, athletic swimmer of the family, whereas Yvonne had been less sure of herself. She'd hated the enforced swimming lessons her sister had excelled at and only felt safe in the water once she had her blow up armbands on. Even then, she wasn't happy unless she was allowed to remain in the shallow end with all the other babies. Mind you, that hadn't stopped her sister dive-bombing her from the side of the pool, causing a wave big enough to splash her in the face and making her choke on the muggy water that smelt of toilet cleaner.

Right now, she figured, everyone else would be home, tucking into slices of bread and butter and dishes of Bird's trifle, which they had every Sunday teatime. And she bet Vee had stolen her job of sprinkling the hundreds and thousands over the cream topping – a treat that had been hers for as long as she could remember and which Vee had always resented her for. In fact, she wouldn't put it past her sister to have dreamt all this up just so she could rush home and be first in line to tear open the packet with her teeth. Spitefully, Yvonne hoped that the hundreds and thousands would spill all over the floor. That would teach her, she fumed.

With little left to do other than keep hoping somebody would find her – a nice blonde surfer who would share his chewing gum with her would do nicely – the little girl made by God walked deeper and deeper into the water until she almost started to float. Incredible really, considering that she didn't have her armbands on. Even more amazing was the fact she should still be thinking of the bright pink nail polish she wanted to buy from Azam's store in town, so that she could paint her toenails the same colour as her mother's.

And then, standing still on the same spot, she fought to keep her balance as the water twirled fiercely around her like a mini tornado, so cold that it made her hold her breath for longer than she'd ever been able to in the games she'd played with her sister in the bath. Of course, Vee had only ever pretended to hold her breath as long as she did, because it wasn't possible that anyone could last as long as twenty-five minutes without taking a single breath of air. Not even the record holders in *The Guinness Book Of Records* had managed that.

As she felt the force of the water threaten to knock her over and frothily trickle into the corners of her mouth and even up her nostrils, as if she was sucking up a milkshake with a straw, she saw the sun dip even lower in the sky. So much so, it seemed to be practically touching the earth. Soon she was bound to see the fairground lights come on and hear the screams of holidaymakers on the sea dragon rollercoaster ride. Nobody would hear her own screams from out here, she realised sadly – not even *Wiley the Wash Monster* who, like her, wasn't allowed out in the dark.

Already, she could see that lights had come on in the lighthouse tower where Phillip always retreated to with a glass of peach-coloured whisky in one hand and the broadsheet pages of *The Financial Times* in the other. Closing her eyes, Yvonne imagined him there. He'd be dressed in a smart pinstripe suit with a red and navy tie held in place with a silver pin and would have his head bent over the yellow pages he found so interesting.

Her mother, dressed in a satin nightgown, would kneel at his feet, smiling up at him as if she counted her blessings every day, and gently remove the polished brogues from his feet. Venetia would no doubt be hovering in the background, pulling faces and pretending to stick a finger down her throat to make herself sick, but all the while secretly wanting to be part of the homely, family scene. Somewhere in the kitchen would be the remains of the Bird's trifle, with one spoonful left in the bowl for her.

Her parents, especially her stepfather, might already be starting to worry about where she was, but only Vee knew for sure. And she wouldn't tell in a hundred thousand years if it meant having that last quivering spoonful of trifle all to herself, as well as getting to lick out the bowl afterwards – which again had always been a special Sunday treat set aside for Yvonne.

I wonder if anyone's been left for dead over a bowl of trifle before, was her very last thought as the sun finally drew its curtains and the light went out altogether.

* * *

THERE WAS SUCH a look of resigned acceptance, of defeat, even, on everyone's faces aboard that even the boat seemed to sigh wearily. On account of the sea being so calm and still, it no longer bobbed jollily up and down on the water as it had been doing. Eerily, all three women stared into the water that was as motionless as a stillborn child and privately grieved for losses that didn't need any explaining.

Yvonne was the first to raise her bedraggled hair and cast steely grey eyes that looked like metal dustbin lids at her mother.

'I died on the beach that day.' Yvonne's face twisted with pain as she touched the egg-shaped bump on her head that continued

287

to throb. Without looking, she knew that when her hand came away there would be blood on her palm – an unnecessary reminder of what had happened.

'And you let her get away with murder, as always,' she accused, not knowing who to look daggers at first – her mother or her sister.

'Is that why you hated her so much? Because of what she did to me?' Yvonne pressed her mother.

'It's not her I hated,' Hazel admitted matter-of-factly, as if hurting people was no longer of any significance.

'So when you said only one daughter was truly special to you…' Yvonne already knew the answer, but felt compelled to hear it all the same.

'Venetia.' Hazel's whole body trembled with emotion just from speaking her eldest daughter's name. 'It's always been Venetia.' Her blurry eyes pleaded for understanding, but couldn't help going off in another direction entirely, ending on Vee's startled face.

'I just never knew it until the day she finally realised that she needed me and that was the day you died, Yvonne,' Hazel confided sadly, as if it still hurt to acknowledge the loss of so many years not knowing how she'd felt about her firstborn.

Sensing that there would be no further elaboration, excuses, apologies or even a long, drawn-out plea for forgiveness from her mother, Yvonne realised that her time had run out. Her story had ended, as surely as her life had that day on the beach fifteen years ago. Her long weekend might have come to an end a little earlier than anticipated, but, whilst she was free to go, her mother and sister had to stay put and see it out to the end.

A SPLASH OF water the size a six-year-old girl would make

falling overboard cascaded onto the boat at exactly the same moment that Venetia tugged a pair of microscopically small earphones from her ears, letting loose the distinctly tinny sound of Radiohead's "Creep".

The irony of the words in the song was not lost on Vee as she dashed to the edge of the boat where Yvonne had disappeared from and frantically searched the water.

'Yvonne. Vonnie,' she screamed to a vast, endlessly hungry ocean that stubbornly refused to regurgitate any of its victims.

Too late. She'd left it too late to intervene or do anything, because as usual she'd been too preoccupied with her own misery, thinking nothing of her sister's sacrifices or suffering. God only knew how many times Vonnie had helped her in the past, looking after her during her night terrors and protecting her from Mr Naughty and Wuffa. Or telling her, in her strict "mother hen" voice, not to call out, 'Please don't hurt me,' when she thought that Mr Naughty was about to drag her into the walls of the lighthouse, but to sit up straight and say firmly, 'I will not let you hurt me.' Odd that her little sister, who had a heart of gold and would try to put squashed worms back together again, could be so tough and ballsy at times.

Shamefully, she could count on both hands the number of times Vonnie had selflessly saved her life – calling for an ambulance whenever she had a chronic asthma attack, or calming her down and helping her to breath during milder spells. Vonnie had wanted to be a nurse when she grew up and the practice had been good for her, she'd claimed, though Vee suspected that she only said this to make her feel better. And now, because of her, she'd never get the chance to do – be – anything. Not now her sister's dreams were at the bottom of the ocean.

Distracted by the sound of the engine starting up, Vee spun

around to see her mother steering the boat in the direction of home. Her heavily ringed hand was pressed firmly down on the speed lever, in full throttle mode, and the kill cord was wrapped around her wrist.

'What are you doing? We have to stay and find her!' Vee out-shouted the spluttering engine and groped her way along the edge of the speeding boat, terrified that she too might tip out if she wasn't careful. 'Mother. Stop the boat right now. Are you mad?' But her plea fell on deaf ears: Hazel did not even glance around, so intent was she on getting back to shore.

By the time Vee made it to the steering controls with every intention of removing the key, the boat was veering wildly out of control and she was thrown violently around the craft's cabin, ending up where she started, at the back of the boat, perilously close to the 20 HP engine.

Momentarily stunned, Vee felt the boat start to loop in an out-of-control circle, which could only mean one thing – her mother had let go of the kill cord. And then there was an ominous shadow standing over her, blocking out the sunlight and the view of the lighthouse in the distance.

HER MOTHER.

'We have to try and find Vonnie,' Vee told her feebly; she suddenly felt incredibly woozy, as if she'd had all the stuffing knocked out of her. Tomorrow her skinny body would be black and blue like a rare steak.

Through blurred vision, Vee saw that her mother carried something long and large in her hand, something she could hardly lift because it was so heavy.

An oar.

'You left her. You left her and the tide came in!' Hazel screamed – a demented sound that could just as easily be mistaken for laughter – as she lashed out with the oar, brutally striking Vee on the side of the head with it.

SHE FELT AS if she were inside a washing machine – continuously being churned around like a pile of dirty old rags in need of a good wash – repeating the same slow spin cycle over and over again, just like in *Groundhog Day* – her whole life spent being thrown from one end of the drum to the other.

But at least she still had a life, which was more than could be said for her poor defenceless little sister – and on that sobering thought, Venetia opened her eyes. But not too quickly, mind, for she was fearful that they were sealed together with her own blood.

The first thing she saw was a flock of black-faced seagulls that looked as if they were wearing zipped-up hoods to hide their criminal faces as they screeched by overhead, on the lookout for swag of the takeaway kind. Next, she saw how incredibly grey and cloudy the sky was, like milky tea that needed a good stir. *There must be a storm on the way*, she guessed, feeling a chill in the air that made her shudder and regret having once carelessly stepped on dead men's graves in St Mary's churchyard. Because that's what it felt like right now – like somebody had just jumped all over her grave – and she'd rather it be anyone other than Yvonne. She couldn't think of anything creepier than being haunted by her own sister, especially if there was any truth in what her mother had said. Was she alone responsible for her sister's death, or did she just want her to think that and take all the blame?

The sound of the engine, now humming gently, intruded on her puzzled thoughts as the boat continued its high-speed passage through the choppy sea. She felt rather than saw the shadows of Hunstanton's famous red cliffs ripple across her face.

She was still on the boat, then. That much she knew for sure. In fact, she was all at sea, at sea, which seemed to make some sort of peculiar sense to her muddled mind. But why on earth her mother had decided to bash her head in with an oar was quite a different story.

Fighting back another wave of nausea that threatened to send her floating back into unconsciousness, Vee closed her eyes once more and tried to remember what really happened on the beach that day.

* * *

THE SEAGULLS WERE, as usual, strategically perched on the crumbling cliff edge or hidden among the sand dunes, hoping for a lone child to come along so they could mug them. Having already spotted their victim, they'd screeched and screamed each other into a frenzy of activity in preparation for operation "ice-cream cone", but today they were out of luck – the little girl, snuggled in a blanket and sitting on a wall in front of the Royal Life Boat Station, not only had a guard of protectors surrounding her, but she didn't even have anything edible in her hand. All she had was a screwed-up napkin that she kept wiping her snotty nose on.

At first, Venetia had enjoyed the attention, with all the fetching and carrying going on by handsome members of the RNLI crew in their bright orange overalls. Not only had she been brought a blanket matching their uniform that made her feel like she was one of them, but also a polystyrene cup of tea with at least six spoonfuls of sugar stirred into it, "for the shock". Meanwhile, members of the public – some of whom she recognised as regular holidaymakers to Hunstanton – looked on helplessly, wanting to lend a hand. Normally she wouldn't get a look in, she realised resentfully, not when her sister was around. Because if anyone got the pick of the black jacks and fruit salads and all the pats on the head by "the greys", as her and Vonnie liked to call old people, it was Yvonne, so it was no wonder she sometimes got really fed up about it.

Behind her, some of the crew were preparing to launch a bright orange rescue boat and kept on shouting instructions at each other in a maritime language she didn't understand. But one thing she did know better than them was that their search would be a waste of time, because they would never find her sister. Not alive, anyway.

Having lured Yvonne to the quietest part of the North Beach where hardly anyone went, except for the odd band of migrant cockle pickers who were always in danger of being caught out by the incoming tide, she'd been determined to get her own back on her sister for yet again receiving preferential treatment from their mother. After all, why should *she* have to carry out the creepy four-inch wide spiders from the beach hut just so precious Vonnie could feel safe? So, by playing the twirling game, she'd had every intention of making Vonnie dizzy enough to spin off, disorientated, into the sand, and that was when she planned to run off and leave her.

Being left alone on the beach, especially as it got dark, would absolutely terrify the wits out of her sister and that would have been punishment enough, but when Vee saw her sister hit her head on a stone and get knocked out, she couldn't believe her luck. She might not have meant to kill her outright, but even so, she hadn't been able to stop herself feeling smug about it. Until she got to thinking that if Vonnie had been everyone's favourite when she was alive, there was no hope for Vee if she was dead.

Already, she knew enough about adults to realise that her sister would, in their soppy minds, become a perfect angel, looking down on them from heaven.

Beyond reproach, Vonnie would become the irreplaceable child everyone mourned and talked about in worshipful whispers in rooms where the curtains were constantly drawn. And for the rest of Vee's miserable life, there would be a suspicious cloud hanging over her dark, mean, spiteful head that meant her mother would look at her as if she were merely a shadow on the stairs she couldn't shake off. And there was every possibility Phillip would do exactly as he'd threatened that day – have her put away.

Just like the annoying man – who reminded her of Pluto the cartoon dog, with his long ears and soppy expression – seemed to want to do, because he wouldn't stop questioning her, as if he didn't believe her story. It was as if he'd seen and heard it all before and refused to have the wool pulled over his eyes. But how many nine-year-olds, who'd left their sister for dead on the beach, could he have come across?

'Can you tell us where on the beach you last saw her? It's vitally important,' he probed efficiently.

Blinking stupidly, Vee shook her head and offered him her empty polystyrene cup in the hope of him sending someone to refill it, but he didn't. He simply looked at her with grave eyes that no longer looked comical. In fact, she felt sure that he'd guessed her secret and knew the disturbing truth and, as a result, she grew increasingly nervous. It had all seemed a game at the time, but now the adults were insisting on turning it into something extremely serious so that it didn't feel like fun anymore. And when she'd wished her sister dead, she hadn't realised that dead meant *forever*. She hadn't actually meant to kill her; just frighten her a bit. After all, actors in films died all the time, yet you still got to see them popping up in different episodes of something else. But then again, losing her father at such an early age... Vee really should have known better.

All at once she was scared of the man everyone called "Coxswain", who looked at her the same way Phillip did. And, feeling as she did, it was no wonder that she couldn't help crying, because he was big and she was small and unexpectedly the crowd seemed less friendly than before. Suddenly the attraction of an extra bowl of trifle for tea and getting to be first to sprinkle the hundreds and thousands over the Bird's dream topping seemed less appealing.

'She's dead. I saw her. She's never coming back,' Vee finally blurted out, and then, seeing the terrified look on everyone's faces, the way they held their breath not wanting to believe, she frightened herself into being sick down herself.

And that's when she saw her...

HER MOTHER.

But her mother wasn't looking at her.

She was gawping disbelievingly at a blonde surfer wearing Union Jack shorts and a look of revulsion that would stay on his face for the rest of his life as he waded exhaustedly through the crowd toward them. In his arms, he carried Vonnie's lifeless body. Both Vee and her mother knew it was her and nobody else, because along the way some kind soul had thoughtfully placed a blanket over her body and they wouldn't have done that for just any old child, would they? But what this person couldn't have known was how that scratchy old blanket would have irritated Yvonne's soft delicate skin and would have ended up in the nearest bin after barely a few seconds. Her sister hadn't been known as "the sea princess" for nothing and could be quite spoilt when it suited her.

Vee sensed, rather than saw, her mother's sharp intake of breath as they watched Yvonne's blood-smeared hand slip out from underneath the blanket and flop uselessly along behind the surfer, who, nervously chewing gum, seemed to instantly recognise the mother of the child because he stopped right in front of her.

Unable to gaze on her dead child a second longer, her mother's enraged, deadly eyes zoomed in on Venetia next – just as Vee had known they would. Perhaps now, her mother would have no choice other than to take notice of her eldest, firstborn, only child. After all, she was all she had left now, no matter the circumstances. But when their glance collided, it felt to Vee like her hair was on fire and she was being burnt alive by her mother's hatred. Nervously, her legs started to jangle beneath her on the wall and she began humming a tune she kept locked inside her head. The same song she relied on, as some people did painkillers, when her father used to visit her in her bedroom and went something like this:-

Shush, now, shush, there's a monster at the door
Shush, now, shush, you've heard him there before
Shush, now, shush, make sure you're not awake
Shush, now, shush, because the bogeyman's no fake

The song was meant to ward off imaginary bogeymen, the kind who preyed on young children in their dreams. Except, in Vee's case, the bogeyman had been her own father and later, after his death, had been replaced with Mr Naughty or Wuffa (she could take her pick). But this time around she wasn't trying to ward off the bogeyman but her mother's displeasure, and she could see it wasn't working. Suddenly everybody moved aside as her mother let out a beastly roar and charged, head down like an angry bull. Nobody tried to stop her because there was *no* getting in the way of a woman as mad as she was, for she would surely toss you aside as soon as look at you.

Lashing out with her fists, she viciously brought down blow after blow upon Vee's head and not a soul intervened, not even when she punched her off the wall onto the sand, giving her daughter a split lip and a bloodshot eye. Even Vee didn't put up a fight, but simply cowered under the blows, curling into a ball and trying to protect her head as best she could. Taking a beating was nothing compared to the emotional torture she had already lived through, so she was pretty immune to physical kind of pain. And, at least her mother was touching her. For once in her life, she wasn't being ignored.

'You were supposed to be looking after her!' her mother screamed – a tormented, blood-curdling sound that would ring in Vee's ears forever. But she'd rather have the sound than not. She'd rather have her mother thrash her half to death than not. And that's what she wanted to tell the braver members of the rescue crew as they finally tore the screaming, spitting, hissing woman off her. Even then, such was the strength and ferocity of her mother's rage that it took four of them to pull her away.

'Get her away before she rips her only other child to pieces', instructed the Coxswain, wiping away a slither of blood from his own lip, where her mother had caught him with one of her talon like nails (not that he didn't deserve it).

Once she was safe, Vee burst belatedly into tears, and this time they weren't even crocodile ones – not that she understood exactly what that meant, but she'd heard Phillip use the expression enough times to know that he was pointing the finger at her in not a very nice way.

'Mummy.' She called out shakily in a little-girl-lost voice that seemed to surprise everyone – from the shocked and tearful holidaymakers to the "must stay impartial and professional at all times" rescue crew. Even her mother was caught unawares by the pathetic tremor in her voice as she got unsteadily to her feet, revealing blood-scuffed knees and a trembling lip.

'Mummy, please.' The vomit-stained blanket slipped off Vee's painfully thin shoulders and dropped to the ground, making a strange shushing sound. For the briefest of moments, Vee felt she knew what it was like to be Jesus removing his cloak in front of a crowd of spellbound followers. Similarly, she realised that she would now have to perform a miracle of her own if she were to survive this day and avoid being put in a home for naughty children by Phillip.

Trembling from head to toe, Vee did something she'd never done before. She held out both arms and asked for the space to be filled by someone other than her father.

'Hold me, Mummy, please. I never meant to…' Her eyes darted over to where Yvonne's crumpled body rested on the sand, half wondering how her mother could stand to let her stay another second under that scratchy blanket.

Sensing her mother was about to do exactly that – remove the blanket from her daughter's body before running off to find Phillip – Vee piled it on all the more, like layers of cheese, lettuce, gherkin, mayo, ketchup and anything else that went to make up a burger-sized lie.

'Don't leave me, Mummy. Not now. I need you, Mummy. Please, don't go,' she begged, for all she was worth.

Watching her mother's face crumple with uncertainty, Vee could tell she was wondering if she'd heard right and watched her repeat the words out loud to herself in a low, quiet mumble only she could detect.

'Don't shut the door on me like you did before.' These were meaningful words for a nine-year-old to use, but Vee had been saving them for this moment. 'When I was with him,' she ground out.

'You were supposed to love me. Not him!' her mother shouted hoarsely, almost accusingly, once Vee's telling words had sunk in. 'Why didn't you?'

Only Vee knew how much it cost her mother to ask that searching question. Only Vee understood why, instead of immediately going to hug her daughter, she hung back.

'I never knew how. Nobody ever showed me,' Vee confessed truthfully, hoping that it would make all the difference.

It did. Must have. Because, before she knew it, her mother had thrown off the last of her doubts, as well as the remainder of the rescue crew who were still trying to restrain her and crossed the distance between them. Then, finally, Vee was being folded into her mother's arms as if she were a delicate lace christening gown that had once belonged to a much-mourned child.

'My child. My precious, most special daughter. You've come back to me. After all this time you've come back to me,' her mother cried in her ear, glossy lips brushing against her skin in an unfamiliar tickle. Such an overwhelming assault of soft flesh, potent perfume, gentle fabric and silky hair Vee had never experienced before, and right there and then, she made a promise to herself to never, ever ask for anything more than this. Except perhaps for her mother to protect her from the person she feared and hated most in the world. The person who had dared call her evil. Phillip.

* * *

SHE SHOULD HAVE had sons. They would have loved her more. More than daughters, anyway. Even if she didn't deserve it, like many a bad mother before her, they would have worshipped her for being beautiful, if nothing else – especially if they'd been born gay. Not only that, if she'd had sons she wouldn't have had to do everything herself, like take out bins, organise services and MOTs on vehicles or fetch down Christmas decorations from the creepy loft. Nor would she have had to learn how to captain a boat single-handedly, as she did now, sailing toward the perilously rocky shoreline where the cliffs and lighthouse were barely visible in the mist.

The imminent threat of a storm worried Hazel more than she cared to admit because she was not a great sailor and therefore needed to get back to the lighthouse before it broke. Already there were rain spots thundering down on the water, making the sea bounce like miniature marbles, and a massive grey cloud had formed above her head that looked like a mountain. She prayed that there would be no lightning – at least not until they got back home, where they'd be safe. If Phillip could see her now, battling his precious boat on a stormy sea, he would not be able to believe it – he'd never thought her very competent. Well, she had shown him, hadn't she? Time had taught her that she hadn't needed Phillip as much as she thought she had, that she could cope on her own. But even so, having a grown-up son around to take care of her would have been nice. Instead she'd landed up with surly, demanding, selfish daughters who did nothing but criticise, think only of themselves and put distance between them.

But no matter what anyone else said, Hazel had been a good mother and nobody could take that away from her. She had done her best. Her very best. But it was never good enough for *them*. She had loved. But not enough, it would seem. She had chastised, but, again, not often enough – especially as far as Venetia was concerned.

Hazel turned to look at her ugly-beautiful daughter who, despite being wrapped in a thick blanket, shivered on the pontoon seat where she slept restlessly. Already she was having trouble breathing, wheezing and whining like a fan belt on a car, and her lips had turned a reptilian bluish green. Nobody would guess her true age of twenty-four from looking at her – she'd always appeared years younger than she was. So much so, she'd been considered stunted, backwards even, and socially retarded for her age. But the long line of dubious teachers and doctors, whose hands she'd passed through, had all been deceived. Because her daughter was capable of immense intelligence and cunning, and it was best you never forgot it.

Hazel had always felt that if you took away the heavy boots, camouflage trousers, ridiculously short hair, tattoos and piercings you would still see that pretty, ever-frowning difficult child of hers underneath. And whenever she caught a glimpse of this same child, the child she'd never been able to get close to, until now – it broke her heart all over again.

Something deep inside Hazel made her want to reach out and touch her prickly daughter, who had always been off-limits to her, like a crime scene with police tape around it, but her hand refused to break the habit of a lifetime and stayed where it was. She couldn't help noticing though how Venetia's nostrils flared angrily even as she slept and could see bruises forming under the transparent skin, like islands on a map. Simply wishing for her hedgehog hair to grow back wouldn't work any more than hoping she would have a smile on her face when she woke, because her unruly, wayward daughter had been born resenting life and wanting to cause harm.

Looking back, it seemed to Hazel that between her and Roger they had bred the very worst of themselves in Venetia and saved the rest, or should that be *best*, for Yvonne. Although she'd spent the best years of her own life denying any resemblance or similarity between herself and her eldest daughter, the truth had come out in the end, because they were the same and always had been. At first she'd battled against it, choosing instead to despise her daughter for taking after her cruel domineering father and stubbornly blaming him for the way she had turned out. There was so much not to like about her daughter that Hazel felt insulted by their likeness and hated having to admit that she and Venetia were fast turning into a pair of doppelgangers. Here was a person she did not like at all – would even go so far as to say she once hated – and yet there was no escaping the disagreeable fact that mother and daughter shared the same deadly, callous nature that made them capable of murder and more.

And if she could no longer escape that unwanted part of herself that was inherent in Venetia, then she also had to admit never being much of a match for Yvonne and her ideals, always falling way short of her expectations. For everyone had loved little Yvonne, who was so stupidly kind and self-depreciating, always putting others first and wallowing in self-pity whenever anyone said anything hurtful to her. Without exception, anyone who was anyone would move heaven and earth to get her sugary sweet attention. There was no denying it. Phillip, every cleaning lady and babysitter she'd ever hired, schoolteachers, doctors and nurses, all the locals, her classmates. God knew, even Hazel had convinced herself that she too was in love with the child, for it had proved impossible not to pretend otherwise. Tragically, it had taken many years before her true affections became known to her, when all the while her sublimated feelings had lain dormant, hidden in her unconscious mind, like the precious jewels in her red snakeskin leather box, only taken out and examined far less.

She had in fact only realised where her true loyalties lay that day on the beach, when her firstborn child held out her arms to her and, for the first time in her life, told her that she needed her. That it was the same day she lost her other daughter was no matter, almost incidental. Because, all at once, a lifetime's worth of hatred and resentment had disappeared, to be replaced by a fierce, protective, maternal love whose existence had never been hinted at before. At long last, Hazel knew what it was to love. She was a complete woman and there would be no further need of pretence.

Even so, she still couldn't shake off the macabre feeling that it was unnatural for a grown woman to love another grown woman – even if the woman in question happened to be her own daughter. Realising they shared the same flesh – that Venetia had actually inherited *her* vagina and probably smelt the same down there as she did – was repulsive to her. Knowing her grown-up child had experienced sexual arousal was something else she consciously had to force herself not to think about. Hazel quickly squashed any hopes that other women might also have the same un-maternal thoughts, because she knew once again that the only one who would have understood where she was coming from was Venetia herself, who no doubt felt exactly the same horror at having inherited *her* vagina from her mother.

If she and Venetia shared the same abhorrent make-up, then they equally lacked the same important gene inherit in most people – the desire to protect life at all costs, especially new life. Whereas most normal individuals would go out of their way to put a fallen fledgling bird back in its nest, risking life and limb on a high ladder to do so, or swerve dangerously to avoid hitting

303

a cute baby bunny that happened into the middle of the road, Hazel and Venetia would not hesitate to stamp on and squash any living creature that got in their way. Because, as far as Hazel was concerned – and she was sure Venetia was of the same mind – nothing was more important than her own life, even that of her daughter's.

It made no sense to Hazel to hear of mothers sacrificing their own lives for their children because, put simply, an adult parent's life was far more useful than a helpless child's. As far as she could see, it did nobody any good in the natural world for any offspring to outlive its mother because without an adult to care for it, it too would die. So in her book it was far better to sacrifice a child or two along the way if it meant ensuring the mother's survival.

Reflecting on survival and realising that she would soon need to single-handedly moor the boat in the tiny cove near the lighthouse, which was always a risky manoeuvre, as well as having to half-drag, half-carry Venetia up all those steps by herself, she once again mourned the loss of having a man around to rely on. But one thing she could count on was her intention to survive no matter what anyone cared to throw at her.

BOTH TWIN BEDS were neatly made up, with the crease-free bedspreads folded down invitingly at the pillow edge. In the background, a clock ticked methodically – not too loud, not too quiet, just audible enough to let you know that time would go ahead with or without you. The dusky pink curtains had been pulled half closed, their heavily hemmed bottoms dragging reluctantly on the floor as if they couldn't be bothered to glide anymore.

Somehow the room seemed more outdated and neglected than it had before, especially now there was no evidence of

Yvonne or Una ever having been here. There was no longer any child's imprint on the covers; no practical holdall belonging to Yvonne, bursting with various discount shampoos, tampons and talcum powders; and no pink messenger bag with a smiling monkey on the front that had once been slung over Una's shoulder.

A Tiffany lamp had been lit in one corner, highlighting the mildew on the walls and ceiling, but despite the glow it cast around the damp room, the atmosphere remained cold and unwelcoming. The reason for that was in a rocking chair positioned next to the window.

Looking skeletal and deathly, Venetia slipped further down in the chair each time she coughed and wheezed, dribbling saliva onto the blanket tucked around her. Totally unaware that she looked more ghostly and frightening than a whole room full of Mr Naughtys or Wuffas, she would have scared herself half to death were she able to catch a glimpse of herself.

But what was bone and what was wood under the blanket was anybody's guess, for the gaunt frame of the chair and Vee's undernourished body blended into one, like a controversial Tracey Emin exhibition.

With her eyes dragged down like a bloodhound's and the grey flesh around her eyes and mouth looking like it belonged on a corpse, Vee felt as if blood was trickling from her lungs into her nostrils, strangling and suffocating her in the process. Having been sat in this chair too long already, she had long since given up trying to make it rock soothingly, for her body was too weak to gain any momentum. More importantly, she didn't feel as if she had sufficient strength even to breathe in the life-saving medication from her inhaler.

But then, with a sarcastic 'Ha' that hurt her ribs, she

305

reminded herself that nobody had offered her any relief so far, just a few reassuring words that "everything would be alright". In fact, there was no sign of an inhaler – preventative or relieving – and so she knew, without being told, that nothing was alright and never would be again.

She might look like an old woman of one hundred, but unlike the elderly victims she'd seen rescued on TV, buried for days in underground bunkers only to be brought out alive with grateful smiles on their faces, Vee sensed that she would not be so lucky. She was a killer, a murderer, and deserved no less. As their old cleaner, Mrs Dunoon, had once warned her for some misdeed or other, she'd "made her bed and now she must lie in it".

But God, it hurt, it hurt so much, and she didn't mind admitting that she was more than a little frightened. She would give anything to see Vonnie right now and have her hold her hand – but not that awful, limp, blood-stained one she'd seen dangling out of the blanket on the beach. Not that one, but one of her nice, soft, pink hands she'd once told her looked like pig's trotters, a remark that had upset her. The names she'd called her all those years ago put her to shame now, for when had Vonnie done her any real harm? It hadn't been her fault everyone favoured her, not really. It wasn't as if she'd gone around demanding attention and preferential treatment – maybe she'd even resented it, as she claimed to have done. And, anyway, how could anyone not prefer Vonnie to her?

And what about her mother? Where was she right now? Shouldn't she be fussing around her, taking care of her every need, if what she said was to be believed? Could it be true that, despite everything, it turned out that she *was* the truly special daughter? And had been all along? If that was the case, that meant *both* her parents had loved her in their own individual ways and favoured her above anyone else. So where did that leave poor little Vonnie, who'd once thought she was so special? Out in the cold, that's where. Had Vee known any of this back then, she couldn't but think how much easier and simpler it would have been to tolerate and even grow to love a sister who was merely second best.

Aware of movement, Vee tried to focus on the elusive shadow that flitted from one side of the room to the other. Always busy doing something, it turned back the bed one minute, filled a glass of water the next and then opened the window, though she couldn't imagine why, because it was freezing in here and she for one couldn't stop shivering so much her top teeth rattled against her lower ones. Feeling a blast of wind on her face, so cold it took away what little breath she had left, she opened her mouth to complain, but no words came out. Without being told, she already knew whom the shadow belonged to – the distinctive Dior perfume she wore preceded her into the room.

When the gentle "never done a day's work" pair of hands reached out to help her up, Vee instinctively wanted to fight them off, but she didn't have the strength.

'Nearly there, that's it.' Her mother's voice was annoyingly cheerful and ordinary. But, even though Vee tried obediently to put one shaky foot in front of the other, she had no idea where "there" was, but she supposed she must have got there in the end because all at once she felt herself sink gratefully onto a soft mattress that made her feel as if she were floating on the sea and staring up at a warm sun. But that only made her think of how her sister had died and so she turned on her side and stared at the window, where one of the pink curtains had been sucked outside by the wind.

'You're mumbling, Venetia. Not making much sense at all,' her mother cooed, again way too bright and upbeat, as if she had a holiday in Greece to look forward to.

'That's because none of *this* makes any sense.' Vee found her hoarse, boyish voice at last.

When her mother eventually stopped fussily taking so much time to tuck her in, their eyes met. In Hazel's vivid green eyes, that still had so much life left in them, Vee could see her own bloodshot pair lifelessly reflected back.

'Should it?' Hazel asked, feeling Vee's feverish forehead.

Vee nodded emphatically, 'Yes. It must in the end.' She might be a bit vague about where she was or what was going on around her, but there was no confusion in her mind about that. 'What happened after Yvonne died?' She tried to keep her voice matter-of-fact, knowing it would do her no good if her mother guessed how desperate she was for answers.

'You don't remember?'

Vee's face went to work, stretching and frowning, but it was no good, she just couldn't think. But then, just as she was about to give up, a spark of memory came to her – and with it a chilling fear. As a result, her eyes narrowed automatically and suddenly she had colour in her face that hadn't been there before. In the blink of an eye, she reached out and grabbed her mother's arm, intent on reminding her that this wasn't the happy girlie sleepover she seemed to think it was.

'Phillip came. He was angry,' Vee whispered in terror.

* * *

UP AND DOWN Hazel paced, not knowing what else to do except perhaps pull out her own expensively-styled salon hair.

And with every impatient step on the bouncy champagne carpet (definitely champagne, not magnolia, and the distinction *did* matter), she felt in danger of losing someone else dear to her. As the disturbing premonition refused to go away, she marched up and down all the more, continuing relentlessly like a groundsman on a tractor mower with a Wembley-sized football pitch to get through.

The sound of the main door slamming was welcome news. Even more so was the sound of highly-polished Oxford shoes tripping hurriedly up the metal treads of the spiral staircase.

'Thank God,' Hazel breathed, immense relief showing on her face as the living room door opened and a man showing off a Tuscan tan and wearing a hand-tailored Savile Row suit came in. Although his tormented face was grey and haggard, he was unable to halt the vulgar flash of gold Rolex from glistening around the room. This, then, was her husband, her rock – Phillip, a gentle silverback of a man, well groomed and with impeccable taste. Somebody she could, and did, rely on one hundred percent.

'Phillip, I'm so glad you're here. I've been going out of my mind!' Ready to pass on all responsibility, Hazel threw herself into his capable arms, only to find them stiff and unbending, denying her the comfort she desperately craved.

When he didn't respond in any way, she stepped back to look at him better. Normally he was so dependable, but tonight there was something different about him. And it wasn't just the fact he'd shaved off his moustache two days ago, revealing a naked top lip she'd never seen before, which unfortunately reminded her of a leering drag queen's whenever it curled into an unpleasant smile.

'Phillip?' She questioned, trying not to stare at his top lip.

'My little girl, dead. I can hardly believe it,' he spluttered brokenly. And then, consumed with his own loss, he turned his back on Hazel, covered his face with his hands and began to weep unashamedly.

She had never seen him cry before – had never known him turn away from her before. Another first seemed to be that he wanted – no, expected – *her* to comfort *him*, or at least that's what the anguished look in his eyes was telling her. But, surely to God, it should be the other way around. She was the natural mother of Yvonne, whereas he was just the stepfather of three years who'd turned his back on his own biological children when it suited him. And now he was doing the same to her. But she wasn't about to let him get away with it.

As she watched the tears spill out of his hands and run down his knuckles, she fought back the urge to throw something. Unable to resist looking around the room for a suitable weapon, her tetchy glance settled on a crystal vase of Madonna lilies whose black furry antlers reminded her of the bearskin hats worn by guardsmen during the trooping of the colour. But, as they had not yet dropped their yellow pollen, she decided that the flowers were far too fresh to waste on him.

Hazel felt a volcanic rage tremble throughout her body that threatened to erupt any minute, again making her want to lash out and hit him over the head with something. How could he do this to her, turn his back on her when she needed him, just like her father and every other man had done? They were all the same – useless, pathetic, weak little boys who cried louder and harder than any woman, who wanted to be mothered and nurtured throughout their ridiculously long lives. But she was tired of mothering him, this boy she'd mistaken for a man, who could no longer take care of her and as a consequence was no longer any use to her. Besides, there was only one person left on earth she wanted to mother and it wasn't him. It wasn't even the precious little girl he was grieving for right now.

She hated him, she realised. But there was no shock or surprise in the revelation; she had hated him for some time, perhaps even for as long as they'd known each other. Love had never really been plausible when all it had taken was a curl of her finger and a lick of her lips to lure him away from his wife of twelve years.

'A beautiful woman is one you notice, a charming woman is one who notices you,' Phillip had once quipped, believing himself clever to have memorised Adlai E Stevenson's famous quote. Perhaps he hadn't intended his derogatory words to be insulting, but she had despised him all the same.

And the hatred, now that she had acknowledged it, would never go away again, no matter how hard she tried. In fact, she could see it haunting her for the remainder of their lives together, which meant that, for the sake for their marriage, she would have to go on pretending.

She couldn't stand it, the thought of continuously having to pretend. Hadn't she had enough of that already? She wouldn't be able to go through with it. It would drive her mad. But wait… she must compose herself, calm down. She had to, or else… She had to think this through more sensibly – plan what she must do next, how she would handle this bolt from the blue. What she really needed was a distraction, something to take her mind off it – that way she could come up with a strategy, a plan, one that wouldn't mean losing the lighthouse or her extravagant lifestyle. She wasn't simply thinking of herself as she plotted, but of Venetia's prospects too. A lot would depend on Phillip's reaction when he found out exactly what happened on the beach as to whether her daughter even had a future.

And then, all of a sudden, there she was. The distraction she'd prayed for.

Speak of the devil… VENETIA, who had, unbeknown to Hazel, crept silently into the room and was now fixing venomous eyes on her stepfather.

'She wasn't your little girl. And you're not her real father,' she hissed dangerously.

Hazel tried not to be fascinated by the water dripping from her daughter's swimsuit onto the carpet, but she couldn't help but be morbidly aware that the wet costume was a match for the one Yvonne had been wearing earlier that day – except that hers was now being cut off her body, piece by piece, as she lay on a concrete slab in a cold morgue somewhere.

'She killed my real father,' Venetia screamed, pointing accusingly at Hazel.

'Stop that, Venetia,' Hazel squirmed uncomfortably, wishing that her daughter didn't look so obviously guilty of something, with her tangled hair, bloodied, scraped knees and swollen right eye that had puffed up like burnt pastry on a meat pie.

'I saw her,' Venetia insisted defiantly, locking eyes with her stepfather and ignoring her mother.

'She doesn't know what she's saying. She's just a child,' Hazel countered, eyes flicking frantically back and forth between her husband and her daughter, trying to read what the other was thinking, trying to second-guess what their next move would be.

Phillip shook all over like a huge Labrador emerging from water and glared right back at Venetia.

'You did this. You were meant to be looking after her!' Phillip towered menacingly over his stepdaughter, who was now backtracking and shaking her head in fear.

'Pure evil, that's what you are,' he snarled. And then, with a forceful flick of his fist, he sent her flying across the room, all the while conscious of how good it felt. Truthfully, he'd always wanted to do that to the child he'd grown to hate, mainly because of the way she'd made Yvonne's life a misery with her relentless bullying, but also because of the feelings of impotency he'd experienced due to never being allowed to do anything about it. On that, Hazel had always been firm.

'No, Phillip. No.' Hazel quickly jumped in his path before he could strike out again, for there was no denying that he intended to do exactly that. In fact, he had the glazed, mad look in his eyes emulated by fighters on the TV, who got into the "zone" before every fight – a place where emotions were not allowed.

As Venetia dazedly picked herself up from the floor, wiping away fresh blood from her cut lip, Hazel signalled for her to leave the room. And when she did not, Hazel lost it…

'Get out if you don't want to end up like your sister,' she screamed, flapping her arms hysterically. Not needing telling a second time, Venetia shot out of the room, bumping into walls as she went and sending the vase of lilies crashing to the floor.

When Hazel looked around for Phillip, she saw him disappear through the sliding glass door onto the tower.

SHE MIGHT ONLY be nine years old, but she had managed to break into the beach hut all by herself by smashing a windowpane with her fist and climbing through the jagged edges of the glass frame, ripping a bite-sized chunk out of her swimming costume in the process.

Once inside, she trailed an incriminating path of wet footprints across the dusty floor. Realising that she had been holding her breath the whole time, she now found it hurt to inhale the stale, mildew air.

Inside, everything was the same as before. There were spider webs strung up in corners whilst a pink feather duster leaned against the side of the hut with the remains of a broken web caught in its feathers. Underneath one of the window shutters was a tiled top table with a couple of deck chairs pushed underneath. On the table there was a loaf of sliced bread and an open tub of butter with a knife stood up in it and a camping gas ring with a kettle perched on top, as well as an array of white china plates that were thicker and uglier than the ones they ate on at home.

If she shut her eyes, Venetia could almost hear the kettle whistling and the sound of her mother sweeping the floor as she hummed a tune she did not recognise. Earlier that day her mother had worn her hair in a lively ponytail that swung from side to side and would have tickled Vee's skin had she been close enough to her. In the air remained the offensive smell of the boiled eggs that her mother had planned on giving them for tea and a lingering, subtle aroma of her Dior perfume that stung Vee's eyes and made them water unexpectedly.

Everything was the same as before. It felt the same. Looked exactly the same. But it was not the same and never would be again. Not now Yvonne was no longer part of their – her – world. She might not have been the precious little angel or princess Phillip claimed her to be, however – the truth was that Vonnie had a nasty temper when provoked and Vee still had the scars to prove it. Even so, she had been the reason they had all gone on living in relative harmony together, and now she was gone they were falling apart, dropping like flies. Her, her mother, Phillip…

She longed to box her sister's ears for doing this to them, and if she was here right now there was no telling what she would do to her. Instead, Vee took out her rage on the beach hut, knocking the kettle, cups and plates to the floor and loving the way they bounced and split into a hundred pieces of fragmented china that cut her feet as she trod on them.

Next she tore the door from its hinges and then, before she knew she was doing it, her spindly legs were galloping down to the sea as fast as they would go and she was standing knee-deep in the dirty grey water that stunk of the public toilets in Lighthouse Close.

'I hate you. Hate you,' she screamed tearfully, kicking out at the lapping water, wanting to strangle every last drop of it.

THERE WAS A delicate chink of glassware as Hazel passed a tumbler of Phillip's favourite whiskey to him and took a sip of something strong herself. Not liking the taste very much, she preferred the frosty feel of the good-quality glass in her hand to anything else and the way it misted up romantically whenever she breathed into it. Not to mention the satisfaction in seeing her Chanel "Monte-Carlo" shade of lipstick stamped on the rim of the glass each time she took a sip. Hazel always found it reassuring to know that she left something of herself behind.

Having followed Phillip out onto the tower, they now stood side by side, gazing out at the black swirling sea that had taken their daughter from them. Only a few inches separated them as they clung onto the metal railing for support, but they did not touch. Nor yet did they speak, for the sound of the waves crashing onto the pebbled shore had far too much to say for themselves.

While she toyed with her drink, Phillip had finished his and was now looking at her through the empty glass with weirdly distorted eyes. Although there was a silence between them that neither wanted to break, there was also an expectant expression on Phillip's face that would not tolerate being kept waiting much longer.

'When they went off to play, I wanted to shout after them, "Be careful". They could so easily have tripped and fallen.' Hazel immediately felt her eyes fill with tears. 'But I never did. And now I can't help blaming myself,' she confessed.

Instead of his being moved, as she'd hoped, Phillip sighed irritably and without thinking tried to take another slug of his empty drink, neither noticing nor caring when no amber liquid hit the back of his throat.

'One of these days, Hazel, you're going to have to face up to the fact that she's not right. She never has been.' His voice wobbled dangerously.

'You never did have much time for her. It was always Yvonne this and Yvonne that.' Hazel was immediately defensive.

'You should have let me lay down the law years ago, like I wanted to… Ironic really, because neither of you will be able to escape it now,' he laughed sarcastically.

As if he'd just hit her, Hazel flinched and took a fearful step back.

'Will you go to the police?' Hazel's hand flew to her mouth as if she couldn't believe she had spoken such words.

'Over her or you?' Phillip let the threat sink in and watched his wife squirm.

'After what you've just said about Venetia… I can't imagine you'd believe anything she said.' Hazel's voice faltered when she saw that her words made no difference. He had already made up his mind.

'I have a far better imagination than you give me credit for,' Phillip went on. 'You see, I always knew there was something you were hiding from me, and now it all makes sense – though I never had you down as a cold-blooded killer until tonight.'

There was a long pause as Phillip leaned over the railings and looked down curiously on the choppy waves below, almost as if he expected to see Yvonne's body floating back and forth in the tide.

'I did it to protect them.' Hazel grabbed the arm of his jacket, making him turn to look at her.

'From what?' He was sceptical. 'What were you meant to be protecting them from?'

'Their father. He…' What couldn't be said hung unspoken in the air between them. And then, cowering beneath his cold stare, Hazel caved in. 'He did things he shouldn't'. At last she had his attention.

'To you? Did he rape you?' Phillip was so horrified, he almost put out a hand to touch her.

'Yes, but what of it?' Hazel smiled inwardly, detecting the first glimpse of sympathy. There was hope yet of regaining his trust and understanding and the knowledge gave her confidence. 'What of it, compared to the girls?' She allowed that implication to hover in the air like a bad smell.

'He raped Yvonne and Venetia?' The allegation almost stuck in his conservative, happily brought up throat. Phillip was a person to whom unpleasant things did not happen. Crime, rape, abuse, theft or even plain old incivility happened only to people he didn't know; those who featured in red top newspapers and lived on sink estates in rundown cities.

'Just Venetia. He always left Yvonne alone.' Hazel thanked God he was coming back on board. Perhaps now he would support her, as he was meant to, and protect her and Venetia from the fallout of what happened on the beach. She had been wrong before – she did need him, he was a good man after all, judging by the way he was reacting to the news about Venetia.

Perhaps he would view her differently from now on, knowing what she'd been through, and might even turn out to be as much of a father to her as he had once been to Yvonne.

'Well, thank God for that. I couldn't bear it, knowing he'd... not to little Vonnie.'

Feeling as if she'd had her handbag snatched from a train, along with her most recent hopes and wishes, Hazel weighed up her husband as if for the first time.

'So it was alright for him to do it to Venetia? You can live with that?'

'That's not what I meant,' Phillip backtracked.

'Isn't it?' Now it was Hazel's turn to be fierce and furious. She wanted to kill him. She'd never wanted anything so much, not even the Tiffany heart bracelet with the £3,650 price tag that was locked away in her red and cream suede jewellery box.

'I've always looked after you and the girls, haven't I, Hazel?' he reminded her gently. 'Been a good husband and father?'

'Nobody could deny it,' she retorted sulkily, shrugging her shoulders.

'But, what you've got to understand is that she was my little "sea princess". And no matter what anyone else says, she loved me as a father. That much I do know.'

So what, she wanted to shout back, just as Venetia would have done. She didn't have to understand anything, not as far as he was concerned. He'd only loved Yvonne because she was beautiful and knew how to sit perfectly still on his lap while he stroked and petted her like he would a gold bar hidden under the floorboards. Hazel knew this because that was exactly how he'd been with her when they'd first married. Yvonne might have unwittingly stolen her husband away from her, but to give credit where it was due, her daughter had known how to work him far better than she ever could.

Clearly choked up and misunderstanding her moody silence for understanding, Phillip held out his empty glass and the faithful fondness Hazel was accustomed to seeing returned to his watery grey eyes.

'Fix me another, I could do with it. You were always good at fixing things.'

'Just not people,' Hazel warned.

If he thought for one minute she was going to mollycoddle him – put him first before her and Venetia – he had another thing coming. Nevertheless, she obediently turned away to do his bidding. Just as she was about to close the sliding door, she thought she heard him whisper something, so she turned back expectantly. But he still had his back to her and was leaning over the railings and staring moodily at the sea below, just as before. As he did not turn around again, she couldn't be sure that he had said anything at all. But there it was again… and this time she heard right.

'Be careful, Hazel. Or she'll have you tripping and falling for the rest of your life,' he whispered brokenly.

Too late she realised what he was about to do and for an interminably long moment held her breath – whether from suspense or shock, she couldn't be sure. But as she exhaled, it felt to her that she blew him off the tower herself, as if he were no more than a flimsy dandelion in the wind. And even then, her screams warning him to, 'Stay back' and 'Don't do it' went undeclared as Phillip toppled off the tower, bouncing once off the white walls of the lighthouse – breaking his left clavicle, scapula and femur on initial impact – then a second time – snapping his sacrum, right tibia and patella – before disappearing into the black sea below.

Before her eyes, all Hazel could see were a hundred thousand pieces of dandelion snow being dispersed on the breeze like parachute balls of fuzzy cotton, which reminded her of childhood picnics in summer meadows. Except those picnics had only ever actually taken place in her imagination, because her mother always ended up spoiling any family outings long before they ever left the house.

But then, as it finally dawned on Hazel what had really happened, that the terrible event unfolding before her eyes was real and not just her imagination playing tricks on her, she screamed, 'Phillip. No. Phillip. No!' She rather enjoyed listening to the sound of her own heartfelt screams. It was true, then. He really had thrown himself off the tower and was now almost certainly dead. Now he was gone, she found herself as devastated as any wife could or should be in the same circumstances. And nobody listening to her tormented wailing would ever think otherwise.

* * *

SHIVERING UNDER THE bedcovers, Venetia's face was trained on the open window, where the curtains danced a lively Charleston in the breeze, and not on her mother, who, having pulled the rocking chair right up to the bed, now sat in it, looking tired and irritable, as if her premenopausal period was about to start.

Vee had something important to say and didn't want her mother's eyes on her when she said it. 'He wanted to kill me. Rip me to pieces. I could see it in his eyes.'

Her throat was dry and her lips were cracked. She could tell her health was deteriorating very rapidly because by now it hurt even to talk. 'I'm not evil.' She fought back tears, focusing hard on the rumbling of thunder and the flashes of lightning through the window as if they were the only thing keeping her alive.

'I know you're not.' Her mother picked up her cold, clammy hand and held it against her cheek for a moment. 'No more than me, anyway.'

'I saw you. I know what really happened that night with Phillip on the tower.' Vee's voice escaped as more of a frivolous whisper than the incriminating hiss she'd intended it to be.

'You've been watching me your whole life.' Sighing disappointedly, her mother placed Vee's hand back on the bedcover, readjusted it once more because it wasn't quite straight enough, and then frowned. 'When are you going to learn that's not good for you?' Shifting in her seat, Hazel slid out the bedside table drawer and took out an inhaler.

Licking her dry lips in anticipation of some much-needed relief, Vee half raised her hand, frustrated to find that the knuckles would not bend into a holding grasp. And then her eyes widened fearfully as she watched her mother hold down her finger on the release button and an ominous hissing sound filled the room – a sound that was at once both familiar and terrifying to her. But she could do nothing except watch helplessly as the gassy compound vanished into the air, along with her chance of living.

'He left me. Just like my father. The only thing keeping him here was Yvonne. That's why he left us,' her mother spat, oblivious to Venetia's fear.

'But I saw you…' Vee was close to forgetting what she had seen, what she remembered, or even why it was important she let her mother know this.

'It doesn't matter what you saw.' Her mother's voice rose to a piercing shriek as she took out another inhaler from the drawer and started emptying that one too.

Collapsing back onto the bed, Vee wheezed and struggled for breath, hating the nasty grey phlegm that shot from her mouth onto the bed sheets, sticking like glue to the 100% Egyptian cotton. The weight on her chest was crushing her and her lungs felt like water bombs about to explode.

'After Phillip… left… we stayed up all night listening to the sea.' Her mother's haunting voice sounded far off, a million miles away but, strangely, the echo of the sea grew closer, until it felt as if the crashing waves were rolling around inside Vee's head, deafening her.

It had been an incredibly long day. So much had happened and she was tired. So very tired, she felt as if she were floating. But then she felt a weight on the bed that wasn't her own. Not only did the extra burden immediately unbalance her, it made her lean to one side, taking her back to the times that she or Vonnie would budge over in bed in order to let the other one in. But this was no six-year-old girl sitting prettily at the end of the bed, with bubblegum-pink cheeks and a Sunday morning smell in her hair – it was her tragically middle-aged mother, who wore heartbreak on her face as well as any size-8 model did Stella McCartney.

'I'm cold.' Vee wasn't sure why she wanted her mother to know this. It couldn't be because she wanted to feel her press her finger on her mouth and shush her gently, could it, as she'd seen her do to Vonnie?

'I want you to know you were always my favourite. Never Yvonne,' her mother whispered conspiratorially, as if afraid that her other dead daughter might yet overhear. 'She never even came close. Why else do you think I protected you the way I did?'

Venetia would have liked to stay and listen to her mother, but she was incredibly exhausted and could hardly keep her eyes open. But, suddenly, they did fly open and stayed wide open, for there was somebody else in the room with them – a malevolent presence that was not entirely unexpected but feared all the same. She could feel it, sense it – smell it, even. And the smell was one she recognised… of a carnivorous, warm-blooded animal.

'It's Wuffa. He's coming for me,' she cried out deliriously, clinging onto her mother's hand.

'They would have taken you away, otherwise. All those terrible things you did to Yvonne… all the hospital emergencies,' her mother carried on, as if she'd never heard her. Then Vee knew shame once again as she felt her organs abandon themselves to the terror of the giant wolf-like dog as the sheets absorbed her vinegary urine. It wouldn't be long before the telltale pungent smell hit her mother's nostrils, causing her nose to crinkle at the corners. Not long at all till she took away her reassuring hand or got up from the bed in disgust, as she'd done all those years ago.

But, surprisingly, her mother remained where she was, still perched on the edge of the bed, and every so often stroked Vee as if she were a sleepy kitten curled up on a satin cushion. But when Vee heard the terrifying lupine snarl coming from the bottom of the bed, the imaginary kitten shot up in alarm, arched its back, hissed loudly and scarpered, making her almost want to laugh. Almost.

Just as she was about to close her eyes again – for truthfully she was finding it more and more difficult to concentrate, let alone stay awake, and her mind felt all fuzzy, like Vonnie's favourite brown felt bear – she felt something wet and warm nudge her arm. Turning her head slightly, she found herself looking into a pair of predatory amber eyes and the long, black snout of a giant wolf. It was Wuffa. He had come for her at last, just as she'd always dreaded.

With an arched back and crouched demeanour, he had somehow managed to stalk his way into the room, carrying himself low to the ground so as not to be observed. On first glance, he was of course fierce and frightening, but now Vee was able to see him better she found his eyes surprisingly kind as well as intelligent.

With hardly any breath left in her, she was having to change her opinion about dogs, fast. Well, about Wuffa anyway. For there he was now, his head laid docilely on the bedcover, looking at her with meltingly affectionate eyes and not a bared canine in sight. Was he big? Yes, massive in fact, and as potentially dangerous as a grizzly bear. His paws alone were the size of plastic sandcastle buckets. But what she noticed more than anything through her blurred vision was the grey hairs on his muzzle and chest, which reminded her of the rare glimpses she'd caught of Phillip shaving bare-chested in the bathroom. It came as a shock to learn that Wuffa was old and had grown tired of carrying children off into the sea in his massive jaws. Reaching out timidly for the wolf's warm, furry head, she allowed her fingers to play in his matted mane, which curled in downward spirals like pretty girl's ringlets. Panting heavily and dribbling saliva on her hand, he seemed ridiculously grateful for the attention. And when she took her eyes off him for a second and looked around for her mother, he whined, wanting her back. But eventually Wuffa sighed and settled down, his huge devoted eyes full of a sadness he couldn't speak or share.

With only a few more minutes to go, somebody else entered the room and joined the other grieving mourners around her soon-to-be deathbed. She knew who it was without opening her eyes. She felt his pain, smelt the blood. It was the headless boy king, who wept over the loss of his dismembered head, which he carried in the crook of his arm. Although Vee did not fear him, it sent shivers down her spine to see the hundreds of arrows embedded in his body and she fought against feeling pity, for she had no strength to waste.

Strangely enough, she felt as if she had climbed the walls of the room to escape such emotions and was now sitting on the ceiling, but perhaps she was just confused? Because it seemed to her that she had left her physical body behind on the bed, like a purse she'd once mistakenly left on the holiday train that used to take her and Vonnie into town. The £2.30 in pocket money had never been returned to her either, she recalled crossly, even though her name and address had been clearly written in exaggerated black capitals inside the purse.

From her elevated place on the ceiling, she continued to look down on Wuffa and the boy king's heads, but wondered why her own broken body had been replaced with a child's – a child who was as instantly recognisable as her own refection in a mirror and who wore a disturbingly familiar old-fashioned swimsuit. A child whose slight body made hardly any indentation on the bed but left a pool of water around her that resembled a chalk mark drawn around a dead body. Her dark eyes were open and fixed on the window, Vee noticed gratefully – for she did not want to look directly into them – and her breathing was as awkward and difficult as she herself had been as a child. Now Vee came to think about it, the child was as still as she was. It was almost as if they had reached the same stage of something – she didn't know what – at exactly the same time.

Tearing her eyes away from the child's grey body, Vee focused instead on the second hand of the clock that somehow made time slow down. She didn't know if that was good or bad, because she felt disinclined to get back in her own body. The thought of having to slip it on again depressed her, just as much as losing a game of Monopoly to her sister might have done. She'd once read somewhere (one of those interesting but useless facts that often spring to mind) that an average of 150,000 people die in the world each day and of that number 7,000 die every hour. Vee couldn't help wondering how many per minute that amounted to, or per second, for that matter, because it felt important to know who would be keeping her company into the afterlife – if there was such a thing. And even if there was, she wasn't sure that it was somewhere she was overly keen to go. The question she dared not ask herself was, would she see Vonnie there? And if so, would her sister be angry? Would she ever be able to forgive her or deign to speak to her again, or would she punish her by grassing her up to everybody else? Wherever she went, Vee figured, her prospects were not good.

She wished she could let Vonnie know that the aftermath of what happened on the beach that day was so very different to what she may have imagined – far from it, in fact. There had been no unexpected joy of sprinkling hundreds and thousands over the Bird's trifle for Vee, or of having an extra-large portion to herself, or even of getting to lick the bowl out afterwards, because everything had happened so fast.

The first person she'd run into on the beach had been the Coxswain outside the RNLI station who somehow or other managed to coax her story out of her and then her mother had come and beaten her black and blue, right in front of everyone. Before she knew it, they'd been back at the lighthouse with the dreadful sound of Phillip's shoes tripping up the stairs. Her heart had pumped so fast she thought it would burst, like that time she swallowed a whole packet of fruit Polos for a dare without crunching and got one wedged in her throat. She could still remember getting into a "pet" (as Phillip called it) and sulking when the ambulance rushing her to A&E refused to switch on the siren as well as the flashing lights.

Such idle reflection couldn't alter her outcome.. No matter how much she might try to delay, He finally came. As soon as his presence was felt in the room, the child disappeared from the bed and she was back in it, rolling in the wet patch left behind.

Ultimately, she had sensed he would be there at the end, because he had never forgotten her and never would. She was, after all, as much a part of his life as he was hers. They may have spent their whole lives glimpsing each other in dark corners and mysterious hallways that led to shadowy, macabre worlds, but this time they would actually come to face to face. She had run out of places to hide, betrayed those who would protect her from *him*, and used up all of her nine lives where he was concerned. And not one person noticed his depraved presence by the bed – not even Wuffa, with his enhanced canine senses. Mr Naughty might have slid in silently, so as not to arouse suspicion, but now that He was finally here, positioned rigidly on the corner of the bed just inches away from her unsuspecting mother, she could no longer deny that this was THE END.

She watched, mesmerised, as his hand stretched out on the cover, skeletal fingers tapping impatiently, as if he were some ordinary soul at a bus stop grown tired and irritable of waiting. What's more, he was so thin his bones creaked with every laboriously slow movement. When Vee dared at last peer closer, she was horrified to see how the skin stretched tightly over his yard-long face and that his black eyes flickered with not so much as an iris or pupil in sight. Not only that, but his shredded clothes looked as if a dozen corpses had previously been buried in them. More frightening still was the ragged slit of his scabby mouth that was quite clearly tired of conversation. And the way his balding head, dotted with sparse long black hairs, resembled the ribbons of squid ink pasta her mother liked to dish up, made her cringe all over.

'Mum. Mummy,' she cried, scared out of her wits. 'I'm sorry. I didn't mean it. Any of it. Make it all go away, please,' she implored.

'You're your father's daughter, alright. I've always said so, haven't I?' Reassuringly, her mother climbed onto the bed and lay down next to her, stroking her damp hair and shushing her gently, so close that Vee could taste her Earl Grey breath. And then, as she felt her own slight body being pulled forcibly into the more womanly curve of her mother's embrace, Vee immediately recognized it as a place she had always wanted to be.

'But I fear it will only get worse the older you get.' Her mother's voice seemed to come out of nowhere, like a car with no headlights in the fog. But Vee was no longer capable of listening. Instead, she drifted in and out of worlds where one minute she was off with Wuffa, then the boy king, then back again with Mr Naughty in the next instance.

Rolling onto her back, Vee stared up at the hypnotic ceiling fan, almost allowing herself to be lulled to sleep by it and the comforting sound of the sea in the distance. After a second or two, she felt her mother do the same. Truthfully, Vee felt that her mother was someplace else too. A place inhabited by both her daughters, perhaps?

Unable to ignore the ominous sound of an owl hooting outside the window, Vee concentrated instead on the whirring blades of the fan above her head. She would never get the chance to take a pleasure ride in a helicopter with similar blades, she realised – not that she'd ever wanted to before, but it would have been nice to have the option all the same. In fact, she'd never been on a plane in her life or gone skiing in Gstaad like her mother and Phillip had. Nor would she ever stay in a log cabin where a chalet girl from Notting Hill called Fuchsia would "knock together" a cinnamon cake for tea that would turn out heavy as a brick.

Such hopes were as dead to her as the bluest of skies, the first sign of snowdrops in spring or a field of red poppies that had sprung up overnight just to surprise her. Even then, as Vee's eyes closed, shutting out any last glimpse of colour, she was acutely aware that these were not her own thoughts but those of her mother's. Because since when had she thought to notice a blue sky, even if it was staring her in the face? And she wouldn't know a snowdrop if she saw one, let alone be impressed by a whole field of wild flowers. She was far more likely to flatten the delicate petals with her Doc Marten boots and not give a damn. So dominant was her mother's power of control over her, she was not even allowed her own last thoughts at the moment of her death without interference.

True to form, her mother would rather have her think of fields of flowers or prom gowns and updos at the hairdressers rather than booze, fags, tattoos and cunnilingus, as would have been Vee's natural wont. It was too late to do anything about it now, though, because already she could sense that her mother had got up from the bed and was moving agitatedly around the room, a bittersweet tang of gin and lemon following her as she turned off the lights and folded things up – something she could never resist doing.

'Time for bed,' Vee thought she heard someone whisper. It

sounded like her mother's voice, younger and fresher from many years ago. Her special night time voice, reserved for her and Yvonne when they were little.

'Don't let the bedbugs bite.'

Her mother's words caused a crinkle to appear at the corner of her mouth and an even bigger smile would have appeared right then, if she could have managed it, because all at once she could smell the sea. She could hear the ripple of water on the sand, taste the saltiness in the air and hear her sister's precious laughter as she ran... ran... ran... down to the sea, laughing – always laughing as she chased the sun's rays towards the clear blue water.

'I'm coming too, Vonnie. Wait for me!' Vee cried out happily. Her legs started to move beneath the sheets, as if she too were running... running... running to join her sister. Because she was...

HAZEL WATCHED HER daughter slip out of the skin she'd worn so miserably all her life and felt mild surprise when her eyelids slid back up again, like a fruit machine that had, for once, struck lucky.

Belatedly, it occurred to her that she would no longer feel her daughter's hot breath on her face that once smelt of Liquorice Allsorts and would never again witness her bite the corner of her lip until it formed an unattractive scab, a habit that always made Hazel want to scold. But for once, she observed gratefully, the angry crease on her forehead had, in death, finally smoothed out. As a result, her daughter no longer looked as cross as a girl always on her period. The face that could have been so pretty and given Yvonne a run for her money had filled out, making Venetia look healthier than when she was alive.

Hazel didn't get mad when a blue bottle fly, which made a

heavy whacking sound each time it bounced off the walls, laid eggs in her daughter's nose, nor did she attempt to swat it away. Instead, she watched, fascinated, hardly daring to move in case she disturbed its burrowing and wondered how new life for some animals could be so easy, barely an inconvenience at all. While others, like her, were made to suffer such unbearable agony.

On that thought, she had fallen into a troubled sleep and dreamt disturbingly of breast-feeding other people's babies. As she slept, her unconscious mind flitted between the present and the past, so that when her eyes flickered open, as they frequently did, she sometimes saw nine-year-old Venetia lying dead on the bed next to her and sometimes the older, grown-up version.

WHEN I FINALLY woke up, I realised that life would go on around me, as it always had. As it did now, judging by the noise going on outside the window, of gulls squawking and squabbling and the sound of waves crashing against the cliff edge. I couldn't decide which was more painful – giving life or taking it away.

Having woken up confused and alone on the bed with barely an indentation on the bedcover next to me where Venetia had spent her last moments, I felt bewildered by the photographs scattered haphazardly around me and couldn't even begin to imagine what the pink ballerina jewellery box was doing on the pillow where Venetia's head should have been.

There was an old creased photograph of Yvonne on a swing, smiling happily at the camera while Venetia scowled in the background, arms folded crossly, looking as if she hated the world and everybody in it. Noticing the sun-scorched grass at their feet and that both heads were bleached by the sun, I estimated the picture to have been taken about fifteen years ago.

There was one of me too, alone on the sea dragon

rollercoaster ride, taken with one of those automatic on-ride cameras that were meant to capture you screaming – except in my case I'd kept my face stonily turned to one side and appeared indifferent. There was another of me behind the wheel of the powerboat over at Seal Island and a self-portrait of me playing a game of solitary bingo at the amusement arcade. Turning the photograph over in my hand, I could see that it had only been printed yesterday – so where were the rest of the photographs, the ones of us together?

Glancing bemusedly at the empty space beside me on the bed, I reached out to stroke its smooth surface and in doing so knocked over the ballerina jewellery box, which spat out a few uninspired bars of "Dance of the Sugar Plum Fairy" before spilling its contents as effortlessly as a tortured prisoner of war would, revealing two almost identical children's death certificates, each dated 3rd August of the same year… fifteen years ago.

As the sadness and ugliness of what had happened dawned on me, and what I'd done, I realised that I had been flitting in and out of a perverse fantasy world the whole time I'd been here. Closing my eyes against the horror of it and hoping that it would all somehow go away, I finally admitted the truth to myself.

'I'd promised myself a long weekend with my children and after fifteen years apart I was determined to make it happen,' I cried tearfully, angrily screwing up the folds of paper in my hand.

'What have I done? God forgive me. What have I done?' I whimpered pitifully in between long, drawn-out sobs. I then threw the jingling ballerina jewellery box at the door, breaking one of the dancer's gracefully upturned arms as it landed with a thud on the floor.

My hopes and dreams had become a living fantasy, a real "castle in the air" fairytale, where I could be anything I wanted.

Where day could become night and vice versa. In the midst of this unreal existence was the promise of reconciliation with my dead children, whom I had miraculously turned into adults, living their lives like characters in a play I'd written especially for them.

I didn't consider myself abnormal for devoting so much of my time to imagining what my children would have turned out like in adulthood, had they lived – for didn't all mothers spend their lives wondering and worrying about exactly the same thing? It wasn't that I was narcissistic, as some might claim – a ridiculous suggestion, considering that I'd never even liked myself, let alone grown to love myself as others did – like Phillip had. But I suppose I was vain enough not to have wanted the grown-up Yvonne to outshine me, because even at six years old she had been a promising beauty. So, having conveniently decided it was highly likely that my daughter would have struggled with her weight in later life, especially after childbirth (she had always been rather too fond of her food), I made sure that she was two-and-a-half stone heavier than she ought to be. And if I did sometimes consider this a little harsh on poor little Yvonne, who had seen beauty in graffiti and would cry over her sister biting the head off a jelly baby, I would tell myself that it was all for the best. And, as for the tomboyish Venetia, who had always scorned both Yvonne and I for our femininity, it seemed almost natural for her to have evolved into a taciturn and sullen lesbian, awkward around people and unable to communicate her emotions without resorting quickly to anger.

Like my firstborn daughter, I knew all there was to know about anger and hatred. It lived inside me, just as it had her. *There weren't many people I didn't hate*, I realised with a jolt. My father, my mother, my devil's spawn half-brothers and sister –

who I still curse to this day – Roger, my own children at times and even Phillip.

Especially Phillip. For there was nothing more devastating for a vain and beautiful woman like me to lose power over a man who once professed to love and adore me. And I still couldn't get over the fact that he had been ready to abandon me that night – just leave me and walk away. How dare he? Who did he think he was to do that to me? I'd once considered myself extremely lucky to have been loved and adored by two husbands, but it was just as I'd told the children – 'I don't mind admitting I really don't know what I did to deserve it.' And I hadn't deserved it. Not their abuse, or their betrayal, either.

For years, Phillip had been threatening to lay the law down where Venetia was concerned, even going so far as suggesting that we involve social services. On more than one occasion, he'd demanded I do something about her terrorising her sister and had intimated that if I would not, he would. Anyone would think Yvonne was his, the way he went on as if he were the only adult interested in protecting her. But they were my children, I had reminded him, not his, and I would deal with them as I saw fit. At least my children were a normal size, and pretty – not obese and ugly like his own biological children, who had turned out to be such a disappointment and embarrassment to him.

That night on the tower, before he... before I... He had looked at me in the same way he did his fat daughters, with horror and scorn, as if he were truly seeing me for the first time. And I felt his repulsion like I would a gold chain done up too tightly around my neck. I could have forgiven him for wanting to beat Venetia half to death for what she'd done to her sister, but not his abandonment and betrayal, which came at a time we needed him most. It was just as well he'd thrown himself off the tower when he did, because I couldn't have allowed him to go to the authorities and let them take Venetia away, nor have her locked up like some captive animal. I could bear anything but that.

There were a lot of things I wished I'd done differently in life, but losing Phillip on the tower that night was not one of them. Besides, once I'd grown accustomed to being a widow again, I was able to reinvent my husband all over again. Only this time I made sure he was very different to the resentful man he'd become over the years; one who better resembled the man I'd first fallen in love with. The new Phillip I created in my mind would not have rejected me or threatened to abandon me, and so he became a man worthy enough to mourn.

When it came to planning his funeral, the rest of his family were appalled to discover his love of competitive outdoor sports and extravagant playboy lifestyle had been obliterated from memory as effectively as a field of wheat under the blades of a combine harvester. In fact, every word uttered by the female vicar – who loved nothing more than to spit out pleasantries at people the same way she did flaky pastry on a sausage roll – had been penned by myself. I'd made sure there was no mention of his sailing club, golf tournaments, tennis matches, weekends away with the boys, drinking till all hours at his private club or rowdily eating out at top restaurants, let alone his fat former wife and obese home-educated children.

Likewise, when it came to choosing a selection of music for him to be remembered by, I deliberately ignored what would have been his obvious choice (he had long been a Def Leppard fan) and instead chose "Goodbye to Love" by The Carpenters, which met with just as much shock from the Ladd family as did the fraudulent eulogy. But I refused point-blank to compromise;

335

in death I had him just where I'd always wanted him, under my control and at my mercy, a man incapable of opposing my views. That pretence would go on surviving, even if he hadn't.

Whenever the situation called for it, such as when I was being grilled about his death or asked about *that* night on the tower, I could always rely on tears filling my eyes as a way of combating questions. Some fell for it and pitied me; others were openly sceptical. But not one of them guessed the truth; that my heart-wrenching sobs were for the baby who'd first rejected me twenty-four years ago. And, knowing what I do now, I realise that I should have fought for my firstborn and wrestled her out of Roger's cruel hands at the first hint of trouble. Or drowned her in the process, because even that would have been a better outcome than what actually happened.

There was of course no possibility of putting things right, not in the real world at least, which was what the whole imaginary "long weekend" had been about. And now I am as alone, as I have always been. Because at last I have let them go. For too long I have endured them inside my head, imagining the best and worst of both of them. My greed even saw me invent a granddaughter for myself, one who would love me far more than my own daughters ever had. But I couldn't even get that right. No matter how hard I tried, I couldn't make my family love me, because deep down I knew I didn't deserve it. How could I?

It seems to me that the love I should have lavished on Venetia all those years ago had arrived at a junction, not knowing what direction it should be heading in. And, being a bad driver (as claimed by both my dead husbands), I had as usual gone in entirely the wrong direction, choosing hatred over love and rejecting my child when it became apparent that she preferred anyone else's embrace to my own.

INTENT ON RETRACING my steps back over the long weekend, I pause outside the neglected lighthouse that stands alone on the cliff edge and has an air of abandonment about it. Cricking my neck, I gaze up at the highest part of the tower. Scared of the incriminating shadows I might see there, I think I hear the crunch of bone slamming against its harsh, unforgiving walls.

Turning quickly away, I walk down to the beach where I follow other people's footsteps in the sand but do not want to think of Yvonne having done the same all those years ago. Never able to shake off the feeling someone is watching me, I stumble past the RNLI boat station, which is eerily empty. Even the Boathouse Cafe that usually does a roaring trade is closed for the winter. I can remember many a time spent there, drinking weak tea from a chipped enamel cup, but these days they refuse to serve me, even though my money is as good as anybody else's.

But nobody can stop me going down to the shore, where I watch the sea lap at my expensive Hunter boots as if it is a tentative kitten tasting milk for the first time and stand for a while outside the rundown beach hut that once knew the bare feet of my children. But the squeal of children's laughter follows me everywhere. Even the sound of the beach hut's doors banging open and shut in the wind cannot drown it out.

Later, at the funfair that now resembles a ghost town, I wonder where all the summer smells have disappeared to. No longer does the stench of cockles in vinegar, fish and chips and candyfloss linger in the air, and there are no bored ponies on the beach dropping shovelfuls of dung. Surprisingly, the sea dragon rollercoaster ride is silent and still on its rusty rails and it needs a lick of paint for its angry mouth, which appears more clownish than frightening, and its tail is tucked under in apparent cowardliness. I find the dodgem cars covered in plastic onesies to protect them from the rain and the carousel horses seem glad of the respite from cantering in circles. In the cold light of a wintry grey day, Blackbeard's Adventure Golf course looks as small as a children's toy set and its fake green grass is covered in a blanket of soggy leaves.

The town itself is also deserted and some shops have even been boarded up for winter. No longer can you buy fake dog poo, itching powder, stink bombs and fun blood from the joke shop, and the sound of revving motorbikes and smell of fumes is gone from the green. I don't know what has happened to *Wiley the Wash Monster* but would give anything to hear its cheerful tooting once again, for everywhere is quiet. Too quiet. I find the silence disturbing. I would even welcome the voice of the bingo caller calling out cheesy comments on the amusement arcade's PA system, but he too has gone home for the winter.

Afterwards, I came here – to St Mary's Church – which has the Le Strange family's name stamped all over it, including the windows. I know I am meant to gaze in awe at the stained-glass windows, particularly the main east window which depicts images of Christ on the cross, but all the same they are just windows to me and do not move me. Unlike the two identical gravestones in the churchyard that have been erected ten feet away from William Webb's grave, a soldier famous for being shot dead by smugglers in 1784.

Here lie my daughters, side by side, buried on the same day with nothing but a few hours separating their deaths. They got their wish in the end, for hadn't they always wanted to be together forever? It had always been that way – them together as Team Cox, with me on the outside of their impenetrable circle, isolated and alone. I might have had them buried together, just as they would have wished, but it hurt bitterly to do so, knowing that they had finally, irreversibly, shut me out of their world. Even so, for my eldest daughter's sake, I'd made sure that Phillip wasn't buried anywhere near them. In fact, he'd gone into a different cemetery altogether, because I'd had him shipped back to Holt in Norfolk, much to his family's relief. But I wasn't sure if the distance between them could ever be enough for Venetia.

As I bend over the gravestones to read their epitaphs for perhaps the thousandth time, I imagine I can hear Yvonne whispering to me.

'You always did let her get away with murder.'

I feel the accusation shudder through me *and* the cold grey headstone bearing my daughter's name, and the fact that Yvonne hasn't raised her voice in anger doesn't surprise me one little bit. Not when I take into account that my youngest daughter had been a gentle child who would have risked her own life to save a torn paper bag from the middle of the road.

Suffering from a habitual sense of rejection I cannot shrug off no matter what, I get to my feet and gaze around me. Not even the trees want me here, I realise, for they arch their gnarled backs away from me and even the fallen leaves keep directing me to the pathway out of here. What little sun there once was is now tucked out of sight behind the church spire, and will not come out again until I leave – of that I am certain. Maddeningly, the crows in their nests no longer cackle and caw but worry me along with their calls of, 'Go, go, go.'

'I want you to know, Yvonne,' I speak aloud, as forcefully as I dare under the predatory eyes of the grave robbing crows. 'That I didn't let her get away with murder in the end.'

And then, feeling a sudden rush of uncontrollable anger, I

wave a fist in the air, alerting the crows to trouble and making them take off in the air like a battalion of World War 1 airplanes swooping over a doomed city. 'Nobody ever gets away with that,' I cry.

IT WAS TRUE. I hadn't got away with it in the end. I had served fifteen years at HMS Holloway for being found guilty of allowing my child to die.

Of course, nobody had been able to prove I actually killed her – Venetia, that is – but nobody could prove I hadn't. In fact, at the time of the trial, most of the incriminating evidence the prosecution had against me was found to be circumstantial, but this in turn was strongly supported by the condemning fact that I could have prevented my daughter's death by calling for help. But I hadn't. So, on grounds of lack of evidence and suspicions of a psychotic, unstable mind, the murder charge had been dropped to the lesser crime of manslaughter and that's why I only served fifteen years in prison. Fifteen years was not a long time, in my opinion, but it was a lifetime without my children. The biggest crime I'd committed, in my book, was never being able to say sorry. Fifteen years of never being able to put things right had plagued me like no disease could.

Unlike a lot of my prison inmates, who hadn't been involved in such a high-profile case and who weren't as beautiful, glamorous or as rich as I was, I'd received support in the form of fan mail from many a sensible person, and offers of marriage too. Others wrote sick, terrible lies about me or claimed that I was a psychopath who would rather everyone close to me die rather than run the risk of being rejected by them. Some supporters even applauded me for what I had done, saying that I'd been right to kill my evil firstborn for murdering her saintly sister. They sympathised with my case and shared the belief that it was better for the child to die rather than abandon her to social services and a legal system that would otherwise have locked her up for good. I sat somewhere in the middle on all this divided opinion and read everything printed about me and my family in a distant way, as if it were wholly unconnected to me.

A lot of things about prison had surprised me. For one thing, the time went quicker than I could have imagined and once I'd got through the first couple of years – which I'd been warned were always the hardest – life inside had become reasonably tolerable. I no longer liked to think about the times I'd been spat at, had urine thrown in my face or been punched in the ribs when the wardens weren't looking. But after months of refusing to react, the bullies had finally grown tired of tormenting me and left me alone.

Thankfully, I'd had a cell to myself that had a small window overlooking a green area that got mown every fifth day in the summer and had two stone monuments in the centre that reminded me of my children's graves. I may never be sure whose face might appear behind the bars in my cell door (friendly or hostile), but one thing I did know was that I would soon see them again… my children. If fifteen years could be considered soon, that is.

And when that time came, I wanted them to be proud of me, so I'd put my time to good use and studied hard, mastering typing skills for the first time in my life and managing to find my way around the internet. More importantly, I'd been awarded a degree in English literature and met somebody who would change my life, later becoming a lifelong friend. The fact that he came from such a highly unlikely source still continues to delight me.

I can still remember the shock on his face when he first called in at my cell, as he was expected to do with any new inmate in the hope of discovering repentance, only to find me just as serenely beautiful and pitiable as ever. My visitor was none other than the Rev John Pickles, the man with the ridiculous basin haircut who had buried Roger. It turned out he was a regular visitor to "Hollers", as us inmates called our home, and liked to think he was offering hope and compassion to those who "needed" it most. He never used the word "deserved", I noticed cynically, in his preaching to sinners.

For the first five years of my prison term he came to see me every fortnight, dressed in his black cassock and white clerical collar that smelt of church mice. But then, having stumbled upon Brian Carpage, a metal-detecting enthusiast from Dereham who wore Hawaiian shirts, smoked Cuban cigars and talked a lot about gutting fish, he abandoned the priesthood, wrote an authorised biography of me entitled *Beyond The Smoke & Mirrors* and started attending book festivals.

After my release from prison, I met up with Pickles – my fond nickname for the former vicar – and Hawaiian Brian, as he'd become known, at The Taverner's Inn in Hunstanton for a best-selling steak and ale pie.

At first, I'd been terrified that Brian wouldn't like me, but thankfully we all got on like a house on fire. Never having had much of a sense of humour myself – a fact they both seemed to find hilarious – I suddenly found a wit of my own and was able to join in with their bitchy laughter, which was invariably at the expense of somebody else. Although Brian could be a little cutting and abrasive at times, I valued his friendship, as well as Pickles', and found myself able at last to relax in their company. As there was no pressure to perform or pretend to be perfect, being around these oddballs was, in a way, strangely liberating for me.

As for the actual day of my release, which I can remember as if it were yesterday, I can picture all the other inmates, dressed in civilian clothes for the first time in years, shaking hands with the prison wardens and being congratulated on being discharged. But as I reached the enormous prison gates – the last to be released that day – there was no hand-shaking or slaps on the back for me. Blinking at the strong sunlight, I took one last, long look back at the cold prison walls and shuddered. My time there was over, thank goodness, but I could still hear the cries of the inmates from inside the prison walls. Their squabbles and vendettas would go on as usual, only without me from now on.

I can never forget the names they called me or the things they accused me of. But although I'd served my time, same as everyone else, the prison wardens continued to eye me suspiciously and whispered among themselves as I passed them on the way out.

'Fifteen years for killing her own child. She should have got life,' I heard one of them say maliciously.

'What sort of mother could do that?' another agreed loudly, not bothering to lower her voice.

In response, I flipped open my gold snakeskin compact mirror and applied the familiar Chanel shade of lipstick that hadn't touched my mouth in 5,478 days, and, admiring my reflection in the glass, adjusted a wayward lock of butter-blonde hair.

'What sort of mother am I?' I turned deliberately to face them, noticing that one or two of the wardens were now decidedly less brave than they had been a minute ago. 'I suppose what you should really ask yourselves is this: did my husband really throw himself off the tower that night, or was that the act of a mother protecting her child from the hell she would have gone through in institutions like that one?' I nodded gravely toward the prison walls before tottering away in a pair of high heels that I hadn't worn in years.

I HAD LOCKED up the lighthouse, covered the furniture in ghostly-looking dustsheets and drawn the curtains, making the rooms come alive with shadows. I didn't know for sure when – if ever – I'd be back.

Earlier, I'd telephoned the agent, a nice, well-brought-up young man called Oliver, who always wore a silver tie pin and cufflinks, just as Phillip had once done, and told him to reduce the price by £15,000 – I wanted shot of the place ASAP. I didn't go on to explain what bad memories it stirred up for anyone who lived there or that I believed the place to be haunted. For how else could it hold all the emotions of my past prisoner and conjure up shadowy images of the people who were irreversibly lost to me?

Having placed my suitcase on the leather passenger seat next to me, I'd started up the Range Rover Sport with the personalised number plate that started with HE11 (my initials – Hazel Eleanor Lucinda Ladd) and was now driving along the A149 King's Lynn road, heading out of Hunstanton.

Concentrating hard on the tarmac in front of me, for I was not the most confident of drivers, I caught a glimpse of the "You are now leaving Hunstanton" sign in the corner of my right eye and felt immense relief. I shouldn't have come. I knew that now. My children were as dead to me now as they'd ever been, and I had to accept that – face facts. If that meant leaving our old home behind, then so be it. Everything they'd said about me was, of course, true. I was – *am* – a cold-blooded killer and my one redeeming feature is that I loved at least one of my daughters, even if I hadn't shown

344

it when she was alive. It was true I would have done anything for her, even murder – and not just the once, but as many times as was necessary. With a self-indulgent smile, I couldn't help but wonder how many other mothers could say the same.

Taking my mind off the long journey ahead and the loneliness that awaited me around every corner, I slipped a disc into the CD player and as the first bars to "My Immortal" by Evanescence registered moodily in my mind, my hand lingered a little too long on the dashboard – because that second was all it took for something to run across the road and crash into the car.

HAZEL KNEW SHE had hit something because she instantly felt the impact and recognised the splatter of blood that hit the window screen. But as yet, in the panic, she was unable to figure out exactly what had happened. Slamming on the brakes, she saw what looked like a folded fur coat flip onto the bonnet and slide towards her, baring white canines in what would be its final death snarl, its legs moving so fast that it looked like an alien creature with too many flailing limbs.

'Oh my God, Laddy,' Hazel cried as the car came to a juddering stop another 329 feet further down the road. Getting out of the car, she found herself staring down at what remained of the poor, mashed-up dog that had tyre marks impaled on its skull. More disgustingly still, there were sirloin steak-sized bits of brown furry dog stuck to the smart chrome grill of her 4x4 and she hadn't a clue as to how she would get them out. As usual, when she needed to flag somebody down for help, there was not a single other road user in sight – which was peculiar for this time of day, even in winter.

Wishing she could magic up a passerby like a rabbit out of a hat, she felt a sense of dread take hold of her, as surely as if a giant hand had grabbed her wrist and was now refusing to let go, because there, in the distance, she could see the lighthouse and almost immediately caught a glimpse of a shadow in the tower window that shouldn't be there. Knowing that the shadow was in fact herself, or a memory of herself, lost in time, she felt the strong pull of belonging to a place that demanded her presence. As she watched the shadow lean closer to the window, hoping for a better look of the people on the ground below, perhaps even longing for a glimpse of her children returning home for tea, Hazel felt her own breath fogging up the glass.

Tearing her eyes away, hoping to break the tower's spell, she saw to her amazement that the dog had vanished. Knowing there was no way that it could have survived the impact or crawled away to die, she was equally shocked to discover that there was no longer a spot of blood or flesh left on the bonnet of her car. Not only did that mean she hadn't killed the dog, because it had never really existed (except in her own head), she took it as a sign that she had broken the condemning analogy she had once used about Venetia and herself – and proved she *was* capable of going out of her way to protect life by trying to avoid hitting an animal that ran out in front of her.

Alone in the middle of the road, dressed in a navy print Jenny Packham tea dress that was ever so slightly too short and a pair of Salvatore Ferragamo heels, Hazel found herself envying the make-believe dog who knew no pain and didn't have to endure days of jumbled confusion the way she did. Pretty soon she even began to wish that a lorry with a sleep-deprived driver at the wheel would come from nowhere and plough into her, for she had nothing left to hope for, not now the fantasy of seeing her children again was over.

How could she be the only survivor, all that was left, when the thought of seeing them again had been the only thing to get her through those fifteen years in prison? Without the promise of seeing them again, there was nothing left to hope for. Or wish for.

It couldn't be true, could it? She could not – must not – believe that her children were dead and gone. Both of them, lost to her. Because that would mean she would have to face up to – and she couldn't – wouldn't… Nothing so terrible could have happened to her, to them, surely? No. It had to be a mistake. Her mind must be playing tricks on her again. She had probably imagined the whole thing. If she could conjure up a dead dog one minute, only to have it vanish the next, then anything was possible. Wasn't it just as likely that her two girls were alive and well and living their own lives, desperate for an opportunity to make up with their long-lost mother and each other?

Yes, they had fought and hadn't spoken to each other in a long time – fifteen years in fact, because they'd never been a family who knew how to forgive. But the more Hazel thought about it, the more convinced she became that she could make things right between them again.

That could even mean they would soon all be together again. She would get in touch and beg them to come back to the lighthouse for a long weekend, during which they would resolve all their issues and become a close-knit family again.

Feeling a lot more light-hearted, Hazel got back into the car and swung it around in an excruciatingly neat three-point turn that didn't once involve a tyre meeting the kerb or the burning of rubber.

Silly me, not knowing my own way home, she thought as she drove past the "Welcome to Hunstanton" sign a few miles further up the road, the same one she'd passed just minutes before.

'I must have gone in the wrong direction, taken the wrong turn,' she muttered to herself. But then, both Roger and Phillip had always accused her of being a dizzy driver, claiming that she was far too dangerous to be behind the wheel and should in fact never be allowed out on the road. The memory made Hazel grin from ear to ear because she happened to agree with them.

'I definitely shouldn't be allowed out at all,' she conceded to her own reflection in the rear-view mirror.

And then, reaching for her favourite Chanel lipstick, she managed to apply a fresh splash of colour to her mouth without once swerving. Truthfully, she was an excellent driver and always had been, even though sometimes it suited her to pretend otherwise. But there was nothing wrong with a bit of pretence now and again, she felt. After all, most women played the same game, didn't they – pretending to be less smart, far more needy, way more pliable or kinder than they actually were, and even darn right incompetent when it suited them.

As the swell of the grey North Sea crept into her field of vision and the whitewashed walls of the old lighthouse grew closer still, the sun came out and lifted her spirits further. So much so that as she drove through the town, she was delighted to see the holidaymakers back, clogging up the pavements, and parents pushing toddlers in buggies smothered in sun-block and ice-cream smiles.

The ponies were also back on the beach, carrying impatient children up and down the same bit of sand they trudged every day in the holiday season, and she was pleased to see *Wiley the Wash Monster* back out on the water, carrying passengers searching for seals and loudly tooting its horn. Everyone seemed to have an ice-cream cone, candyfloss, stick of rock or bag of chips in their hand, and music from the funfair made the meltingly hot tarmac streets vibrate. She even caught a glimpse of the sea dragon rollercoaster ride thrashing its long tail as it sped along the metal tracks with armfuls of screaming passengers aboard.

In Hazel's mind, everything was as it should be. So content was she to see the return of the summer, she even found herself smiling at the heavily made-up young girls who chewed gum in a very unladylike fashion and wore the tiniest of shorts in their bid to attract boys, but she couldn't help wondering if they were a secret disappointment to their mothers. After that, nothing could stop her thinking of her own children or wondering what they were like now they were older.

Her excitement to see them grew more intense. Perhaps they were already here in Hunstanton? She could pass either one of them on a street corner and not instantly know them, not after being estranged from them these last fifteen years. She couldn't help wondering what they looked like, how they'd turned out. Was Yvonne as beautiful as she'd always promised to be? Had Venetia finally outgrown her awkward, antisocial stage and grown less violent?

They could be at the lighthouse right now waiting for her, she realised. And then, feeling her foot press down impatiently on the accelerator, Hazel warned herself to slow down. She must stay calm, take it easy – or how else would she be able to resolve a lifetime of wrongs in one weekend? She would no doubt have to tread on eggshells around them, especially where Yvonne was concerned. Because no matter what happened, she mustn't let them find out her true feelings. They must never find out that their mother had spent her whole life hiding the love she felt for one of them and disguising the hatred she felt for the other.

'Soon, they will come. Soon, the pretence will start all over again.' Hazel said out loud, wondering how she would keep her secret...

THANKS

To my husband, Darren, who shared the dream and made *The Long Weekend* the first novel he has ever read all the way to the end. For Mike Sherman, who supplied the wonderful photographs of Hunstanton and to the seaside town itself, that inspired me to write the book. Whilst all of the places featured in this novel are real, I have taken a few liberties here and there. For instance, the sea dragon rollercoaster ride is just a children's ride and not the terrifying experience it is made out to be and the description of the lighthouse is all mine. But if, like me, you find the characters and location intriguing, why not take a long weekend in Hunstanton yourself? You can even book to stay at the lighthouse, like I did (if you dare). That way you'll be able to retrace Hazel's steps for yourself, just as she does in the book.

Jane E James enjoys living the 'good life' in the Cambridgeshire countryside with her husband and four dogs. She likes being a little bit mysterious too, like her books.

www.janeejames.com

The author's photograph is reproduced with the kind permission of Alex Drury Photography of Stamford.